THE
VILLAIN'S
DAUGHTER

THE
VILLAIN'S
DAUGHTER

ROBERTA KRAY

sphere

SPHERE

First published in Great Britain in 2010 by Sphere

Copyright © Roberta Kray 2010

The moral right of the author has been asserted.

A CIP catalogue record for this book
is available from the British Library.

Hardback ISBN 978-1-84744-242-0
Trade Paperback ISBN 978-1-84744-243-7

Typeset in Garamond by M Rules
Printed and bound in Great Britain by
Clays Ltd, St Ives plc

Papers used by Sphere are natural renewable and
recyclable products sourced from well-managed forests and certified
in accordance with the rules of the Forest Stewardship Council.

Mixed Sources
Product group from well-managed
forests and other controlled sources
www.fsc.org   Cert no. SGS-COC-004081
© 1996 Forest Stewardship Council
FSC

Sphere
An imprint of
Little, Brown Book Group
100 Victoria Embankment
London EC4Y 0DY

An Hachette UK Company
www.hachette.co.uk

www.littlebrown.co.uk

THE
VILLAIN'S
DAUGHTER

Chapter One

The two men strode through the door at precisely five o'clock, bringing with them an unwelcome rush of chill November air. They were both tall, in their thirties and dressed in smart dark suits. One was sporting a blue tie and the other a red. From the similarity of their sharp-featured faces, Iris guessed they were related.

Blue tie approached the desk and gave a cursory nod. 'We're here to see Lizzie Street.'

She returned the greeting with her recently acquired 'professional smile', not too slight, not too wide. 'I'm afraid there's someone with her at the moment. If you'd like to take a seat and—'

'Who? Who's with her?' red tie interrupted rudely.

Iris gave him a look, her eyebrows lifting. She didn't much like his attitude or his tone but was careful to keep her own response polite. 'If you wouldn't mind waiting, just for a few minutes?' She gestured towards the shabby collection of chairs, the once plush fabric worn thin by years of use.

It was blue tie who replied. 'Thanks, but I don't think so.' He glanced deliberately at his flashy gold watch. 'We're a little short on time, darlin'. We'd like to see her now if it's not too much trouble. Chris and Danny Street.'

'Ah,' Iris said uneasily. So these were the sons. She had heard of them, of course, but had never had the pleasure of meeting them before. They both had reputations, but the younger one, the red-tied Danny, was particularly renowned. The kindest description she had heard was 'short-tempered', the worst something she didn't want to dwell on. 'I'm sorry, I didn't realise.'

Chris Street nodded again.

But the uptight Danny wasn't quite so forgiving. 'What's the hold up, ginger?' he said, leaning down to push his face aggressively into hers. He slammed his fist down on the desk. 'We ain't got all fuckin' day!'

Iris jumped back.

Chris Street placed a restraining hand on his arm. 'Cool it, okay? It's not the lady's fault.' He stared at him and then looked back at Iris, his thin lips shifting into a smile. 'I apologise for my brother. He's a touch . . . upset about things.'

With her stomach shifting, Iris tried her best to remain calm. In her mind, however, there was 'upset' and there was just plain deranged. She'd been in the job three months and had never encountered anything quite as alarming as this. What was she supposed to do? As she reached for the phone, intending to pass the problem on to someone more senior, the two of them suddenly took off and headed down the corridor. Jumping up, she anxiously followed in their wake. 'Hold on . . . you can't . . . look, if you could just wait a minute . . .'

But it was too late.

They crashed into the lounge.

It was only ten minutes since she'd shown the man called Wilder in. He turned, frowning at the intrusion.

'What the fuck are you doing here?' Danny Street snarled at him.

As the two men advanced towards each other, Iris didn't hang about. Rushing back to reception, she hammered on the door to the director's office and quickly pushed it open. 'Mr Grand? Mr Grand, we've got trouble!'

'What?'

Without waiting to explain, she dashed back to the room.

By the time she returned, it had already kicked off. The three men were involved in a grunting, fists-flying, all-out punch-up. She had more sense than to try to intervene. At five foot five, and skinny with it, she was hardly likely to make much of an impact. Two against one was hardly fair, but Mr Wilder, at least for the moment, seemed to be holding his own. As they smashed against a table, she winced at the sound of splintering wood. Then all three of them, along with two large vases, crumpled in a heap to the floor.

Gerald Grand came storming in, followed by one of his gofers. His mouth dropped open. 'Please, gentlemen!'

As they rushed to separate the brawlers, Iris glanced across at the woman who was clearly at the centre of it all. Elizabeth Anne Street, known to her friends as Lizzie, was in her late forties and was wearing a hip-hugging, silky blue designer dress, sheer stockings and a pair of Manolo Blahnik high heels. She had diamonds in her ears and her tinted blonde hair had recently been waved. As if more amused than disturbed by the bust-up, a hint of a smile played around the corners of her scarlet lips.

Iris shook her head. Lizzie Street was well known in certain circles – the kind of circles that it paid to keep away from. For the past ten years, ever since her husband had been jailed, she had been running, and rapidly expanding, his business interests. Perhaps 'business' was too respectable a word; if the rumours were true, the Streets were behind most of the violent crime, drugs and prostitution in the area.

Still, even if she'd felt inclined, there was nothing much Lizzie could have done to prevent this particular row. Two weeks ago a bullet had passed clean through her heart. Now, laid out in a top-of-the-range polished coffin, she had no choice but to lie back and witness the consequences of her death.

Iris refocused her attention on the room, or the viewing lounge, as her boss always insisted on calling it. Personally, she didn't care for the term. It reminded her of airports, of departure lounges and people flying off to foreign places. But that, perhaps, was the intention: the cold harshness of death being somehow tempered by the prospect of a warm, blue-skied, idyllic destination.

She sighed as she surveyed the damage. As well as the shattered table, a pair of heavy velvet drapes had been dragged down from the window. The jagged remains of the vases were scattered across the carpet, and the beautiful lilies lay crushed and scattered around them. There were even splashes of blood on the walls – not a good look for a funeral parlour. However, all the men were safely back on their feet.

Gerald Grand, his forehead gleaming with sweat, was fussing around the two brothers, his obsequious hands busily sweeping off the dust from their shoulders. 'I can only apologise,' he murmured. 'I have no idea how this could have happened.'

Iris raised her eyes to the ceiling. Gerald had no idea either as to who had actually started the fight, and probably didn't give a damn. Placating the Streets was his only interest. Not that she was surprised; the funeral taking place tomorrow was the biggest, and by far the most expensive, the firm had seen in years. As she glanced down again, she saw Wilder standing in the corner. He had a red-stained tissue pressed against his nose. She had the impression he was grinning but couldn't be sure; his hand was obscuring his mouth.

4

Gerald Grand threw Iris a sideways, accusatory look as if this was all her fault. He jerked his bald head towards Wilder. 'Get him out of here!' he hissed.

Iris didn't know whether he meant from the room or from the building entirely, but as Wilder was still bleeding she didn't have the heart to show him the door. Instead, she led him out into the corridor and then through to the staff area. Her first act was to switch the kettle on. If there was one thing her mother had taught her, it was the comforting value of a cup of tea.

Wilder lowered himself on to one of the cheap plastic chairs and put his elbows on the table. 'Sorry about all this.'

Iris took the first-aid box out of the cupboard, tore off a large wad of cotton wool and passed it over. 'There's no need to be sorry. From what I saw, it wasn't down to you. That Danny was itching for a fight from the moment he arrived.'

'Family reunions,' he said wryly, dabbing at his nose.

'Family?' Iris could see no physical resemblance between those two crude dark-haired thugs and this sleek blond man. Well, admittedly not quite as sleek as when he'd first come in, but still a cut above the Streets.

'Lizzie Street is my mother.'

She stared at him, amazed. He hadn't mentioned it when he'd arrived for the viewing and his name had given her no clue. 'They're your brothers?'

'Stepbrothers,' he quickly corrected her. 'She married their father, the delightful Terry Street. So no blood relation, thank God.'

'I'm sorry. I mean, about your mother.'

'Don't be. She was a scheming bitch.' He gave a laugh as he caught her expression. 'Don't be shocked. You wouldn't be if you'd ever met her. She dumped me with my gran when I was seven and moved in with Terry and his three brats. That was twenty-five years ago. Still, I thought it only right to come and pay my last respects.'

Iris was sympathetic. She knew how it felt to be abandoned by a parent. However, she didn't know what to say next, so turned away to make the tea. 'Do you take sugar?'

'Just milk, thanks. Are you sure you should be doing this? I don't think your guvnor would approve.'

'It doesn't much matter what Gerald does or doesn't approve of; I'm only working here short term. Anyway, I imagine he's too busy sucking up to your . . . your stepbrothers to be worried about what I might be doing.'

'True enough.' He transferred the grip on the cotton wool to his left hand and held out his right. 'The least I can do is to introduce myself properly. Guy Wilder. Nice to meet you.'

'Iris,' she replied, taking the hand. Noticing the grazes on his knuckles, she was careful not to shake too hard. 'Iris O'Donnell.'

'Irish, I take it.'

'Historically,' she said, 'but I was born here.'

He smiled. 'Irish Iris. I wouldn't like to try repeating that too many times when I'd had a few.'

She smiled back, gazing into his eyes. They were blue, dark-lashed and curiously intense. 'You don't sound as if you're from round here.' His voice was as smooth as his appearance, not posh exactly, but . . . She searched in her mind for the right description. Seductive was the first word she came up with.

'Well, that's something I have to thank my mother for. "A good education, Guy, that's what really matters." So she paid to send me to the kind of school where you get your head shoved down the toilet until you learn to speak like everyone else. Fortunately, I'm a quick learner.'

Iris laughed and then, aware that she was still staring a little too intently into his eyes, quickly lowered her gaze. 'Has your nose stopped bleeding yet?'

Guy Wilder took the cotton wool away, glanced down at it

and nodded. 'Just about. Thank you.' He sat back and looked around, taking in the peeling wallpaper, the stained counter by the sink and the general run-down nature of the room. 'I'm still trying to figure out why Terry chose this place.'

Iris stirred the tea and put the two mugs on the table. 'Why? You think he'd have got a better deal from the Co-op?' Suddenly aware that it was his mother's funeral she was joking about, she felt a deep flush rise to her cheeks. 'Oh, I didn't . . .'

'It's okay. You can skip the sensitivity. Consider yourself off duty for the next five minutes.' He paused. 'I just expected him to go for somewhere more upmarket, more ostentatious. This is hardly the Ritz of funeral joints, is it? And Terry always likes to make an impression, even when his heart is only theoretically broken.'

Iris sat down. She couldn't tell how much of Wilder's cynicism was bluff and how much for real. Since coming to work at the small family firm of Tobias Grand & Sons, she had witnessed many different responses to death; not the full gamut perhaps, but enough to inform her that the big, dramatic displays of tears and hand-wringing were not necessarily a reliable indicator of those who were grieving most. She thought of the pain she would be feeling if her own mother had died. 'It's not so bad. Maybe he wanted somewhere local.'

'Or cheap.'

'Not that cheap,' she said, recalling the expensive coffin, the flowers and all the other fancy extras the Streets had ordered.

Wilder grinned at her. 'It will be if he doesn't pay.'

Now that he had moved the cotton wool, Iris had the opportunity to examine his face more closely. Despite the swollen nose, he was still what she would describe as classically handsome. His cheekbones were high and he had a firm if rather stubborn mouth. It wasn't, however, an easy face to read. 'I take it you and Terry Street don't get along?'

Wilder sipped his tea. His eyes suddenly narrowed. 'If you're asking if I hate his guts, if I think he's got away with murder – then yes, it's safe to say we don't get on.'

She felt a shiver run through her. Was he suggesting what she thought he was? 'You mean . . .?'

'Terry's due out in less than a month and his whore of a wife didn't even pretend to be faithful.'

Iris flinched, partly at the description of his mother, but also at the underlying accusation. Her voice was no more than a whisper. 'You think he . . . he murdered her?'

'Well, bearing in mind that he was safely behind bars two weeks ago, I can't hold him directly responsible but, as the saying goes, there's more than one way to skin a cat.' He put down the mug and shrugged. 'But then again, I could be wrong. Dear old Lizzie made plenty of enemies in her life. There were times when I felt like shooting her myself.'

Iris relaxed a little. Perhaps it was only the bitterness talking. 'And what do the cops think?'

'That she deserved all she got – although, naturally, it's not the official party line. That leans more towards a gangland killing. Still, I doubt if they're putting too much effort into the investigation. No point wasting valuable resources on the likes of my mother.'

There was a short silence.

'I'm sure they'll find whoever did it,' she said.

'To be honest, Iris, I don't really care.'

But that, she suspected, was a lie.

Wilder pushed back the chair and got to his feet. 'Right, I'd better get going. Thanks for the tea and sympathy. You're an angel.' He dropped the bloodstained wad of cotton wool into the bin by the sink. 'Perhaps I can return the compliment some-time. I run a bar on the High Street. Drop in if you're ever passing.'

She opened her mouth intending to ask what it was called, but then changed her mind. The offer was, in all likelihood, more of a polite gesture than any firm invitation. She stood up too. 'Wait here a moment. I just want to check that the coast is clear.'

'Don't worry about it. I'm not bothered about those two morons.'

She laid her hand on his arm as he went to leave. 'No, I'm sure you're not, but you won't be the poor sap doing all the clearing up when it kicks off again.'

His gaze slowly slipped down to her hand before his mouth curled into a smile. 'Iris O'Donnell,' he said, 'you're a very practical woman.'

Chapter Two

Luke Hamilton walked into the kitchen and dropped his brief-case on the floor by the table. He took off his jacket, threw it over the back of a chair and sighed. His afternoon meeting had not gone well – the client had ripped his ideas to shreds – and then there had been a problem with the trains at Liverpool Street. He had spent over an hour in the pub before finally forcing his way on to an overcrowded cattle truck.

Iris was standing by the stove, stirring one of her stews. In the past they had taken it in turns to cook but now, with him working longer hours, she usually had a meal on the table by the time he got home. This had been a novelty at first, but now he resented it. Or, more to the point, he thought that she should resent it. The old Iris, the sassy one with attitude and passion, would have told him to make his own damn dinner.

She looked over her shoulder. 'Good day?'

'Not especially.'

When he didn't elaborate, she turned back to the stove. 'Me neither. There was a punch-up just before we closed. One of the lounges took a right battering. You should have seen the state of it. I had to stay and help clean up.'

'Really.' Luke wasn't surprised. He wasn't particularly interested either and made no attempt to hide it. Opening the fridge, he grabbed a beer and flipped off the lid. He couldn't understand why she was still working at that place. A few weeks was all it was supposed to have been, a gentle introduction, after what had happened, back into the world of employment, but three months on she was still there. How anyone could bear to be surrounded by dead bodies all day was beyond him. It gave him the creeps just thinking about it.

'It was Lizzie Street's family,' she said.

Luke leaned against the counter and shook his head. The name didn't mean anything to him.

'You remember?' Iris prompted. 'It was on TV, in the papers. She was shot in her house a couple of weeks ago.'

He snorted. 'Hardly news round here.' The borough of Kellston, for all its aspirations, for all its fancy new apartments and shops, was still fundamentally an East End dive full of villains, tarts and junkies. Hemmed in between Bethnal Green and Shoreditch, it also wasn't far from the gloomy streets of Whitechapel, where Jack the Ripper had gone on his murderous spree. He wondered why he'd ever agreed to move into the area, although he already knew the answer – to please Iris. This was where she'd been born, where she had last seen her father and where, somewhere in the back of her mind, she undoubtedly hoped to see him again.

'She's being buried tomorrow.'

'You shouldn't be working there,' he said. 'It's not safe.'

Iris lifted her slim shoulders and smiled. 'It was a punch-up, Luke, not a massacre. I think I can just about handle the dangers of a funeral parlour.' She caught his eye, saw the look in it and smartly returned her attention to the pan. What he really

11

meant, she thought, was that her job wasn't suitable for the partner of an 'executive'. Ever since his promotion, Luke had become increasingly pretentious. Everything now was about appearances, about money and status. He'd changed. She gazed down into the brown sludge of beef and vegetables. Or maybe she was the one who had changed.

'You could do better,' he said, refusing to let it drop. 'I've heard there are vacancies at Cleary's. With your experience you'll get an interview, no problem. Why don't you give them a call?'

Iris felt her stomach shift. The thought of returning to that cut-throat world, of working for yet another advertising firm, filled her with dismay. What did it matter what sort of tea you drank or what kind of washing powder you used? It was all so meaningless. She took a deep breath. 'It won't be forever. I'm only covering while their usual receptionist is away.'

'But you'll think about it?'

'Yes,' she lied. 'Of course I will.'

'Good. Your talents are wasted on that place.'

With a thin smile, Iris spooned the stew out into bowls and placed them on the kitchen table. That he believed the best use of her talents lay in persuading people to buy what they didn't really need both saddened and confused her. She had only got the job at Tobias Grand & Sons by chance, but for the moment, it suited. Concentrating on other people's grief had proved to be a surprisingly effective way of dealing with her own.

They sat down and ate in silence for a while.

'Perhaps we should think about moving,' Luke said. 'A fresh start.'

A flutter of panic rose in her throat, giving her voice a tight uneasy edge. 'You want to move away?'

'Not out of London, just somewhere more . . .' He took a mouthful of food and chewed. 'I don't know. Somewhere safer.'

Iris raised her head and gazed out of the window. From here she could see the floodlit perimeter wall and the locked, heavy-duty security gates. Silverstone Heights resembled an inner-city prison, the only difference being that it was designed to keep the less desirable locals out rather than in. The complex of apartments was exclusive in every sense of the word. It had been Luke's idea for them to live in this splendid isolation; she would have preferred to be out in the real world, but occasionally compromises had to be made. 'You mean somewhere with more ferocious guard dogs?'

'You know exactly what I mean,' he said irritably. 'Kellston might be up-and-coming, but it's taking a damn long time to get there.'

And it would take even longer, Iris reckoned, if the wealthier residents continued to segregate themselves from the general population. It was an opinion, however, that she chose to keep to herself. Luke often got grouchy when he'd been on the booze and he'd clearly had a few already. His brown eyes were bright and his cheeks were growing pinker by the minute.

'Take what happened to that woman, for example,' he continued. 'It's not right. People aren't even safe in their homes any more.'

Iris was tempted to retort that from what she'd heard about the activities of Lizzie Street, the local crime figures, were likely to go down rather than up, at least temporarily. But that would only give him an excuse to start banging on about guns and gangsters and how 'decent people' couldn't sleep safely in their beds at night.

Luke shovelled the stew into his mouth, barely tasting it. He took a swig of beer. The more he thought about moving, the more attractive the idea became. He was earning good money now and could easily afford to have an address that didn't result in the lifting of his colleagues' eyebrows every time he mentioned it. And it would be better for Iris too. This flat, this whole area, held too many bad memories. Although he had, briefly, come to terms with the prospect of being a father, he felt a guilty relief that it wasn't going to happen. Parenthood wasn't what he'd planned for this stage of his life.

'I don't want to move,' she said softly.

Luke didn't reply. She wasn't thinking straight and hadn't been ever since the miscarriage.

Every conversation he had with her these days held undercurrents of tension; it was all about what wasn't said rather than what was. He didn't know how to change it and a part of him, although he wanted to be closer to her, dreaded being pulled down again into that whirlpool of emotion. How long was it supposed to take for a woman to recover? It was almost six months now and she was still a shadow of her former self.

Iris could see the frustration on his face. He had been patient at the beginning, loving and supportive, but had gradually grown more impatient as time passed by. She wished she could explain how she felt, but she couldn't. She might only have been ten weeks' pregnant, but the loss was so profound she was still struggling to come to terms with it.

Seeing her stricken expression, Luke felt a pang of conscience. 'Why don't you splash out and buy yourself something nice for Friday.'

'It's only a meal,' she said. 'I don't think Michael's expecting us to dress up for the occasion.'

'Michael?'

'His birthday.' She paused, frowning. 'Why, what did you mean?'

'Oh God, not this Friday. It's the Christmas do at Rufus Rigby.'

She groaned. 'But it's only November.'

'They always hold it in November. Any later and half the clients won't turn up. You know that.'

Iris blinked at him. She didn't know any such thing. He had only been in the job for twelve months and this time last year they'd been too busy with the move to even think about parties. 'Why didn't you tell me?'

'I did. I told you weeks ago.' He tilted his head towards the calendar stuck to the fridge. 'I even wrote it down.'

'Then why didn't you remind me? I said last night that I'd booked a table.' She realised he couldn't have been listening to her – just as she had not been listening to him. It was symptomatic of the general breakdown in communication between them. 'So what are we going to do?'

'You'll have to rearrange. Tell him we can't make it.'

She shook her head, annoyed. 'I can't do that.'

'Why not? We can change it to Saturday.'

'It won't be his birthday on Saturday.'

Luke shrugged. He could see she was upset, but refused to feel bad about making the suggestion. Michael O'Donnell was fond of a pint and, with nothing better to do, he'd probably spend most of the day in the pub with his mates; by seven o'clock he'd be completely smashed. Even if the dates hadn't coincided, Luke wouldn't have relished the prospect of spending the evening with him. As it was, there was no way he was going to pass over one of the most important networking occasions of the year for a cheap meal with a lousy drunk.

'I thought you liked him.'

Luke stared at her. He could see the direction this was going in and tried his best to cut her off. 'I do. Of course I do. For heaven's sake, it's got nothing to do with that.'

'Hasn't it?' Iris narrowed her eyes and stared back. 'You haven't seen him in ages. Every time I go round, you make some excuse. You're always making excuses and now—'

15

'That's rubbish. I've just been busy.'

'You find him embarrassing.'

'Don't be ridiculous,' he snapped.

But Iris knew it was true. She couldn't deny that Michael could get a little loud when he was on the booze – it didn't take much encouragement for him to burst into song or to start regaling total strangers with some of the more colourful stories of his life – but he had a good heart and was the nearest thing she had to a father. 'He's been good to me.'

Luke shrugged. When he'd first encountered Iris, he'd been completely bowled over by her. Infatuated, even. With her slim figure, long red hair and green-grey eyes, he had thought her the most stunning girl he had ever met. And it wasn't just her physical attributes, or her zest for life, which had fascinated him so much: he'd also been intrigued by her association, if only marginal, to the villainous underworld of London. Back in Manchester, he'd even bragged to his pals about it. But things had changed a lot since then. Now he preferred to keep his mouth buttoned about some of the less savoury pastimes of her relatives. 'This party's important; it's my job we're talking about.'

'Michael's birthday is important too.'

'I'm sure he'll understand.'

Iris bridled at his dismissive tone. 'Understand what? That I'd rather swig champagne with a bunch of overpaid, immature morons than spend the evening with my own uncle?' She bit down on her lip. It was an unfair retort and she instantly regretted it. She had only spoken so rashly because she resented his presumption that Michael should take second place to his glittering career.

'Well, if that's how you feel,' Luke said, abruptly standing up and snatching his jacket off the back of the chair. His eyes flashed with anger. He got as far as the kitchen door, glanced along the hall and stopped. 'I'm going to the study. I've got work to do.'

Iris pushed aside the bowl and put her elbows on the table. She knew he would have flounced out of the flat if he hadn't been so worried about all the muggers lying in wait for him.

Chapter Three

Iris turned up the collar on her coat as she walked through the gates. She was glad to be outside; the atmosphere over breakfast had been as frosty as the winter air. Luke hadn't come to bed, making a point by spending the night in the spare room. He was not a man who dealt well with conflict and for all his newly acquired sophistication was still more than capable of behaving like a sulky teenager. He had eaten his toast in silence, his eyes occasionally flicking up to stare at her accusingly. She had felt the tension between them like a thread pulled tight and about to snap. In the end, unwilling to have the argument hanging over them all day, she'd offered up another of those compromises.

'What if I call Michael and see if I can arrange to take him for lunch instead?'

He had thought about this for a few seconds before replying, 'I'll be at work. I won't be able to make it.'

'I know.'

But even in victory, Luke was incapable of being gracious. 'If you'd just listened to me in the first place . . .'

Iris frowned as she crossed the road. She was sure Michael would understand, but she didn't want him to have to. He'd been good to her since she'd come back to Kellston.

Meeting the jailbird uncle she hadn't seen in years, whom she only barely remembered, had been a daunting prospect, but he'd instantly put her at ease and made her feel not just welcome, but cared for too. Now a week didn't go by without them seeing each other or talking on the phone.

As she cut down on to the High Street, Iris began to think about her father. She still automatically scanned the faces of every passing male of a certain age, hoping to catch a glimpse in their features of the man who had disappeared nineteen years ago. Would she recognise him? She was sure she would. Unlike her mother, she refused to believe that he was dead.

Kathleen O'Donnell hadn't been happy about her only daughter moving back to Kellston. She had screwed up her eyes, put her hands on her hips and stared at her. 'I don't think it's a good idea. You're both earning good money. There are plenty of nice places you could live.'

'What's wrong with the East End?'

'It's not safe, love. It's full of . . . well, junkies and the like.'

Which had been pretty much Luke's opinion too until Iris had managed to persuade him otherwise. She smiled wryly. That was back in the days when she could persuade him to do pretty much anything. She shoved her hands deeper into her pockets and tried not to think about the call she would have to make to Michael.

Iris gazed around as she walked, taking in the familiar landmarks: the infant school she had attended, the small expanse of the Green, the old sweetshop on the corner that was now an organic farm store. She passed Ruby's, the jewellers, and noticed how smart it had become. Yes, things had changed in her absence, but not beyond recognition.

19

It wasn't hard to explain the pull this place exerted on her; it was where she'd been born and where she had lived for the first seven years of her life. Most of her memories were happy ones. Having spent so many of the subsequent years moving around, shifting from one part of the country to another, she was desperate to find somewhere that would finally feel like home.

Iris stepped up the pace, feeling the cold start to bite. She took a deep breath. It was weeks since Bonfire Night, but she could still detect the lingering smell of fireworks. It was one of those smells that conjured up her childhood, her father's fingers wrapped tightly around hers, that distant time – maybe the only time – when she had felt completely safe and secure.

Tobias Grand & Sons lay in the less developed, northern end of the High Street, the premises jammed between a florist and a charity shop. Here all the establishments were a little scruffier than their southern counterparts, and the exterior of the funeral parlour, like its neighbours, was in sore need of a lick of paint. As Iris approached, she noticed that a small crowd had already gathered at the entrance. Two plumed black horses, along with a Victorian-style glass hearse, were also standing in wait. Some of the people had probably been drawn by the spectacle – this was going to be a traditional East End funeral – others, including members of the press, by the prospect of seeing Terry Street come to bury his murdered wife.

Iris slid between the onlookers, opened the door and quickly closed it behind her. She shrugged off her coat. It was warm inside and the heady scent of lilies wafted through the air. The reception area was in the process of being cleared, all the furniture being pushed back against the wall to create a wide open space for the mourners to congregate before proceeding to the church. At the back there was another smaller room where the grieving widower, with his prison escort, would be able to spend some private time with his sons.

Gerald Grand, dressed in full funeral regalia, was strutting around, barking out orders. He gave her a brief nod as she came in. His long, rather hang-dog face looked even more lugubrious than usual and a pale sheen of sweat glistened on his bald head. It was a big day for Tobias Grand & Sons and the consequences, should anything go wrong, could be more than financial. He was right to be anxious. Neither Terry Street nor his offspring were the forgiving sort.

Iris took her coat and bag through to the kitchen area. She checked her reflection in the mirror, smoothed down her hair and hurried back to help. Within half an hour she had despatched the order of service cards to St Mark's, made sure all the flowers had been delivered and sorted out the refreshments. As requested by the Streets, she placed a pot of strong ground coffee in the private room, along with a jug of fresh milk and a bowl of sugar. The best china was out on display. For the reception area, there were two large urns, one of tea, one of hot water. There was also water, orange squash and instant coffee for anyone who could be bothered to make it.

It was five to nine when Iris next checked her watch. Everything was quieter now, everything in place. A sense of calm had descended on the room. As she glanced around, she noticed Toby leaning idly against the wall with a Starbucks cup in his hand.

'Keeping busy?' she said.

He raised the cup and grinned. 'Just steadying myself for the big event.'

Gerald Grand's son was twenty-six, the same age as herself, but she always thought of him as younger. With his silky blond hair, pale skin and wide blue eyes he had the look of an overgrown choirboy. He was both feckless and charming, a combination that attracted countless numbers of female admirers. Iris, however, wasn't one of them. Not that she disliked him. Far from it. For all his faults, he was still good company.

Although ostensibly a partner in the firm, Toby rarely spent much time there. Funerals, as he frequently insisted, were not his thing although he didn't have any objection to picking up a pay cheque at the end of every month. This funeral, however, was different. Lizzie may not have been the most popular woman in the neighbourhood, but she was still the wife of Terry Street. And Terry had enough 'celebrity' friends to make this an occasion worth attending.

'If you want your picture taken, you'd better get out there now before the paparazzi find someone more interesting to snap.'

Toby flashed his white-toothed smile. 'More famous perhaps, but never more interesting.'

'You wish.' She glanced at her watch again. 'We'll be opening the doors soon. Think there'll be a big turn out?'

'There'd better be or Mr S will be none too pleased.'

Iris moved the Book of Remembrance into the centre of the table, opened it to the first crisp white page and smoothed out the sheet. Beside it she had placed a pen attached by a chain to a solid black holder.

Toby peered over her shoulder. She could smell the lemony scent of his expensive aftershave. 'He'll be reading that from cover to cover tonight. Let's hope our guests can come up with a few good things to say about her.'

Terry Street arrived at ten o'clock, securely cuffed to one prison officer and accompanied by another. He was brought in amidst the flash of camera lights. By then the reception area was packed. For the past hour it had felt more like a party than a funeral, a gathering of old friends slapping each other on the back and exchanging stories.

Everyone fell quiet as he walked in and then a murmur of sympathy rippled through the crowd. He stopped to shake hands, to exchange a few words with the assembled mourners.

Iris watched from the other side of the room. A lean, gaunt man in his early sixties, Street was impeccably dressed in a dark blue pinstriped suit, white shirt and tie. His thinning hair was grey and swept back off his forehead. She saw his eyes flick quickly around, but couldn't tell whether he was searching for one particular person or simply checking out the attendance figures.

As he grew closer, Iris heard his voice for the first time. It was unexpectedly soft and low but also slightly raspy as if he was suffering from a bad cold.

Toby leaned forward and whispered in her ear. 'Shot in the throat,' he said as if reading her mind. 'Lucky to survive.' He gave a chuckle. 'Well, lucky for him. I'm not sure about the rest of us.'

'Toby,' she remonstrated. She was not so much concerned with the content of the comment – there was probably some truth in it – as worried that he might be overheard.

As she looked more closely, Iris noticed the ugly white scars extending up from beneath the collar of Street's shirt. She glanced away, not wanting to stare and a few seconds later he entered the private room. The door was open and as her gaze slid back, she saw the cuffs being removed from his wrist. He stepped forward then and embraced his two sons.

Chris and Danny Street had arrived twenty minutes earlier. Chris's other half, a tall leggy blonde with long straight hair down to her waist, had been hanging from his arm like the original trophy wife. There were no signs on the older brother's face of the altercation that had taken place yesterday. The younger one, however, was sporting a split lip and some bruising to his cheek.

'Shame I missed the fun at the viewing,' Toby said.

'Serves you right for skiving off.'

'I prefer to call it working from home. I see Deadhead took a beating.'

'Deadhead?' she repeated quietly.

23

Toby lowered his voice too. 'Danny Street,' he murmured. 'A full-on nutter if ever I met one. Crack, H, coke, booze – you name it, it's all there swimming around in his bloodstream. He takes the bloody stuff for breakfast. That is one crazy guy. Twisted too, if you get my meaning.'

Iris was pretty sure she did. She remembered the man's dark glaring eyes as he had slammed his fist down on the desk. A shudder ran through her. 'He was none too pleasant yesterday,' she said resentfully. 'He even called me "ginger".'

Toby laughed, his breath fluttering lightly against her ear. 'So it was you, not Wilder, who landed one on him.'

She smiled, almost wishing it was true. Then, reminded of Lizzie Street's son, she rapidly scanned the reception area. 'Do you think he'll come? Guy Wilder, I mean. Do you think he'll turn up?'

'Not if he's got any sense.'

'But it's his mother's funeral. Can't the family put aside whatever grievances they have for just one day?'

Toby laughed again. 'Ah, my sweet Iris,' he said teasingly, 'what a lot you have to learn. Families like the Streets don't put aside anything, not even to bury their dead.'

She was prevented from making a reply by the approach of Gerald Grand. He was heading for the private room with a group of five serious-looking men in tow. Three of them she recognised as being old-school villains, the type who had been active in the sixties and seventies and were now eking out their pensions by writing and promoting their memoirs. The other two were younger, faces she hadn't seen before. They were, perhaps, trusted members of Street's firm.

'The chosen few,' Toby said, echoing her thoughts.

The last thing Iris saw, before the door closed, was Chris Street taking a miniature bottle of whisky from his pocket and pouring it discreetly into his father's coffee.

She returned her attention to reception and did the rounds again, making sure everyone was happy – or at least as happy as they could appear to be in the circumstances – and that they knew refreshments were available. She made a few cups of tea and passed them to anyone in need. She also provided some gentle reminders about the book sitting on the table. Everything was running smoothly and she wanted it to stay that way. Any complaints would inevitably find their way back to Terry Street and his worryingly violent sons.

Iris knew the faces of a few other people who were present, mainly B-list actors and actresses. How well they had actually been acquainted with Lizzie, she could only guess at. She had the feeling they were there more for the publicity than through any genuine sense of grief. The men were all in sharp suits, the women in fashionable black dresses, veiled hats and gloves. If she hadn't known it was a funeral, it could easily have passed for a rather sombre West End film launch.

It was ten-twenty when Terry Street emerged from the room again. He went, along with his prison escort, to see the body of his wife and reappeared ten minutes later. That he had not been allowed to spend any time alone with her might have struck Iris as tragic if Guy Wilder's words hadn't been revolving in her head. 'He's got away with murder . . .'

Street's face was tight as he came out, closed down and impossible to read. Retracing his steps, he moved through the reception area, stopping again to accept the condolences of anyone who offered them. The prison officers nudged him gently forward. There was a schedule to adhere to.

Iris followed them outside. The crowd had expanded now, snaking down the street for as far as the eye could see. A long row of shiny Daimlers were lined up behind the hearse. Most had been hired for the occasion; Tobias Grand & Sons didn't have the money to keep such a fleet on standby. The car at the very front, however, was a blue Peugeot – this was the prison vehicle that would transport Terry to the church. As he climbed into the back, one of the plumed horses pawed at the ground and snorted out a steamy cloud of breath.

While the other mourners found their seats in the cars behind, the press leapt into action, grabbing sound bites from anyone prepared to give them. And there wasn't a shortage of volunteers. Iris lifted her brows as she heard praise for Lizzie's 'charity work', her strong family values and her contribution, through her various businesses, to the regeneration of the local economy. No mention, naturally, of any of the more dubious enterprises she had been involved in.

'Makes you laugh, doesn't it?' a voice beside her said.

Iris turned, surprised to find Guy Wilder standing beside her. He was dressed casually in blue jeans and a leather jacket. Apart from a little pinkness around the base of his nose, his face, like Chris Street's, had escaped relatively unscathed from yesterday's incident. She gave a faint smile, not sure what to say to him.

'My mother, the loving matriarch,' he continued caustically. 'If she's listening, she's going to be lapping it up. Saint Lizzie! Still, she probably deserves to be sainted, just for putting up with Terry for so many years.'

Iris left a short pause before replying. 'You're not going to the church then?'

He shook his head, his gaze fixed firmly on the hearse as it started to pull away. 'I've already said my goodbyes.'

Then, without another word, he moved swiftly off in the opposite direction to the cortège. She watched for a while as he wound his way through the onlookers. His head was down, his shoulders hunched. She felt a pang of pity. For all his apparent bitterness, it still wasn't right that a son should be absent from his own mother's funeral.

Iris wrapped her arms around her chest and shivered. It was

cold and she didn't have her coat. A chill wind cut through her thin blouse, boring into her bones. Time to go back in before she caught pneumonia. Time to start the dreary process of clearing up. She had been hoping for some help from Toby, but he was nowhere to be seen. Had he gone to St Mark's? Perhaps he was hoping for an invitation to the gathering afterwards.

As Iris headed back inside, she experienced a peculiar pricking on the back of her neck.

Frowning, she turned and instinctively looked across the road. A small, wiry man, in his late sixties or maybe even older, was staring straight at her. Despite his age, his eyes were sharp and sly. It was not a casual or even vaguely leery kind of look. It was nothing short of confrontational. Even when she returned his gaze, he didn't look away. It was as if he wanted her to know he was there, wanted her to feel uncomfortable.

For a few seconds their eyes remained locked and then he suddenly ducked his head and disappeared into the crowd.

Chapter Four

Alice Avery put on her green scrubs, her apron and a pair of thin latex gloves. She looked in the mirror and patted her stomach, aware of the extra weight she had accumulated since turning forty. Her face had grown plumper too and she pulled in her cheeks for a second, trying to recapture the more sculpted contours of her youth.

To avoid the crowds, Alice had used the back door and made her way down the old stone staircase to the basement of Tobias Grand & Sons. It was only here, in these cool sterile rooms, that she could truly relax. This was her territory, both familiar and comforting. She could not say for certain exactly when or why the world had become such a threatening place, she could only remember the frantic beating of her twenty-three-year-old heart as she walked through the hospital ward and her growing dread of having to deal with the demands of yet another living, breathing patient.

It was not that she disliked people – on the contrary, she had always had a burning desire to help them – but she somehow lacked the means to connect. Efficiency, she could do, hard work was second nature to her, but that other necessary element, the ability to communicate, was missing from her personality. Her briskness, matched with her natural reserve, had the unfortunate effect of conveying a certain lack of compassion. Which was why, after numerous discussions with Sister Lewis, she had eventually been forced to accept that nursing was not for her. Although dismayed at the time, feeling herself a failure, she was grateful now for the well-intentioned advice that had propelled her into an occupation where she was both satisfied and happy.

Well, she *had* been happy until a week ago. And of course she still was in many ways, more so perhaps than she had been for years. But she was scared too. She knew that what she had done was wrong, that it went against everything she believed in. And if anyone found out . . .

A shudder ran through her.

Alice quickly turned her attention to the job in hand. She had to stay calm, to try and put it behind her. The cadaver had already been taken from the refrigerated unit and laid on the table. It was a male in his late sixties who had died suddenly from a heart attack. She was glad of that. Not that he had died, obviously, but that he hadn't been the victim of a car crash or some other disfiguring incident that might involve a large amount of complicated restructuring. A run of sleepless nights hadn't done much for her concentration. The more straightforward things were today, the better.

Sometimes she worked with the radio on, but this morning she wasn't in the mood. After she had checked for evidence of a pacemaker – the guys at the crematorium didn't need any explosive surprises – she got on with the cleaning. Alice was not the type of person who could completely disassociate herself from the corpse she was working on. Although she viewed the body as a shell or a skin that had been shed, and thus felt no particular feelings for it, she respected the soul it had once contained. She also couldn't help musing on what their life might have been like. Had the person been popular, successful or had they struggled like her? Had they loved, been loved? She searched for evidence of their history in the flesh and bones that were laid in front of her. She studied their nails and hair, their scars and imperfections.

As she massaged the limbs, working out the rigor mortis, Alice was already constructing in her head an image of the kind of life Joseph Bayle may have led. He had been a thickset man, jowly, with rough hands and knuckles. Not a white collar worker, that was for sure. His nose had been broken more than once and a fading anchor tattoo decorated his left bicep. He was a man who had travelled widely perhaps, but had chosen to return to the East End. Maybe he had lived in one of the little two-up, two-down terraces that were widespread in the area. There would probably be a widow, children and grandchildren too.

Alice made the necessary incision in the carotid artery and began the process of injecting the formaldehyde, watching as the fluid began to spread through the vascular system, plumping out the tissue. Soon the body would achieve a healthier colour.

People were either revolted or intrigued by what she did, usually a combination of the two. Back in the days when she'd still attended dinner parties – the few friends she had were always trying to matchmake, to fix her up with another 'sad and single' – the revelation that she was an embalmer had more often than not stunned her prospective suitor into silence. Had she told them she was a nurse, their reaction would have been quite different. *That* profession was acceptable, praiseworthy, even downright sexy in most men's eyes. But working with the dead was just creepy. Most of the guys she'd met were too busy worrying about where her hands had been earlier to even think about getting to know her better.

But none of that mattered now. After nine long years of celibacy, Alice finally had someone in her life again. She smiled as she picked up the trocar, a long metal tube with sharp blades at one end and a point for attaching a hose at the other. After putting the hose in place she connected it to an aspirator, a device for creating suction. Alice pierced the abdomen just above the navel and skilfully punctured each of the major organs in turn, keeping the instrument in place long enough for their fluids to be drained.

She thought of him gently touching her, caressing her. Of his lips lightly brushing against the nape of her neck, of his hands roaming down to cup her breasts, to touch her stomach, and then his legs sweetly forcing hers apart. No one had ever touched her quite like that before or whispered such seductive words. The kind of words she should have been disgusted by, but . . .

After death, the contents of the organs began to decompose, creating a build-up of gases and bacteria. All kinds of smells, including bile and urine, could emanate from the corpse. Once the draining process was complete, Alice connected the trocar to a bottle of cavity fluid. This was another important stage of the process. It was essential to cleanse the body as thoroughly as possible. Inserting the trocar again, she waited as the fluid flowed into the body, providing a fresher smell and quickly firming up the tissue.

When this was done, Alice carefully sutured the hole where the trocar had been inserted and checked her watch. Just over an hour and a half since she'd begun. All she had left to do now was the cosmetics, the part of her job as important as anything that had gone before. For those who came to view the body, what they saw in that time would leave a lasting impression. Which was why it was not just important but essential for her to make Joseph Bayle look as peaceful as possible. And why she had to keep her mind on the job.

Was it wrong to feel so thrilled, so excited by him? The breath caught in her throat. She already felt like she knew every inch of his body. As if he'd been seared on to her skin, burnt into every inch of her flesh, he was as much a part of her as her own beating heart.

Alice shook her head, trying to concentrate. Joseph Bayle still had most of his own teeth, so she didn't need to put in any dentures or pad the mouth out with cotton wool. She did, however, have to ensure that his mouth remained closed. She did this by threading a length of string through the lower jaw, into the upper, through the septum of the nose and back down again, tying the ends together. The eyes were the next thing she addressed.

She thought of his eyes, of how beautiful they were, how clear and enquiring. When he looked at her he saw the real Alice, not a dull, drab female heading towards middle age, but a woman of intelligence and sensitivity – a woman, most of all, who was still desirable.

Gently she placed the plastic lens-like caps under the lids, their textured surface, along with a dab of Vaseline, ensuring that the eyes remained closed. Some embalmers used glue, but she didn't care for it herself. She cleaned the body again, then washed and dried the few remaining strands of thin grey hair. Next, she shaved his face and neck, removed a few stray hairs from the nostrils and tidied up his fingernails.

All that was needed now was a little light make-up. She turned and took the cosmetics bag off the counter. This was where she had to be especially careful: the trick was to add subtle shades to the bloodless face whilst keeping the appearance as natural as possible. She applied a layer of fine translucent foundation, blending it with her fingertips, and then added a tiny amount of colour to the cheeks. A final dab of lipstick, massaged into the lips, completed the task.

Alice stood back and viewed her work. She was pleased by it, satisfied that she had done a good job. No, better than that – an excellent job! If there was one thing she excelled at, it was breathing life into the bodies of the dead.

Chapter Five

By midday, the reception area had been cleared of its debris and the furniture returned to its rightful position. Iris had swept the heap of polystyrene cups and plastic spoons into a black bin liner, run a damp cloth over all the surfaces and even given the carpet a quick vacuum. Although this fell outside the realm of her more usual secretarial duties, she wasn't going to complain; her main priority these days was just keeping busy. And making sure she kept her job.

Like so many other small firms, this one was finding it tough in the present economic climate. There was no shortage of prospective clients – as Toby delighted in pointing out, people were always going to die – but getting them or their relatives to choose Tobias Grand & Sons above the competition remained a major problem. The funeral parlour may have stood in the High Street for over a hundred years, but tradition had ceased to count for much.

However, a large and very public funeral like Lizzie Street's was always good for business. It would get Tobias Grand & Sons's name mentioned in the local papers and even on the regional news – the kind of publicity money couldn't buy. This was probably why, after his return from Kellston Cemetery, Gerald Grand was looking so pleased with himself. Or maybe it was simply relief that everything had gone so well. Obviously no unexpected punch-ups or other graveside disputes had marred the smooth running of the ceremony.

He gave Iris an unusually wide smile, thanked her for all the cleaning she'd done, and then disappeared into his brother's office. Whether he had gone to pass on the good news or, more likely, to start the joyous process of compiling the bill, was anyone's guess. William Grand dealt mainly with the financial side of the business.

'The Brothers Grimm' was how Toby always referred to them, having little respect for either his father or his uncle. It made Iris laugh although she always felt guilty about it afterwards. Well, guilty about William at least, who was always scrupulously polite to her. Ten years younger than Gerald, he was the very opposite to him in personality: a reserved, grey man who never said more than he had to. He floated around the premises as quietly as a ghost. If it wasn't for the invoices he periodically placed on her desk, Iris could easily forget he even existed.

Toby was convinced that William had the 'hots' for Alice Avery and teased the poor woman mercilessly about it. Her cheeks would blush bright red whenever Toby was on the attack, her shy shoulders hunching in defence, her eyes becoming liquid. Iris always did her best to deflect the worst of his onslaughts, either by glaring at him or trying to provide some diversionary snippets of gossip, but rarely to much effect. Once Toby got his teeth into someone he never let go.

'You shouldn't do that,' Iris had remonstrated more than once, usually after Alice had scuttled back down to the basement.

'Why not?' he always retorted. 'Those two are perfect for each other. They just need a shove in the right direction.'

35

But Iris wasn't so sure. If, as the saying went, opposites attract, then William Grand was the last person Alice would be interested in.

The afternoon was quiet and at four o'clock, with no one else in reception, she took the opportunity to give Michael a ring. When he answered the call, she could hear the sound of voices and loud music in the background. He was, she guessed, in a pub somewhere. 'Hi, it's me. Where are you?'

'What?'

'It's Iris.'

'Hello, love. Sorry . . . sorry, it's noisy in here. I can't hear you too good. I'll go outside, shall I?'

From the tone of his voice she could tell he didn't really relish the prospect of stepping out into the cold winter air. Or was perhaps just unwilling to give up the comfortable seat he was occupying. 'No, it's okay. I need to talk to you but it can wait.' It didn't seem right shouting down the line that she wouldn't be able to make it on Friday evening. Better to buy him a drink and do it face to face. 'Where are you?' she said again. 'I'll be finished in an hour or so. Can we meet up?'

Iris paused as she stepped through the door, her ears protesting at the noise. She couldn't believe how crowded it was. The Hope & Anchor, situated close to Kellston Station, was not so much an old-fashioned East End pub as one that no one had bothered to redecorate for a decade or three. It had been neglected to the point where it now seemed almost deliberately retro. The brown lino flooring was scuffed and stained and pocked with cigarette burns. An old, scarred counter arced around the right-hand side. To her left were a couple of slot machines and a juke box that was pounding out 'Mack the Knife' by Frank Sinatra. *Oh the shark has pretty teeth dear . . .*

It was only as she was forcing her way through a sea of black designer clothes and recognising a few faces from the morning that she realised what was going on. This dingy backstreet pub was, amazingly, the venue for Lizzie Street's wake. Of course, it wasn't strictly a wake – these were supposed to take place before a person was buried – but she couldn't think of what else to call it.

'What are you doing here?' she said when she eventually found Michael. He was at a table near the back, the last third of a pint of Guinness sitting in front of him. She bent to kiss his cheek, catching a pungent whiff of his alcohol-laden breath. 'Isn't this a private do?'

'Nah, not that private,' he said, shifting along the bench to make room for her. 'Everyone's welcome.' He patted the seat. 'Come on, love, sit down.'

Unconvinced, Iris remained standing. She was uncomfortable at the thought of gatecrashing such an occasion.

His smiling blue eyes gazed up at her. 'I'm just paying my final respects, sweetheart.'

More like taking advantage of the free drinks that would have been on offer earlier, she thought. Michael O'Donnell could sniff out a freebie from a mile away. 'You didn't even know her.'

'Sure I did. Me and the lovely Lizzie went to school together.'

Iris stared down at him, amazed. 'You never said.'

'Did you ever ask?' he replied with a grin. He rummaged in his pocket and produced a grubby tenner. 'What are you having?'

'It's okay,' she said, waving the note aside. 'I'll get these.'

At the bar, she had plenty of time to look around. The three curvy barmaids were run off their feet; there was nothing like a good funeral to get the tills ringing. Especially if the old faces were present. Everyone wanted to ingratiate themselves, to ply the 'boys' with drinks and compliments. Terry Street might have been returned to his lonely prison cell, but his attention-seeking cronies were more than happy to fill the gap.

Iris noticed Toby across the far side of the pub. So this was where he'd been all afternoon. He and the volatile Danny Street were standing together, knocking back shorts and laughing loudly. Since when had those two become so pally? Not that she was overly surprised. Toby was one of those typical, middle-class guys, resentful of their comfortable background and fascinated by the world of crime. Rubbing shoulders with the local sharp-suited villains was probably his idea of living dangerously. After a minute she spotted Chris Street too, deep in conversation with a pair of hard-looking bruisers. Neither of the brothers seemed particularly upset – nor, come to that, did anybody else. Of course, wakes were not supposed to be dreary affairs, but the degree of mourning in this room was so negligible as to be virtually absent.

One of the girls eventually took her order. Iris bought a pint of Guinness and a large red wine, elbowed her way back through the crowd and sat down beside Michael. 'Why did they choose this place?' As soon as she said it she was reminded of Guy Wilder's very same question about Tobias Grand & Sons.

'It's one of her joints – or rather, one of Terry's. The first place he bought after he made a few quid.' He finished his pint and immediately started on the next. He nodded towards the bar. 'No point letting all those readies drop into some other land-lord's pocket. They'll make a decent wad today.'

Hardly the point, Iris thought, although not a startling revelation either. Villains like the Streets were not renowned for their sentiment, especially when it came to the cold hard business of profit and loss. 'So what was Lizzie like?'

Michael lifted his broad shoulders and shrugged. She waited, but he still didn't speak.

'You said that you knew her.'

'Ah, that was a long time ago.'

Iris sensed his reluctance, but it only fuelled her curiosity. 'So what was she like back then? Come on, I'm interested. I'd like to know.'

Her uncle gave a soft sigh, glanced around as if to check that no one else was listening and then leaned closer to her. 'Hot,' he murmured in her ear, 'the hottest girl I've ever met.'

She smiled. 'And?'

'And smart with it. That girl had looks *and* brains. She always knew exactly what she wanted.'

'Did you two . . .?'

Michael sat back and laughed. 'Are you kidding? We were mates, we used to bunk off school together, but that was all. Even at that tender age, the lovely Lizzie had ambition, and grubby little oiks like me didn't fit into her plans for the future.'

'Is that just a tiny hint of resentment I can hear?'

He took another swig of his pint and gave her a sideways look. 'I'm way too old for regrets, love.'

Which provided Iris with a timely reminder of why she was here. She still had to tell him that she couldn't make the meal on Friday. 'You're not old,' she insisted. At forty-eight he was only two years younger than her father. Which, in turn, reminded her that it would be *his* fiftieth birthday soon. December 30. It was one of those landmark dates that would normally be marked by a family celebration.

'I feel it,' Michael said. 'My bones are starting to creak.'

As Iris looked at him, she wondered how much of her father, how much of Sean O'Donnell, she might be seeing too. From the small but precious collection of photographs she possessed, they had clearly been physically similar when they were young: the same height, the same solid build, square jaw, blue eyes and black curly hair. Streaks of silver were running through Michael's hair now, but it was still as thick as when he'd been twenty. Although the booze hadn't done much for his appearance, reddening his cheeks and thickening his waist, he was still a handsome man. There was every chance that her father – *if* he was still alive – might not look too different.

She was taking a sip of her wine, preparing herself to make the necessary excuses for Friday, when Michael put his pint down on the table and began to talk again. 'Lizzie had big plans, starting with getting out of this Godforsaken hole, but it all went wrong for her. Got up the duff, didn't she, when she was fourteen, got landed with a kid she didn't want and . . .' Then, remembering Iris's miscarriage, he stopped suddenly and scowled. 'Shit. Sorry, I didn't . . .'

Iris laid her hand on her arm. 'It's all right. I'm not made of porcelain. I won't shatter if you mention babies.'

'I didn't mean to . . .'

'I know,' she said, leaning affectionately against him. She sometimes thought Michael grieved more for the loss than Luke ever had. 'It's okay. As it happens, I met him yesterday. Lizzie's kid, I mean. Except he's all grown up now.'

'Guy?'

She nodded. 'Yeah. He came in to see her at Tobias Grand & Sons. Unfortunately, his timing wasn't great. The Streets arrived ten minutes later and . . . let's just say that the reunion wasn't a happy one.'

'Tore the place up, did they?' He laughed. 'I bet that arse-licking guvnor of yours was none too pleased.'

'Not overjoyed, no.'

Michael laughed again, but then suddenly grew serious. He gazed almost mournfully down into his drink. 'She really loved that kid, you know. Worshipped the ground he walked on.'

'Did she? Only I heard that . . .' Iris hesitated, in two minds as to whether she should repeat what Guy Wilder had said. She couldn't claim that he had told her anything in confidence but

40

then again he had just been in a nose-bleeding scrap with a couple of thugs while he was supposed to be viewing the body of his mother. People came out with all kinds of regrettable comments when they were grieving or in shock.

'That she was a heartless bitch who dumped him with his gran?' Michael suggested, saving her the bother of wrestling too hard with her conscience.

Iris stared down at the table.

He saw the look on her face and nodded. 'Well, Lizzie had her reasons. She knew what Terry Street was like, the kind of life he lived. There were things she wanted – money, power, the good life – but she wasn't stupid. Nah, never that. She knew there'd be a price to pay. Terry's world was hard and vicious. You know what I mean? Big risks, but with big rewards too. She was determined to give that kid all the chances she never had, but to distance him from all the bad stuff too. She was just trying to keep him safe.'

Iris thought of a confused seven-year-old boy separated from his mother whilst she chose to take care of another man's kids. 'He might not have seen it that way.'

'At least he's still alive – which is more than can be said for Liam.'

'Who?'

'Terry's eldest. Shot, weren't he? Same time as his old man. Got his stupid bleedin' brains blown out when he was seventeen.' Michael took another gulp of his Guinness, his tongue sliding quickly across his lips to lick away the residue of foam. 'So maybe Lizzie had a point after all. Trouble is, love, you can't live in that world without getting infected by it. It eats into you, destroying anything good or decent. In the end she grew as cold as Terry . . . and as brutal.' He paused again, shook his head and gave a soft cynical sigh. 'The silly cow never learned; no matter how good or bad, she always had to be the best at *everything* she did.'

41

Iris, surprised at how much he knew about Lizzie, couldn't resist asking the million-dollar question. She kept her voice low. 'So who do you think killed her?'

'Take your pick. The list of suspects is as long as your arm.' He looked up, slowly scanning the crowd. 'Half of them are probably here. She didn't go out of her way to make herself popular.'

Iris followed his gaze, her eyes eventually alighting on Chris Street again. Had Guy been serious when he'd made the accusation about his stepfather? Could one or both of Terry's sons have been responsible for her death? She was about to ask more when Michael flapped his hand. 'Anyhow, sweetheart, enough of all that. You didn't come here to get the lowdown on Lizzie. What was it you wanted to see me about?'

'Oh, yes,' she said reluctantly. 'It's about Friday . . .'

Chapter Six

Michael was as understanding as she'd guessed he would be. He laughed and shook his head. 'So that's what the long face has been about. You had me worried there. I was starting to think it might be something serious.'

'It *is* serious,' she insisted. 'It's your birthday. I'm really sorry – I'd get out of it if I could but . . .'

'Lord, I have one of those every year. And that young man of yours has his job to consider. It wouldn't look too good if he skipped his own work's party, would it?'

He was, she thought, a lot more considerate of Luke than Luke would ever be of him. 'We can still get together for lunch.'

'That would be grand,' he said, putting his arm around her and giving her a squeeze.

Toby chose that moment to bounce into view. His blue eyes were shining brightly and it was clear that it wasn't just the drink he'd been on. He had the fast-talking, overconfidence of someone who'd been sniffing the white stuff.

'Hey, gorgeous. How's it going? Looking lovely as always. You should have told me you were coming. Not a bad turnout, is it?

There must be half of Kellston here.' He looked at her breasts rather blatantly before turning to Michael. 'Aren't you going to introduce us?' Then, before she had the chance to reply, he put out his hand. 'Hi, I'm Toby. I have the pleasure of working with Iris.'

'Toby *Grand*,' Iris said pointedly in case Michael chose that moment to make an ill-judged comment about Gerald. Not that Toby would be offended – he always enjoyed slagging off his father – but she had no intention of getting involved in a public exchange of insults about her employer.

'Michael,' her uncle said, shaking the outstretched hand. 'Nice to meet you.'

'Likewise. I was just off to the bar. Can I get you another?'

Never one to look a gift horse in the mouth, Michael nodded. 'That's very good of you, son. I'll take a Guinness and Iris will have . . .'

'Iris is fine,' she said firmly, worried that if Toby stayed for much longer, his new best friend might decide to join them too. After what had happened yesterday she had no desire to renew the acquaintance.

Michael, eager for the pint but aware of a certain atmosphere, looked from one to the other. Then, either mistaking the ensuing silence for a cue to make himself scarce or simply in need of a pee, he stood up and headed for the Gents.

Toby slid into the space beside her. 'I didn't expect to see you here.'

'I could say the same.' She picked up her glass. 'So what's with you and Danny boy? I thought you couldn't stand him.'

'Just doing my duty,' he said, grinning widely. 'Making sure I keep the punters happy. As Pa would say, you can't over-estimate the importance of customer service. We're going on to a club later. Fancy joining us?'

Iris couldn't imagine anything she'd like less. 'No thanks.'

'Come on,' he urged. 'It'll be a laugh.'

'Other plans, I'm afraid.'

'What kind of plans?' Then, before she had the opportunity to come up with anything even vaguely plausible, he threw a sneaky glance in the direction of the Gents. 'Oh, right. I get it. Something you'd rather your better half didn't know about, huh?'

Iris frowned. 'What are you talking about?'

'Well, you'd usually be at home by now, putting on the dinner and waiting for your loved one to return. Instead, here you are snuggling up to—'

'Snuggling?' she said.

Toby tapped the side of his nose with a finger. 'Hey, your secret's safe with me, darling. Everyone's entitled to a little fun. I won't tell if you don't.'

Had it been anyone but Toby, she would have been offended. As it was, she knew that he was too much under the influence to be thinking even faintly straight. 'I hate to disappoint you, sweetie, but he's actually my uncle.'

'Really?' Hoping for something much more scandalous, Toby didn't attempt to hide his disappointment. 'You never told me you had relatives round here.'

'There are lots of things I don't tell you.' She crossed her legs and glanced down at the glasses on the table. 'I thought you were going to the bar.'

'You said you didn't want one.'

'I don't.'

It took a few seconds for the penny to drop and then Toby giggled. 'You trying to get rid of me, Iris?'

'God forbid,' she said, smiling back. 'But I need to talk to Michael. Family stuff. You don't mind, do you? We can catch up tomorrow. You can tell me all about your great night out.'

Still laughing, Toby got to his feet. 'It's a date,' he said, blowing her a breezy kiss before heading back across the room.

She took a few sips of her wine and wondered what kind of a mood Luke was likely to be in when he came home that night. Although it pained her to admit it, she wasn't looking forward to seeing him. Recently, it had all been niggles and rows, minor squabbles that escalated into bigger arguments. She understood his frustration – he wanted the old Iris back, the fun one with drive and attitude – but she couldn't fake what wasn't there. They were both stubborn and the more he pushed, the more she resisted.

'Pssst.'

Iris looked up at the sound, surprised to see an old man standing beside her. He was wearing a grubby grey overcoat and a red scarf pulled tight around his neck. It took her a moment to place him and when she did her heart gave a jolt. He was the same man who'd been in the High Street that morning, the one who'd been staring so determinedly at her.

'Yes?'

'Got the time, love?'

She gazed at him for a moment and then looked down at her watch. 'Ten past six.'

'Ta.' Then he leaned down, getting too close to her face. His oily voice was hardly more than a whisper. 'You and me need a little chat.'

'Do we?' she said, automatically shifting back. His breath was bad and his body reeked of stale sweat and tobacco. 'What do you want?'

His thin cracked lips crawled into a smile. 'It's more like a matter of what *you* might be wantin'.'

Her eyes widened. 'I'm sorry?' Alarm bells were starting to go off. She had clearly been landed with the local nutter. Quickly, she looked around. She didn't feel threatened exactly – the pub was full of people – but she didn't fancy spending any more time with him than she had to. Where the hell was Michael? It didn't take this long to have a pee. Then, to her dismay, she suddenly caught sight of the top of his head in the middle of the crowd at the bar. Realising that Toby's offer of a free pint was unlikely to materialise, he'd decided to buy the round himself.

'I'm waiting for someone,' she said, as if the old man might be in the process of propositioning her.

'Don't you want to know where your daddy is?'

Iris's mouth dropped open. She could feel the blood draining from her face, a coldness running through her. The response, when she finally got it out, sounded thick and croaky. 'W-what do you mean? Who are you?'

'Just a friend,' he said, 'a friend who wants to help.'

'What do you know about my dad?'

'Not here,' he said, glancing uneasily over his shoulder. 'Meet me tomorrow night, half-six at the Monny. You know where that is?'

Iris nodded, too bewildered to say anything else.

'Half-six,' he repeated. 'Don't be late, eh?'

Then without another word he turned and walked away. Iris, unable to move – she felt as though her legs were full of lead – watched as he pushed rudely through a small group of people and swept out through the rear set of doors. There was a brief gust of winter air and he was gone. She was still in a state of shock when Michael came back with the drinks.

'What's the matter, love? You look like you've seen a ghost.'

'Do you know that man?'

'What man?'

'The scruffy one, the old guy in the red scarf.'

'Nah, I didn't see him.'

Iris, a delayed shot of adrenalin rushing through her body, suddenly jumped up. She wanted to run out of the pub, to chase after him, but then had second thoughts. She sat back down again.

'What's up?' Michael said, looking worried. 'Did he . . . did he do something to you?'

She was about to blurt it all out, but then changed her mind. Michael, like her mother, was convinced that Sean O'Donnell was dead. She didn't want to go causing any upset. But there was another reason for her silence too. She couldn't bear to hear what she knew he would say – that the old man was crazy, that she shouldn't take any notice of him. Sometimes the truth was too hard to take. A little bit of hope, she decided, was better than none.

'No, er . . . nothing like that. Just a tramp trying to cadge a few quid. Maybe I should have given him something. He looked kind of hungry.'

'He'd only spend it on the booze.'

Iris squeezed out a smile. 'Yeah, you're probably right.'

It was another half-hour before she felt comfortable about leaving. She didn't want Michael to think that she was rushing off, but as he had recently got into conversation with a trio of middle-aged but well-preserved ladies who had joined them at the table, she knew he wouldn't miss her too much. With his usual gift of the gab, he was regaling them with stories of the good old days. One of the women in particular, a giggly blonde with a generous amount of cleavage on view, was giving him the eye. And Michael, always up for a flirt, was giving it straight back.

'I'd better make a move,' Iris said. 'Luke's going to be back soon.'

Despite his pulling prospects, Michael didn't hesitate. He started getting to his feet. 'I'll walk you home.'

But Iris shook her head, put a hand on his shoulder and gently pushed him back down again. 'Don't worry, it's early. I'll be fine.' She didn't want to cramp his style. It was only a ten-minute walk back to Silverstone Heights and her thoughts were still spinning from what had happened earlier. She needed time alone, time to think.

He hesitated, but she was insistent. 'Stay where you are.' She leaned down and kissed him on the cheek. 'I'll call you, okay?'

Iris turned up her collar as she stepped outside; the temperature had dropped a few degrees since she'd first arrived. Digging into her pockets, she found her gloves and pulled them on. There was snow forecast and she gazed up at the dark sky. Then she set out for the flat. She had only gone a few yards when she heard the thin clatter of the pub doors closing again.

'Hold on!'

She turned and jumped, hearing her own harsh intake of breath as she saw Chris Street striding towards her. His sharp face was lit by the overhead lamps. She could see that he was smiling, but with the kind of smile that didn't quite reach to his eyes. 'I wanted to apologise,' he said as he drew up beside her, 'for what happened yesterday.'

'There's no need,' Iris said nervously.

'There's every need. It all got out of hand. Feelings were running high and you got caught in the middle. It was out of order. We're not normally that uncivilised. I'm sorry if we scared you.'

Not half so much as he was scaring her now, she thought,. Despite his smart appearance and polite words, she sensed an ulterior motive. He'd had the last hour to express his regrets. If it was that important to him, why hadn't he done it while she was inside? 'That's all right. I understand. People get upset when . . . I'm really sorry about your mother.'

Immediately, she knew it was the wrong thing to say. She saw his whole body stiffen. 'My mother died years ago.'

Iris bit down on her lip. 'Sorry,' she said again. 'I meant . . .'

'It's all right.' The superficial smile immediately appeared

49

again. 'You weren't to know. I just wanted to make sure that you were all right.'

Iris forced a thin smile in return. 'I'm fine.' In some respects she found him more disturbing than his younger brother. Danny might be crazy, but he was visibly crazy – what you saw was what you got – whereas Chris had a more frightening mask of normality.

'That's good,' he said softly.

She went to move forward, but he wasn't finished yet. Taking a small step to the side, he effectively blocked her path. 'I hope Jenks wasn't bothering you.'

'Who?'

'The Weasel,' he said, 'the old guy you were talking to.'

Iris felt her heart begin to hammer. The Weasel? She sensed that this might not be the time to tell the truth. Instead, she tried to look nonplussed. Pretending to think about it, she furrowed her brow. 'Oh, *him*,' she eventually managed to say. 'You mean the old tramp, the smelly bloke? He was only asking me the time.'

'And?'

She shrugged. 'That was it.'

A hard edge entered his voice. 'It doesn't take that long to ask the time.'

Iris stared up at him, her hands clenching into two tight fists in her pockets. She was still scared, but now she was oddly uplifted too. If he was so concerned about what the old man had said then maybe there was some truth in it. 'I don't know. He was going on about how busy the place was. I think he was trying to tap me for a few quid. I-I wasn't taking much notice. I just wanted to get rid of him.'

Chris Street gave her a long, hard look and then his features gradually relaxed. 'That's all right then,' he said smoothly. He reached out and gave her a friendly pat on the arm. 'I just wanted to make sure he wasn't bothering you. He has a habit of making up all kinds of stories. I'm afraid old Jenks isn't all there in the head department.'

And it took one to know one, Iris thought. 'Right.'

Finally, he stood aside. 'Well, take care of yourself.'

Iris looked into his cold eyes and didn't like what she saw. 'Thank you. I will.'

Chapter Seven

He takes a long, deep breath before opening the folder and removing the contents. This is a luxury he rarely allows himself. Today, however, is a special occasion. Today he has seen his little girl again. It may have only been a glimpse, but it was better than nothing. The funeral, and its attendant crowds, provided him with the perfect opportunity to stand only feet away from her.

With care, he spreads the nineteen precious photographs out, one for every year they have been apart. The memory of that separation still fills him with grief, the pain as fiercely sharp as if it had happened yesterday. How agonising it had been! Kathleen could have left with him, but she wouldn't. Not that he blames her — her choices were hard ones.

He reaches out and with a finger gently traces the contours of his child's face. He touches the freckles that run across the bridge of her nose, the rosebud mouth and silky red hair. He can still remember holding her as a baby, can still recall the sweet smell of her skin. He remembers her tiny fingers and toes. He feels his stomach twist. Other men craved sons, but not him; he had been overjoyed at the birth of a daughter.

If only Kathleen had trusted him, trusted to the love they'd once had for each other. He had made mistakes, done terrible things, but they could still have had a future together. When he'd tried to get in touch again, she'd gone. Ten months it had taken him to track them down, but she still refused to change her mind. A clean break, she'd insisted, begging him to leave them alone. He could still see those green-grey eyes, full of tears and pleading. 'Please. If you truly love us, then you'll let us go.'

Kathleen, with all those crazy Catholic notions of hers, had blamed herself, had believed it was all her fault, but it wasn't — unless loving someone was a sin. He scowls. The Church, he thinks, has a lot to answer for. But he'd agreed to let them go . . . if not completely. For the past nineteen years he's been paying someone to keep track of their movements, to deliver one treasured photograph of Iris every year. He deserves that one small consolation, doesn't he?

Rubbing at his eyes, he sighs. He's paid a hefty price for his mistakes. Iris is grown up now, but that doesn't mean she has no further need of a father. There can only be one reason why she's come back to Kellston and it has to be to do with him. She must be searching, just as he is, for what has been lost.

Does Iris imagine he abandoned her? To think of it provokes an ache deep inside. Because it isn't true. He's always been watching over, making sure that she's safe. At the beginning he sent money too, but Kathleen always returned it. Fuck her! His hands curl into two tight fists. The knowledge of this, no matter how hard he tries, always makes him angry. Surely he was entitled to provide for his kid even if he couldn't see her? There was principle and there was just downright stupidity. Kathleen was always too damn proud for her own good.

He stares down at the photographs. Well, he has stuck to his side of the bargain and, after nineteen years of silence, has the right to claim back what is his. That isn't too much to ask, is it? And now that Lizzie is dead, now the bitch is six foot under, there are no more obstacles. He's been hiding away for too long. It's time to step back into the light. It's time to reach out to his little girl again.

Chapter Eight

It was Thursday morning and time was dragging by. Iris found herself constantly raising her head to look at the clock on the wall, frustrated by how slowly the red second hand was revolving, by how much longer she would have to wait. She was counting down the hours until her appointment with Jenks and it wasn't doing much for her concentration. William Grand had already returned two letters with an embarrassing number of typos.

'Er, sorry, I'm afraid there are . . .' He was not a man who liked to complain and had passed the sheets over with stumbling apologies, as if the fault was somehow his rather than hers.

The letters were important, both concerning an increasingly complicated repatriation. The dead man, being held in cold storage downstairs, had been with them for two months now, his body at the centre of an acrimonious family row. The wife wanted Connor Hills returned to Ireland, the son to have him buried in England. Solicitors had become involved and irate letters were flying back and forth.

At one o'clock, the corrections having been made, Iris went to the kitchen and put the kettle on. She retrieved her tuna sandwich from the fridge, peeled off the plastic wrapper and stared at it. Anxiety had blunted her hunger. She hadn't eaten since the half slice of toast she had forced down at breakfast and butterflies were flapping in her stomach. She hadn't told anyone about her meeting with Jenks, not even Luke. Not that she'd had the opportunity. He hadn't rolled in until after midnight and by then she'd already been in bed. A year ago she'd have given him hell – he hadn't even bothered to call her – but instead she had closed her eyes tight and pretended to be asleep.

Alice Avery came into the kitchen with a tentative smile. She seemed, if it was possible, more jittery than usual. 'No Toby today?' she said, her eyes darting left and right as if he might suddenly jump out and start tormenting her again.

Iris, glad of the distraction, raised her brows and grinned. 'Don't worry. He's probably sleeping it off.'

'Sorry?'

'He went clubbing last night, out on the town with the delightful Danny Street. He wouldn't be my choice for a dancing partner but hey, there's no accounting for taste.'

'No,' Alice said.

There was a short silence.

As that conversation clearly wasn't going anywhere, Iris tried a different tack. 'Keeping busy?'

Alice sat down. 'So-so.' As she placed her hands on the table-top, Iris noticed that they were trembling.

'Are you okay?'

'I'm fine.'

Iris frowned. She neither looked nor sounded fine. Usually they got on pretty well; they weren't exactly bosom buddies but had developed what she liked to think of as a decent working relationship. At the very least, Alice was usually fairly relaxed with her. 'What's wrong?'

'Nothing,' she replied with unusual brusqueness. But then,

having second thoughts, she shook her head. 'I don't know. Could I ask you something?' It was a purely rhetorical question so Iris didn't bother to reply. 'Have you ever . . . I mean . . . have you ever done . . . have you ever . . . I don't mean anything illegal but . . .'

Iris waited patiently, willing her to spit it out. She didn't believe her capable of anything even faintly immoral; Alice was one of the most upright people she had ever met. After a few seconds had passed, she gently urged her on. 'But?'

'Well, have you ever done something that you knew was—'

Unfortunately, William Grand chose that very moment to walk into the kitchen. Iris silently cursed him for his bad timing. He nodded at them both, switched on the kettle and hovered while it boiled again. Unlike Gerald, he didn't consider tea-making to be part of Iris's duties and always made his own. He looked over his shoulder at Alice. 'Everything all right with Mr Bayle?'

She lowered her head, avoiding his gaze. 'Yes, all done. He's ready for viewing.'

'Good, that's good. I'll have him moved.' He paused as if about to say more, gave her an odd look and then turned abruptly back to the kettle.

Iris glanced from one to the other, sensing an atmosphere. Alice was blushing bright red and she wondered, not for the first time, what made her tick. The woman must be in her early forties, but still had all the awkwardness of a teenager. However, Toby was right – there was a certain frisson between her and William Grand. Well, so what if there was? Alice could do worse. If she liked the quiet sort, then William wasn't a bad bet. Iris made a brief study of him, ticking off the usual boxes: he was the right age, early forties, a bit on the grey side but nice-looking enough, solvent and interested.

Maybe, in the interests of love, she should make herself scarce.

But before she had the chance, Alice grabbed her mug, muttered some garbled words about having things to do and rushed back downstairs.

William, who was looking rather pink himself, departed shortly after.

Iris stared down at her uneaten sandwich and sighed. The course of true love, as she was more than aware, rarely ran smoothly. Should she go after Alice? She decided not. For one, the contents of the basement always made her feel uncomfortable and for two, the moment had passed. Whatever Alice had been trying to say, she was clearly not in the mood to proceed with it now.

Iris dumped the sandwich in the bin, and with nothing else to do went back to work.

The afternoon rolled by with more speed than the morning. Gerald Grand was back in the office and, like the devil, believed in making work for idle hands. As such, she had a heap of filing dumped on her desk. The phone was busy too, a response perhaps to the publicity over Lizzie Street's funeral. By four o'clock there were three new funerals booked in with all the accompanying arrangements to sort out. There were also a couple of viewings that fortunately passed with none of the drama of the last one. With bereaved relatives to deal with, flowers to order and plenty of paperwork, Iris didn't have time to dwell on her own worries.

When five-thirty came around, she still had an hour to kill before her meeting with Jenks. She could go home and wait, but was worried that Luke might be there; it was unlikely – he never usually got back before seven – but not impossible. And if he was there, how was she going to explain why she needed to go out again? If she told him the truth he would try to talk her out of it or, at best, insist on going with her. And she didn't want that. This was something she had to do alone.

Iris gazed up at the two high windows. For privacy's sake, the lower ones were obscured so no one could see in. Snow had started to fall, drifting gently down from the sky. She watched as the flakes fell lightly against the panes, clinging briefly to the glass before melting away. Stay or go? If she went, she'd only be walking around in the cold for the next hour or so. Better to stay here in the warm. There was, much as it grieved her, plenty of filing left to do.

Iris strode briskly down Market Road, hearing the thin layer of ice crunch under her boots. There was still ten minutes before her appointment, but having worried so much about being early, she was now afraid of being late. She followed the road down to the large square where a general market was held every Saturday. In the centre, known to the locals as the Monny, was the War Monument, a tall, concrete obelisk flanked on all sides by a flight of steps.

Despite the weather, a few drunks were lounging around on the steps, either disinclined to give up their regular spots or simply too inebriated to move. Iris slowly circled round, making sure that Jenks wasn't there. She glanced at her watch. Still eight minutes to go. Withdrawing to the north side, she shook out her umbrella and went to stand in the covered area outside the cinema, joining a couple of other girls who were probably waiting for their dates to arrive.

From here she could easily monitor the two entrances to the square and she kept her eyes peeled while her thoughts began to wander. It had never been entirely clear to her why her father had left. Mild interrogations of her mother – she always got upset, even tearful, if Iris pressed too hard – resulted only in the repetitive and by now almost word-perfect response: 'Things weren't working out between us, darling. It was no one's fault, but we decided it was better to split up.' None of which adequately explained why he hadn't been in touch again. Some men could leave their children without a backward glance, but not him – he had not been the type, she was certain of it. Iris could still feel her small hand held securely in his. He would never have abandoned her like that. There was something she hadn't being told. And Jenks, surely, had confirmed that suspicion last night. Why else would he have approached her?

Iris, feeling the cold, stamped her feet on the ground and made another fast survey of the square. Unlike Luke, she never felt nervous when she was walking around this area alone. The difference was that his head was full of horror stories about the East End – most of them historical – and hers full of nice, safe memories from her childhood. In truth, neither of them was right: he was too cautious and she was probably too careless.

This evening, however, she couldn't see any danger in what she was doing. There were plenty of other people, mainly commuters cutting through the square on their way home. Some were walking straight across, others stopping off for a drink at the pub on the corner. The Hare & Hounds was doing brisk business; as the door opened and closed, a brief snatch of the Stereophonics floated out across the air.

As she waited her thoughts began to race. Michael, his mouth loosened by drink, had once hinted at another kind of trouble as regards her father but, when she had questioned him, had instantly backtracked, admitting only that Sean may have had some financial problems. Her dad, she knew, had been no angel – in his younger days he had spent time in jail for theft – but had cleaned up his act when he'd got married. Or had he? His criminal record was something else that her mother didn't like talking about.

Iris checked her watch again. It was bang on half past six. Where was Jenks? She had already decided that when he arrived she wouldn't do anything stupid like going to a quiet place with him. Whatever he had to say, he could say to her in public. That's if he ever turned up. She was starting to worry about that.

And she wasn't the only person who was worried. Although one of the girls had been met by her boyfriend, the other still remained. She was a blonde skinny teenager, only fifteen or sixteen, dressed in blue jeans, a denim jacket and the kind of cut-off slogan T-shirt that exposed her bare midriff to the elements. Her wide black-lined eyes briefly met Iris's but then quickly veered away again. She placed a hand on her hip and tried to look casual. Iris could understand how she felt; being stood up was bad enough, having it publicly witnessed was a humiliation too far.

Another ten minutes passed.

By now Iris was starting to despair. She suspected the worst: Jenks wasn't going to show. If she had any sense, she'd cut her losses and leave. But what if he'd been held up? What if he was on his way? The chance was slight, but it wasn't impossible. She'd give him another five minutes.

A lanky teenage boy appeared, offered a sullen muttered apology to the remaining girl and led her into the cinema. The girl glanced back over her shoulder as she went inside. Iris couldn't tell if the look she gave her was pityingly sympathetic or simply gloating.

She stamped her cold feet on the ground and raised her eyes to the sky. This was ridiculous. She should go. But still she couldn't quite bring herself to do it. Instead she cut across the square and walked very slowly, almost at a snail's pace, around its perimeter. The snow fell softly around her. She made several more circuits until her watch read seven. By now she knew it was pointless. Jenks wasn't coming.

Despondently, Iris wrapped her arms around her chest.

It was time to give up. It was time to go home.

Chapter Nine

Albert Jenks was backed up against the wall, his mottled hands raised in a shaky gesture of defence. His face was still stinging from the slaps. A steady trickle of blood flowed from his nose; he could taste it on his lips, on his tongue. His breath was coming in short, fast bursts and each exhalation increased the pain in his chest.

'Yer . . . yer old man won't be 'appy about this,' he managed to splutter.

Danny Street cocked his head and grinned. 'Oh, no need to be worrying 'bout that, Weasel.' He left a disconcerting pause. 'Who do you think sent me?'

An icy chill swept down Albert's spine. He cowered in the corner, his eyes never leaving Street's. 'I don't get it,' he whined.

'Lizzie can't protect you no more. She's six foot under, case you ain't noticed. Poor old bitch. Always thought she were so fuckin' smart but . . .'

Albert opened his mouth, but quickly snapped it closed again. Usually, he could worm his way out of any tricky situation, but at the moment everything he said only increased the younger man's hostility. Danny Street wasn't normal. You couldn't reason with him; he wasn't right in the head. Best not to give him an excuse to lash out again.

Danny frowned, took a few steps back and gazed critically around the room. It was sparsely furnished with a battered green sofa, a table, an old tasselled lamp and a couple of chairs. The carpet was threadbare. A pair of flimsy curtains, pulled tight across the window, prevented anyone from seeing in. The room was overly warm – the central heating was on high – and the heat accentuated the stinking odour of fear and sweat. 'Bit of a shithole, Weasel, if you don't mind me mentioning it. You didn't spend all that extra cash on home improvements, eh?' He snorted at his own joke. There was an overflowing ashtray balanced on the arm of the sofa and he reached out and deliberately flipped it over. His voice had become low and menacing. 'You think he don't know what you've been up to?'

Albert shook his head, the action increasing the terrible ache in his temples. He drew his sleeve across his nose and looked down at the blood. 'W-what do you mean?'

'Don't fuck me about!' Danny's eyes flashed bright with anger. He took three fast strides, his right hand raised and clenched into a fist.

Albert instinctively cried out and covered his face, waiting for the blow that never came.

Only inches away, Danny stopped and laughed again. Leaning forward, he hissed into Albert's ear. 'Didn't take you as the nervous sort, Weasel. You gettin' jumpy in your old age?'

Albert knew he'd been rumbled. It had been a mistake, a bloody big mistake, to get involved with the likes of Lizzie Street. He should never have told her that the O'Donnell girl was back living in Kellston. He'd been greedy; that was the beginning and end of it. He'd seen a chance to make a few extra quid, and with Terry off the scene . . .

'How much did she pay you?' Danny whispered. 'What's the going rate these days for a double-crossing, lowlife grass?'

'I never told her nuthin' important. I swear.' Albert laid his hand on his thumping heart. He swallowed hard, his Adam's apple jumping wildly in his throat. 'She just . . . just . . . she said Terry never talked no more, didn't tell her stuff.'

'And why do you think that was?'

'Dunno,' Albert muttered. Then, as he caught sight of the big man's fist twitching again, he sensibly added, 'Because he don't trust her.' He looked up pleadingly. 'It was only a few quid, son. I shouldn't have done it, I know I shouldn't, but things have been tight since your old man went away. I've only got me pension.'

'He's still paying you, paying you to keep yer big gob shut about his private business.'

Albert nodded. He couldn't deny it. But the small monthly allowance he received was barely enough to pay his bar bill. Once he'd been Terry Street's eyes and ears, doing the rounds of the local pubs and clubs, listening in to conversations and picking up all those tiny but essential snippets of information. Not much on their own, but if you had the nous to put them together . . . And Albert had always had a talent for that. He could sniff out something dodgy in a matter of seconds. Not only had he possessed the crucial ability to merge into the background, but had also known, at least by sight, every local villain in the neighbourhood. If there was a job going down, it had never taken him long to suss it out – and his employer had paid generously for the information. But that had been then. Times had changed and it was getting on for ten years now since Terry had been banged up.

Danny Street shoved his face into Albert's and glared at him. 'You never 'eard of loyalty, arsehole? You betrayed him. Dad told you to keep her away from her. And what did you do?'

Albert shrank back, taking refuge in repetition. 'It weren't like that. It weren't. I were only playin' her along. I never told her nuthin' important.'

'So what did you tell her?'

A series of sharp stabbing pains rolled up Albert's arm and through his chest. His breathing felt shallow and constricted. While he struggled to reply, Danny turned his attention to the room again.

'You hear about people dying in dumps like this. Not being found for weeks, months even. Getting eaten by cats and all. You got a cat?' He pulled a mock sympathetic face. 'Ah, shit no. You ain't got no one, have you, Weasel? No friends, nuthin'. No one gives a fuck about you. You could be rotting here for years before the council finally turn up to collect the rent. Although I suppose the smell might eventually bother the neighbours.' He gave a light shrug of his shoulders. 'But then again, would they notice the difference? You've been stinking out the place for the past twenty years.'

Albert had one last chance and he had to make the most of it. He took a deep breath and heaved the words out. 'Lizzie only wanted to know about the girl.'

Danny stared back at him. He looked genuinely baffled. 'What are you talking about? What fuckin' girl?'

Until this point Albert hadn't been certain about how much Danny knew, but now the answer was clear – sod all! He didn't have a clue. This simple fact not only revived his courage, but also gave him the leverage he needed, something to bargain with. His hopes immediately revived. There was still a chance of getting out of this with his skull intact. For the first time that evening, a tentative smile found its way on to his lips. 'Ain't Terry mentioned her?'

'You're talking shite,' Danny said. His eyes were beginning to blaze again. 'Why should he be arsed about some bloody girl?'

'For the same reason Lizzie was.'

Danny took a threatening lunge forward. 'Meaning?'

Albert jumped back, his spine pressing hard against the wall. He was too old, too tired for this kind of stuff. Even in his youth he'd relied entirely on his wits. His voice leapt up an octave or two. 'You'll never find out if you don't listen, son.'

Danny's face crunched into indecision. His instinctive urge was to try to beat it out of him, but some remaining seed of rationality held him back. A dead Jenks wouldn't be able to talk. Instead, he bared his teeth, wrapped his fingers around Albert's throat and spat out an order: 'Tell me!'

'Let go of me first.'

Danny's fingers tightened for a second, but then gradually loosened again. 'Start talkin', you pathetic streak of piss or I'll put yer fuckin' head through the window.'

Albert moved away from the wall, rubbing resentfully at his throat. He staggered over to the armchair and stood behind it. It might not offer much protection, but at least it was something. He stared at Danny. How Terry had managed to spawn such an ignorant piece of scum was beyond him. Terry Street was a bastard, there was no disputing that, but he'd always been a charming bastard.

'Well?' Danny snarled.

Albert's tongue snaked out and made a fast circuit of his dry, cracked lips. He wasn't sure how much to say. Too little and Danny would squash him like a bug, too much and he would have Terry to answer to. 'It's to do with your Liam, ain't it?'

At the mention of his dead brother, Danny's face grew even harder. 'What about him?'

Albert quickly shook his head. 'I can't say more than that. Talk to yer old man. He'll tell you. He'll put you straight.'

'And how am I supposed to do that? Give him a bell? In case it's slipped your mind, he's not staying in a fuckin' hotel!'

65

As Danny advanced on him again, a new, even more violent pain spread suddenly through Albert's chest. With a choking sound, he jerked back and crumpled. He could feel his knees buckling as he slowly collapsed on to the floor. The room was starting to dissolve.

Danny Street leaned over, his eyes wild and angry. He began to shake him. 'What are you doing? Wake up, you fuckin' bastard! Wake up!'

Chapter Ten

Iris unlocked the door and stepped into the flat. It was dark and silent. She flicked on the light in the hall. No Luke. He was late home again. Was she relieved or resentful? A bit of both, she decided, as she went through to the kitchen and plucked the bottle of brandy from the cupboard. She didn't usually drink spirits, but this counted as medicinal; her teeth were still chattering from the cold.

She took a hefty gulp, screwing up her face as the strong brandy slid down her throat. Then she poured another stiff measure into a glass. She felt utterly deflated. Jenks had raised her hopes before cruelly dashing them again. Sitting down, she placed her elbows on the table, closed her eyes and groaned. Why hadn't he shown up? Perhaps Chris Street had been right: Jenks wasn't all there. But, on the other hand, he was 'there' enough to know that her father was missing.

The phone began to ring. Thinking it could be him, she leapt up and snatched the phone from the cradle. 'Hello?'

Her mother's voice floated down the line. 'Hello, darling.'

Of course it wasn't Jenks. He didn't even have her number.

Iris tried to hide her disappointment. 'Hi, Mum. How are you?'

'I'm all right. What's wrong?'

'Why should anything be wrong?'

But Kathleen O'Donnell had a sixth sense for trouble, especially when it came to her daughter. 'Is it Luke?'

'No, it's nothing to do with Luke. I was just . . . just thinking about something.' She paused, but decided there wasn't any point in lying. 'Well, about Dad, actually.'

'Oh.'

Iris could tell from her tone that she wasn't best pleased about the subject matter. Wincing, she sat down again and took a swig from the glass. She tried to think of a diplomatic way of putting it, but couldn't come up with one. 'Why do you think he disappeared?'

Kathleen gave an exasperated sigh. 'He didn't disappear, darling. There wasn't anything mysterious about it. We split up. He simply packed his bags and left.'

'And never came back.'

'No,' she said shortly.

'Except people don't just do that, Mum.' Even as she said it, Iris knew it wasn't true. Every year thousands of people walked out of their homes never to be seen again. But she didn't want her dad to be one of them. She couldn't bear the thought of it. 'There's more to it than that. There has to be.'

'Why do you want to dig all this up again, Iris?'

But Iris didn't see it as digging. She hated the expression. She had a right to know the truth, didn't she? 'Was he in some kind of trouble?'

There was a brief hesitation followed by a laugh that sounded false. 'For heaven's sake! What are you talking about?' Her voice grew tighter. 'Has Michael been saying something?'

'No, he hasn't.' Iris raised her eyes to the ceiling. Her mother, for reasons she had yet to fathom, didn't like Michael O'Donnell and was never slow in sharing the fact. 'Why should he?'

'Because I know what he's like. He's full of tall stories. You can't believe a word he says. I hope he hasn't been—'

'He hasn't,' Iris said swiftly, not wanting to add to the ill feeling her mother already harboured. 'This has nothing to do with Michael.'

'Someone's been putting ideas into your head.'

Iris thought of the old man in the grubby raincoat. 'No one,' she lied. 'I've just been wondering why you're so sure that he's . . . that he's dead.'

There was a long pause and then her mother's voice grew softer. 'Because he loved you, darling, because no matter how he felt about me, he'd never have abandoned you. And I know we moved around a lot, but Michael always had our address. There was nothing to stop him from getting in touch if he'd wanted to.'

There wasn't much Iris could say to that. She felt guilty now about even asking – any talk of her dad always caused distress – so she simply murmured, 'Yeah, okay. I'm sorry.'

'Now are you sure everything's all right? I mean between you and Luke?'

'Fine.'

'Because every couple goes through difficult patches, especially after—'

'I know,' Iris interrupted, perhaps a little too quickly. She had no desire to get into an embarrassing counselling session with her mother. She knew exactly what she was thinking – that losing the baby had caused a rift between her and Luke and of course she was right. But it was their problem and no one else's. They would either work through it or they wouldn't. Changing the subject, she made small talk for the next few minutes and then said her goodbyes. 'I'll call you at the weekend.'

It was only as she put the phone down that she thought of

another question she could have asked. If her mother was so certain about it all, why hadn't she had her husband declared legally dead ages ago? Nineteen years was a long time to be missing. If she had ever wanted to get married again . . . but that was another odd thing: Kathleen O'Connell was an attractive woman but, apart from the occasional date, had never once – at least to Iris's knowledge – been seriously involved with anyone else. Why was that? She could hardly be pining, not if the split had been mutual, and she couldn't have been without opportunities.

Iris knocked back the brandy and poured herself another. Too many confusing thoughts were spinning around in her head. Restless, she went to stand by the window. Gazing out over the pinprick map of lights illuminating Kellston, she began to wonder if Luke was right – perhaps they did need a new start. Coming back here had been like chasing after a rainbow: a pretty dream, but not exactly practical.

She turned to view her surroundings. The flat was rented and the ultra-modern kitchen, all snazzy, new and neat, wasn't really to her taste. There was an almost unnerving sterility about it. The walls were a stark brilliant white and everything shone too brightly. She preferred a more old-fashioned style, the kind of surroundings she'd been comfortable in when she was growing up: a big wooden table in the middle of the room, a pile of pans and clutter. But perhaps that was her problem: she had got into the habit of always looking back instead of looking forward.

And where had that got her?

Perhaps what had happened earlier was a sign that she should stop pursuing the past. There was no real mystery as to how Jenks had found out about her missing father. Michael had a loud voice, especially after a pint or two, and could easily have been talking in any number of pubs. It wouldn't have taken the old man long to figure out that she was Michael's niece and that

70

there might be a few quid to be made from leading her on. There could be all kinds of reasons why he hadn't bothered to show up – the most likely being that a better opportunity had come his way.

It was another half-hour before Luke walked through the door. He was carrying a fancy bouquet of yellow roses, all crinkling cellophane and flowing ribbons. 'Sorry about last night,' he said, giving her a shame-faced grin. 'I should have called. I meant to, I really did.'

Iris took the flowers and stood on her toes to kiss him. Determined to make the effort, she had washed her hair and changed into a dress. 'Thank you. They're lovely.'

'You look great,' he said, standing back to admire her. 'What's the occasion?'

'No occasion. I think what you meant to say is that I always look great.'

'Absolutely,' he sensibly agreed. Leaning forward, he wrapped his arms tightly around her. His mouth nuzzled softly against her neck. 'Only tonight you look even greater than usual.'

'Good answer,' she said before gently pulling away. She walked across the kitchen and put the flowers in the sink. 'There's a bottle of wine in the fridge. I don't feel like cooking. Should we order a takeaway?'

'Sounds good to me.'

As she poured some water into a vase, Iris heard him clear his throat.

'Er . . . I got some news today.'

She glanced over her shoulder. 'Good or bad?'

'They want me to go to Brussels,' he said. 'On Monday. It's the Fernley contract. You know, the perfume people. I didn't think they'd consider me but . . .'

71

As Iris looked at his face, full of pride and excitement, she felt her heart contract. She should be glad for him and she was . . . except she didn't want him to go away. Not right now. Not while all this weird stuff about her father was going on. 'How long for?'

'Oh, just for the week. Less than a week. I'll be back on Friday.'

'Ah, so that's what the roses are really for,' she said only half-jokingly.

Luke walked over, wound his arms around her waist and kissed her again. 'You don't mind, do you? I won't go if you don't want me to.'

She wanted to say, *No, stay with me*, but she couldn't. It wouldn't be fair. Opportunities like these didn't come along every day. 'Of course I want you to!'

'And I'm really sorry about Michael's birthday. We'll make it up to him as soon as I get home.'

She leaned back against his chest, her hands folding over his. They had been together for five years and most of those had been glorious ones. They were an established couple, a good couple. Some things, the good things, were worth fighting for. They'd been through rough times recently, but they could get over them.

Couldn't they?

Chapter Eleven

Alice watched as he moved around the room, her eyes avidly tracing the smooth planes of his body, his muscular legs and pale strong arms. She was drinking in every detail as if she might never see him again. Astounded, as always, by the fact he was with her, she pulled the rose-coloured duvet up to her chin and smiled. She was always amazed by his utter lack of self-consciousness; she would no sooner parade naked in front of him as stab a man to death.

'There's something I need to ask you,' Toby said, reaching down to pick up his jeans.

'What's that?'

'Promise me you won't get mad? I know I swore I'd never ask again but . . . but is there any chance that you could help me out?'

Alice felt her heart sink. 'Helping out' was a euphemism for what she'd spent the past week stressing about. Could she really bring herself to do it again? She didn't want to say no – she never wanted to say no to him – but instinctively she hesitated. 'I-I thought it was only supposed to be the once.'

'Me too,' he sighed, 'but you know what the Streets are like. Once they get their claws into you . . . I wouldn't ask, I really wouldn't, but you know how I'm placed. This way I can pay off what I owe them without getting any bones broken.' He zipped up his jeans and gazed mournfully at her. 'You will help, won't you?'

'I want to,' she said. 'But . . .'

'But?'

Alice lowered her chin into the duvet. 'I'm not sure if I can. I don't . . . I mean, it's not, not right, is it?'

'So what's right?' he said sharply. But then he threw back his head and laughed. 'Alice, love, you're so wonderfully strait-laced.' Sitting down on the edge of the bed, he leaned forward, gently pushed her hair aside and kissed her neck. 'That's why I adore you so much.' He kissed her again, this time on the mouth. 'But when you think about it, it's not actually harming anyone, is it? Come on, please say yes. Please.'

Harm, she thought, was a relative concept. Anyway, it wasn't so much about damage as morality. She wanted to say yes, but still she held back. It was mainly because she didn't feel com-fortable with it, but also because she wanted him to work a little harder at persuading her. If nothing else it was a means of keep-ing him with her for a while longer. 'I don't know.'

His mood instantly changed again. Frowning, he stood up, grabbed his shirt off the chair and shrugged it on. 'Well, I sup-pose I could do it on my own, but if one of the Brothers Grimm turn up, I'll be done for. I mean, how the hell am I going to explain that?' He paused, forcing out a trembling smile. 'Still, if you can't bring yourself to do it, I'm not going to try and force you. It's your decision. You have to do what you feel is right.'

Alice felt the breath catch in her throat. 'Would they really hurt you?'

'What do you think? I owe them over twenty grand. I don't imagine they'll be taking me to court to get it back.' He bowed his head, his blue eyes filling with fear. 'I've fucked up, Alice, big time. I never wanted to put you in this situation, but it's my only way out. I don't know how I'll cope if—'

'Of course I'll do it,' she said, unable to bear the terror in his voice. There was no way she could refuse when the man she loved needed her so much.

'Are you sure?'

'I'm sure.'

He smiled, leaned down and kissed her again. 'God, you're such an angel. What would I do without you?'

'So long as it's the last time.'

'Yes, absolutely. I promise. Thank you.'

Seeing the relief in his eyes was enough to enable Alice to temporarily push her conscience aside. What he was asking of her might not be right, but it wasn't so dreadful either. No one was going to get hurt. No one was going to die. What was that saying – what the eye didn't see, the heart didn't grieve over? It was the kind of quote her mother would have claimed came from the Devil's mouth, but Alice instantly put that thought aside. The last thing she wanted to think about – especially when she was sitting naked in bed – was her mother's thin-lipped disapproval.

'Although there is one other thing,' Toby said. 'I hate to ask, but next time could you make sure that . . .'

He bent to whisper the rest of the request in her ear.

As she listened, Alice flinched. 'What?'

'I know,' he said, grasping her arms and pulling her closer. 'I don't like it either. I really don't. But that's the deal – that's what he wants. I've told him it might not be next week, even next month, but he's prepared to wait.'

Alice shivered under the duvet. She knew if they were caught,

75

she'd not only lose her job, but her reputation too. How would she cope with the shame? But then how would she cope without Toby? He had brought a joy to her life, an incredible passion she had never felt before. Without him, everything would be grey and meaningless.

'I'd better get off,' he said.

It was nine o'clock and she didn't inquire as to where he was going. She didn't want to know. No, that wasn't true. She did want to know, but was too scared to ask. He'd never stayed the night and she had never had the courage to request it. Alice was aware that the affair had to remain a secret, at least for now. As Toby never stopped telling her, it had nothing to do with their age difference. He'd be proud to take her out to any restaurant or bar, but it was better that they weren't seen together in public. 'The old man's such a dinosaur. He wouldn't approve. He'd find a way to get rid of you, Alice, and I couldn't bear that. The idiot wants to marry me off to some dull undertaker's daughter.'

Alice ached at the thought of it. 'You're too young to get married,' she said quickly.

Toby gave her a wink as he headed for the door. 'I'll call you.'

She listened to his footsteps in the hall and then a few seconds later heard the front door slam. He was gone. And suddenly it seemed as if he had never been there. Alice bowed her head and hugged her knees. Was she happy or sad? She wasn't sure if she could differentiate between the two any more. She buried her face in the duvet and tried not to cry.

Chapter Twelve

Iris had managed to wangle the afternoon off. This had been achieved by waiting until Gerald Grand was out of the building – he would never have agreed at such short notice – and then approaching William with a sob story of how her uncle had fallen, sprained his ankle and needed her help. She felt guilty about the lie, but it wasn't a complete fabrication: by the end of his birthday celebrations Michael probably wouldn't be able to stand up.

As she was leaving the office, William had cleared his throat. 'Er, could you spare a moment? I just wanted to ask. Do you . . . do you think Alice is all right?'

'Alice?'

He shifted uncomfortably in his chair. 'You don't think she's been acting a little oddly?'

Iris couldn't remember a time when Alice didn't behave that way. 'Not really. What do you mean?'

William thought about it for a second, frowned and then shook his head. 'No, no I'm sure you're right.' He gave a light wave of his hand as if to dismiss both her and the subject. 'I'll see you on Monday. Have a nice weekend.'

It was only as she closed the door that Iris remembered the conversation she'd had with Alice the previous afternoon. Perhaps there was something troubling her. Still, whatever was on her mind was her business rather than anyone else's.

They were joined for lunch by Michael's pal, Rick Howard, and his wife Kavita. Michael had refused the offer of a restaurant and chosen instead to go to his favourite pub, the Dog and Duck. Iris thought it a vaguely threatening kind of place with too many young, bored men idling away the afternoon but it had, for her uncle at least, the overwhelming advantage of being within staggering distance of his flat on the Mansfield Estate.

Kavita, or Vita as she was more commonly known, was the only real friend Iris had made since coming to Kellston. She was a smart, slim, dark-haired woman in her early thirties, pretty but tough, and more than capable of holding her own with some of the friskier locals. She had a first-class law degree and although she could have made big money in the City, had chosen instead to work for a small Kellston firm. One of the major reasons for this was undoubtedly her husband's past.

Iris looked over to the pool table where Rick was currently lining up a shot. He was a large, easy-going bear of a man, good-looking, dryly amusing and almost fifteen years Vita's senior. She wasn't entirely sure what bound the two of them together. Perhaps it was sheer obstinacy. Vita's parents had vehemently opposed the match. This wasn't, as Iris had first imagined, down to any objections on religious or cultural grounds – her family was actually quite liberal – but more to do with Rick having spent so much time in jail. He had a record as long as his arm. Although not a villain in the true sense of the word – he lacked the concentration or the single-minded determination to make a true success of crime – he had never been able to resist the lure of the sure bet, of the badly planned job that couldn't possibly go wrong. It was a miracle that Vita had managed to keep him out of trouble for the past four years.

Iris glanced down at her plate. She was no longer hungry. The current trend for good pub food had passed this establishment by; lunch, if you wanted something hot, consisted of a microwaved baked potato or anything fried with chips. She pushed the remains of her limp ham and tomato sandwich to one side and took a sip of orange juice. With the Rufus Rigby party to attend tonight, she'd decided to stay off the booze.

'So?' Vita said, nudging her elbow.

Iris looked at her. 'What?'

'You know what. You've had a face on you ever since you arrived. Is it Luke?'

'No, it's nothing to do with him.'

'Your mother then.'

'No.'

'Work?' Vita picked up her pint of lager, took a large swig and then slapped her hand down on Iris's arm. She laughed. 'Oh God, I know what it is. You're having a secret, sordid affair with that infamous seducer Gerald Grand.'

Iris sighed. Only Vita could have come out with such a comment. 'If you could just rein in your insane fantasies for a moment . . .'

'Not until you come clean.'

'Okay, okay. I'll tell you.'

The other woman's eyes grew wide as Iris explained about how Albert Jenks had been watching her outside the funeral parlour, how he'd later approached her in the pub and the arrangement he'd made for them to meet the following evening. 'You did what? Are you completely mad?'

'Keep your voice down,' Iris said, glancing anxiously towards the pool table. 'I wasn't in any danger. He's an old man, he wasn't about to . . .'

'Yeah, well, he might have been a pensioner, but you didn't know who was actually going to turn up. You could have been met by anyone.'

'It was at the Monny at half past six. There were lots of people around.'

'And how many do you think would stop and help if some nutter did have a go? This is Kellston, Iris. No one gives a damn or if they do they're usually too scared to do anything about it. You have to be careful.'

Iris shrugged. 'Well, it doesn't matter now. He didn't even show.'

'Why didn't you call me?'

'Why do you think?' Iris gazed into Vita's large brown eyes. 'You'd have tried to talk me out of it, and with your powers of persuasion you'd have probably succeeded. And then later I'd have regretted not going. I know I would. I had to give it a shot, at least try to find out if he had any useful information.'

Vita nodded. 'Okay, I get it. And yes, I may have raised some of the more obvious objections, but if you'd been that determined . . . well, Rick and I could have come along too. We could have hung around the square. No one would have known we were with you. At least that way you'd have had someone watching your back.'

Iris hadn't thought of that. But then she hadn't been thinking logically about anything much recently. She nodded. 'You're right.'

'Promise me you won't do anything crazy like that again.'

'I swear,' Iris said, obediently raising her right hand. She had a lot to thank Vita and Rick for: Vita for standing by her through the past six months – not the easiest of jobs in the circumstances – and Rick for getting her the position at Tobias Grand & Sons. He worked there part-time, sometimes as a driver, sometimes as a pallbearer, and when the vacancy for a new receptionist had come up had managed to get her an interview with Gerald.

'So what are you going to do now?'

'Forget about it,' Iris said. 'What else?'

Vita hesitated for a moment and then said, 'I suppose I could ask around, see if anyone knows this Jenks bloke. If he's local, and he probably is, then one of my more dubious clients might have heard of him.'

'Could you?' Last night Iris had been determined to move on, to put it all behind her, but now she jumped at this fresh opportunity.

'He's probably some kind of shyster. You do realise that, don't you?'

'Yeah, but I'd like to know for certain. It was all so . . . so weird, him coming up to me like that. The more I think about it, the more I think that he must know something.'

'Yes,' Vita agreed, 'that your father took off nineteen years ago and was never heard of again. Kellston's not that big a place, Iris, and people have long memories. As soon as he realised you were Michael O'Donnell's niece, he may have thought he could play you for a sucker, string you along in exchange for a few quid.'

'I did consider that.'

'But it didn't stop you going to meet him.'

Iris shrugged again. She knew that what she'd done was foolish, but if she had the opportunity she would, in all likelihood, do the same thing again. 'There was only one way I was going to find out. I agree that it was stupid, and a long shot at best, but I couldn't ignore it. I couldn't ignore him. I had to follow it up.'

Vita took another swig of her drink. She put her glass down, folded her arms and put on her serious face. 'Have you talked to Michael about any of this? I don't mean about last night – I can see why you wouldn't want to mention that – but just about your dad in general.'

'He says exactly the same as my mother. It's as if they worked it out together; their stories are virtually word-perfect.'

'That could be because they're both telling the truth.'

'Or because they're both hiding something.'

Automatically, they swivelled their heads to stare at Michael. He was still playing pool, his focus entirely on the game. 'You think he knows more than he's letting on?'

'I've no idea. He's like Mum; I can't get anything out of him. He'll give me the official party line, but then if I press him, he clams up and starts acting all shifty.'

'Ah, shifty,' Vita said. 'I know that look. Rick was born with it. Fortunately, I have my methods for getting at the truth.'

'Care to share them with me?'

'I would, but in all honesty I don't think they're applicable when it comes to your uncle.'

It took a second for Iris to cotton on. 'Oh, please,' she said, wrinkling her nose. 'Spare me the details.'

Vita laughed, but then grew thoughtful again. 'You know, it could be that Michael simply doesn't like to talk about it. Perhaps it's too upsetting. I've known him for years and I wasn't aware he even had a brother until you turned up.'

'You think I'm wrong, that I'm being paranoid?'

'No, don't be daft. I think you have to go with your gut instinct – wherever it leads you. And, so long as you swear not to keep me in the dark, to not go swanning off for any more meetings with strange old men, I'll do everything I can to help.'

Iris gave a mighty sigh of relief. She loved her uncle and she loved Luke too, but she hadn't realised until this moment just how alone she actually felt. 'Thank you,' she said, leaning over to give Vita a hug. Convinced that her family were hiding the truth, it felt good to have a friend to confide in.

Chapter Thirteen

Despite the credit crunch, Rufus Rigby hadn't stinted on the Christmas party. The West End venue was all mood lighting and soft-pile carpets. The buffet was excellent, the champagne free-flowing and the guest list must have numbered a couple of hundred. There was a jazz band playing and the dance floor was full. Iris limped over to a chair after yet another toe-crushing experience with one of Luke's superiors. And it wasn't just her feet that were suffering; she could feel her jaw aching too. She'd had a fixed smile on her face for the past two hours.

Still, this evening was all about making an effort. For Luke's sake, she'd put on the little black dress, the high heels and the pearls. Her long red hair was tied up in a complicated series of twists and knots and her make-up had taken an eternity. A new start, that's what she'd promised herself, and okay, she may have backtracked a little by agreeing to let Vita make some enquiries about Jenks, but that didn't mean she wasn't moving forward as regards her relationship with Luke. She had been doing her best to sparkle, laughing at his bosses' jokes and flirting with them just enough to prove how very attractive they were without crossing any boundaries. Once upon a time this juggling act had come quite naturally to her, but now she found it both tedious and tiring.

Iris sipped on the chilled champagne and tried to spot Luke in the crowd. She hadn't expected him to stay by her side all night – these occasions were as much about networking with the clients as rewarding the efforts of the workforce – but he'd disappeared twenty minutes ago and she hadn't seen him since. She glanced surreptitiously at her watch; it was ten past ten. The do would go on for ages yet, probably not breaking up until the early hours of the morning.

A brunette in her mid-forties, dressed in a long green skirt and low-cut top, wandered past, stopped, retreated and then slumped down on the chair beside Iris. She kicked off her high heels. 'Shit, I hate these parties.'

Iris smiled. 'Join the club.'

The woman took the bottle from the ice bucket on the table, checked how much was left inside and filled up her glass. She drank half of it down in one and then topped up. Turning, she looked Iris up and down and said, 'You don't work for these jerks, do you?'

'No.'

'And you're not a client?'

'No,' Iris said again.

'Well, that's something.'

Iris took a moment to study her new companion. The deep-set eyes were a cool shade of grey and the mouth, victim perhaps of a little too much cosmetic filler, had a rather bee-stung appearance. 'So do you work for the company or . . .?'

'God, no. I'm only here to embarrass my husband.' Reaching for her glass, she took another hearty swig. 'Sadly, I'm not pissed enough yet.' She emitted a sound that was halfway between a sigh and a groan. 'As if I haven't got anything better to do than waste my time on these big-mouthed, lecherous, groping losers . . . no offence to whoever you're here with, love.'

'None taken,' Iris said.

The woman laughed, flinging a generously ringed hand into the air. 'I'm Sandra by the way. Don't mind me; I'm always bitching about something or other.'

'Iris,' she replied.

'So what line are you in?'

'I work for an undertaker.'

Sandra laughed again. 'Poor you! You spend all day working with the dead and then have to come out at night and play with the zombies.'

Iris grinned. 'I hadn't quite thought of it like that before.'

'So which one is yours? I take it you're here to support your other half. It's a gruesome duty, but one we're obliged to perform. Thankfully, it only comes round once a year.'

'Luke Hamilton.' Iris scanned the room again and eventually spotted him near the bar. He was talking to a slim, rather striking girl with honey-coloured skin and sleek fair hair. 'Over there,' she said, 'the guy in the grey suit.' And then, realising that this description applied to half the men in the room, she added: 'The tall one talking to the blonde in the red dress.'

Sandra's brows shot up. 'He's a looker,' she said. 'Do you think it's safe to leave him alone with her?'

'Oh, I'm sure he can take care of himself.'

'My dear,' she said, leaning forward to place her hand firmly on Iris's arm, 'I hate to mention this but in my experience, it's usually the taking care of themselves that ends with some poor woman's heart being broken. If I was you, I'd get over there right now and claim what was rightfully mine.'

But Iris had never been the jealous type – and certainly not the type to act like some crazy possessive girlfriend. However, she did find herself staring rather hard at the girl. She was pretty, there was no denying that. 'Do you know who she is?'

Sandra shook her head. 'Jen, Jody, Jade? I don't know; they all look the same to me. Some bitch in the sales department. They come and go. They're all young and ambitious and don't care what they have to do to get to the top.'

Iris had the feeling she was speaking from bitter experience. 'So where's your other half?'

Sandra lifted her shoulders in a small indifferent shrug. 'So long as he's not within twenty yards of me, I'm happy.'

And then Iris, for some reason she wasn't quite sure of – perhaps just because of Sandra's comment or because it had been on her mind so much recently – began thinking about her parents. Had they been so unhappy that they couldn't bear the sight of each other? She had not felt it as a child, had always thought of them as thoroughly content, but maybe they had taken care to hide their true feelings from her. She wanted to ask Sandra why she stayed with this man who clearly made her so miserable, but didn't have the heart to go there. This evening was supposed to be about being positive, about supporting Luke and moving forward; she couldn't afford to start slipping back.

'Perhaps you're not that bothered.'

'What?' Iris said, glancing back at Sandra again.

The woman nodded towards the dance floor. Luke and the girl had moved away from the bar. The blonde had curled her arms rather intimately around his neck and was nestling against his shoulder. Her long fair hair, the kind of hair that was reminiscent of Chris Street's trophy wife, fell in a long silky curtain down her back. Luke was leaning in close and whispering something, but she couldn't read his lips. Iris felt a tiny shiver of doubt, but quickly dismissed it. At the end of the day it came down to trust; either she believed in him or she didn't. There couldn't be anything going on or Luke would never have insisted on her coming. It was just a dance, a dance between colleagues.

It was another hour before Iris decided she'd had enough. Sandra had wandered off in search of more champagne and hadn't come back. The scarlet woman had disappeared too and Luke was now deep in conversation with a huddled group of clients. Having endured three more dances and too many corny pick-up lines from a number of guys drunk enough to chance their luck with a girl who appeared to be on her own, she decided her duty was well and truly done.

Iris made her way over to Luke and told him she was going home. 'I've had a really good time,' she lied. 'I'm just a bit tired, that's all. It was a hectic day at work. You don't mind, do you?' She omitted to tell him that she'd taken the afternoon off, but there was no reason why he should ever find out. 'You don't need to come with me.'

He seemed relieved that she wasn't asking him to leave too. 'Well, let me get you a cab at least.'

'No, really, I'll be fine. Don't worry. There'll be plenty out-side.' She stood on her toes and gave him a kiss. 'You enjoy yourself. I'll see you later.'

As it happened, there wasn't a taxi in sight when she stepped out into the crisp night air. She waited for a couple of minutes, but then decided to start walking towards Leicester Square. The longer she hung around, the colder she was going to get. Then, as she was turning the corner, she spotted a bus that was heading for Kellston. It had just pulled up at the stop and she had to do a teetering run in her high heels in order to catch it. Luckily, the driver wasn't the type who waited until you were almost there before gleefully closing the doors and accelerating away.

Iris thanked him for waiting, bought a ticket and found a free seat about halfway back. She was aware of a pervasive smell of alcohol coming from the other passengers, but there were no obvious drunks in evidence. The traffic, she thought, shouldn't be too bad at this time of night. With luck she'd be home within half an hour. Maybe even less. She stared out of the window at the bright lights and the crowds. Even after a year she still hadn't got used to the size of London. As a child she hadn't been aware of its immensity; her little carefree world had revolved around the much quieter streets of Kellston.

Once the bus had freed itself from the tangle of the West End, it sped along at a good pace. Iris, reviewing the evening, found herself pondering on the warning Sandra had given. Was the blonde really a threat? If so, maybe she shouldn't have left Luke alone. There was such a thing as asking for trouble – but then again there were such things as loyalty and trust. Luke might have his faults (who didn't?), but infidelity, as far as she was aware, wasn't one of them. She hadn't been the easiest person to live with for the past six months, but all that was going to change. From now on, she was going to concentrate on what was important.

Iris wondered what Michael was doing and whether he was still in the pub. The Dog and Duck kept long hours and didn't usually close until well after midnight. Hopefully, Rick and Vita would still be there. She didn't like to think of him celebrating his birthday without friends. Not that he didn't have a wide circle of acquaintances – other than his compulsory absences at Her Majesty's Pleasure, he had lived all his life in Kellston and seemed to know half the population. However, she wouldn't trust many of them to see him safely home.

And then she started thinking again about what Michael knew, or didn't know, as regards what had happened to her father. Perhaps Vita was right about the reason he didn't like to talk: her parents' separation, and Sean's subsequent disappearance, was clearly surrounded by more than her own personal pain and confusion. Sometimes the things that hurt most were the things that were hardest to talk about.

Iris was still dwelling on this when she realised that she'd overshot her stop. Standing up, she rang the bell, but by the time the bus halted again she was at the south end of the High Street. Getting off, she looked around her. She was never normally down this way, but fortunately it wasn't too far a walk back.

After the warmth of the bus, the air felt even colder than it had before. She rubbed her hands together, pulled up the collar of her coat and set off for home. This part of the long High Street was virtually unknown to her. The majority of shops lay in the middle section and Tobias Grand & Sons was at the northern end. It was only as she was crossing the road that she noticed the blue neon sign in front of her: Wilder's. She almost stopped dead in her tracks – not the wisest thing to do when cars were hurtling towards you – but somehow, amidst the blaring of a few angry horns, she managed to make it to the other side. Iris understood now why Guy hadn't given her the name of the bar he owned; he must have presumed, after introducing himself, that she'd put two and two together.

Trying not to look too obvious, she gazed casually in through a narrow transparent strip in the otherwise opaque window. It was busy. She searched the faces for Guy Wilder, but couldn't see him. And then, just as she was about to go, he walked straight into her line of vision. Dressed in the kind of suit that must have cost more than she earned in six months, he stood out from the crowd. But it wasn't just his clothes that made him shine; he was the kind of man who had a certain aura about him.

Guy had stopped to talk to a couple sitting at a table and Iris watched as he leaned down, chatting and laughing with them. She knew that she should walk away, go straight home, but couldn't resist lingering for a few seconds longer. There was no harm in looking was there? It was only when he glanced up that she realised what a mistake that had been. As his eyes met hers, she jumped swiftly back. She could feel her cheeks blazing red. Mortified, she quickly moved off.

Iris had only gone five yards down the street when she heard the door to the bar opening. A brief snatch of music, of voices, floated through the air.

'Iris O'Donnell. Is that you?'

She could have ignored him, but she didn't. She could have kept on walking, but she didn't. Instead she turned around and smiled.

Guy Wilder smiled back. 'Not running off, are you? I believe I owe you a drink.'

Chapter Fourteen

Inside, the place had a laid-back lounge bar type of feel. The red walls were covered with old black and white movie-star photos: Bogart and Bacall, Cary Grant, Bette Davis. A number of soft leather sofas and chairs were arranged around low tables. The lighting was subdued, the music smooth and the atmosphere easy and relaxed. Most of the patrons appeared to be in their late twenties, early thirties, but there were older people there too. It was the kind of establishment where anyone could wind down after a long, hard day at the office.

Guy Wilder led her through to a more private area at the back. She was aware of several female heads turning to watch them; the eyes were mainly concentrated on him with just a few fleeting glances in her direction – as if to judge and assess the possible competition. As she took off her coat to reveal the little black dress, he gave her an admiring glance. 'You look amazing.'

'Thank you,' she said, gracefully accepting the compliment. Then, as she sat down, a horrifying thought leapt into her head: what if he imagined that she'd got all dressed up for *his* benefit? 'Actually, I was at a Christmas party. I was a bit tired so I decided to call it a night but, of course, I couldn't find a cab. A bus came along, so I jumped on that, but I missed my stop and ended up down here. That's why I . . . I was just . . .' Iris realised she was starting to ramble and abruptly shut up.

But Guy, if he noticed her discomfort, tactfully glossed over it. 'Well, God bless London Transport. It seems the fates have conspired to bring you to my doorstep. Let me get you that drink. A glass of wine or would you prefer champagne?'

Iris had drunk enough champagne for one night. She thought about asking for a coffee, but changed her mind. Perhaps she was in need of something stronger. 'Thanks. A glass of red would be nice.'

Guy disappeared for a minute and then returned with a bottle of Cabernet and two glasses. She stared at the bottle; she had only been intending to stay for the one. He must have seen her surprise because he smiled. 'Don't worry, we're not obliged to drink all of it.'

Iris wondered just how transparent she actually was. 'So, how have you been?'

'Oh, getting by. Doing my best to contain my grief.'

She gave him a look.

He winced. 'Sorry. I've got in the habit of doing that, of hiding behind sarcasm. It's not an attractive trait, is it?'

Iris gave a light shrug. 'You've not had the easiest of times. I guess it comes down to whatever gets you through.'

Guy poured two glasses of wine and passed one over to her. 'Cheers,' he said. His blue eyes gazed intently into hers. 'Here's to . . .?' He paused. 'To new beginnings, new friendships . . . and buses that never stop where they're supposed to.'

Iris laughed as they lightly chinked their glasses together. She glanced around. 'I've never been here before. It's nice.' She inwardly flinched at the word she had used. *Nice?* Who on earth would want to hear their bar described in such an insipid fashion? 'I mean, it's very . . . stylish. I like it. I love the décor. To be honest, I wasn't even aware that it was here. I haven't been down this end of the High Street since I moved back to Kellston.'

'And when was that?'

'A year ago,' she admitted. Iris was aware that she had used *I* instead of *we* and immediately thought of Luke. But she wasn't deliberately hiding anything. Or maybe she was. Maybe, just for a few minutes, she wanted to be a different Iris O'Donnell, a woman who wasn't burdened by all the pain and grief of the past six months. 'I grew up here, but we moved away when I was seven. I'm glad to be back, but the area has changed a bit over the years.'

'And not necessarily for the better,' he said. 'So where are you living now?'

Iris pulled a face, feeling a need to apologise for her choice of accommodation. 'Silverstone Heights.'

'Ah, one of the chosen few. So how does it feel to be up there on the hill looking down on us poor minions?'

Iris felt a hot glow spread through her cheeks. She bent to pick up her glass, taking a large gulp of wine before she answered. She knew how the locals felt about the flats, that the people who lived in them believed they were a cut above the rest of the population, and she couldn't blame them for thinking that way. The development, with its locked gates and hi-tech security systems, said as much about the people who chose to live there as those they were trying to keep out. 'It wouldn't have been my first choice, but I needed somewhere in a hurry.'

'You don't have to justify it,' Guy said, grinning. 'There are plenty of times when I'd have welcomed that kind of protection. I've been broken into twice this year. You'd have thought, with my mother being who she was and all, that they might have given me a wide berth, but no such luck. The junkies have no respect for anyone, not even the hard-working sons of local villains.' He stopped and took a breath. 'Talking of which, I should apologise again for that unfortunate scene you were forced to witness. I'm sorry, really sorry. I hope the Streets didn't give you any trouble over it.'

Iris, recalling her disturbing conversation with Chris Street outside the Hope & Anchor, hesitated before she answered.

A frown crunched on to his forehead. 'They didn't have a go at you, did they?'

'No,' she said quickly. 'It was nothing like that.'

'But?'

Iris wasn't sure if she should tell him. He had his own problems to deal with and his own simmering resentments. She knew how he felt about the Streets and didn't want to add fuel to the fire.

Guy leaned forward to refill her glass. Iris, surprised by the fact she'd already emptied it, made a mental note to drink this one more slowly. *So much for only staying for the one.* She glanced at her watch; it was almost midnight. Still, Luke wouldn't be back for ages yet and even if he did get home before her she could always claim that she'd run into Vita. The moment the excuse entered her head, she baulked at it. What she was doing was completely innocent and yet she was already thinking like some cheating girlfriend, busily making up excuses in case she got caught out.

'You don't have to tell me if you don't want to,' he said.

Iris lifted her eyes and what she saw made her heart shift. It wasn't just his good looks or his charm – she felt a weird, inexplicable connection to him, something she couldn't explain. 'It was nothing to do with you.'

He sat back, crossing his legs. 'Well, contrary to whatever impression I may have made – and I'm sure it hasn't been a good one – I am capable of discussing subjects other than myself.'

'I . . . I didn't mean that.' She knew he was just teasing her, but couldn't bring herself to respond in the same light-hearted tone. Suddenly, making a decision, she said, 'Have you ever heard of a man called Jenks? He's an oldish guy, looks kind of scruffy. He was in the Hope & Anchor on Wednesday night, you know at the . . . the wake. He said something to me . . . he . . .'

'Go on,' Guy said.

Iris ran her tongue along her lips. They felt parched and dry. How much should she tell him? 'It's nothing really, he just said that he might have some information about my father.' She briefly lowered her eyes before lifting them to meet his gaze again. 'He disappeared years ago. It's a long story. I won't bore you with it. I shouldn't have taken any notice, but you know what it's like when someone catches you off guard. There are all these things you think about later, about what you should have said, should have asked, but I was too shocked at the time. He wanted me to meet him on Thursday evening. I didn't say yes or no but . . . well, I went along but he didn't turn up.' She paused and took another sip of wine. 'Anyway, all that aside, Chris Street approached me after I'd left the pub and started interrogating me as to what Jenks had wanted.'

Guy stared hard at her. 'And what did you tell him?'

'Nothing,' she said. 'I told him he'd only asked me the time.'

He let out a long relieved sigh. 'Thank God for that.'

'What do you mean?'

'I take it you haven't heard.'

She could tell from his face that this wasn't going to be good news. Her heart began to hammer. 'Heard what?'

At that very moment a tall, elegant black man walked by the table and nodded at them. Guy beckoned him over. 'Noah,' he said, 'have you got a moment? This is Iris, Iris O'Donnell.'

95

Noah leaned across, smiled and shook her hand. 'Nice to meet you.'

'And you.'

'Noah, for his sins, is my partner in the business,' Guy said. He looked up at him. 'Could you do me a favour and get Iris a brandy.'

Iris frowned, shaking her head. 'What? I don't want a brandy.'

'No,' Guy said, 'but I think you're going to need one.' He nodded at Noah. 'You'd better make that two.'

'Sure,' Noah said. He glanced briefly at them both before retreating to the bar.

'What is it? What's going on?' Despite the warmth of the room, she could feel a chill running through her. Recalling what he'd mentioned just before his business partner had arrived, she said, 'What haven't I heard?'

Guy seemed reluctant to pass on the information. 'It was in the evening paper.'

'I haven't read the evening paper.'

'It's about Albert Jenks,' he said carefully.

And now, seeing the expression on his face, the chill in Iris turned to ice. 'What about him?'

She knew the answer even before he gave it. Her hands were clenching, gripping her thighs, even as he spoke.

'I'm sorry but . . . he was found dead last night.'

'Oh my God,' she murmured. She bent down towards the table. A long strand of her hair came loose and fell down around her face.

Noah arrived with the brandies, put them on the table and discreetly left again.

'W-what happened to him?' she eventually managed to stammer out.

Guy reached out and touched her gently on her arm.

'Someone broke into his flat yesterday afternoon. He was beaten up, but it seems he died from a heart attack.' He picked up the glass and pressed it into her hand. 'Take a sip,' he said. 'It's good for shock.'

Iris did as she was told. Her head was spinning as she felt the warmth of the brandy slide down her throat. And she remembered drinking another glass of brandy the night before, the night she'd been supposed to meet Jenks at the Monny. She had sat there in the kitchen, cursing him for not turning up, when all the time he'd been lying dead in his flat. She shuddered. 'Who could do that?' she asked. 'He was an old man. Who could do something like that?' As she tried to make sense of it, a terrible thought came into her head. She could see Chris Street's eyes boring down into hers. 'You don't think . . . you don't think it could have been . . .?'

'It could have been anyone,' Guy said. 'Don't go jumping to any conclusions. Jenks was trouble, Iris. He may have been old, but that doesn't mean that he was good.'

'He still didn't deserve to die that way.'

'Probably not,' he said.

Hearing the reservation in his voice, Iris looked sharply up. 'I take it you knew him rather better than I did.'

'Not really,' he said. 'I made a point of keeping well away. Unlike my mother.' He lifted the brandy glass and looked at her over the rim. 'I suppose you have the right to know this.' Guy hesitated before he spoke again. 'Jenks used to work for Terry Street. After Terry went down, she took over the business, along with all his snouts. Jenks was paid to gather information, anything that might be useful. He was good at it, very good, and he didn't give a damn about who might get hurt in the process. Let's just say he wasn't called the Weasel for nothing. He'd have grassed up his granny if there was a few quid in it.'

Iris nodded. *The Weasel.* Of course, that's what Chris Street

97

had called him. 'So he might not have been lying. He may have known something about my father.'

'If you don't mind me asking, Iris, who exactly *is* your father?'

If it hadn't been for the shock she was feeling, she might not have spoken so freely. Guy Wilder, after all, was a virtual stranger. 'His name's Sean O'Donnell. He split up with my mum nineteen years ago, but then just disappeared. We never heard anything after that. She reckons he's dead and . . . I don't know, perhaps she's right. Even if he hadn't wanted to see us again, he'd have kept in touch with his brother. He and Michael were close.' She took another sip of brandy. It seemed to be having the desired effect. The initial shock had worn off and although she couldn't claim to be thinking with absolute clarity, she was at least able to string a few coherent sentences together. 'Actually, my uncle used to know your mother. Michael O'Donnell?'

He shook his head. 'It doesn't ring any bells.'

'Well, it was a long time ago. They went to school together, but I think they stayed in touch for a while after that. Actually, I think he had a bit of a crush on her.'

Guy thought about it some more. 'Hold on. A biggish guy, dark curly hair?'

'That's him.'

His mouth broke into a wide smile. 'Jesus, yes, I do remember. Sometimes he was with her when she came to pick me up from my grandmother's.'

'Not Terry?' she said, confused.

'No, never Terry. I couldn't stand the man – and vice versa. Michael was okay though. Yeah, he was one of the good guys. We used to go the park sometimes, kick a ball around. My God, is he still living here?'

'He's lived in Kellston all his life. I don't think he'll ever move away.' Iris wasn't overly surprised that their paths hadn't crossed again. Michael wouldn't be seen dead in a bar like this and she couldn't see Guy Wilder popping into the Dog and Duck for a pie and a pint.

'So you're Michael's niece. How amazing is that? I wonder if we ever met when we were kids.' He left a short pause and then grinned. 'No, I don't reckon we did. I wouldn't have forgotten *you.*'

Was he flirting with her? Perhaps just a little. But then he was in the type of business where flirting with the female customers was virtually obligatory. It probably came to him as instinctively as breathing. Had it not been for the brandy – and the champagne and the wine – Iris wouldn't have said what she said next. 'Michael believes that she only left you with your gran to protect you; that she didn't want you getting involved in all the nastiness of Terry's world.'

Something in Guy's face instantly closed down. 'Then Michael, no offence, is talking through his arse. What you have to understand about my wonderful mother is that she didn't have an altruistic bone in her body. The only person she was ever concerned about was herself.'

Iris could hear the anger in his voice and regretted having spoken. She had clearly overstepped the line.

There was a short, awkward silence before Guy apologised. He ran his fingers through his hair and groaned. 'Sorry. I'm really sorry. I didn't mean to snap. I've been all over the shop recently.'

'It's okay. I understand.'

Guy nodded and quickly changed the subject. 'So what exactly did Albert Jenks say to you on Wednesday night?'

Iris didn't have to think about it. The words had been revolving in her head for the past forty-eight hours. 'He just leaned down and said: *Don't you want to know where your daddy is?* That's all, nothing else – well, apart from to meet him at the Monny at half-six.'

'And you went?' he said. 'You went alone?'

There was an edge to his tone that reminded her of Vita's similarly incredulous response.

'Yes, I know,' she said defensively. 'It was a stupid thing to do. I'm aware of that. But what would you have done if it was your dad?' Immediately, she bit down on her lip. Had she put her foot in it again? She had no idea who his father was and strongly suspected that he might not either.

But Guy simply shrugged. 'The same as you, probably.'

She let out a sigh of relief. 'So what should I do next?'

'What do you mean?'

'Well, the police are going to be making inquiries. Should I tell them about it? Should I tell them how Chris Street was asking questions about him?'

'No,' he said sternly. 'You don't. Absolutely *not*. There's nothing to directly connect the Streets to what happened to Jenks.'

'You can't be sure of that.'

'And you can't be sure of the opposite either. Look, the Weasel's been working for them for years. Why should they suddenly turn on him?'

'I don't know. Why do villains usually turn on each other?'

Guy shook his head. 'It's not a good idea to start pointing the finger. The Streets are powerful people. You don't want to get on their wrong side.'

Iris lifted her brows. 'Says the man who was rolling around on the floor with them a couple of days ago.'

He smiled at the quick retort. 'Yeah well, I haven't got the brains I was born with. You, on the other hand, are an intelligent woman and should know better. Keep your head down and your mouth shut. Believe me, it's the best advice you're going to get.'

'But come on,' she said insistently, 'the old man arranges to meet me and then gets murdered. Is that just a coincidence?'

'Yes, more than likely it is. I'm sure he had his grubby little fingers in lots of pies. You wouldn't have been the only person he was trying to screw over.'

Iris didn't even try to keep the disappointment from her voice. 'Do you think that's all it was? Some kind of con?'

'I don't know,' he said, 'but if you want to find out, then you're going to have to be smart about it. If Jenks knew something, then other people must too. Tread carefully and you might find out. Making an enemy of Chris Street, however, is not going to open any doors for you. Honestly, I know what I'm talking about.'

'So what *do* I do?'

'You play it cool. I may be able to help, point you in the right direction at least.'

Iris looked hopefully at him, her spirits rising. 'Could you? Are you serious?' And then, as soon as she had asked, she felt guilty about the excitement she was feeling. A man had died and all she was thinking about was herself.

'Don't expect too much. I can't promise anything.' From his pocket Guy took out two of his business cards along with a pen, and passed them over to her. 'Here, keep one of these and write your number on the other.'

Iris scribbled down her mobile number and was about to add the number at the flat when she thought again. What if he called and Luke answered the phone? If she told Luke the truth – that she was searching for answers about her father – he would only get into one of his black moods again. He was convinced, like her mother, that Sean O'Donnell was dead and thought Iris's preoccupation with his disappearance both maudlin and unhealthy. For a second she sat with the pen poised over the tiny oblong of card. Then, in case her mobile was switched off, she quickly added her work number.

Guy took the card, looked down at it and nodded. 'And will

you swear that you won't do anything without talking to me first?'

'Of course not.'

'Promise me,' he said.

'Okay, I promise.' She glanced at her watch; it was getting on for twelve-thirty. She'd better make a move before Luke got home. She got to her feet. 'Thanks for the drink, but I have to go. It's getting late.'

'I'll order you a cab.'

She waved the offer aside. 'No, don't bother. I can walk. It's only down the road.'

'Not at this time of night,' he said firmly. 'Do you really think I'm going to let you wander around on your own? This is the East End, Iris. Tough as you are, I don't fancy your chances against some of the lowlifes out there. There's a cab firm just round the corner. I've got an account with them. They'll send a car in five minutes.'

Iris, on reflection, decided not to argue. She'd made enough rash decisions for one night. It was time to start acting sensibly.

Chapter Fifteen

Iris had not slept well, tossing and turning throughout the night, her brief interludes of sleep invaded by nightmares where a bloody and beaten Albert Jenks was leering maliciously down at her. At three in the morning she had woken abruptly, recalling Vita's offer to make some inquiries about him. Panicking, she had leapt out of bed and gone to find her phone. Vita often worked on Saturdays and if she innocently started asking questions about a man who had been murdered . . .

It had been too late to ring, and so she had sent an urgent text instead. *Plse don't mention Jenks to anyone. V important. Will call later. Iris x*

Then, feeling too anxious to go back to bed, she had curled up on the sofa, switched on the TV and watched an old film until she finally dozed off again. She had woken, cramped and aching, at around eight o'clock. Since then she had taken a hot shower and made some breakfast.

Luke, who had not come home until after two, had just got up. Unaware of the restless night she had spent, he was now nursing a hangover in the kitchen. She passed him a bottle of aspirin and put the kettle on. Outside the snow was falling again, drifting down in a squall of fast, steady flakes and making even the shabby rooftops of Kellston look like something from a fairytale. She stood by the window and watched as the world turned white around her.

Luke made a soft groaning sound as he rubbed at his forehead. 'Oh God, why did you leave me there, babes? You should have made me come home with you.'

Iris turned and smiled. 'I'd have liked to have seen your face if I'd tried. I got the feeling you were in the middle of trying to clinch a deal.'

'Was I?' he said, frowning. 'I don't remember much about it. Did you get home okay? Well, obviously you did, but I shouldn't have let you come back alone. What was I thinking of?'

'Hey, don't worry about it. I'm old enough to take care of myself.'

As she went over to him, he reached out and wrapped an arm around her waist. 'Yeah, I know you are but—'

'It was still early and I was tired. There was no point in you leaving too.' Iris didn't want him feeling guilty, especially when her own conscience was bothering her so much. She felt bad about keeping secrets; it was hardly the ideal foundation for the fresh start she'd been planning on. Perhaps she should come clean about what had happened last night, about seeing Guy Wilder. But then he didn't even know who Guy was. And if she did start explaining, she would have to tell him about going to meet Jenks too. And that was a conversation she felt way too tired to have.

Iris bent down to kiss the crown of his head and at that very moment her mobile started ringing. Jumping at the sound, she quickly freed herself from Luke's embrace. Grabbing the phone from the counter, she flipped it open and stared at it. Even though she knew it was too early to expect any news from Guy

Wilder, she was still hoping that it might be him. Or even Vita. Instead, it was her work number flashing up. She thought about not answering it, letting it go to voicemail, but then wondered if it was Toby. And if it *was* Toby, his new friendship with Danny Street might prove useful to her.

'Hello?'

But it was only a very apologetic William Grand on the other end of the line. 'I'm really sorry to disturb you on a Saturday.'

Iris wished she hadn't picked up. There was only one reason why he would be calling her and she didn't want to hear it.

'I'll understand if you're busy,' he continued. 'I know that it's short notice. And I wouldn't ask, I really wouldn't, only Gerald's in bed with the flu and I've had a call-out that I need to attend. I've tried getting hold of Toby, but he isn't answering his phone.'

Smart Toby, she thought. As William obviously wasn't going to cut to the chase any time soon, Iris did it for him. 'You want me to cover, right?'

'If it isn't too much trouble, and only for an hour. There's a viewing booked for eleven. Mrs Bayle's coming in to see her husband and I might not be back in time. I suppose I could put her off, try and schedule it for later in the day but . . .'

Iris sighed. The prospect of viewing the body of a loved one was traumatic enough without having the appointment postponed at the last minute. Did she really have it in her heart to refuse? 'No, its okay, it's fine. I'll do it.'

'Thanks. That's really good of you. Everything's prepared here; you can show her through whenever she's ready. Oh, and I'll leave the keys next door with Janey. If I'm not back before you leave, you will remember to lock up, won't you?'

As she put the phone down, Luke – having caught the gist of the conversation – scowled at her. 'Why on earth did you say yes? I was hoping we could spend the day together, maybe go

105

out and grab some lunch. You haven't forgotten that I'm off to Brussels on Monday?'

Sensing the onset of another row, Iris immediately tried to lighten the mood. Rushing over to him, she wrapped her arms around his neck. 'No, of course I haven't forgotten, sweetheart, but it'll be a while yet before you can face any food. Anyway, it's only for an hour. I'll be back before you know it.'

'Those people take advantage,' he said resentfully.

'Gerald's got flu, William's had an urgent call and some poor woman wants to see her husband before he's buried. I could hardly say no.'

But from the expression on his face, she could see that he'd expected her to.

Iris still had twenty minutes to spare before Mrs Bayle was due to arrive. She decided to stay in the florist and talk to Janey, the owner of the shop. In all honesty, she didn't relish the thought of being alone in the building next door. Although, as she considered it more, she realised that it was actually the fact she *wouldn't* be alone that made her feel so queasy. She had not yet grown accustomed to the silent contents of the basement.

Janey, oblivious to her fears, was breezily chatting away about Lizzie Street's funeral. Had Iris seen that actress off the television? She wasn't quite so good-looking in real life, was she? It only went to prove what those make-up artists could do. Still, it gave hope to the rest of the female population. And what about Terry Street? 'He's got old, hasn't he? I feel sorry for him. You'd have thought they'd have let him off the last few weeks of his sentence, compassionate whatsit and all; I mean, you can't be needing more compassion than when your missus has just been murdered.'

Iris, keeping one eye on the door to Tobias Grand & Sons in case the widow arrived early, was happy to simply stand and listen. Janey was in her mid-forties, a tall, stick-thin woman with a wide mobile mouth. She could talk for England and the only encouragement she needed was the occasional nod or comment of agreement. Her curiosity about the event was understandable; there wasn't much of interest that ever happened in Kellston. Also, with all the floral wreaths and arrangements that had been ordered, the funeral had provided a much-needed boost for the shop.

'I hear that son of hers didn't even bother to turn up.'

Iris's attention was instantly focused. 'What?'

'Her own son,' Janey continued. Her voice was a mixture of astonishment and accusation. 'Her stepsons were there, but not her own flesh and blood. How could anyone be so callous?'

Iris, recalling what Guy had said – and what she had witnessed – felt an instinctive urge to defend him. 'I don't think it's that straightforward. He did come to see her.'

'Did he?'

Iris regretted having spoken. What went on next door was private, confidential – or at least it should be. She was aware of Janey's eyes gazing greedily towards her, eager for a juicy snippet of gossip. She could also imagine Gerald's reaction if he ever got to hear that she'd been passing on information about what had happened on the day before the funeral. Her only option, she decided, was to backtrack as quickly as she could. 'Well, I think so,' she said casually. 'I'm not completely sure. Maybe I've got it wrong. But families are complicated, aren't they? You never know all the facts.'

Janey looked disappointed. She had no interest in the facts; it was only rock-solid hearsay that she craved. 'So you didn't actually see him?'

Iris, without lying outright, gave an ambiguous half shake of her head whilst making a show of glancing at her watch. 'Blimey, is that the time? I'd better open up.'

She took the keys, made a hasty exit and unlocked the door to Tobias Grand & Sons. Stepping inside, she paused for a second, breathing in the quiet. At the same time she expelled a sigh of relief. That had been a close call; she would have to learn to keep her big mouth in check in the future, especially if she wanted to keep Guy Wilder on side. He'd be none too pleased if he found out that she'd been talking about him. Not to mention how Gerald would react. Discretion, as he never stopped telling her, was an *essential* part of the business.

After placing her coat on the back of her chair, Iris went through to the kitchen and put the kettle on. She wondered if she should check on Mr Bayle, make sure that everything was okay, but only got as far as the door before her nerve failed her. It wasn't as if she'd never seen a dead body before, but she had never viewed one alone. Feeling slightly guilty, she took one look at the coffin and turned away. She could trust to the excellent ministrations of Alice; no one could make a corpse look more peaceful.

Mrs Bayle, with the punctuality of the older generation, arrived at precisely five to eleven. She was a local woman, small and wiry, in her late sixties. Her iron-grey hair was cut short and her face was etched with the kind of lines that spoke of a less than stress-free life. She was wearing an old tweed coat that had clearly seen better days.

Iris was concerned that she might be upset or offended at being dealt with by the office junior. Gerald possessed, if nothing else, a certain gravitas and William had a natural compassion. She, however, was merely the receptionist. But Mrs Bayle had more important things on her mind than who was showing her through to the viewing lounge.

'So, dear,' she said. 'Is he ready for me?'

Iris nodded. 'Would you like a cup of tea before . . .'

'Ta, it's nice of you, but I'd just as soon go through.'

'Of course,' Iris said. 'If you'd like to come this way.'

They didn't speak as they walked along the corridor. Iris opened the door and stood aside. 'I'll leave you alone.'

'Oh, that's all right, dear. There's no need to go.'

Iris hesitated, unsure as to whether Mrs Bayle was being merely polite or if she was actually being requested to stay. But then the woman linked her arm through Iris's and there was no choice but to accompany her to the coffin.

Alice, as expected, had done an excellent job. Mr Bayle looked more peaceful in death than he had possibly ever done in life. There was a faint pinkness to his cheeks and lips. His features showed no evidence of any suffering – perhaps there had been none, she didn't know – but instead had that easy, rested appearance as if he were merely sleeping.

'He was a waste of space, really,' his widow said, gazing soulfully down at him. 'Still, I'll miss the old bugger. You get used to having them around, don't you?'

Iris, who had only been used to Luke for the past five years, wasn't sure how to respond. 'Were you married for long?' she eventually said.

'Forty years, give or take.'

Iris gazed at the man in the coffin again. She could not imagine how it would feel to live with someone for so long. This was a time, she thought, to deliver some profound and comforting words. Unfortunately, she couldn't think of any. Instead, she said: 'Do you have any children?'

Mrs Bayle's face fell a little. 'We only had the one. Our Alan's working abroad. He'd like to be here, but things are tight and with the cost of air travel and all . . .'

Iris experienced a sudden surge of anger towards the son who couldn't be bothered to return for his father's funeral, but she felt guilty about it straightaway. It was not her place to cast aspersions. Maybe she was misjudging him; after all, she had no idea what the relationship between the two of them had been like. Immediately she thought of Guy and his mother. But then again, funerals weren't just about the dead – they were about the living too, about who was left behind, and this poor woman could have done with some support. Keeping her thoughts to herself, she said: 'I'm sure he'd be here if he could.'

A soft, barely discernible sound emanated from the back of Mrs Bayle's throat. It could have been agreement or a stifled sob. Iris instinctively placed her hand over the older woman's, giving it a gentle squeeze of sympathy.

Eventually, Mrs Bayle reached out and touched the body of her husband. Not on his hands or face, but on the shoulder of his slightly shiny suit. Her fingertips lingered for a few seconds before she withdrew them and nodded. 'Thank you,' she murmured.

Iris wasn't sure if she talking to her or the husband. Suddenly, she felt weighed down by a terrible sadness. Part of it was down to Mrs Bayle's loss, which seemed so profound after all the time the two of them had spent together, but part of it was to do with her own father. If he was dead, had there been anyone to grieve for him? She couldn't bear the thought of him lying alone in some cold mortuary, unidentified, uncared for, with no one to whisper that final goodbye.

Mrs Bayle turned away, her farewells completed.

Iris, still with a lump in her throat, showed her back through to reception. Although she knew Luke expected her home within the hour, she paused by the door and said, 'Are you sure you wouldn't like to stay a while, have that cup of tea?'

'Thank you, dear, but I'd best be getting on.' Reaching out, she patted Iris on the arm. 'You've been very kind.'

Iris stood and watched as she walked down the snow-filled street, a small, lonely figure despite the crowds. It was Saturday, with only four weeks left to Christmas, and the shoppers were out in force. Even though this wasn't the popular end of the High Street, there were plenty of bargains to be had in the charity shops. She thought how terrible it must be to walk amongst those people, all of them unknowing and indifferent to your grief. Mrs Bayle would not be having much of a Christmas this year.

Iris was still standing there, lost in thought, when William returned five minutes later.

'Still waiting?' he said.

She shook her head and sighed. 'No, she's been and gone.' Following him inside, she picked up her coat. 'Well, I'll be off if you don't need me for anything else.'

'No, you go. And thank you for coming in. I wasn't sure what time I'd get back.'

'It's okay,' Iris said. She was glad now that she'd done it. Mrs Bayle, with her stoical attitude, had helped put her own problems in perspective. The widow had also helped focus her mind as to what she had to do next – no matter what the consequences, she was going to find out what had happened to her father.

'So, how's your uncle?' William said.

Iris, forgetting about the excuse she had made yesterday, stared blankly back at him for a moment. 'What?'

'His ankle?'

'Oh, yes. Right. Sorry, I was miles away. Not too bad, thanks.' Then, worried that she might have to tell more lies, she raised her hand in a quick wave and shot out through the door.

Iris had only got a few yards down the street when she became aware of unwanted company. Glancing over her shoulder she saw a big man in an overcoat twist his face away too sharply. She watched, her heart starting to thrash, as he sauntered over to a shop window and peered inside. Iris couldn't say for certain how she knew that he was following her; it was an inexplicable sixth-sense thing – the same as she'd experienced when Albert Jenks had been watching her on the day of Lizzie's funeral. The thought of *his* fate made her swallow hard. Should she carry on or go back? She was tempted to go on, the street was busy enough, surely nothing could happen to her here, but was too afraid to take the chance. Not wanting her shadow to know that she'd spotted him – what if he panicked, made a move? – she made a show of rooting in her pockets, pretending she'd mislaid something and then walked casually back to Tobias Grand & Sons.

William looked surprised to see her again.

'I . . . er . . . forgot my phone.' Back in the safety of the undertaker's, Iris felt suddenly stupid. Perhaps she had just imagined it all. Nerves did funny things to the psyche. But still she glanced towards the door, worried that her pursuer might follow her in. Going over to her desk, she opened a drawer and pretended to retrieve her mobile. Then, sitting down, she quickly made a call to Luke. Even if this was all in her imagination, she was too scared now to walk home alone.

'Hey,' she said when he finally answered. 'I'm all done. Why don't you come and meet me? We can grab some lunch on the High Street.'

'I'm already cooking. I thought I'd surprise you. It's only spag bol but—'

'No, that's great.' She took a small, despairing breath. 'I'll come straight back then. I'll see you soon.' What she had wanted to say was *Please come and fetch me*, but if she had done that, she would have had to explain why – and explaining why she thought some thug might be following her was all too complicated. She sat and stared at the wall.

'Is everything all right?' William asked.

Iris glanced over at him. She was feeling a growing panic about having to go outside again. 'Yes, I'm just . . . er . . .' Then she made a decision: paranoid or not, there was no way she was walking home alone. 'You don't have the number for a local cab company, do you?'

If William was surprised by the fact she wanted a taxi to take her the short distance back to Silverstone Heights, he didn't show it. Instead, he grabbed his overcoat and gestured towards the street. 'Come on. You don't want to be wasting good money on cabs. I've got the car outside. I'll give you a lift.'

'But that means there won't be anyone here.'

'Well,' he said, 'they're hardly clamouring at the doors, are they? I think I can be spared for fifteen minutes. And after what you did this morning, it's the least I can do.'

Iris couldn't tell if he was simply being kind or if he'd somehow picked up on her anxiety. Perhaps William Grand was more perceptive than she'd thought. Either way, she wasn't going to look a gift horse in the mouth. 'Thank you,' she said, her voice filled with gratitude. 'That would be great.'

As they left the building, Iris's eyes raked the High Street searching for her shadow. She looked all around, but there was no sign of him. Still, just because she couldn't see him didn't mean he wasn't there. She kept close to William as they headed for the car.

Chapter Sixteen

There were two things Alice Avery was thoroughly ashamed of: one was what Toby had persuaded her to do the previous week; the other was her loathing for her mother. As she stood in the kitchen, wearily stirring the pan of tomato soup, she tried to close her ears to the constant barrage of whining and complaints. Quite what her mother had to moan about was beyond her; she was in good health (despite her constant protestations to the contrary), had a nice flat in a friendly retirement complex, a good social circle and was relatively comfortably off. George Avery, a man who Alice couldn't even remember, had died when she was only a baby. She couldn't help wondering if he had gone to his grave with a grateful smile on his face.

Janet Avery was not an easy person to like. She was a bitter, disappointed woman and, as she never failed to point out, most of that disappointment was rooted in her only child's failures – her failure to be beautiful, to be witty, to have a stunning career or to get married and provide the grandchildren that she felt were due to her. Alice regretted all these things too, apart from the lack of kids. She had no desire to pass her own flawed genes on to another generation, or to have those innocent souls tormented in the same way she had been.

That Alice had not succeeded in life was hardly surprising. All she could recall, right from childhood, was impatience, derision and a continuous mocking. This had grown even more intense when, at the age of seventeen, she had hit that moment of teenage blossoming. She had never been exactly beautiful – she had inherited her father's blander features – but, with her youth, auburn hair and ivory skin, she had briefly shone. It was a time she should have been able to make the most of, but even then, perhaps *especially* then, her mother had gnawed at her confidence, laying seeds of doubt in her mind and preventing her from taking the chances that might have changed her life.

'Is that soup ready yet?'

Alice flinched at the sound of her voice. 'Two minutes,' she called back. Leaning down, she took the hot rolls out of the oven and placed them on a warmed plate.

Her mother came into the kitchen, frowned and glared into the pan of soup. 'You haven't overheated it, have you?'

'No,' Alice said.

'You haven't let it boil? You know it spoils the taste if you let it boil. I can't cope with boiled soup – you know what it does to my digestion.'

'Why don't you sit down, Mum, and I'll bring it over.' Alice was only able to keep her cool because of Toby. Knowing that he was there for her, the one bright spot in her otherwise dull and dreary life, gave her the will to carry on. She took a deep breath, trying to think of the good things in her life rather than the bad. Toby Grand was at the top of the list, but the fact she had her own place, small and cramped as it was, came a close second. At least she had some privacy, a chance to get away from her mother's watchful gaze. Even though she was forced to visit almost every single day, and was always subjected to the same nasty snipes and criticisms, the knowledge she had a bolt-hole kept her spirits just about intact.

Alice put the bowls of soup and the rolls on the table. She sat down and attempted a smile.

'Let's eat, shall we?'

'If you can call it eating,' her mother said. 'It's not exactly substantial, is it?'

'I thought you liked soup.'

'I *do* like soup, just not every day.'

'You don't have it every day,' Alice said impatiently. Juggling her work commitments in order to be free for lunch was a constant problem. Why wasn't she ever the slightest bit grateful? 'We had a casserole yesterday.'

Janet Avery pulled a face as if her daughter was being deliberately argumentative. 'I only mentioned it. There's no need to get in a huff.'

'I'm not . . .' Alice managed to stop herself in time. Rising to the bait would only give her an excuse to have another go. Not that she needed an excuse; the old woman had been getting under her skin for the past forty years. She could still recall her mother's glee when she'd given up nursing, a profession she had never wanted her to enter in the first place. *What did I tell you? You're not a people person, dear. You need to find something more . . . suitable.* Alice, however, had managed to find a profession that disgusted her even more. That was probably the reason why she'd stuck with it for so long.

For a couple of minutes they slurped their soup in silence.

Eventually, the day never being complete unless she'd managed to provoke her, her mother put down her spoon and stared. 'So what are you looking so pleased about? I suppose it's some man or other.'

Alice blushed. 'Don't be ridiculous!'

'I don't know why you bother. They never stick around, do

they dear? Here today and gone tomorrow. You're not wife material. You're hardly girlfriend material either. I'd have thought you'd have learned that by now.'

Alice tore her roll into several more pieces. As her fingers clawed at the bread, she tried to keep hold of her temper. 'I've no idea what you're talking about.'

Janet Avery shook her well-groomed head and smiled. It was the kind of smug, self-satisfied smile that gave Alice the urge to hurl the remainder of her soup over her. She silently counted to ten. It didn't matter what was said, she would not give her the satisfaction of reacting.

But her mother wasn't giving up. 'So what's he called then, this latest *beau* of yours? Someone to do with work, is it?' She gave a long sigh. 'I suppose he's married, that's why you want to keep quiet about it. He'll only use you, Alice, use you and then cast you aside. They're all the same. You should have learnt that by now.'

Alice stared at her mother, examining the newly waved grey hair, the sagging cheeks and tight prim mouth. Only she could use an old-fashioned word like beau and then go on to suggest that she was involved in some sordid affair. 'I've told you. There isn't anyone.'

'I hope it's not that Gerald Grand. I've always had my suspicions about him. He's got a lecherous look. Oily, if you know what I mean.'

As it happened, Alice did know what she meant. The idea of Gerald's hands roaming over her body was enough to make her shudder. 'Oh, please,' she said, 'give me some credit.'

Her mother, disappointed, turned her attention back to the soup.

Alice thought about Toby and a warm glow crept over her. Secrets were all very well, but there were times when she wanted to shout from the rooftops, to tell the whole world that *she* was the one he had chosen to be with, that *she* was the one he slept with at night. Well, perhaps not for all of the night, but she understood why that wasn't possible. Toby was only protecting her, protecting them both from his father's disapproval.

'I saw the funeral on the news. I suppose you sorted out that Street woman.'

By 'sorted out' Alice knew she was asking whether she had embalmed her or not. She also knew, from the gleam in her mother's eye, that she was eager for some juicy gossip on the subject. It would give her something novel to pass on to the other old crones who were part of her cynical, malicious group. 'No,' she said abruptly, 'I didn't. There's been a murder inquiry in case you'd forgotten. All that was dealt with before she came to Tobias Grand & Sons.'

'But you still saw her. You must have done.'

'No,' Alice replied, although it was a lie.

'Him, then,' her mother persisted. 'You must have seen *him*. Did he look like he was grieving? Rumour has it they didn't get on. You were there the morning of the funeral, weren't you?'

Alice didn't want to get into a discussion about Terry or Lizzie Street. In fact the very mention of any member of the Streets was enough to remind her of what had taken place last week. The shame of it brought the redness back to her cheeks. If there was a judgmental God – and she lived in dread that there might be – she would never be forgiven for what she had done.

Chapter Seventeen

Luke was looking none too happy as she stepped through the door of the flat. 'Where have you been?' he said irately, as if she were hours rather than minutes late. 'I've been trying to call.'

Iris realised that she'd turned her phone off when Mrs Bayle had arrived and had forgotten to turn it back on again. 'You know where I've been. What's wrong?' All kinds of ideas, products of her guilty conscience, sprang into her head – that Vita had called and inadvertently mentioned Jenks, that Guy Wilder had dropped round and told him about . . .

'It's Michael,' he said.

From his expression she knew it wasn't good news. She felt the breath catch in her throat. 'What is it? Is he all right?'

'Don't worry, he's fine.' Luke said quickly. Then he paused. 'Well, not fine exactly, but it's nothing terminal. He's in the living room.'

She rushed through to find Michael perched on the edge of the sofa. He had a bowl of red-stained water and a bottle of TCP sitting on the coffee table in front of him and was dabbing somewhat ineffectively at his forehead with a damp cloth. His face was covered in cuts and bruises. Iris crouched down, putting her hands on his knees. 'Oh God, what happened?'

'He got in a fight,' Luke said sharply, as if to discourage her from showing too much sympathy. 'Down the pub.'

'Here, let me do that,' Iris said, removing the cloth from her uncle's hand.

'I'm all right, love,' he said. 'I can manage. It's nothing. There's no need to fuss.'

But she could see how pale and shaken he was and, as he made no further objections, she started to clean his wounds. He winced as she gently cleared the blood away. Iris glanced over her shoulder at Luke. 'Can you get me some fresh water? And you'd better get a drink for our wounded soldier here. There's brandy in the kitchen cupboard.'

'Brandy?' Luke repeated. His forehead scrunched into a frown.

'Yes,' she said insistently, glaring back at him. She could tell that he wasn't overjoyed at the prospect of having to waste his vintage Armagnac on the likes of Michael O'Donnell. As he left the room she wondered if he'd notice the rather large dent she'd made in the bottle on Thursday night. Still, she had more important things to worry about at the moment.

'Come on, then,' Michael said, 'let's get it over with.'

She stopped her ministrations and looked at him. 'What?'

His blue eyes gazed back at her with a mixture of shame and embarrassment. 'Scrappin' in a boozer at my age. It's a disgrace, eh? Tell me I ought to know better.'

Iris gave a soft laugh. 'I'm not your mother.' Although she couldn't claim that she approved, she wasn't about to lecture anyone – least of all her uncle – on how they should or shouldn't behave. Everyone did things they weren't proud of from time to time. She hadn't exactly been Ms Perfect herself over the last few days.

'I wouldn't have come here, love. It wasn't my idea. You don't need the hassle, do you?' He reached out and took her hand. 'I know you don't. It was Rick who brought me. To be honest, I didn't have a clue where we were going. If I had, I wouldn't have agreed. What, with the knocks and all, I was a bit out of it.'

'Don't be ridiculous,' she said, squeezing his fingers between her own. 'Rick was right. You're always welcome – whatever state you're in.' Now that she'd established his injuries weren't too severe, she was beginning to relax. There was a nasty cut above his right eyebrow, but it wasn't deep enough to need stitches. The rest, although none too pleasant to look at, appeared to be fairly superficial. She glanced over her shoulder again. 'So where is he? Is Rick still here?'

Michael shook his head. 'Nah, he had to get off. He promised to pick Vita up from work.'

Which served as a timely reminder to Iris that she still had to talk to her friend about the recently deceased Albert Jenks. But she quickly pushed the thought aside. Now wasn't the time to be dwelling on that. 'So what was this stupid fight about?'

'Whatever,' he said with a shrug. 'Somethin' and nothin', some cocky geezer with a gob on him. I should have walked away but . . .'

'But?'

'Well, I'd had a pint or two – you know how it is.'

'Not exactly,' Iris said.

Michael let go of her hand and grinned. 'Sorry, I didn't get much kip last night, what with the birthday and all. I was still a bit out of it and then this jumped-up little git bumped into me and spilled my pint and started mouthing off. And then . . .'

Iris was starting to see how one thing had led to another. 'Okay, I get the picture.'

Luke came back with the clean water and the brandy. 'Here,' he said, placing the glass on the coffee table.

'Ta, son,' Michael said, immediately reaching out for it. He took a large mouthful and licked his lips. 'Ah, that's good stuff!'

'It should be,' Luke replied. 'It's not your cheap rubbish. And you should sip it, not gulp it.'

Iris saw Luke flinch as the remaining contents of the glass quickly disappeared down Michael's throat. Then she watched as Luke's eyes carefully scrutinised the couch in case her uncle had spilled any brandy or blood on the soft brown leather.

'Perhaps you should get him another,' Iris said wickedly. 'In fact, why don't you just bring in the bottle?'

Luke gave her a look – one of those *What on earth did you suggest that for* kind of looks.

So to keep the peace, she suggested instead: 'Or there's beer if you'd prefer it, Michael. There's plenty in the fridge.'

Michael, glancing at them both, thought about it for a second. Perhaps he read something in Luke's face because, although he had clearly enjoyed the brandy, he gave a nod and said, 'Yeah, ta, a beer would be good.'

'And then we'll get some food inside you. I bet you haven't eaten a thing today. It's spag bol; there's plenty to go round.'

After the beer had arrived, Iris spent the next ten minutes cleaning up the rest of Michael's injuries. She put a sticking plaster over the cut on his eyebrow and then went in search of Luke. She found him standing by the kitchen window with his arms folded ominously across his chest.

'What's the matter?'

'What do you think?' he said. 'Why did you have to invite him for lunch?'

'What do you want me to do – send him packing? He'll only end up down the pub again. At least this way I can keep an eye on him.' Iris paused before imparting the next piece of bad news. 'In fact I've asked him to stay over. I don't think he should be alone at the moment.'

'For God's sake,' Luke hissed. 'How long for?'

'I don't know, just until he's properly back on his feet. He could have concussion or anything. Anyway, what difference does it make; you'll be away all next week. He can stay in the spare room for a few days.'

'He stinks,' Luke said.

'I'm sure he knows how to use the shower.'

'I was hoping we could spend some time together before I go to Brussels – just the two of us. It's not that much to ask, is it?'

Iris put an arm around his waist and hugged him. 'Hey, I'm really sorry, babe. You're right. I should have asked you first.'

But Luke wasn't going to be appeased. He had descended into one of his petulant moods. 'He's not your responsibility. If he chooses to get drunk, to get in fights, you shouldn't have to pick up the pieces.'

'It's not to do with responsibility,' she said. 'He's my uncle and I care about him. I don't want him out there, getting into even more trouble.'

'Fine,' Luke said. Pulling away from her, he whipped his jacket off the back of the chair.

'Where are you going?'

'To see Kieron. We've got some papers to go through before Monday.'

'You didn't mention it before.'

He shrugged. 'No, well, I was going to try and do it over the phone, but as we've got the pleasure of your uncle's company for the foreseeable future, I may as well go round in person. It'll be easier that way.'

'Why don't you stay and have some lunch first? You've gone to all the bother of making it.'

'I'm not hungry. You have it. I'll see you later.' Luke stopped by the door. 'Oh, and your mother rang.'

Iris frowned. It was only a couple of days since she'd last talked to her. 'What did she want?'

'I've no idea. Why don't you call her back and find out?'

And on that happy note he was gone. Iris heard the front door slam. She sighed, turned back to the window and gazed down on the residents' barking bays. A minute later Luke appeared and climbed into his black BMW. She waited, her hand raised in a wave, but he didn't bother looking up.

By three o'clock, Michael was fast asleep on the sofa. Iris turned the TV down and covered him with a blanket. Back in the kitchen, she quietly closed the door and reached for the phone. Who to call first – her mother or Vita? She decided on the latter. While the number was ringing, she kept her fingers crossed that Vita had received the text she had sent.

'Hi.'

'Hi, it's Iris. How are you doing?'

'Yeah, I'm okay. How's Michael? Rick told me what happened. I wanted to call round and check on him but . . . Well, I thought you might have enough to deal with without two more uninvited guests showing up.'

Iris smiled down the phone. What Vita really meant was that she knew Luke had been none too pleased by the unannounced arrival of an unkempt, smelly and somewhat battered Michael O'Donnell and had discreetly decided not to make matters worse. 'Look, will you thank him for me? Rick, I mean. It was good of him to take the trouble.'

'To be honest, he wasn't sure what to do. He felt like he was just dumping him, but that wasn't the intention. He'd have brought him back here only we've got Candice for the afternoon and—'

'That's okay,' Iris said. Candice was Rick's twelve-year-old daughter from his previous marriage. He'd had enough problems getting access in the first place; the last thing he needed was for her to report back to her mother on the kind of disreputable company he kept. 'Anyway,' she said, echoing Luke's earlier words, 'he's not your responsibility. You don't need my drunken, bloodied relatives littering up your living room.'

Vita laughed. 'It wasn't really Michael's fault. And he wasn't pissed. I mean, he'd had a couple of pints, but he was far from wrecked.'

'I always knew the Dog & Duck was trouble,' Iris said, shaking her head. 'It's a dump. It's full of dealers and wasters. The whole place smells of grief. I don't understand why he drinks there.'

There was a short silence on the other end of the line. 'He wasn't in the Dog. Didn't he tell you?'

Iris frowned. 'No, he didn't.'

'Oh,' Vita said.

Iris waited, but when Vita didn't go on, she said, 'Are you going to enlighten me?'

There was another hesitation. 'Er, he was . . . he was in the Hope & Anchor.'

'What?' Iris pressed the phone closer to her ear. Although Michael had gone to the Hope for Lizzie Street's wake, it wasn't – so far as she was aware – one of his more regular haunts. Although it was understandable why he'd been there on Wednesday night, she couldn't see why he'd gone back. 'What was he doing there?'

'I take it Michael hasn't been too forthcoming.'

'He just said that he'd had a few and then got in a scrap with some guy who bumped into him.'

'Oh,' Vita said again.

Iris felt her heart sink. She swallowed hard before she spoke again. 'Tell me.'

'I only know what Rick said but—'

'Tell me,' Iris repeated more insistently. She had the feeling that she wasn't going to like it, but pressed on regardless. 'Please. I want to know. I *need* to know. Michael's claiming it was just a stupid row, but there's more to it than that, isn't there?'

'I take it he didn't tell you who the other guy was?'

'No.'

'It was Danny Street.'

Iris took a quick breath. Her throat felt tight and dry. She put her hand to her chest. 'What?'

Vita sighed down the line. 'God, I'm not even sure if I should be telling you this. Rick says I shouldn't, that I shouldn't worry you, but I think you have the right to know. You see, it wasn't accidental, Michael being in the Hope today. He went there deliberately. He said he had some business to sort out and . . . and if Rick didn't like it that was fine, but he was going anyway. So of course Rick got worried and went along. Michael would-n't explain what the problem was, but he was pretty fired up and then the minute Danny Street arrived he went for him.'

'Danny Street?' Iris repeated, barely able to believe what she was hearing. 'But that guy's an out-and-out nutter. And twenty years younger. Why the hell would Michael want to pick a fight with him?'

'You're asking the wrong person.'

Iris thought back to the conversation she'd had with her uncle at the wake. 'Was it to do with Lizzie Street? Was that why he was having a go?'

Vita audibly cleared her throat. 'That might have been part of it. Rick isn't sure. It all happened so quickly. Only . . .'

'Only?'

'Rick thinks it was more to do with you.'

'Me?' Iris said, by now completely stunned. 'What? Why should it have anything to do with me?' For a few confused seconds she completely blanked out. She knew that Vita was still talking, saying something else, but she had stopped listening properly.

'Iris?'

'Yeah, sorry, I'm still here. But I don't even know Danny Street. Well, I've met him once, but that's all. Why should they be rowing about me?'

'I don't know. You'll have to talk to Michael about it. Rick didn't hear much, but he did hear your name mentioned.'

Iris had a sudden, disturbing thought. She remembered Chris Street cross-examining her outside the pub. She recalled his dark scrutinising eyes, his insistence that she tell him what the old man had wanted. Her voice, when she spoke again, had a touch of panic in it. 'Jesus, this isn't connected to Albert Jenks, is it? With my father? Maybe that's what this is all about. Do you think it could be? Oh God, this is all just so weird.'

'Hey, calm down,' Vita said, 'don't go jumping to any hasty conclusions. Have a chat with Michael first, find out what his side of the story is.'

'He's already told me his side and it was a pack of lies. And did you hear what happened to Jenks? He was killed, Vita, or as good as. Someone broke into his flat and he had a heart attack and—'

'Yeah, I saw it in the paper. It doesn't mean that he's connected to this. Why should he be? Any little bastard could have broken into his flat. We're hardly living in the most salubrious of areas. Don't go putting two and two together and coming up with five.'

Iris, her fingers gripped tight around the phone, was about to retort *And what if I'm coming up with four?* when, at the other end of the line, she heard the sound of a door opening and voices in the background.

'Look, I'm really sorry. Candice has just arrived. I have to go. Are you all right?'

'Of course,' Iris lied. 'I'm fine, I'm fine. Don't worry.'

'We'll talk later. And in the meantime, you'll have that chat with Michael?'

'You can bet on it,' Iris said. She put the receiver down with a frown on her face. What the hell was going on with Michael? She'd had enough of all these secrets and lies. It was time to get to the truth.

Chapter Eighteen

Iris had gone straight to the living room intending to shake Michael awake, but on seeing him fast asleep with all the cuts and bruises on his face, she hadn't had the heart to disturb him. It could wait, couldn't it? Whatever the truth, it could wait an hour or so.

But, as it turned out, an hour had turned into three and Michael was still asleep when Luke got home. There was no way she could start that particular conversation while he was in the flat so she'd had to bite her tongue. They had spent a quiet evening sitting in front of the TV with a couple of DVDs and a takeaway pizza. Iris, desperate for answers, had blindly watched the films rolling by in front of her, her eyes frequently flicking sideways to glance at Michael as if she might somehow glean the answers she craved just by looking at him.

Now it was Sunday morning and Luke had decided that he wanted to go and buy a Christmas tree. Iris, after another restless night, was tempted to make an excuse, to say she didn't feel well so that she could be alone with her uncle, but then felt too guilty to go through with it. Today was Luke's last before he went to Brussels and the least she could do was spend some quality time with him.

However, when he decided to go out and defrost the windscreen of the car, Iris grabbed the opportunity for a quick word with Michael.

'So,' she said, sitting down at the kitchen table and fixing her gaze on him. 'Are you going to tell me what really happened yesterday?'

'Huh?' Michael said, acting as if he didn't understand. 'I've already—'

'I mean the truth, rather than another of your highly imaginative tall stories. Like why you were scrapping with that anonymous "little scrote" in the first place. I take it you can bring his name to mind now or have all those knocks to your head affected your memory?'

Michael glanced briefly down at the table before raising his eyes again. 'If you already know the answer, love, why are you asking me?'

'Danny Street,' she said, shaking her head. She was unable to keep the exasperation from her voice. 'What on earth were you thinking of? The guy's crazy; he'd kill you soon as look at you. What's going on, Michael? You got some kind of death wish?'

Michael simply shrugged. 'What can I say? He wound me up. He was badmouthing Lizzie, slagging her off. I couldn't just stand by and let him get away with it. She might not have been perfect, far from it, but she kept that family together when Terry went down. She kept the business running too. If it hadn't been for—'

'So it had nothing to do with me?'

Iris could see that her question had taken him by surprise – and his subsequent hesitation lasted a little too long.

'You?' he repeated, his tongue sliding quickly across his lips.

Then he added, unconvincingly, 'Why should it have anything to do with you?'

'I've no idea.' She glanced anxiously towards the door, worried that Luke might suddenly reappear. 'But I understand that my name was mentioned.'

'Nah, you've got that wrong. Who told you that? It was about Lizzie, love, nothin' else.'

'So why didn't you say that yesterday?'

'I dunno.' He shrugged again. And then, blatantly playing for time, he picked up his mug, buried his bruised face in it and took a long slurp of tea. 'It was all kind of blurry, you know, when I got here.'

But Iris didn't believe him. 'Look at me,' she said, 'and swear that my name wasn't mentioned.'

It took a while for his guilty blue eyes to meet hers. 'Well okay, maybe it was, but only—'

Iris drew in a breath. 'I knew it.' Her heart had begun to beat faster. She could feel the blood rushing into her cheeks. 'Was it about Dad? It was about Dad, wasn't it?'

'What?' Michael said. 'No, of course not. Why should it be?'

She reached across and grabbed his hand. 'You have to tell me, whatever it is. I have to know!'

'It's nothing to do with Sean,' he said, pulling away his fingers. 'Jesus, whatever put that stupid idea in your head! I was pissed off, that's all, about how Danny Street treated you. He thinks he's the big man, the way he likes to push women around. It's not right. He's got no right.'

Iris was confused, but then it suddenly dawned on her that he must have heard about Danny's less than chivalrous behaviour at Tobias Grand & Sons on the day before Lizzie's funeral. Knowing what Michael was like, she had deliberately kept the details from him. 'How did you hear about that?' A wave of disappointment flowed through her, followed by a wave of relief.

The disappointment was down to the fact she had hit another dead end as regards the disappearance of her father, the relief that the Streets, hopefully, were not connected to it.

'I dunno. Someone must have mentioned it.'

It didn't take her long to figure out who it had been. 'Toby,' she said with a sigh. The two of them must have got talking after she'd left the pub. And God alone knew what kind of exaggerated version Toby had provided him with. 'You don't want to listen to a word he says,' she added, even though it was too late. 'He wasn't even there. He doesn't know the first thing about it. And anyway, Michael, it's not down to you to fight my battles. I'm all grown up now; I can take care of myself.'

The conversation was interrupted by the return of Luke. An abrupt silence fell over the kitchen as he walked in through the door. 'Should my ears be burning?' he said, looking from one to the other.

'No,' Iris said, getting to her feet. 'I was just giving Michael a lecture on the dangers of scrapping in pubs. Are we ready to go?'

Luke nodded. 'Ready when you are.'

As Iris left, she glanced over her shoulder. 'I haven't finished with you yet. We'll talk later.' Michael didn't seem overjoyed at the prospect.

As soon as they arrived, Iris knew she'd made the right decision. Getting out of the car, she waited as he bought a Pay & Display ticket and stuck it to the inside of the windscreen. Then they walked together into the Columbia Road Flower Market. Iris loved this place: the noisy crowds and bright stalls, the wonderful scents and colours; it was a full-on, heavenly assault on the senses and her spirits were instantly lifted. There was so much to see, to smell, to hear. Even her taste buds were on fire with the drifting aroma of fresh coffee, bread and something wonderfully spicy that she couldn't put a name to.

132

She suddenly felt happier than she had for days. 'This was a good idea,' she said, gazing up at Luke and linking her arm through his. Although she suspected he had only come here to get away from Michael, she didn't care. Just for a while, she was determined to put all her worries behind her.

As they strolled down the centre of the crowded market, their feet crunching on the thin layer of snow, Iris remembered all the times she had come here as a child. They had never bought much – they'd never had much money and only a tiny scrap of yard to plant things in – but she had always been allowed to choose some bulbs, a few hyacinths or tulips, which she'd put carefully in the ground and which would miraculously send up their green shoots a few months later. She smiled at the memory. Occasionally her mother would buy cut flowers, a small spray of freesias in summer, a few daffodils in spring.

It wasn't so much the buying that mattered, she realised, as the being here. The market wasn't just a place to buy stuff: it was where you went to look and smell and touch. It was where you went to listen to the vendors, to mingle, to touch shoulders with your neighbours and feel a part of something. When people talked about the East End it was usually about the crime, about the grimness and the grief. But there was no evidence of any of that in the busy street she saw before her.

Iris immediately understood how just being in the right place at the right time could put everything else into perspective. She had been stressing too much recently. Although she still had questions about Albert Jenks and his approach to her, they were questions that she suspected would never be answered now.

As Luke stopped to study a row of Christmas trees – he always took an eternity before choosing anything – she hung on to his arm and gazed around. Her eyes alighted first on a

133

row of winter pansies. The velvet flowers in shades of golden yellow, deep red and purple made her smile. It would be nice, she thought, to have a home with a garden rather than living in a flat. On the stalls to their left was a selection of tall, leafy ferns, bamboo and bay trees, and to their right a selection of brightly coloured gladioli. Further along she could see roses, white chrysanthemums and a dramatic display of exotic orchids.

Iris sighed with pleasure. It wasn't just the wonderful array of flowers and plants that made her feel so good, it was the whole atmosphere of the place. This was the East End she had yearned to return to with its hustle and bustle, its heart and soul. This was where she'd been born and where she belonged.

'So what do you think?' Luke said. 'This one or this one?'

They appeared much the same to Iris. 'I don't mind. They're both nice. You decide.'

But Luke, as ever, couldn't quite make his mind up. Iris let go of his arm as he poked and prodded at the two trees. Then, as she could see that a decision wasn't likely to be made soon, she said: 'Look, while you're doing that, I'll nip across to the deli. I'll only be five minutes.'

'Okay,' he said.

Iris walked down the street, weaving in and out of the crowd, breathing in the fragrance of the market. There was a short queue at the deli. While she waited, Iris examined the goods on offer and when she got to the counter bought a hunk of blue brie, fresh bread, three homemade chicken pies and a carton of stuffed olives.

It was as she was leaving the shop that Iris and a tall, broad man in an overcoat accidentally collided. Or at least she thought it was accidental. A second later she knew better. The man's hand gripped the upper part of her left arm causing her to drop the carrier bag. As the food spilled out across the pavement, he quickly pushed her back against the wall. Leaning down, he stared into her face.

'What are you doing?' she said, confusion quickly being replaced by panic. She struggled to free herself.

But his grip only tightened. 'I've a message for you, Iris O'Donnell,' he hissed.

She instantly stopped struggling. He knew her name. *How did he know her name?*

Iris stared up at him, her eyes wide and scared. Her assailant, in his forties she thought, had soft, almost flabby features, as if the weight of his skin was too heavy for his face. But there was no disputing his strength. She could feel his fingers digging angrily into her flesh. 'What do you want?'

The big man paused. As if revelling in the fear he was creating, a tiny smile crept to his lips. He glanced to his left and right in case anyone was watching. It was at that very moment that she recognised him. He was the man, she was sure, who'd been hanging around outside work yesterday.

He bent even lower until his jowly face was almost touching hers. She could smell onions on his breath. 'Tell yer daddy that we're waiting for him.'

Iris swallowed hard. 'W-what?'

'You 'eard,' he said. 'Just do as you're told and pass the message on. And pass this on too – if he wants his precious daughter to see another Christmas, then he'd best start co-operating. He gave her arm one final squeeze for good measure. 'You got that, love?'

Her heart was thrashing in her chest. 'But—' she began. He didn't give her a chance to finish.

'No fuckin' buts, sweetheart. This ain't a bleedin' debate. And don't even think about going to the law. If you do, you'll regret it – and yer old man will regret it too.' He let go of her arm, straightened up, and took a step back. 'Keep yer gob shut, eh?

135

We'll be in touch soon.' Then he turned and walked away. A few seconds later he was lost to the crowd.

Iris stood rooted to the spot, gently rubbing at her arm. Her lungs were pumping out her breath in short, fast, frightened bursts. Jesus, what had just happened? She was barely able to process it. It was like a loop going round and round in her head. Especially those words he had uttered at the start: *Tell yer daddy that we're waiting for him.* Could it be possible that he was still alive, after all? That Albert Jenks *had* known where he was? And then the full thrust of the stranger's threat suddenly registered in her brain. They expected her to contact her father and she didn't have a clue as to where he was.

Suddenly Luke appeared at her side, dragging the tree behind him. 'Here you are. I thought you said five minutes.'

'Sorry,' she muttered, trying to pull herself together. 'There was a queue. And then someone bumped into me and . . .' She gazed down at the food scattered on the ground, at the huddle of tiny green olives by her feet. Then she looked up again at Luke, at his familiar face, at the lock of brown hair that fell over his forehead. Surely he would notice there was something wrong? Surely he would notice how scared she looked?

But he was too preoccupied with his recent purchase. 'You like it?' he said. As if he'd grown it himself, he gestured proudly towards the tree.

Iris nodded. 'It's great.' This was the point where she should tell him everything. So what was holding her back? A part of her longed to explain, longed to sink against his chest, to feel him hold her safely in his arms. But another part drew back. He was due to go to Brussels tomorrow and all she'd be doing was landing him with a heap of worry. Or maybe that was just an excuse. She was certain that he would insist on going to the cops. And she couldn't do that, wouldn't do that, if it meant putting her father in danger.

'We'll get back then, shall we?' Luke said, stamping his feet impatiently on the ground.

Iris gave another nod, not trusting herself to say any more than she had. Her legs were still shaking as she linked her arm through his again. As they made their way back to the car, her frightened eyes scanned the crowd for any sign of her assailant. But if he was still there, he was well hidden.

Chapter Nineteen

Iris was aware of a silence in the flat; in the living room the TV was off and the sofa was empty.

'Michael?' she called out, but there was no reply.

She walked into the kitchen where she found a scribbled note lying on the table. *Ta for everything. Have gone home. M.* Iris knew why he'd left in such a hurry – he didn't want another grilling. But now, more than ever, she needed to talk to him. If anyone had an idea of what lay behind the threats she had received today, it was Michael.

'He's gone,' she said, retracing her steps and flapping the note under Luke's nose.

'Well, he probably wants to be at his own place.'

'But he shouldn't be alone. It's too soon.'

Luke shrugged, not even trying to look concerned. 'He'll be fine, babe. Don't worry about it.'

'Perhaps I should go round, check that he's okay.'

'For God's sake, give the guy a break, can't you? He just needs a bit of peace and quiet.'

Iris frowned. For the second time she was tempted to tell him about the man in the market. If Luke came with her to see Michael then maybe, between them, they could force him to talk. But she instantly dismissed the idea. The only talking Luke would be doing was to the cops.

'So are you getting those decorations, babe, or not?'

While he began sorting out the stand for the tree, Iris went to the bedroom and dragged down the cardboard box from the top of the wardrobe. December started next week, but she wasn't feeling festive. Her mother had never put the tree up until a week before Christmas. Anyway, she had more important things on her mind than baubles and tinsel. At the thought of what had happened in the market, her legs began to shake again. As her knees buckled she sank down on the bed and buried her face in her hands. What should she do? For a minute she was too overwhelmed to do anything. Then, reaching into her bag, she pulled out her mobile and tried to call Michael. It went directly to voicemail. She hesitated before leaving a message, unsure of what to say. She didn't want to scare him off, to make him think that she was going to start cross-examining him again, but she needed some answers – and quick. 'Er . . . it's me. It's Iris. Will you call me when you get this message? *Please.* I just want to know that you're okay.'

Luke came into the room and stared at her. 'He's a grown man,' he said. 'He doesn't need you fussing. Why don't you give the poor guy some space?'

Although what he really meant, Iris thought, was that he was glad Michael had gone and didn't want her encouraging him to return. 'You know what,' she said, standing up. 'I'm just going to nip round. I bet he hasn't even got any food in.'

'Are you kidding?' Luke said.

And seeing his expression, Iris knew he wasn't going to forgive her in a hurry. 'I'm sorry. Look, I won't be long, I promise. I'll be back in an hour or so.' She thought about asking if she could borrow the car, but then changed her mind. Leaving any decent car in the vicinity of the Mansfield Estate was tantamount to asking for trouble; the kids who lived in those blocks would have it away before she'd even crossed the threshold. Luke could have offered to drop her off, but he didn't. He simply pulled a face and then retreated to the living room.

Iris grabbed her coat and made for the door.

She walked with her head down against the cold winter air. In her hurry she'd forgotten her scarf and gloves, but she wasn't going back for them now. While she advanced up the High Street, her freezing hands bunched deep in her pockets, Iris rehearsed what she'd say to Michael. It would be no good if the words were to tumble out in any old order. She had to be smart about it; she had to be prepared.

Over the years, things had been kept from her – she was certain of it. However, getting Michael to reveal them could be tricky. But then again, she had just been threatened. Surely no family secret was important enough to put her life in jeopardy? She shivered, remembering what the thug had said.

Suddenly Iris became aware of how stupid it was for her to be walking alone after what had happened. She quickly glanced to her left and right, before looking back over her shoulder, but no one appeared to be following. Anyway, they wouldn't have another go so soon – would they? No, she decided. She was safe for a while. They would give her a few days' grace, time to contact her father, before putting any more pressure on her.

Ten minutes later, as she passed Tobias Grand & Sons, Iris thought she glimpsed a light behind the opaque glass. It was only there for a second, as if a door had opened and then swiftly closed again. She paused, wondering if she'd imagined it, but then noticed Toby's racing green Toyota parked in the street. Perhaps there had been another call-out. With Gerald ill, and

William possibly occupied elsewhere, it would have been left to Toby to step into the breach. Iris gave a wry smile. He'd have been none too pleased at having to drag himself out of bed after a late Saturday night. At any other time she would have stopped to stay hello, to see if he needed a hand, but today she was too busy with her own problems.

Iris went into the Co-op on the corner and picked up a basket. Whizzing down the aisles she grabbed milk, bread, butter, eggs, bacon and cheese. To these she added a selection of ready meals. They weren't exactly a healthy option, but even Michael could manage to remove something from a packet and throw it in the microwave. As she was about to pay, she noticed the bottles of spirits lined up behind the counter. She shouldn't be encouraging him to drink, but if there was one sure way to loosen Michael's tongue . . .

It was still early afternoon, but already it was growing dark. The sky was low, a soft grey blanket beginning to wrap itself around the three looming towers of the estate. Iris stepped up her pace as she walked through the gateway; this wasn't the kind of place to loiter even in broad daylight. Michael lived in Haslow House to the left. She glanced up at the rusting balconies, the cracked and peeling paintwork, and thanked God that he was on the second floor. At least she didn't need to use the lift.

It was only as she was jogging up the worn stone steps that it occurred to her he could be out. She should have stopped off at the Dog on her way here. More than likely, he was propping up the bar. But, surprisingly, and much to her relief, she saw a light in his window as she turned the corner on to the walkway.

Iris knocked on the door and waited. There was no response. She pressed her face to the window glass, but the mustard yellow curtains were pulled tight. She tried knocking again. Pressing her ear against the wood, she listened for the sound of

141

any signs of movement from inside. Nothing. Putting the carrier bags on the ground, she knelt and opened the letterbox. 'Michael? Michael, it's me, Iris.'

She peered in at the small gloomy hallway. Nothing stirred. 'Michael?' she called out again.

Now she was starting to get worried. What if he'd suffered a delayed reaction to the blows from the fight? What if he'd collapsed and was lying helpless on the floor inside? Iris had a spare set of keys for emergencies. She stood up straight, pulled them out of her bag and stared at them. Did this qualify as an emergency? He could have simply come back, pulled the curtains against the cold, left the light on and gone down the pub. Really, she ought to check the Dog out first, but she didn't relish the thought of dragging the shopping back down the steps. And what if he wasn't there? She'd have to come all the way back up. All of which was a crazy waste of time if Michael *was* in need of help.

Iris tried his phone one last time. She leaned in against the door again and listened for the sound of ringing, but there was none. Eventually it went to voicemail. With no means of knowing whether his phone was actually turned off or if he was just sitting in a pub and avoiding her calls, she decided to take the bull by the horns. Michael might not be overjoyed by the fact she'd let herself into his flat, but she'd rather risk his displeasure than his life.

She took a breath, unlocked the mortice and then turned the key in the Yale. Pushing open the door, she called out again. 'Michael?'

As soon as Iris stepped foot inside, she sensed that the place was empty. She closed the door behind her and listened again. The flat had a curious quality to it, a kind of stillness even though it was not entirely quiet: the radiators gurgled, the fridge hummed and the clock on the wall emitted a soft, steady tick.

Even though she knew it was pointless, Iris made a rapid check of all the rooms. It was only when she'd established that there was no body laid out on the floor that she allowed herself to relax. Going through to the kitchen, she put the carriers bags on the table and started to empty them. The fridge, she noticed, was almost empty. She piled in the food and put the bottle of whisky on the counter by the sink.

Iris paused, deciding what to do next. What she *should* do was head straight over to the Dog, but a little voice was whispering in her ear. Why not take the opportunity to have a quick look round? Perhaps, somewhere in the flat, was a clue to the whereabouts of her father. Iris pulled a face. It wasn't right to snoop – but then lying wasn't right either. And she was sure that Michael had lied to her. This morning's scrap with Danny Street had been about more than good manners.

Before she could let her conscience get the better of her, Iris started on a fast sweep of the flat. The place was untidy but relatively clean. Starting with the kitchen, she checked all the cupboards and drawers but found nothing more than a few tins of baked beans and a pile of old bills. In the living room, she rooted through the newspapers lying on the coffee table and then opened and closed the scratched mahogany cabinet. There was nothing in there either apart from an almost empty bottle of vodka. It was only when she came to examine the small round table by the sofa, the table which had the phone standing on it, that she noticed the scrap of paper. It had a number scrawled across it and Iris knew that number by heart. It was her mother's!

Iris's heart gave a start. So far as she was aware, her mother and Michael hadn't spoken in years. So why on earth was her number written here?

Iris leaned over, picked up the phone and dialled 1471. She listened to the BT message reciting her mother's number.

Michael had been called yesterday morning at a quarter to eleven. Although she had no means of knowing whether he had actually taken the call – he could have written down the number later – it seemed too much of a coincidence that half an hour after it had come in he'd been on his way to pick a fight with Danny Street. She tried 1571, but there were no recorded messages.

Iris was still pondering on what all this might mean when she heard the key turning in the lock. Smartly, she backtracked to the kitchen, opened the fridge and took some of the contents out.

'Michael,' she called out. 'Don't worry. It's only me.'

He came through to the kitchen, looking bemused.

'I'm really sorry,' she said. 'Only I was worried about you. I brought some food round and when you didn't answer the door, I thought . . . well, to be honest I panicked a bit so I let myself in. I hope you don't mind.' As if she had only just arrived, and was still in the process of unpacking the bags, she started to put the food back in the fridge. She felt guilty at the subterfuge, but not entirely sorry.

'I popped into the Dog for a quick one,' he said.

'You weren't answering your phone.'

'Oh,' he said, taking it from his pocket and staring at it.

Iris, still feeling awkward, forced a smile on to her lips. 'It doesn't work if you don't turn it on.'

'No,' he said. 'Well, thanks for the food. You needed haven't bothered. I was going to nip out later.'

'It'll save you the bother. You should be resting, not running around.' Iris nodded towards the whisky. 'And I bought you a bottle. I thought you might be in need.'

Michael's eyes instantly lit up. 'Ah, sweetheart, that was good of you.'

Iris suspected that he had only left the pub because he'd run

144

out of cash. Her uncle had not worked, at least not legally, since an accident at the car factory over ten years ago. Having sustained a back injury, he was now living off disability benefit. She had witnessed no particular evidence of any lasting damage – he had no problem playing endless games of pool – but it wasn't her place to pass judgement.

Iris picked up a couple of glasses from the draining board. 'Hey, why don't we have a quick drink before I go?'

Michael, perhaps questioning her motives, narrowed his eyes a little. But seeing as she had bought the bottle, he could hardly refuse. 'Sure,' he said. 'Why not?'

Iris added a generous splash of water to her whisky, but Michael took his neat. They sat down at the kitchen table and she waited until he'd taken a few sips. 'So, how are you feeling now?'

'Not bad,' he said, his fingers tentatively lifting to touch the cuts and bruises on his face. 'Not so bad at all. I think I'll live.'

Iris nodded. 'That's good, Michael, because we've still got some talking to do. We never did finish our conversation, did we?'

'Didn't we?' he said, acting all innocent.

'Don't give me that,' she said, smiling again. 'I can read you like a book. You rushed off the minute my back was turned. And I know when you're lying. Tell me the real reason why you were fighting with Danny Street.'

'I've already—'

'The *real* reason, Michael, not that pile of old crap you told me earlier.' She leaned across the table and looked hard into his eyes. 'Because something happened in Columbia Road today, something nasty, something that scared the hell out of me. So I want the truth and I want it now. I'm sick of being lied to!'

He stared back at her for a moment. His voice, when he replied, sounded brittle and fearful. 'Ah, Jesus,' he said. 'What happened?'

Chapter Twenty

Michael jumped up after she had told him and started to pace the kitchen. 'The bastards! The fuckin' bastards!'

Alarmed by his reaction, Iris stood up and grabbed his elbow. 'Sit down,' she said. 'This isn't achieving anything. Just sit down and tell me what you know.'

'Did he hurt you? Did he—'

'No,' she said. In truth her arm was still aching from where the brute had dug his fingers into her flesh. She made an effort not to rub at it. Her priority now was to calm Michael and find out what was really going on. 'Please sit down,' she said again.

This time he complied and sank wearily into the chair. He put his elbows on the table and covered his face with his hands. 'Shit,' he murmured.

'I need the truth,' she said. 'I'm entitled, aren't I? Whatever your reasons for lying and I understand that it was probably to try to protect me – well, it's too late for that now. I'm already involved. I've been threatened. And I need to know why this is happening.' She took a deep breath. There was still the all-important question she had to ask. 'Is my dad still alive?'

'No,' Michael said, immediately removing his hands. He left a short pause and shook his head. 'No, he can't be.'

Iris felt her heart leap. 'You're not certain?'

He knocked back his drink, reached out for the bottle and poured another generous measure. 'It's been nineteen years. Don't you think he would've contacted me?'

'I don't know,' Iris said. 'I don't have any clear idea of why he left in the first place.' Recalling what the man at the market had said, she added: 'Was he in trouble with the police?'

Michael was obviously surprised by the question. There was a short silence. 'The police?' he repeated slowly.

But his surprise, she decided, was more down to the fact that she knew he'd been in trouble than out of any kind of incredulity. 'He was, wasn't he? And it must have been something serious or—'

'It wasn't his fault,' Michael said. He rubbed his face again and ran his hands through his dark curls.

Iris felt her heart shift again. 'So the cops *are* interested in him?' She took another drink. The whisky was so diluted she could barely taste it. Perhaps she'd skip the water on the next round. That there would be a next round, she was now in no doubt at all. Michael was up against the ropes, struggling with what he should and shouldn't say, and she intended to knock the truth out of him. And if that meant staying until every last drop of the whisky had been drunk, then so be it!

'Come on, Michael,' she urged. 'This has gone too far. You have to talk to me.'

He gave a small nod, reaching for his glass again. 'Your dad . . . well, he got himself into a bit of a fix.'

'A fix?'

'He had money problems and . . . and he was in deep and looking for a way out. I told him not to get involved, but he wouldn't listen.' Michael shook his head. He paused as if unsure

147

whether to go on. Iris waited patiently. Eventually, he gave a sigh and continued. 'You ever hear of a guy called Davey Tyler?'

She thought about it. 'No.'

'He was a local villain, nothing big time. He made a living out of robbing warehouses mainly – electricals, stuff like that. Your dad and him, well, they weren't exactly mates, but they used to drink in the same pubs. Acquaintances really, rather than mates. But they got talking one night and . . . and Tyler made Sean an offer. He needed a hand with a job and offered to split the profits with him.'

'A job?' Iris said. 'You mean a robbery?'

Michael nodded. 'And not at some warehouse. It was a private house Tyler had targeted this time.' He hesitated again. 'Sean wouldn't have considered it normally, but he was desperate for cash. He had the loan sharks on his back, making all kinds of threats. Sean made a mistake, love, a really bad mistake. Sure, he'd been in trouble in the past – we'd both done stretches inside, both mixed with the wrong sort of people – but he'd turned his back on all that. From the moment he met your mum, everything changed. He didn't want to be involved in that stuff any more.'

Iris topped up his glass and hers. She took a large gulp of whisky, certain that what she was going to learn next would be best heard with more alcohol flowing through her veins. 'Go on,' she said.

'The house,' Michael muttered, 'well, it wasn't just any old house. It was Terry Street's place.'

'What?' she spluttered.

'I know,' he said. 'It was crazy, bloody crazy. And if I'd known what the two of them were planning, I'd never have let Sean go ahead with it. I'd have found a way to stop him. Tyler had a grudge you see; he was sick of Terry Street and his firm poncing off him, coming round to take a share whenever he pulled off a successful job. This way he reckoned he could get his own back. He knew the place must be swimming in cash, full of all sorts of other goodies too. It was alarmed, of course, but Davey Tyler was a dab hand at disabling most of those systems; they weren't as sophisticated as they are these days. He reckoned they could be in and out in twenty minutes and half a million better off.'

Iris raised her eyes to the ceiling. She was trying to stay cool, to take it all in, but her mind was doing somersaults. 'I take it things didn't go exactly to plan?'

'You could say that. It was a Saturday night and the Streets were supposed to be out. There was a charity do in Hackney, some boxing event, just an excuse for a piss-up really, but the local press were going to be there and Terry always liked having his face in the paper. It wasn't Lizzie's scene so she was at the Hope, keeping an eye on things. The boys were all sleeping over with mates. Terry dropped them off on his way, but Liam changed his mind at the last minute, decided he wanted to go to the boxing do instead. Anyway, something happened – Liam wasn't feeling so good, I think – and Terry had to take him home. They turned up just in time to—'

'Catch them in the act,' Iris whispered.

Michael gave a soft groan. 'He was never the violent sort, love, you know that. Sean wouldn't hurt a fly.'

Iris felt her stomach shift. 'What do you mean?'

'He had no idea that Tyler was carrying.'

She jumped back in her seat. 'Jesus! He had a gun?'

'And Terry, having found a strange van parked up in his drive, walked in with a sawn-off. I don't know where he got it; perhaps he always had one handy in the boot of his car. Tyler panicked, started firing, and the next thing Sean knew, the two of them – Terry and Liam – were both on the ground. Tyler scarpered pronto, but your dad tried to help. The kid was already dead, but he did all he could to save Terry. And he called an ambulance from the house phone before he left.'

'He left him there?' Iris said, her eyes widening.

'He was scared, sweetheart. He was terrified. He did his best but . . . he didn't know what else to do.'

Iris swallowed the rest of her drink and poured another. This was all too much to take in. The man Michael was talking about bore no relation to the father she remembered. *That* man had been sweet and gentle, full of love and affection. It was hard to reconcile him with this stranger who had broken into someone else's house, witnessed a killing and abandoned a man who could have been dying.

Seeing the expression on her face, Michael reached out and covered her hand. 'I swear he didn't know about the shooter. But once it was done, there was no going back. He had to make a run for it.'

It was then she started to think about the terror her father must have felt, the horror. She swallowed hard. 'So Terry must have seen him? He knew who was there that night, who killed his son?'

'That's why Sean had to take off; he had no other choice. If Terry pulled through, he was dead meat. And even if he didn't make it, the cops had a recording of Sean's voice from when he called 999. Basically, he was up shit creek without a paddle.'

'So what did he do? Where did he go?' Iris said.

Michael shook his head. 'I didn't ask. I didn't want to know. If I was to take a wild guess, I'd say Ireland – plenty of quiet places there where you can keep your head down for a while. But I could be wrong. Tyler got on a plane and pissed off to Spain. Maybe your dad did the same.'

'With what?' she said. 'I thought he was broke. I thought he didn't have any . . .' She stopped dead and stared at Michael. When she spoke again her voice was full of incredulity – and revulsion. 'Ah, Christ,' she murmured. 'It was the money from the house, right? He'd just seen two people shot, seen a kid killed, but he still walked away with the cash.'

'It wasn't like that,' Michael said.

'So what was it like?' she said, angry now. She couldn't accept what her father had done. This was the man she had longed to see again, whose face she'd searched for in the street. That her own flesh and blood could commit such a callous act . . . She pulled her hand away from Michael's. She felt like weeping.

'It wasn't that . . . planned,' he insisted. 'Everything happened so quickly. After he'd tried to help Terry, he . . . he just picked up the holdall again. He didn't even think about it. It was only a few thousand.' As soon as the comment had slipped from his mouth, Michael pulled a face, knowing it had been the wrong thing to say.

Iris raised her hand to her mouth and chewed on her knuckles. There were so many more questions to ask, but first she had to absorb all of this. Although what she needed was a clear head, she automatically took another drink. There was still part of her that was in denial, a part that wanted to blunt the sharp edges of what she was learning.

Michael had the sense to keep silent for a while.

Eventually, Iris looked at him again. 'I want to know everything,' she said. 'What happened next? He came to you, right?'

Michael furrowed his brow as if trying to recall the exact chain of events. 'He called me about an hour later. By then I already had a fair idea of the amount of trouble he was in. I'd been at the Hope, having a drink with Lizzie, when the cops arrived. I could see that it was going to be bad news. They told her there had been a break-in, that . . . that Liam had been—'

'And then?' Iris interrupted, not wanting to hear that word *killed* again.

'I put two and two together, didn't I? I knew Sean had been

151

out on a job, that he'd been doing over some house with Davey Tyler. I prayed it was a coincidence. Fuck, I prayed that it wasn't the Streets' place, but in my heart . . . well, I guess I knew. I went home and waited for him to call.'

Now Iris waited too, giving him time to get his thoughts together.

Michael cleared his throat. Like a drunk on the wagon, he gazed longingly at his glass, but didn't take a drink. Perhaps, just for once, he felt the need to be sober. 'When he called, I arranged to meet him at Bethnal Green Tube. I could tell from his voice what state he was in. He was at his wit's end, love, completely desperate.'

Iris nodded, not trusting herself to speak.

'I knew he was going to have to leave sharpish so I packed a bag for him. It was a change of clothes, nothing much, and a bit of cash in case he needed it.'

'Which he didn't,' Iris said sarcastically.

Michael looked at her and shrugged. 'Okay,' he said understandingly, 'I know how you must feel. This is a lot to take in, but what you have to remember is that your dad wasn't a bad man. He made mistakes, Iris, big mistakes, but if he could have turned back the clock on that night he would.'

Iris flapped a hand, not wanting to hear any more about her father's so-called conscience. 'So what about Mum,' she said. 'When did she find out about all this?'

Michael frowned again, a deep wrinkling of his brow, as if that particular memory was still raw in his mind. 'I went to see her straight after. I told her everything. She was . . . she was devastated, shell-shocked. I remember her sitting there and . . . that *look* in her eyes. It was as if all the light had suddenly gone out of them.' He visibly shuddered and this time reached for his glass. He swallowed the whole of his drink and quickly poured another. 'I told her she should leave, take you and get the hell

152

out of there. It wasn't the cops I was worried about so much as Terry's men. If they caught a sniff of who'd been at the house they'd be straight round to see her.'

'She must have been terrified,' Iris said.

'Yeah, she was. Of course she was.'

Iris shuddered. 'So Dad couldn't even talk to her himself? He couldn't even bring himself to do that? He left you to do his dirty work.'

'There wasn't time,' Michael sighed. 'And anyway, he knew it was pointless. What he'd done – well, she was never going to forgive him. It was over between them, finished.'

'And me?' Iris couldn't stop herself from asking. 'Was he finished with me, too?'

'Ah, love,' he said softly, 'that was the hardest thing he ever had to do, leaving you behind. You were his little girl. He loved the bones of you.'

Iris twisted the glass between her fingers. She felt like smashing it against the wall, throwing it on the floor. Her teeth were clenched tightly together. 'But not enough to stay.'

'Would you have preferred it if he'd put his hands up and admitted what he'd done? If he'd gone to court, got sent down?'

'At least I've have got to see him,' she said bitterly.

'You don't mean that.'

And he was right. She didn't. Not really. How could she have wanted him to be locked behind bars? 'But he could have found a way to stay in touch. It's been nineteen years, Michael, without a single bloody word.'

'That's why I'm sure he can't be alive. He'd never have done that to you – or to me.'

But Iris wasn't so sure. She wasn't sure of anything now. Half an hour ago she'd have sworn her father wasn't capable of the kind of actions Michael had described. Her world had been turned upside down and she was starting to look at things differently.

153

'So,' she said, 'that's when we left Kellston? That's when Mum took me away?'

'No, I couldn't persuade Kathleen to leave that night. She was scared, but she was stubborn too. She said that if she ran, she'd look guilty, and she didn't intend to be looking over her shoulder for the rest of her life.'

Iris wondered if that had been a brave or stupid decision. What would *she* have done in the same position? It was a question she didn't have an answer to.

'Anyway,' Michael continued, 'it was another week before Terry Street was well enough to be able to talk to the cops. Not that he did – do much talking, I mean. Terry liked to sort things out his own way. He told them there had been a couple of guys in the house, but he hadn't seen them clearly; it had been dark inside and it had all happened too fast.'

'And they believed him?'

'I doubt it,' Michael said. 'But what could they do? There weren't any useful forensics, fingerprints or the like. So long as Terry stuck to his story, the cops could only make their own enquiries, start checking out the likely suspects and calling on their grasses for any interesting rumours that might be doing the rounds. Both Davey Tyler and Sean eventually got added to their list, but it was a bloody long list and they weren't exactly at the top of it. Neither of them had a record for breaking into houses, and Terry Street had plenty of enemies.' He paused, his eyes darting around the room. 'It was over two weeks before they turned up on your mum's doorstep, asking after Sean.'

'What did she tell them?'

Michael took a while before answering. 'What we'd agreed,' he said. 'That they'd split up a few days ago, that he was a useless good-for-nothing loser who'd taken off with some slapper. The neighbours could have told them otherwise, especially about the length of time he'd been missing – they couldn't have

154

seen him for over a fortnight – but they were never too fond of the filth. Anyhow, I don't think any of them would've believed that Sean was involved.'

'And the police accepted that?'

'Why not?' Michael said. 'He wasn't the most likely of suspects and your mum was pretty convincing. There wasn't any good reason to go searching for him.'

'But what about the voice?' Iris said. 'What about the recording they had from when he'd dialled 999?'

Michael nodded. 'Thankfully, it wasn't that clear – and Sean was speaking very quickly. Kathleen swore that it wasn't his voice.'

Iris sat back in her seat, trying to absorb it all. She thought about her mum, about her nice, respectable mother, sitting in front of a couple of policemen and lying through her teeth. Perhaps her father wasn't the only person she didn't know too well. Had she lied to help him escape or just to save her own reputation? She must have been stunned. She must have been angry and bitter. Iris knew how it felt to have been deceived. She thought about all the lies she'd been told through the years. It was a shock finding out the truth like this, but now wasn't the time to dwell on it. She had to press on, to discover as much as she could. If Michael stopped talking, he might never start again.

'So why didn't Terry Street come after you? I mean, when he got out of hospital. You're my dad's brother. He must have—'

'No,' Michael interrupted. 'I've got Lizzie to thank for that. She told him I'd been drinking in the Hope all evening – there were plenty of other witnesses too – and managed to persuade him that I couldn't have had anything to do with it. She made him promise that he wouldn't take it out on me or your mother. If it hadn't been for her . . . well, fuck knows what Terry would have done.'

155

It crossed Iris's mind, and not for the first time, that he and Lizzie might have been closer than Michael was prepared to admit. Then she thought about the awful situation her dad had landed other people in. While he'd gone on the run, her mum and Michael had been left to face the music.

Michael raised his glass to his lips again. 'Terry had his priorities. He knew who'd pulled the trigger that night. He knew who'd killed his son, and it wasn't Sean.'

'But he was there. He was still a part of it. And it strikes me that Terry Street isn't the type to walk away from *any* kind of payback. An eye for an eye and all that. By hurting you or Mum, he could at least have got some revenge.'

Michael pulled a face. 'I don't know how Lizzie persuaded him – and I never asked. Perhaps Terry needed to have her on side. She was the one, after all, who was going to have to keep things ticking over while he was stuck in that hospital bed. He was relying on her to take care of the kids *and* the business. If she asked a favour of him, he was hardly in a position to refuse. Anyway, however she did it, I never had any trouble.'

Iris wasn't entirely convinced by the explanation, but sensing that Michael wasn't going to elaborate, she changed the subject. 'Did Terry Street ever catch up with Tyler?'

It was getting dark outside and the kitchen was filling with shadows. Michael stood up, walked across the room, and turned on the light before sitting down again. Iris had the feeling he was playing for time.

'Did he?' she asked again.

Michael gave a thin smile. 'Why do you think he's been inside for the last ten years?'

Iris sucked in her breath, feeling her heartbeat starting to accelerate again. 'He . . . he . . .'

'It took Terry years to track him down, but he never stopped looking. The great Spanish dream didn't work out too well for

Davey Tyler and eventually he came home. It didn't take long for Terry to hear about it and when he did . . .'

'He made him pay,' Iris said.

'When the two of them finally met up again, there was a fight. You don't need to be a genius to guess the outcome. Terry claimed self-defence, but the jury wasn't having it. He was found guilty of murder and the judge sent him down for fifteen years.'

Iris had only a vague idea of how the system worked, but had a notion that most people only served about two-thirds of their sentence. On top of that, she remembered how she'd heard that Terry was due out soon. She took a large swig of her whisky before asking the next question. 'Do you think he killed my dad too?'

Michael hesitated, but only for a second. 'Look, I'm not going to lie to you, love . . . not any more. I don't believe Sean would have kept silent for all these years, not unless he hadn't been able to get in contact. And there's only one reason why he couldn't have done that.'

Iris took a moment. When she spoke again, her voice had an edge of bewilderment. 'So why the hell was I threatened today? If Terry *did* kill him, then Chris and Danny Street must know that.'

'Perhaps someone's been stirring, telling them he's still alive.'

'But that doesn't make any sense.' Suddenly, despite all her earlier ill-feeling, Iris felt an instinctive rush of hope at the thought she might actually see her father again. 'Surely, if they're reacting like this, it means that Terry *didn't* kill him. He couldn't have. Dad could still be out there somewhere.'

'Or someone's just winding up the Streets. Just because you leave a man for dead, doesn't mean that he actually is. Maybe someone's been whispering in their ear.'

'But why would anyone—'

Michael sighed. 'God, Iris, you're talking about a family that has pissed off more people than the fuckin' Mafia. Claiming that your dad's still alive could just be a way of winding Terry up – especially as he's coming out soon.'

Iris, although she didn't want to believe it, could see the logic in his argument. 'So what do we do next?'

'*We* don't do anything,' he said firmly. 'I'll sort it.'

Iris stared at him. She snorted. 'And how exactly are you going to do that? By having another go at Danny Street? As I recall, that didn't go too well last time.'

Michael automatically raised his hand to touch the bruises on his face. 'I won't have them hassling you.'

'Yeah, well,' she said, 'maybe there are better ways of sorting this out than trying to beat someone's brains to a pulp.'

'What do you mean?'

She had an idea, but wasn't in the mood to share it. 'Just promise me you won't do anything until we talk again. Swear to me, Michael. I need time to think.'

Iris set off for home, her head full of the robbery and the terrible things her dad had done. She was halfway down the street when she realised that she hadn't even asked about her mother's phone call. There were so many other questions that needed to be asked too, so much more to be explained. Michael may have revealed some of the story, but she wasn't convinced that it was everything. This, she was certain, was only the beginning.

Chapter Twenty-one

It was nine-thirty on Monday morning. Iris was sitting at her desk in reception, trying to concentrate on the copious amount of paperwork Gerald Grand had miraculously managed to generate from his sickbed. However, her mind was preoccupied with other matters. The conversation with Michael was still revolving in her head; she hoped he wasn't going to do anything stupid.

She had Luke to worry about too. It had been after five when she'd finally got back to the flat. For the second time that day, she'd arrived home to discover a scribbled note sitting on the kitchen table. Luke's had said simply: *Back later.* There had been no further explanation or any indication of where he had gone. Clearly irritated by her absence on the eve of his departure to Brussels, he had taken off in one of his all too familiar huffs. Iris had wandered into the living room. The Christmas tree, still bare and undecorated, had stood accusingly in the corner, listing a little to one side.

Iris could have, maybe *should* have called him, but had chosen not to. He probably wouldn't have picked up anyway. In the event, he had strolled in at around ten o'clock, looking more cheerful than she'd expected and claiming to have been for a drink with his old friend Martin. Iris had her suspicions. Unless the macho, rugby-playing Martin had taken to wearing a particularly pungent perfume, she may well have something else to worry about.

Iris sighed and stared down at her desk. Was it possible that Luke was cheating on her? She recalled the sleek blonde girl at the Rufus Rigby Christmas party and screwed up her face. There had been something about the girl, about the way she had reached out and touched Luke's arm. Or was that just paranoia talking? Iris couldn't deny that their relationship had been rocky recently. Well, not only recently if she was being strictly honest . . . she couldn't remember the last time she'd felt truly close to him. And she wasn't only thinking about sex. They seemed barely able to have a conversation these days without it degenerating into a pointless, petty squabble.

Iris looked up at the computer, typed in a few more lines and then pressed the delete button to correct her mistakes. Her fingers were refusing to co-operate today. 'Come on,' she muttered to herself, 'concentrate.'

But again her thoughts drifted off. On her way back from the Mansfield Estate, she had made the decision to tell Luke everything, to stop keeping secrets, but last night hadn't seemed like the right time. This morning hadn't felt any better either. It was best, she'd decided, to leave the revelations until he came home. He didn't need her problems distracting him while he was trying to work. Anyway, by the time he got back everything might be sorted out.

Did she really believe that? Probably not, she admitted. Problems like these were too big to go away in a hurry. Which was why she needed some serious help. Having run through the rather short list of possibilities – quickly eliminating both Michael and the police – she had eventually picked up the phone and called the one person who might be able to give her some useful advice. There was no love lost between Guy Wilder and the Streets, but at least he understood how they operated. She had called at eight o'clock last night and if Guy had been surprised to hear from her so soon after their exchange on Friday, he hadn't shown any evidence of it.

'Something's happened,' she'd said. 'I can't talk now. Would it be possible for us to meet up tomorrow?'

'Of course. Come to the bar. About six? Is that okay? We shouldn't be too busy then. You can tell me all about it.'

Iris scowled at the computer screen. No matter how she tried to justify it, she still felt a sense of guilt over not coming clean with Luke. How much of that decision had actually been down to trying to protect him, and how much to avoiding the inevitable row? He wouldn't have been pleased that she'd failed to mention the threats made at the market. Even less pleased, perhaps, that she'd dropped into a bar after the Rufus Rigby party and shared a bottle of wine with a virtual stranger. She could imagine the questions that would follow: why didn't you tell me? What were you trying to hide? And if she'd told him she was meeting Guy Wilder again . . .

Iris ran her fingers threw her hair. That was the trouble with lies – one small one led to a larger one and before you knew it, you were embroiled in a complicated web of deceit. This knowledge should have helped her to understand why neither her mother nor Michael had been entirely straight with her but, even though she was aware of the hypocrisy, she still felt angry at them both. So angry, in fact, that she hadn't even been able to call her mother yet. It was best to wait until she was feeling calmer. Some words, said in haste, could never be taken back.

As the door to Tobias Grand & Sons opened, Iris looked up to see Toby walking in. He shook the snow from his hair and grinned. 'Morning, hun. How are you today?'

Iris, glad of the distraction, glanced deliberately at her watch. 'What are you doing in at this time? I thought you usually avoided the boring Monday to Friday routine.'

'Ha ha,' he said, coming over to perch on the corner of her desk. 'I'll have you know that I'm an extremely hard-working member of this thriving family business.'

Iris was about to make another quip when she remembered seeing Toby's Toyota yesterday afternoon. Maybe, just for once, he had been putting in the hours. 'Ah, yes, I suppose the boss has been keeping you busy now he's confined to his bed. I hope he hasn't been spoiling that hectic social life of yours.'

'No chance,' Toby said, laughing. 'I never let anything as tedious as work stand in the way of a good weekend. In fact, I spent the whole of it in bed – and believe me, it had nothing to do with feeling under the weather.'

'Ugh,' Iris said, waving a hand. 'Spare me the details.' Then, confused as to why his car should have been parked outside, she added: 'So there weren't any call-outs on Sunday?'

Toby laughed again. 'How would I know? I don't make a habit of answering the phone when I'm otherwise occupied. Anyway, Grimm Junior would have dealt with anything like that.' He paused and looked at her. 'Why do you ask?'

Iris gave a casual shrug. 'Just wondering.' Toby wasn't telling the truth, but she didn't know why. Maybe there was a perfectly good reason for why he should lie about not being here – except right now she couldn't think of one. Of course there was always the possibility that he'd lent his car to someone else, but that didn't seem very likely; Toby's gleaming green Toyota was his pride and joy. 'Oh, it's just there was a viewing on Saturday, and William was busy so I had to come in and cover. I thought you might have been roped in too.'

'No chance!' Toby exclaimed. 'Wild horses wouldn't drag me into this place at the weekend.' He swung a leg against the desk, his heel tapping against the wood. 'Dropping like flies, are they? It must be the cold. Still, we can't complain. It's all good for business.'

Iris raised her brows. 'If you say so.'

She was about to discreetly pursue the matter of the car when William came out of his office and interrupted the conversation.

'You couldn't nip downstairs with these, could you?' he said, placing a sheaf of papers in her hand. 'They need to be signed by Alice.'

Iris wasn't over fond of the basement and always avoided it if she could. There was something about its sterility, about that eerie hum of refrigeration that always made the hairs on the back of her neck stand on end. She could cope with dead bodies once they were lying serenely in their coffins, but was disturbed by the procedures that enabled them to look so peaceful. The thought of seeing a pale, cold corpse laid out on the embalming table filled her with horror.

As she hesitated, Toby swiftly got to his feet and said, 'No worries. I'll do it.'

Iris, relieved, passed the papers over to him. 'Thanks.' As he walked away, she had her second guilty feeling of the morning – by allowing Toby to make the delivery, she was probably condemning Alice to yet another round of his ceaseless teasing. Should she stop him and insist she go herself? No, it was too late for that now. Anyway, Alice would have to learn to fight her own battles. As soon as the thought entered her head, Iris felt bad about it. There were some people who were just too quiet, too reserved, to handle the likes of Toby Grand.

William was still standing over her. Iris looked up at him and sighed.

'Yes,' William said apologetically, as if her sigh had been

directed at him. 'More correspondence as regards Mr Hills, I'm afraid.' He laid another pile of papers on her desk. 'I think he might be with us for quite some time.'

Iris thought of Connor Hills, chilling quietly in the basement, and felt a stab of annoyance at the warring relatives, the wife and son, who couldn't come to a civilised decision about the poor man's place of rest. 'Why don't they just cut him in two and have half each?' she snapped. Then, aware that her comment was somewhat lacking in compassion, she quickly added, 'Sorry, but it just doesn't seem right.'

Surprisingly, William smiled. 'No, you've got a point. Something along the lines of the judgement of Solomon? It might work a treat. Perhaps I'll suggest it in my next letter.'

'I suspect you'd find yourself at the bad end of a writ.'

'Could be worth it,' he said.

Iris smiled back up at him. Over the past few days, she'd been revising her opinion of William Grand. Perhaps he wasn't quite as dull as she'd originally thought. As he returned to his office, it occurred to her that he wasn't the only one she'd got wrong: Michael's recent revelations had revealed another side even to her nearest and dearest. How had they managed to keep their secrets from her for so long? Perhaps she wasn't quite the judge of character she'd always believed herself to be.

Chapter Twenty-two

The radio was playing in the basement. Alice, who had her back to the steps, jumped as Toby came up behind her and slid his arms around her waist. 'Hey, gorgeous.'

'What are you doing?' she whispered, turning to glance anxiously over his shoulder in case someone might be following.

'Don't stress. I'm on my own.' He laughed as he flapped the papers in front of her. 'And I've got a perfectly good excuse for being here: Grimm Junior needs your autograph on these.'

But Alice couldn't help stressing. Naturally she felt fearful about their relationship being discovered – Gerald Grand, she was sure, would put a stop to it – but another, more pressing cause for anxiety was laid out on the embalming table behind her. It wouldn't take Toby long to notice who she had almost finished working on and when he did . . .

'What's wrong?' he said, letting go of her and stepping back. 'Aren't you pleased to see me, babe?' His teasing tone lasted only a moment before his gaze came to rest on the table. 'Shit!' he exclaimed. 'What the fuck are you doing?'

Alice, who hated any kind of conflict, felt a lump come into her throat. She stammered out her reply. 'W-William told me it was urgent, that she needed attending to today.'

'But I called you. We talked yesterday. I told you to leave her, that she was the one. I *told* you that, Alice, and you agreed.'

She bowed her head. 'I know but . . . but William insisted it was done this morning. I couldn't refuse.'

'Don't be ridiculous!' he spat back at her, his face creased with anger. 'You could have made some excuse, told him you had an emergency at home. You could have said that you'd come in this evening and do it.'

'I'm sorry,' Alice murmured. 'I didn't think.' She gazed down at the young, blonde woman lying on the table. Catherine MacDonald was a pretty nineteen-year-old who had died tragically from an overdose. A post-mortem had been done before William had collected her from the hospital on Saturday. On Sunday, Toby had come in to see if she was 'suitable'.

'Didn't think?' he repeated sarcastically. 'Well, that makes a fucking change, doesn't it?'

Two deep crimson patches burnished Alice's cheeks. She was lying about William's insistence on having the embalming done this morning. In truth, having seen her, Alice had simply felt unable to go through with Toby's plan. Hadn't the poor girl suffered enough? The thought of Danny Street being anywhere near the body filled her with revulsion.

Toby glared at her. 'She would have been perfect and now you've gone and ruined it all.'

'I'm sorry,' she said again, reaching out to touch his arm. Alice always found herself apologising even when she wasn't in the wrong. In the back of her mind she could hear her mother's familiar reproaches: 'Why do you let people walk all over you? Haven't you got a mind of your own?'

He shrugged off her hand. 'It's a bit late for that.'

166

'But there'll be others,' she said defensively. 'You know there will.'

'I've already told him,' Toby retorted bitterly. 'I've made the arrangements. What the fuck am I supposed to say now?'

Alice bit down on her lip. 'Just tell him the truth – that her parents are insisting on seeing her this afternoon, that there's nothing you can do it about it.' She hoped Toby wouldn't check with William or Iris, but didn't think he would. He wouldn't want to draw attention to his interest in Catherine MacDonald.

Toby's eyes flashed. 'You know what he'll do to me if he thinks I'm messing him around? He'll break my bloody legs, Alice. Is that what you want?'

She instantly shrank back. 'Of course I don't. I wouldn't ever do anything to—'

'But you already have. Can't you see that? I thought you cared about me. You said you did. And now look what you've gone and done.' His gaze slid back to the body of the girl. 'You've landed me right in the shit.'

Alice was aware at this point of the contradiction in her feelings for him. The anger had dissolved from Toby's face to be replaced by a sulky, self-pitying expression. She thought it was curious how you could love someone and at the same time not actually like them very much. Toby was selfish, self-absorbed and utterly insensitive to others. In fact, it was doubtful if he had ever felt any real emotion towards anyone else. And yet, despite knowing all this, she still wanted him more than any man she had met before. It was perverse . . . and yet oddly exciting too.

Toby threw the papers on to the counter and sighed. Eventually, grudgingly, he shook his head and said: 'I'm sorry. I shouldn't have had a go at you. It was just . . . just the shock.'

'He'll understand, won't he? Danny Street, I mean.'

Toby shrugged. 'Are you kidding? He's hardly the understanding type.'

'But I can back you up. I can tell him what happened.' Alice was surprised by her own audacity. The thought of talking to a psychopathic gangster like Street filled her with dread, but if it meant that Toby could be spared . . .

'No,' he said, forcing out a smile. 'Thanks, but there's no point in you getting your legs broken too.'

Before Alice had a chance to respond, Toby quickly turned away and headed back up the steps.

Chapter Twenty-three

It was a good ten minutes before Toby reappeared. Iris looked up, expecting him to stop and chat, but he walked straight past without even acknowledging her. There was a dark scowl on his face. She wondered what could have happened in the basement to have changed his mood so drastically. Mild-mannered Alice was hardly the type to cause offence. She watched as he paced restlessly around reception. His lips were moving but no sound came out; it was as if he was rehearsing a conversation he was about to have. After a while, he pulled his phone out of his pocket, stared at it and then abruptly put it away again.

'You okay?' Iris asked.

Toby visibly jumped. 'What?'

'Has something happened?'

'Why should anything have happened?'

Iris thought his voice sounded unusually defensive. 'Because you look like you've just been handed a death sentence.'

'Yeah, well,' he said bitterly, 'that's the business we're in, isn't it – death and despair.'

Iris stared at him. 'And since when did that ever bother you?'

Toby Grand had all the sensitivity of a brick wall. He didn't do sympathy or compassion. Death, for him, usually meant only the happy ching ching of the cash register.

'I've got a call to make, okay? You know, one of those *difficult* kind of calls – discussing arrangements with a relative.'

Iris didn't believe him. There was no reason for him to be making a call like that from his mobile. Why wasn't he using the office phone? And anyway, Toby rarely dealt directly with the public. He left all that to his father and William. 'All right,' she said. 'I was only asking.'

Toby gave her a look as he pulled on his overcoat. He crossed reception, yanked open the door and glanced back over his shoulder. 'Do us a favour, will you? Tell Grimm Junior that I've had to go out.'

'Where shall I say—'

But the door had already closed behind him. 'Don't mention it,' she murmured. Iris wondered what he was up to – something dodgy knowing Toby. She hoped it wasn't connected to the Streets; those two sharks would eat him up and spit him out without a second's thought. She was reminded of the threats that had been made at Columbia Road Market. Her stomach shifted at the memory. The Streets were dangerous, unpredictable men who would stop at nothing to get what they wanted. It wasn't a happy thought. Just how far would they go in their attempts to flush out her father?

It was a question she didn't dare dwell on.

Iris returned her attention to the letter she was typing and tried her very best to concentrate.

It was shortly after one when Iris went to the kitchen. She found Alice sipping on a mug of soup, one of those packet things that you added water to. Her dark hair, freshly cut, was sleek and glossy, and she was wearing more make-up than usual.

In fact, everything about Alice Avery seemed slightly different: her clothes were smarter and she'd even gone to the trouble of painting her nails.

'Hi,' Iris said, before delving into the fridge for her pasta. She put the kettle on and sat down on the opposite side of the table. 'How's it going? Don't usually see you at lunchtime.'

'My mother's out with friends. It didn't seem worth going back to the flat so . . .'

Iris nodded towards the soup. 'Is that all you're having?'

'I'm on a diet.' She patted her stomach and smiled. 'Trying to lose a few pounds.'

Ah, Iris thought, so maybe there was a man on the scene after all. She was about to come out with one of those confidence-boosting phrases, something along the lines of her being absolutely fine as she was, but then changed her mind. It might sound rather patronising. Instead she ripped the plastic fork off the back of the carton and began to eat. 'So what's bugging the beautiful Toby today?'

There was a short pause. 'What do you mean?'

'Well, one moment he's absolutely fine, joking around like he usually does and then he goes downstairs to see you and comes back looking like he's just had his face slapped.' She laughed. 'You didn't, did you?'

Alice, looking flustered, picked up her mug and promptly put it down again. Her eyes remained firmly focused on the table. 'Of course not. He only dropped off some papers. I-I barely talked to him. It wasn't anything to do with me.'

'Oh, that's weird. I wonder why—'

'It wasn't anything to do with me,' Alice repeated, her voice rising to a thin anxious squeak. 'Nothing at all.'

Iris stared at her and nodded. Clearly Toby wasn't the only one feeling defensive. 'No, I'm sure it wasn't. I didn't . . .' She shook her head. Whatever had happened in the basement – and she was certain something had – Alice wasn't prepared to share it. 'All I meant was that you shouldn't take him too seriously. He's a pain in the ass, but he doesn't mean any harm.' Iris, even as she was speaking the words, wasn't entirely convinced that the latter part of the statement was true. Toby, for all his charms, had a mean streak; there was a thin line between teasing and bullying and he had crossed it on more than one occasion.

'I don't,' Alice said. She forced a smile, but her lower lip was trembling.

Iris was beginning to wish she'd never raised the subject. The last thing she'd wanted to do was upset her. 'Look, if there's ever anything you want to talk about . . .'

'I'm fine, really I am.' Alice hurriedly scraped back her chair and stood up. 'I have to get on.'

'You haven't finished your soup.'

But Alice, like Toby before her, was already making a hasty exit.

At five o'clock precisely, Iris put on her coat, said goodnight to William and headed for home. Outside, what remained of the snow had gathered in the gutters and turned to slush. She crossed over and walked quickly along the High Street, pausing only once to gaze into the window of the jeweller's. The reason for this, she told herself, was that she was thinking of buying Luke a new watch for Christmas. But this wasn't the only reason she stopped. Worried that she might be being followed again, and unwilling to glance over her shoulder continuously, she had come to an abrupt halt outside Ruby's in the hope of catching out any shadow.

But no one behind her faltered. No one stopped dead in their tracks or did anything even faintly suspicious. Iris couldn't deny she was afraid – who wouldn't be with the Streets on their case? – but knew she had to stop the fear from overwhelming her. If she wasn't careful she would become completely paralysed by fright.

She didn't hang about for long. Apart from the fact she was in a hurry – she was due to meet Guy Wilder at six – she wasn't really in the mood for considering what gift to buy Luke. She'd received only one curt text since he'd left that morning: *Arrived safely.* Not even a kiss. Not even a 'Call later'. Despite his good mood of the previous evening, she was still, she suspected, in his bad books after abandoning him for Michael. Her doubts about his fidelity started niggling again. Frowning, she pushed them to the back of her mind. She already had enough to deal with.

Iris passed by the café, its windows steamy and opaque, and continued along the High Street. Across the other side of the road, the small Green had a scattering of pure white Christmas lights twinkling in its trees. At any other time she might have found the sight entrancing, but in her present mood she couldn't conjure up much festive spirit.

As she passed through the main gate of Silverstone Heights, Iris looked up at the three 'For Sale' signs and was glad she and Luke hadn't committed to buying a place. In the current economic climate, property was hard to shift. She found herself wondering how many couples were forced to stay together through financial commitments when the relationship had long since run aground. Not that she and Luke had reached that point yet but . . .

Iris jogged up the stairs to the second floor and unlocked the door to the flat. She figured she should just about have time to grab a shower and get changed before going to meet Guy Wilder. She could have gone straight to the bar from work and saved all this crazy dashing around. Why hadn't she? Because she felt it was only polite to freshen up, to put on some clean clothes. Except she knew that wasn't the only reason. She wanted to make a good impression. She wanted him to *like* her. But that was only, she inwardly insisted, because she needed his help. It had absolutely nothing at all to do with that lean sculpted face or the way his gaze seemed to reach into the very heart of her.

Twenty minutes later, showered and with her make-up done, she was still trying to decide what to wear. Something casual, she thought, but not too casual. There was a thin balance between looking good and looking like you'd tried too hard. Black? That was always a safe bet, but she'd been wearing black last time she saw him. She tried on a few more items before finally settling on a pair of slimline dark grey trousers and an emerald green shirt. The green, she knew, accentuated her red hair.

Iris checked her watch. It was ten to six. She had to make a move. The sensible thing to do would be to take the car – that way she couldn't drink anything but coffee. It was important to keep a clear head, to be able to tell her story as succinctly as she could. After picking up the keys, she juggled them in her hands for a few seconds, but then put them back down on the table. Maybe a glass of wine, or two, was just what she needed.

Chapter Twenty-four

Vita Howard pushed back her long dark hair and smiled across her desk at the young man who had turned up just as she was leaving. Neal 'Duggie' Duggan was knocking on nineteen, but with his slight skinny frame, smooth face and big blue eyes could easily pass for several years younger. He was a throwback to an earlier era, an Artful Dodger who made his living from picking pockets.

'So,' she said, 'you in bother again, Duggie?'

He threw up his hands in mock horror. 'Aw, Mrs H. Have a bit of faith. You think I'm gonna make the same mistake twice?'

It was over nine months since Vita had last seen him. He'd been up on charges of theft after being caught on CCTV skilfully relieving a local magistrate of his wallet, a pack of cigarettes and a mobile phone. Fortunately the film had been grainy enough to cast some doubt on the identity of the thief. When push came to shove, one grey hoody looked much the same as another. She had managed, after weeks of hard work, to get the charges dropped.

'Okay,' she said. 'So if it's not my professional services you're after . . .?'

Duggie leaned forward and grinned at her. 'I've always reckoned that one good turn deserves another.'

Vita raised her brows, still smiling. For all her disapproval of the way he made his living, she had a sneaky regard for him. He was, despite his faults, curiously endearing. He was also one of the few clients she had who wasn't dependent on drugs; Duggie got his rush, his kicks, from 'spreading the wealth' of the richer inhabitants of the area. The truth, of course, was that he only spread it as far as the local bookies and his favourite pubs.

'You've lost me,' she said.

Reaching into his pocket, he took out a brown leather wallet and slid it across the desk. 'I didn't realise.' He pulled a face, his mouth turning down at the corners. 'I'm sorry. If I'd known who he was . . .'

It took Vita a few seconds to recognise it. The wallet belonged to her husband, Rick. She picked it up, flipped it open and peered inside.

'I saw the photo of you and when I checked the name and . . . well, I reckoned it had to be your old man.'

Vita nodded. The photo was a few years old, a close-up snap that accentuated her large dark eyes. She stared at her own reflection for a moment before checking that both of his credit cards and his bank card were in their usual place. It was only as she looked in the section at the back that she got an unexpected surprise. There was a hefty wad of notes sitting there. Frowning, she wondered what Rick was doing with so much cash. He'd been pleading poverty for the past couple of weeks. Even yesterday, when his daughter had come round, she'd been the one who'd had to fork out for the rented DVD and a pizza.

'It's all there,' Duggie said, as if her expression was down to some form of suspicion. 'I ain't touched a penny, honest. I swear on me life. Six hundred quid.' He grinned again. 'I counted it.'

Vita glanced up at him. 'When did you take this?'

'Ah, you're not gonna get mad, are you? It was a genuine mistake. Like I said, if I'd had any idea—'

'Duggie, love, I'm not getting mad. Not at all.' She forced another smile, trying to hide her confusion. 'But will you please just answer the question. When did you take it?'

He glanced at his watch. 'I dunno. It was today though. About lunchtime? One?'

Vita was tempted to ask why it had taken him five hours to return it, but she'd already guessed the answer. No one like Duggie was going to hand over this amount of cash without a few second thoughts. 'Well, thanks,' she said. 'I guess.' She screwed up her eyes and stared at him. 'Although, as you took the damn thing in the first place, I'm not entirely sure how much gratitude I should be showing.'

'True enough. Still, at least I did the right thing in the end.'

Vita couldn't argue with that. 'So where was he when you nicked it?'

'Oh, he was outside Belles.'

'What?' she said, unable to disguise the sharpness in her voice. Belles was a sleazy lap-dancing joint in Shoreditch and its clientele was mainly City boys, wheelers and dealers, bankers and brokers looking for somewhere to squander their bonuses. Most of Belles' business was done in the evenings, but there was a healthy lunchtime trade too. And if everything she'd heard was fact, there was no shortage of sex and drugs for sale. What the hell had Rick been doing there?

Duggie, aware that he'd put his foot in it, shifted uneasily in his chair. Quickly, he tried to retrieve the situation. 'I'm not sayin' he'd been inside, Mrs H. I didn't see him coming out or nothin'. I just mean he was near the club. There was a crowd, you see, standing around and . . .' His response petered out into a shrug.

'It's okay,' she lied. 'It doesn't matter.'

But Duggie, unwilling to be the inadvertent cause of a marital rift, couldn't leave it alone. 'Or maybe it wasn't outside Belles at all. Shit, I could be well wrong. Now I come to think, it might have been the High Street. Yeah, yeah I think it was.'

Vita looked down at the wallet again. She had got as much out of Duggie as she was likely to and now wanted to be alone. 'Well, thanks for returning it,' she said. It was hardly moral to reward criminality, but he probably expected something for his trouble. Taking out a fifty, she offered it to him. 'Here.'

Duggie sat back and shook his head. 'Nah, I don't want nothin'. I couldn't. It wouldn't be right, would it?'

'Take it,' she insisted. 'Go out and enjoy yourself. Just promise me that you won't nick anything else tonight.'

He hesitated, his gaze fixed on the note. His nicotine-stained fingers crept towards it, but then withdrew again. 'Nah, I can't. You were good to me, Mrs H. No one else gave a fuck, but you stood up for me. You worked real hard to get me off those charges and I won't never forget that.'

'Please,' she said, dropping the note in front of him. 'I want you to have it. I'll be offended if you refuse. Look on it as a reward for doing the right thing.'

Duggie's precarious sense of right and wrong had its limits. He didn't need telling twice. Swiftly slipping the fifty into his pocket, he scraped back his chair and stood up. 'Ta. If you ever need anything . . .'

'I'll be sure to call.'

'I mean it,' he said. He paused, his big blue eyes gazing down at her. For a second, with his pale cheeks flushing red, he looked as awkward as an adolescent.

'Now fuck off,' she ordered, 'before I change my mind.'

Vita took a deep breath as he closed the door behind him. She was oddly touched by what he'd said and done. There wasn't much to recommend working in a place like Kellston, but rare experiences like this made it seem worthwhile. However, if Duggie's act had temporarily restored her faith in human nature, it hadn't done much for her faith in her husband. She picked up the wallet again and turned it around. Rick had been robbed over five hours ago. Why hadn't he told her? He must have noticed it was missing by now. There was only one reason why he wouldn't have called and that was because he didn't want her to know – and the only reason for that was because he'd had a wad of dodgy cash on him.

Her heart sank as she thought about him being at Belles. She wasn't quite sure what she was more stressed about: the idea of him ogling some curvy bimbo with a bra size she could only dream about or that he'd slipped back into his former ways. No, he couldn't have. He'd promised her – no more jobs, no more crime, and definitely no more time.

So what was he doing with six hundred quid in his wallet?

Vita snatched her mobile out of her bag, pressed one on the keypad and then instantly hung up again. This wasn't the kind of conversation to have over the phone. If she wanted to know the truth she'd have to ask him face to face.

Chapter Twenty-five

Iris hesitated before pushing open the door of Wilder's. Was she doing the right thing? She was suddenly assailed by doubt. Maybe, by enlisting Guy's help, she was only going to make matters worse. Things were complicated enough without involving someone else in the mix. But then again, what choice did she have? Her problems weren't going to disappear of their own accord; either she took control of the situation or became another victim. If the Streets found her dad before she did, Sean O'Donnell was done for. If they didn't, *she* was in the firing line.

Iris steadied herself and stepped inside. As Guy had predicted, the place wasn't busy, but there were enough tables occupied for it not to seem too empty. Her eyes quickly swept the red-walled room, but there was no sign of him. Noah, however, was standing behind the bar.

Iris smiled, relieved to spot a familiar face. It might be the twenty-first century, and she might be a modern woman, but she still felt faintly uncomfortable about walking into bars on her own. She went over to him and placed her bag on the counter.

'Hi,' she said, 'How are you?'

Noah didn't smile back. Instead he gave a small nod and said rather brusquely, 'Guy's upstairs. He won't be long.'

Iris hovered for a second, not sure whether to order a drink or not. Was it her imagination or could she sense frostiness in the air? She hoped it wasn't to do with her. She opened her mouth, intending to embark on a little small talk, but then smartly closed it again. There was something in Noah's expression that told her it would be a waste of time. 'Okay. Thanks. I'll just take a seat then, shall I?'

His only response was a slight, indifferent shrug of the shoulders.

Iris, feeling awkward, turned and walked away. She chose a table in the far corner, well apart from the other customers. Once she'd sat down she wished she'd bought that drink. She was in need of some Dutch courage. Noah's attitude hadn't done much to help her nerves and she wondered if he knew why she was here. If he did, he probably had a right to be annoyed. Guy had enough issues with the Streets without her adding to them.

With nothing else to do, she stared at the framed print directly in front of her. It was an old movie still of Humphrey Bogart and Lauren Bacall, a promotional photo for *To Have and Have Not*. Now *that*, she decided, was sexual chemistry. You only had to look at them to know they would end up together. For a while she pondered on what that mysterious connection was, that vital crazy spark that could so easily grow into a raging fire.

'Sorry to keep you waiting.'

Iris looked up to see Guy Wilder standing over her. He was dressed in a pair of dark jeans and a crisp white shirt. His fair hair was damp – he must have been in the shower – and slicked back from his forehead. Her heart gave a tiny leap. It was just the surprise, she told herself, and yet knew that it was

181

something more. It was a thought she quickly pushed to the back of her mind.

'It's okay. I've only just got here.'

'Didn't Noah get you a drink?'

She glanced over towards the bar. 'Erm . . .'

Guy, following her line of vision, grinned. 'Oh, right. He's still got a strop on, has he? Don't worry, it's nothing to do with you. He can be a right moody sod when he puts his mind to it. I hope he wasn't rude.'

'No,' she lied. 'He just seemed a bit . . . distracted.'

'Woman trouble, I'm afraid. He thinks she's messing him about – hell, she probably is – so he's venting his frustration on the rest of the world. Look, let me grab a bottle and I'll be right back.'

Iris watched as he strolled over to the bar, leaned over and said something to Noah. Noah's gaze immediately flicked towards her and she looked away, embarrassed by the idea that he might think she'd been badmouthing him. She stared down at the floor. She was starting to have those doubts again. Perhaps she shouldn't have come.

A short while later, Guy returned with a chilled bottle of Chablis and two glasses. 'I hope you don't mind white,' he said. 'You all right?'

Iris nodded. Her lips tried to smile, quivered and didn't quite make it.

'Stupid question,' he said, sitting down across the table. He poured the wine and passed her a glass. 'Here, drink this.'

She took a sip. 'I don't want to cause any trouble.'

'I've told you,' he said, glancing briefly over his shoulder. 'Noah's foul mood has nothing to do with you. I swear.'

Iris wanted to believe him, but wasn't sure if she did. However, it wasn't the main thing on her mind. Her worries went far beyond Noah's opinion of her.

'So I take it there have been some developments,' he continued. 'Why don't you tell me what's been happening.'

Iris took a moment to gather her thoughts. Seeing as she was here, she may as well go through with it. But where to begin? She hardly knew Guy Wilder. Her trust in him could be completely misplaced. She looked across the table. He was still patiently waiting. Could she really confess to what her father had done? The very thought made her stomach turn over. It wasn't just the shame of it, although that was bad enough, but there was an element of danger too – confiding in Guy would mean sharing a secret that had been buried for years. It would mean one more person knowing what her father had done. She was tempted to stand up, to say she'd made a mistake, that she had to leave . . . but then she remembered the thug's hand on her arm and the hissing menace of his threats. No, she couldn't deal with this on her own. She had to tell him some of the story at least.

Iris cleared her throat and, hesitantly at first, began to talk. She started with the fight Michael had got into on Saturday and what Vita had said about her name being mentioned. From there it was only one small step to the threats that had been made at Columbia Road Market. At this point she abruptly stopped again.

Guy leaned forward, his elbows on the table. 'I'm presuming there's a good reason why the Streets want to find your father after all this time.'

Iris hesitated again. Even though she wanted to tell him – and she wasn't sure if she did – she couldn't find the right words.

'It's only a wild guess,' Guy said, 'but seeing as your father disappeared nineteen years ago and seeing as it's nineteen years since Liam Street was murdered—'

Iris, who'd been playing with her glass, looked up sharply. 'He didn't do it!'

Guy raised his brows.

'He *didn't*,' Iris said insistently. 'It wasn't him.'

'But?' He paused. 'There is a but coming, isn't there?'

Iris sighed. She should have realised that he'd make the connection. Liam had been his stepbrother after all. Her voice, when she spoke again, was barely audible. 'How much do you know?'

Guy heaved out a breath, gave a light shrug of his shoulders. 'Not much. I was just a kid when it happened, twelve or so. I know that a couple of guys broke into the house, that Terry and Liam came back unexpectedly . . .' He stopped and shrugged again. The outcome of that fateful night was already known to both of them. 'The cops never arrested anyone and Terry probably wasn't that forthcoming with any information he did have; his idea of justice has never been connected to a courtroom. Years later he finally caught up with one of them. Davey Tyler, yeah?'

Iris nodded. 'It was Tyler who had the gun.' And once those words were out of her mouth there was no going back. For a second she paused, but could see no real harm in telling him the truth now. What was the worst he could do? Report it to the police? But somehow she knew he'd never do that. Quietly, stumblingly, she repeated all of Michael's revelations. It only took her a few minutes, but by the end she felt exhausted.

There was a short silence after she had finished.

'Shit,' he murmured, gazing down into his glass.

Iris saw the expression on his face and her heart sank. Why had she told him everything? Why had she bared her soul to him? Jumping to her feet, she said, 'Oh God, you don't need this. I'm sorry.'

But Guy stood up too. 'What are you doing?'

'Leaving you in peace. This is my problem, not yours. I shouldn't have—'

'Sit down,' he insisted, taking hold of her elbow. 'Please.'

She hesitated, but slowly sat back down again.

'I can help,' he said, 'if you'll let me, if you'll just give me a chance.'

Iris looked at him.

'What's the alternative?' he said. 'Going to the cops? That doesn't seem such a great idea if your father *is* still alive.' He paused. 'Do you think he could be?'

Iris shook her head and sighed. She was still trying to work that one out herself. 'God knows. But if the Streets think so, then Terry couldn't have found him. And that means it's possible, doesn't it.'

'Maybe your uncle knows more than he's letting on.'

'Not to mention my mum. Some family, huh? All these things they conveniently forgot to mention over the years.'

'Christ,' he said, laughing, 'you never met my mother. If we're going to start comparing dysfunctional families, you'll have some competition on your hands. You sure you're up for it?'

Iris finally managed a smile. 'I don't want to drag you into all this. But . . . but for as long as they think my dad's still out there, they're not going to leave me alone.'

'So let me talk to them,' Guy said.

'What?' She remembered the last time he'd met the brothers at Tobias Grand & Sons. It hadn't been the most sociable of occasions. 'From what I recall, the three of you don't exactly get on.'

'Getting on has nothing to do with it, Iris. I can still have a word. I can try to put a stop to all this. That family don't give a damn who they hurt, whose lives they ruin. They trample over other people without a second thought. Nothing matters to them. *No one* matters.'

Iris heard the sudden anger in his voice and knew that he was speaking from bitter experience. Was that why he was offering to

185

help? From the little she knew of his past, it was still clear to her that the Streets had left an indelible mark. Perhaps he didn't want the same thing to happen to her. Or perhaps he would simply jump at any opportunity to thwart their plans, to settle some old scores. 'But what are the chances of them listening to you?'

'Pretty good as it happens.' He picked up his glass, took a drink and put it down again. 'Danny's a waste of space, but Chris isn't stupid. He might hate my guts – and the feeling's mutual – but he knows a good deal when he hears it.'

'A good deal?'

'Yeah, he'll listen to what I have to say. I can't promise anything, but I can put the pressure on. My mother and I didn't have the most perfect of relationships, but she told me stuff, lots of stuff. I've enough shit on those two to send them down for the next twenty years.'

Grateful for his support, but still unsure of his motives, Iris shook her head. 'I still don't understand. Why should you . . .? I mean, why get so involved in all this?'

A tiny frown settled on his forehead. 'I thought that's why you came here. I thought you wanted my help.'

'I did . . . I *do*, but not at your expense. They're hardly going to welcome your interference, are they? And that could make life difficult. You've got your business to think about.' She glanced towards Noah who was busy serving a customer. 'I don't expect you to put yourself in the firing line. That's not fair.'

'Some things are more important than business.' He gave her a wry smile. 'Look, I know what you must be thinking – why's he doing this? What's in for him? And you're right to be asking those questions. The truth is, I'm not being entirely selfless. I despise the Streets. I loathe them with a vengeance. And yes, if helping you out means that for once I can stop them from getting their own way, then it'll be more than worth it.'

'But that's why I don't want to get you involved in all this. I only came for some advice on how to get them off my back. I've no idea where my dad is so I can hardly pass a message on. But if they're not aware of that, then . . .'

'Then they're not going to stop until they get what they want.'

Her stomach lurched as the full meaning of his words hit home. Iris covered her face with her hands. 'Oh, Jesus.'

'It's okay,' he said softly. Reaching out, he took hold of her hands and laid them back on the table. 'You're not on your own. Let me do this for you. Let me help.'

Iris was aware of the warm pressure of his fingers against hers. *Not on your own.* The relief of hearing those words was enough to make her want to weep.

'Hey,' he said, 'there's no need to look so pleased about it. I'm not that bad an ally to have.'

'No, I was only . . .' She stopped, temporarily unable to articulate her emotions. A lump had come into her throat. For the first time, she became aware of the music that was playing: Tom Waits was drifting through the speakers, crooning *Blue Valentine* in those deep, hoarse tones of his. 'Thank you,' she finally mumbled. She barely knew Guy and yet she instinctively trusted him. 'Are you absolutely sure about this?'

'I've never been more sure of anything.' His blue eyes gazed directly into hers. 'One good turn deserves another. You were kind to me that day I came to see my mother. You could have just thrown me out but . . .' He paused. 'Anyway, you and me, we're cut from the same cloth. We've been through the same things. We understand one another.'

Iris was reminded of that feeling she'd had when they'd first met, that peculiar and unnerving connection between them. Was it simply because they'd both been separated from a parent or was it something more?

Letting go of her hands, Guy lifted his glass and offered up a toast. 'So here's to us. To the good guys.'

187

'To the good guys,' she echoed, chinking her glass against his. She was about to ask what happened next when Guy made a rapid survey of the bar and pulled a face. The place had filled up since she'd first come in and there was a small crowd gathering at the bar. 'Sorry, but I'd better get back to work or Noah really will have something to complain about. You don't need to rush off though. Stay and finish your wine.'

Iris tried to hide her disappointment; she'd been hoping for a chance to talk some more and the thought of drinking on her own didn't really appeal. 'That's all right,' she said, getting to her feet again. If there was one thing she didn't want, it was to outstay her welcome. 'I should be making a move. I've got things to do.' In truth, the only things awaiting her were an empty flat and an evening stressing over what Luke might be getting up to in Brussels. Even as the thought crossed her mind, she was aware of her own hypocrisy. She had no right to be questioning what he might be doing when she was wishing she could spend more time with the man in front of her.

'I'll get you a cab,' he said.

'There's no need,' she replied, looking down at her watch. It was still early, barely seven o'clock. 'I'm only going down the road. I'll be fine.'

'It's no trouble.'

'Really,' she insisted.

He walked with her to the door, leaned down and kissed her lightly on the cheek. 'Try not to worry. I'll call you. I'll call you soon.'

Iris tried not to show her pleasure. She could have interpreted the kiss as a purely sociable gesture – he probably kissed people goodbye all the time – but was suddenly sure that it represented something more. Somehow it seemed to seal an understanding between them.

Chapter Twenty-six

Outside the bar, Iris wondered what to do next. With her evening having been unexpectedly cut short – she should have realised Guy would have to work – the hours seemed to stretch out in front of her. She didn't fancy returning to the flat with only her own fears for company. Instead, she took the phone from her bag and rang Vita. The call was answered straight away.

'How's things?' Vita said. 'You fancy meeting up? I'm in Connolly's.'

'Great. I'll see you in fifteen minutes.'

Iris walked at a brisk pace, alert to any stranger who might be paying undue attention to her. She was not too worried; there were still plenty of people around. Safety in numbers, she thought, although that hadn't stopped the thug in Columbia Road Market from . . . Hurriedly, she shrugged off the memory. If she started dwelling on that, she'd never dare go anywhere alone.

As she made her way up the High Street, Iris ran through her conversation with Guy. Was it really possible that he'd be able to persuade the brothers to back off and leave her in peace? And if he did, what was it going to cost him? Why should he put himself on the line for her like that? It was the final question that really set her thinking. In truth, she hadn't stopped thinking about Guy Wilder from the first day they'd met.

And what about Luke? She still hadn't heard anything more after his brief text this morning. That was almost twelve hours ago. As she marched along the pavement, kicking through the slush, she found herself assessing their relationship. She couldn't deny that it had been good at the beginning. They'd had plenty in common: drive and ambition, making money, *spending* money, having fun. God, they'd had so much fun– they'd been out at different clubs, different bars, every weekend and half the week nights too. Manchester had been their playground and they'd made the most of it. It had been one long party, a party that had continued after they'd come to London. It had been great until . . . Well, her unplanned pregnancy had put an end to all that. Suddenly, they'd had to stop thinking about themselves. Their lives had been turned upside down. Luke had tried to be pleased, to be supportive, but his heart hadn't been in it. Becoming a father had been the last thing on his mind.

Iris bowed her head. She couldn't blame him for feeling resentful. A baby had never been part of the deal and it wasn't his fault that their relationship had suffered. She was as incapable of talking about the loss as he was. He wanted to move on, to put it all behind them, but she couldn't do that. She couldn't go back to the life they'd been leading before.

Iris was still trying to sort out her conflicting emotions as she approached the café. Situated on the corner of the High Street and Station Road, it was renowned for its decent food and drink. It was also the only place in the area that stayed open all night. As she walked in through the door, she was hit by a rush of warm air.

About half the tables were occupied, some by smartly suited businessmen grabbing their last few minutes of peace perhaps before returning home, others by groups of teenagers, all dressed in the same hooded tops and expensive trainers. Eventually she noticed her friend sitting in the corner with a load of books and papers strewn in front of her.

Iris made her way across the room.

'Hi there.'

Rising from her seat, Vita gave Iris a quick hug. 'Hey, how are you?'

'Okay. Not bad. What are you doing here?'

'Escaping,' Vita said. 'The Bitch is round the house, putting on the thumbscrews. I thought I'd make myself scarce before I said something I might regret.'

Iris grinned. The Bitch was Rick's ex and Candice's mother. Even though Joanne and Rick had split long before Vita came on the scene, the woman still insisted on treating her like a shabby little husband stealer.

'What's she after this time?' Iris said, pulling up a chair.

'Same as ever: cold, hard cash. Candice, apparently, is in danger of becoming a social outcast if she doesn't get to attend the school skiing trip to Switzerland. *All her friends are going, she'll be left out if she doesn't, blah, blah, blah.* God, that twisted cow treats me like dirt – Joanne, I mean. I wouldn't mind, but I'm the one who usually ends up paying the damn maintenance, not to mention all the latest must-have gadgets of the twenty-first bloody century. She ought to try being a bit more polite or I may just slam shut the door on my rapidly dwindling bank account.'

Iris looked at her. It wasn't like Vita to sound so bitter; she'd long ago accepted that Rick had responsibilities and would normally be the last person on earth to complain about them. Through her work, Vita witnessed too many single mothers

struggling to bring up their kids to not be aware of the difficulties they faced. Petty crime was often their last resort and
when they got caught, she was always there to try to defend
them. 'And that's the only reason you're so pissed off?'

'Reason enough,' Vita huffed.

The waitress came over and Iris ordered a cappuccino. Vita
asked for another espresso and the girl nodded before removing
the two small empty cups already sitting on the table and
returned to the counter.

'You not planning on sleeping tonight?' Iris said.

Vita gestured towards the heap of papers. 'I need the caffeine.
I've got a ton of work to catch up on.'

'And I'm disturbing you. Sorry, I'll just have this coffee and
then I'll be off.'

Vita sat back and sighed. 'No, don't go. You're not disturbing
me. I'm glad to see you, I really am. And I should be the one
who's apologising. I shouldn't be taking any of this out on you.
I've just had a really shitty day.'

'And the delightful Joanne turning up hasn't helped.'

'You can say that again.'

Iris had come to the café intending to have a chat about
Guy's offer of help, but now she dismissed the idea. Vita had
enough worries of her own. 'So tell me about this lousy day of
yours. Have a good rant – you know you'll feel better for it!'

Vita laughed. 'You could be right there.'

The waitress came back with the coffees and they stopped
talking while she placed them on the table. After she'd gone,
Vita gave another sigh, pushed her books aside and said, 'It's
Rick.'

Iris raised her brows. 'Rick?'

'I think he's up to something – you know, something not
quite . . .'

Iris didn't need her to spell it out. It had always been a worry that Rick might revert to his former ways. No matter how much he wanted to go straight, the temptation – especially in a place like Kellston – would always be hard to resist. 'What makes you think that?'

'Well, unless you're going to tell me that Gerald Grand has begun paying a fortune for the stately bearing of his coffins, I can't see any logical explanation as to why Rick should have six hundred quid stashed away in his wallet.'

'What?'

'Yeah, quite,' Vita said. She drank a mouthful of espresso and went on to explain about Duggie's visit. At the end of the story, she gave Iris a rueful smile and said, 'I'm not sure what to be more worried about – all that cash mysteriously appearing or the fact he was in that sleazy strip joint this afternoon.'

'You don't know for certain he was there.'

'As good as,' Vita said. 'I've never seen anyone backtrack as quickly as poor Duggie. I think he was trying to spare my finer female feelings.'

'And have you asked Rick about the money?'

'Yeah, and you know what he said?'

Iris waited.

'That he won it on a horse,' Vita continued, 'a bloody horse! Although of course when I asked him what this incredible sprinting nag was called, he couldn't quite remember. He couldn't quite remember where it had been running either.' She banged one of her books down on top of another and scowled. 'He was lying through his teeth. I know he was. And he claimed that he hadn't noticed his wallet was missing, which is ridiculous bearing in mind that he can't go more than two hours without at least one visit to the pub.' She stopped and took a breath. 'And then, in the middle of it all, that bitch arrived and I just had to get out.'

'Did you ask him about being at Belles?'

Vita shook her head. 'To be honest, I didn't tell him about Duggie either. I said the wallet had been dropped off anonymously at the office, that I didn't know who'd handed it in. It probably sounds awful – shit, it is awful – but I'm still trying to make sense of it all. I figured if I mentioned Belles that he'd get even more defensive and then I wouldn't stand a chance of getting to the truth.'

'I can understand that,' Iris said. Feeling the need to be more reassuring she added: 'But none of this means that he's involved in anything serious. He loves you too much to fuck up, Vita. He knows what the deal is. He knows you'd walk if you ever found out that he was getting in bother again.'

Vita ran her fingers through her hair. 'Except he's too damn stupid to think I ever *would* find out.'

Iris, seeing the pain in her friend's face, quickly took her hand. 'Hey, he may have made some mistakes in his life, but he's kept out of trouble for the past few years.'

'What do they say – leopards never change their spots? I mean, the very reason I got to know him in the first place was because the law was on his back. Just my luck that he chose my firm of solicitors to bring all his problems to.'

'We're not talking leopards,' Iris said. 'We're talking about the man you fell in love with, the man who's managed to stay on the straight and narrow since the two of you got hitched. Do you really believe he's going to throw all that away for a few quid?'

'Six hundred quid,' Vita reminded her.

Iris acknowledged the number with a nod. 'Okay, I can see it looks bad, but unless you talk to him properly you could be jumping to all kinds of wrong conclusions. You need to sit down, have a proper chat.' Which was rich coming from her, she thought. She and Luke hadn't had a decent conversation in months.

'You know who owns Belles, don't you?'

Iris shook her head.

'Those twisted lowlife Streets. If he's got himself involved with them . . .'

'The Streets?' Iris repeated, startled. She jumped back, letting go of Vita's hand. After leaving Guy, she hadn't expected to hear that name again tonight. It seemed the brothers were starting to haunt her.

'What's the matter?' Vita said.

Iris took a second to think through the implications. 'You don't think he went there to find Danny, do you? Michael did take a bit of a beating on Saturday. The two of them are mates. What if Rick decided that some payback was in order?'

Vita laughed. 'Who, my Rick? No, he's not the type. He always runs a mile at the first hint of trouble. I'm not saying he can't take care of himself – he's big enough *and* ugly enough – but it's really not his style. Anyway, he's more than aware that it was Michael who started it all in the first place. You can hardly pick a fight with a nutter like Danny Street and expect to walk away unscathed.'

'I suppose.'

Vita drank some more of the strong black coffee. 'I'm starting to wonder if I know him at all. Maybe he spends every spare hour in places like Belles.'

'You don't really think that.'

'I'm not sure what to think any more.' She sank her chin into her hands and looked at Iris. 'I'm starting to wonder how much he had in his wallet *before* he left the club. What's the cost of a private lap dance these days?'

'Oh, come on. He's not like that.'

'He's a man, isn't he?' Vita said.

Which made Iris wonder about Luke, and what the nightlife was like was in Brussels. The city was more renowned for

195

chocolate than steamy sex but, if you had the right company, you wouldn't even have to leave your hotel room to get into mischief. She found herself pondering on the fair-haired girl again, about the pungent smell of perfume that had lingered on Luke's collar.

'Oh God,' Vita groaned. 'If I don't watch out, I'm going to end up as one of those women who are always suspicious, always double-guessing what their husbands are up to. Before you know it, I'll be going through his pockets, checking his phone and employing private detectives to follow him around.'

Iris grinned. 'It hasn't quite come to that, has it? Maybe he did get involved in something less than legal, but he's very nearly been caught out. You might not be aware of all the details, perhaps you never will be, but the very fact you know about the cash means he'll think twice about doing anything dodgy. He understands what the deal is between you two. He might take a chance once, but he won't do it again.'

'Yeah, you could be right,' Vita conceded. 'Perhaps I will have that little chat, make sure he's clear about where I stand on the subject. Then I'll give him the cold shoulder treatment for a few days just to make sure he gets the message.'

'Lucky Rick.'

'He deserves it. Anyway, enough about my wonderful life. Where have you been, all dressed up?'

Iris glanced down at her clothes. 'I'm not dressed up.'

'You're telling me you went to work like that?'

'Well, no,' Iris admitted. 'I had a meeting with someone this evening.'

When she didn't go on, Vita said, 'Are you going to enlighten me? Or it a big secret? I hope you haven't been playing fast and loose now that Luke's safely across the other side of the Channel.'

'No,' Iris retorted, feeling her cheeks redden slightly. 'There's no secret about it. I just thought you had enough on your plate without having to listen to my problems.' She paused to finish her coffee. 'Actually, I've been to see Guy Wilder.'

Vita frowned. 'Lizzie Street's son?'

'That's the one. Do you know him?'

'Only by sight. He runs that bar down the other end of the High Street, doesn't he? Tall, blond guy.' She stopped to gaze at Iris for a few seconds before she continued. 'Good-looking geezer. Bit of the Daniel Craigs about him, yeah?'

'Really,' Iris replied casually. 'I can't say I've noticed.'

'Then you need your eyes testing, sweetie.' Vita leaned forward and smiled. 'Now, are you going to spill or do I have to wrestle you to the ground and force it out of you?'

'It's not like that. There's nothing . . . *going on.*'

'So why did you go to see him?'

Iris realised she'd already said too much. It was the second time tonight her mouth had run away with her. Unlike earlier, however, she didn't have any qualms about confiding in Vita; her loyalty and friendship, along with her ability to keep a secret, was beyond doubt. Accordingly, she recited the tale for the second time. By the time she got to the end, her friend was looking aghast.

'Jesus,' she said.

Iris groaned. 'I know. It's terrible. How could he have done that?'

But it wasn't what her father had done that was bothering Vita. 'Shit, Iris, it's you I'm worried about. You were threatened! You have to go to the cops, tell them what's been going on.'

'How can I?' She glanced quickly round the café and lowered her voice. 'If my dad *is* out there somewhere, he could end up being arrested. A part of me hates him for what he did, but I don't want to see him behind bars. I can't take that chance.'

'You can't take the chance of those two thugs having another go either. Next time it's going to be more than a warning.'

Iris swallowed hard. She'd thought the same thing often enough, but hearing it said out loud made it seem even more real. 'I know that. But Guy can talk to them; he's their stepbrother after all. They might not get on, but that doesn't mean they won't listen. He can explain that I don't have a clue where my dad is. I just want to be left alone.'

Vita narrowed her eyes. 'I don't like it,' she said. 'You've only just met this man. Why's he going out of his way to help you like this? What's in it for him?'

Iris, hearing an echo of what Guy had said earlier, lifted her shoulders in a tiny shrug. She could have explained about his history with the Streets, about how much he hated them, but knew that would only give Vita something else to latch on to. Now wasn't the time to start talking about any of that airy-fairy stuff like 'connections' or 'feelings' either. It wouldn't wash. Vita was in lawyer mode – and lawyers liked the cold, hard facts. 'Does it matter? It's not as if I've got that many options. If he can help, then why not?'

But Vita wasn't convinced. Folding her arms across her chest, she took on a stern look. 'Well, he's either after your body or he's got some other motive. Be careful, Iris. Don't be too trusting.'

Iris nodded back at her. 'I won't,' she said. 'I promise.' In her head, she knew that Vita was right, that she shouldn't go jumping headlong into a risky alliance with a man she barely knew. However, her heart was saying something completely different.

Chapter Twenty-seven

It's the waiting that drives him crazy, the having to stand back and wait. Every hour feels like a day, every day like a lifetime. His face twists with frustration. He bangs his fist against the window ledge and a sharp pain runs through his knuckles. Raising the hand to his mouth, he sucks hard on the broken skin.

The scheming bitch Lizzie is dead and buried. That, at least, is something to celebrate. He's only sorry that it was so quick. He wishes she could have suffered more, died more slowly – but money's tight these days and little extras like those come with additional charges. Still, it was a job well done. It pleases him to think of her lying in her coffin, of the worms slowly wriggling their way towards her corpse.

He stares out across the moonlit rooftops and knows that he's grown cruel. Through the years he's become cold and rotten inside. The bitterness has eaten away at his soul. It would have been different if Kathleen had made a different choice. There have been other women in his life, plenty of them, but when he tries to conjure up their faces he can't. They were nothing to him. She was the only one who mattered.

And now?

Now he's not sure what he feels for her. Not hate, but not love either. He might call it sadness if he was still capable of such an emotion.

The fury slowly rises in him again. To try and calm himself down, he recites what he will say to Iris when he sees her again. Her forgiveness is what he craves most. Will she ever understand? He paces from one side of the room to the other, muttering under his breath. He will plead with her. Yes, he will get down on his knees and beg if he has to. One way or another, he will make her understand.

Chapter Twenty-eight

Iris awoke to the smell of toast. Her head felt fuzzy and for a second she tensed, wondering if she was in the throes of a hangover. But then she recalled the night before, the single shared bottle of wine, and relaxed. Vita had come back to the flat, but they had stopped drinking by ten o'clock. Turning over, she stretched out her arms and yawned. She was just about fit for work, fit to face the world. Pulling on her dressing gown, she went through to the kitchen and found Vita fully dressed and seated at the table. Piles of paper were spread out in front of her and she was busy scribbling notes in a legal pad.

'Morning. What time is it?'

Vita glanced at her watch. 'Ten past seven. Sorry, did I wake you?'

'No, not at all. You sleep okay?'

'Like a baby.' Vita grinned, nodding towards her phone. 'That's because I've got a clear conscience – unlike Rick. He's been sending me texts since six o'clock this morning.'

'You did tell him you were staying the night, didn't you?'

'Course I did. I'm not a complete sadist. Anyway, he'd have

sent out a search party if he hadn't heard from me. But he knows he's in the doghouse. He's worried that I might not be coming back.'

Iris poured herself a coffee, sat down and picked up a piece of toast. 'So when are you going to put the poor guy out of his misery?'

'I haven't decided yet.' Vita shrugged. 'This afternoon? Tomorrow? When he's had sufficient time to ponder on the error of his ways.'

'God, you are going to make him suffer. I'm glad I'm not married to you.'

They looked at each other and laughed.

'Seriously though,' Vita said, 'I want him to be clear about where I stand, about where we *both* stand. I couldn't bear it if he went back to jail. I couldn't. And sod it, I refuse to be one of those sad prison widows, queuing up every Saturday to catch a couple of hours with the man they love.'

Iris, as well as sympathising with her friend's position, felt a tiny pang of envy. Vita was only reacting so strongly because she loved Rick so much. For all their differences, the two of them had a strong and special bond. Whereas she and Luke . . .

'And why should I have to go through that,' Vita continued, 'just because he can't resist the temptation of making a fast buck? It's not as though we're on the poverty line. We might not be rich, but we're hardly starving either.' She pulled a face and groaned. 'Oh, what am I doing? I spent last night boring you to death with all this. Just tell me to shut up.'

'It's okay,' Iris said. 'You've a right to be upset.'

'And you've a right to not have to listen to my constant whining. Especially now. You've got enough on your plate. Look, do you want me to stay here with you while Luke's away? I don't like to think of you being on your own while all this crap's going on.'

Iris considered it. In some respects she'd welcome the company, but Vita's continuing absence wouldn't do much for her relationship with Rick. She glanced out of the window and towards the high perimeter wall. 'Thanks, but this place is pretty secure. I'll be fine. I'll be okay.'

'Or you could come and stay with us. At least that way there'd always be someone around.' Vita put her elbows on the table and frowned. 'I'm worried about you.'

'Don't be,' Iris said. 'I'll be careful. I promise. And this place is like Fort Knox; nobody's going to get in without an invite.'

At a quarter to nine, they climbed into Vita's bright red VW Golf. Iris had thought about borrowing Luke's car while he was away – it would save her having to walk to work and back on her own – but had decided that the hassle outweighed the benefits. By the time she'd found somewhere to park, she'd probably still have a ten-minute tramp back to the funeral parlour. They left the complex, drove along Silverstone Street and joined the traffic on the busy High Street. Shortly after, they pulled up outside Tobias Grand & Sons.

'Thanks for the bed,' Vita said. 'And if you change your mind about coming to stay . . .'

Iris smiled. 'I appreciate it – and the lift. I hope you sort things out with Rick.'

'I'll do my best. Call me, yeah? Let me know how it's going.'

'Will do.'

Iris got out of the car, looked back and waved. She had just reached the door to the funeral parlour when a rather dishevelled Toby appeared by her side. He'd obviously been out on the lash; his face was ghostly pale and there were dark circles under his eyes. His left hand, as determined as a junkie's, was firmly clutching his fix of Starbucks.

'Good night?' she asked.

Ignoring the question, he stood leering towards the Golf. Vita was just pulling away. 'Who's the cute chick?'

'Chick?' Iris repeated, raising her brows. 'Does anyone other than you actually use that term these days?' It amazed her that Toby was still capable of thinking about sex when he was clearly so hung over.

He grinned. 'Well, pardon me for being so retro. She got a boyfriend?'

'She's not your type.'

'All the cute ones are my type.'

'Yeah, well this one's happily married.' At the moment it wasn't strictly true, but Iris refused to share that nugget of information. Toby might have his charms, but sniffing round her friend like a dog on heat wasn't one of them.

After another brief glance over his shoulder, Toby got out his keys and unlocked the door. 'There's no such thing as *happily* married women. Believe me, I've talked to enough of them.'

Iris shook her head. She doubted if Toby ever did much talking when it came to his relationships. Before he could start to question her on Vita's vital statistics – there was only so much he could see through the windscreen of a car – she quickly changed the subject. 'So how come you're opening up this morning? In before twelve, two days on the run – it must be a record.'

'Very funny,' he said, 'As it happens Grimm Senior's still sick as a pig and Junior's got a home visit so naturally I offered to step into the breach.'

Iris suspected that there hadn't been anything voluntary about it. Gerald Grand, despite his illness, must have applied the thumbscrews: *No opening up, no wages at the end of the month*. It was the only reason Toby would have dragged himself out of bed before midday.

She followed him inside, took off her coat and placed her bag on the desk. 'There's an appointment at ten. The Elliots. Are you dealing with them?'

'Hey babe,' he said, 'I'm here to deal with anything that arises.'

Iris frowned at him. A Mrs Jean Elliot, along with her husband, was coming in to discuss the funeral arrangements for her brother. 'You will try to be . . . well, just the slightest bit sensitive?'

Toby ran his fingers through his uncombed hair and grinned. 'What's the matter, hun? You think I can't do caring?'

'I'm sure you can,' she said, sitting down, 'but I haven't seen much evidence of it to date.' William had left a pile of typing for her. Flicking through the sheets of paper, she noticed yet another two letters to go out regarding the final burial place of Connor Hills.

'Ah, Iris.' Toby leaned in close, breathing out a gust of last night's stale beer. 'Have a little faith. I was born and bred to the funeral business. I have sympathy and compassion oozing from my bones.'

'Yeah, right. And, no offence, but it's not the only thing you're oozing. You might want to brush your teeth before they arrive. You stink of booze.'

Toby drew back a little, pulling a face. 'What's bugging you today? You get out the wrong side of bed?'

At least it was her own bed, she thought. Toby probably didn't even remember whose duvet he'd spent the night under. And yes, she was feeling tetchy. Luke still hadn't bothered to ring. All she'd received since he'd got to Brussels was that one grotty text. Of course she could easily call his mobile, but that felt a little desperate as if she might be checking up on him. And that, of course, would be exactly what she was doing. The idea that he might be with someone else make her stomach turn over. What she still hadn't figured out was if that was because she still loved him or simply couldn't bear the thought of being deceived.

'It's nothing personal,' she said, gesturing towards the papers on her desk. 'I've just got work to do.'

Toby gave a snigger. 'Nothing that can't wait. It's not as if any of our clients are actually *going* anywhere.'

Iris gave him a dark look.

'Okay, okay, I get the hint,' he said. And with that, he walked off and disappeared into his father's office.

Iris turned on the computer and started typing. While she worked, she thought about last night, first about Guy Wilder and then about Vita and Rick. She was on her third letter when a terrible notion occurred to her. A chain of apparently disconnected events abruptly came together in her head: Rick had been at Belles, the Streets owned the club, the Streets had threatened her, Rick had suddenly acquired a large amount of cash.

A cold, dread feeling invaded her stomach. No, she was wrong. She had to be. But Rick was a mate of Michael's, which could mean that he knew all about her missing father. Could he have been the one who'd tipped off the Streets that the daughter of Sean O'Donnell was back in Kellston? Rapidly she dismissed the idea. It couldn't be true. She'd already been here a year – why should Rick choose to tell them now? But, unfortunately, there was a ready answer to that: Candice's mother was putting pressure on him to come up with more money. Perhaps he had simply grasped the opportunity of making some easy cash. Iris shivered. She had thought Albert Jenks was the one who'd been causing trouble for her, but maybe the culprit lay closer to home.

Iris shook her head. She didn't want to believe it and had no real evidence that it was true. Rick was a friend. He was Vita's husband. Surely he wouldn't deliberately place her in danger?

She was putting two and two together and coming up with five. And yet . . .

For the next half hour she dwelled on the possibility. It all made sense in a sick kind of way. Rick might have suggested to the Streets that she'd come back to meet her father – or at the very least that she knew where he was hiding. That kind of information would be worth six hundred quid to the likes of the Streets. And Rick might have made even more. There was no knowing how much he'd already spent before the light-fingered Duggie had relieved him of his wallet.

But Iris still wasn't convinced. As soon as one voice in her head talked her round to the idea, another gave a perfectly legitimate reason as to why he wouldn't do it. Rick was, in all probability, completely innocent. Would he really betray her like that? She thought of all the evenings she had spent in his company, all the hours they'd spent chatting and drinking together. They weren't close – not like she was to Vita – but they did have some kind of friendship.

Iris came to a decision. There was only one sensible way to put her mind at rest. She would have to talk to Michael and find out how much Rick Howard really knew about the past.

Chapter Twenty-nine

It was getting on for ten by the time Toby reappeared. Iris stopped typing and looked up at him. He had his jacket over his arm and was heading for the door.

'See you later,' he said.

'What are you doing?'

'An emergency. Got to go.'

Iris immediately thought of Gerald Grand. 'Is it your dad? Has something happened?'

He waved a hand dismissively. 'No, he's fine. It's nothing to do with him.'

'What then?'

'It's . . . er . . .' With his brain still on standby after all the alcohol he'd drunk, Toby struggled to come up with an adequate explanation. 'Does it matter? I've just got to go out, okay?'

She glanced at the clock. 'Yes, it matters. The Elliots are due soon. How long are you going to be?'

'No idea. A while. An hour or so.'

Iris glared at him. 'So what the hell am I supposed to tell them?'

'Oh, shit.' Toby screwed up his face, rushed back into the office and came back with a lumpy black file. He dumped it in front of her. 'Here, this tells you everything you need to know. Just go through the list inside. You can do it. You'll be fine.'

'No!' Iris protested. 'You can't leave me to deal with this. I've never done it before. I can't—'

'Course you can,' he said. 'It'll be good experience if you're going to stay here.'

'Who said I was going to stay? I'm only covering while Maggie's on leave.'

Toby shrugged. 'Postpone it then, rearrange, do whatever you like. Although the Brothers Grimm might not be too pleased to know you've turned away good customers. And, in case you're interested, I heard it on the grapevine that Maggie isn't coming back. Seems she wants to spend more time with that new sprog of hers. So, if you want to take her place permanently, now would be a good time to try and make a good impression.' He took out his phone and stared at it as if expecting it to ring at any second. 'Look, I've got to go. Do whatever you want. See them, don't see them. I don't care.'

And before Iris had a chance to say another word, he was out of the door.

'Hey!' She leapt up, intending to chase after him, but then slowly sank back down again. What was the point? Toby was a law unto himself and nothing she said or did was going to alter that. She looked at the file and then at her watch. There were only a few minutes left before the Elliots were due to arrive. She had to decide what was worse, cancelling the appointment or bluffing her way through it. It didn't help that her confidence was at rock bottom. A year ago she wouldn't have thought twice about whether she could cope, but now she was as nervous as a teenage apprentice. When she'd been working for the advertising company, all that had mattered was money and contracts, but there was far more at stake here: there were people's feelings and emotions.

Cursing Toby, she quickly skipped through the file, trying to absorb as much of the information as she could. There was so much to take in: the type of service, the coffin, flowers, cars, obituaries, eulogies, catering. She wasn't even sure where she was supposed to start.

Just when she'd decided that it might be better to postpone than to try and muddle through, the door opened and Mrs Elliot walked in. She was a tall, thin woman in her late forties, smartly dressed, with ash blonde hair and a tight smile. Her husband, a much smaller man, shuffled in behind her.

Iris shook hands with them both, said hello and introduced herself as Gerald Grand's personal assistant. It was a slight exaggeration, but she sensed that this woman would be none too pleased if she knew she was dealing with the office receptionist. 'I must apologise. I'm very sorry, but Mr Grand has been taken ill. I can rearrange the appointment if you like or if you don't mind going through the details with me . . .'

Mrs Elliot looked her up and down. 'Well, it's not what we were expecting.' She took a moment to consider the options, but then removed her coat and held it out to Iris. 'I suppose you'll do.'

Iris tried not to feel too flattered by the vote of confidence. 'If you'd like to come this way.' She led them through to a more comfortable room, offered them tea, which they accepted, and then rapidly backtracked to reception where she locked the front door – she couldn't be in two places at once – and put the phone on answer machine. She wondered if she ought to call William, find out when he was due back, but then decided it might cause more problems than it would solve. If she was going to stay working at Tobias Grand & Sons, it wouldn't be smart to make an enemy of Toby.

In the kitchen, Iris made a trio of teas and took them back to the lounge. Then, after picking up the file and her pen, she tried to look as though she knew what she was doing. 'Now, is there anything that—'

'We'll start with the service,' Mrs Elliot said. Fortunately, she turned out to be a woman who knew exactly what she wanted and all Iris had to do was to scribble down her instructions. And there were plenty of those. It was only fifteen minutes later when they came to the choice of coffin that Mr Elliot finally made a contribution.

'Bloody hell,' he murmured, peering at the catalogue on his wife's lap. 'They don't come cheap, do they?'

Iris opened her mouth, intending to say that their prices were very competitive, but then smartly closed it again. She was worried about sounding like a pushy salesperson. But then again, she *was* working for Tobias Grand & Sons and was right, surely, to be espousing the fairness of their rates. Thankfully, she was saved from making a decision by Mrs Elliot's firm announcement.

'We'll have the oak, thank you.'

'Oak?' Mr Elliot questioned.

'And what's wrong with the oak?' Jean Elliot turned to glare at him. 'I suppose you'd rather see him dumped in the ground in a cardboard box.'

'I didn't say that.'

'You didn't need to. We all know how you felt about Jonathan.'

'All I'm saying is that things are a bit tight at the moment.'

'Yes, well we all know why that it is, don't we? If you spent less time in the pub and—'

'You saying that Johnny boy didn't like a drink?' He snorted. 'As I recall, the whole reason we're here is that he drank himself to bloody death.'

211

Iris looked from one to the other. She glanced down at her file, but there was nothing in its pages to deal with marital disputes. Hoping to avert yet another funeral – Jean Elliot appeared more than capable of murder – she quickly interrupted.

'There's really no need to make a decision now. You can take the catalogue home with you, have a think about it and call us when you've made up your mind.'

'It's the oak,' Jean Elliot said again.

Her husband gave an ugly sneer, but this time kept his mouth shut.

'Very well,' Iris said.

The two were still bickering as they left. Iris was glad that she'd managed to make a reasonable job of taking down the details, but was relieved to see the back of them. She had heard that funerals often brought out the worst in families and was beginning to understand how.

She was in the process of typing up the notes when her mobile rang. She checked the number and saw that it was unavailable. Immediately, she thought it must be Luke calling from Belgium. *About time.* 'Hi,' she said, but the only sound from the other end was silence. 'Hello? Luke?' The line wasn't dead. It had that curious kind of silence as if someone was waiting to speak. 'Hello?' she said again. 'Is that you?'

After waiting a few more seconds, she shrugged and hung up.

Less than a minute later, it rang again. 'Luke?' she repeated. Again, there was that odd silence. Was it just a bad connection from Brussels? She waited, uneasily aware of a few faint sounds coming down the line. Breathing perhaps? Or she could just be imagining it. 'Hello?' she said once more, waiting a while before disconnecting.

Iris laid the phone on her desk and stared at it. She wasn't sure if she wanted it to ring or not. If it was Luke, then yes –

she'd be relieved – but she wasn't convinced that it *was* him. It was ten-thirty, not the kind of time he'd normally call when he had a morning full of meetings. Although having neglected to speak to her for so long, he might be having a crisis of conscience.

When the phone went off again, she jumped. Warily, she lifted it to her ear. This time she said nothing. There was another short silence and then she heard the sound of breathing – that kind of low, heavy breathing that was only meant to threaten.

Iris felt her heart begin to thrash in her chest. Her mouth went dry. 'Who is it?' she eventually managed to mumble.

The heavy breathing continued.

Jabbing at the button, Iris cut the connection, turned off the mobile and threw it across the desk. For a while she just sat there, overtaken by panic. Her hands were shaking and she clenched them into two tight fists. A wave of fear rolled over her. It was not the content of the call that scared her as much as the knowledge of who was behind it. The Streets, quite clearly, were still determined to bully her into submission.

For the next five minutes, Iris didn't move. She kept her wide eyes fixed firmly on the phone as if her malicious caller might somehow have the power to make it ring again.

Chapter Thirty

It was a while before Iris recovered enough to start thinking about what to do next. Her first instinct was to grab her coat, head for home and lock herself in, but that wouldn't do much for her future employment prospects. It was over an hour since Toby had disappeared and there was no sign of William either. If she left the office unattended, she'd need to come up with a damn good excuse – and a couple of heavy breathing phone calls would hardly cut it.

Eventually, she came to the conclusion that she was probably as safe here as anywhere else. A sense of outrage was beginning to grow inside her. It wasn't exactly replacing the fear, but was helping her to cope with it. How dare the bastards do this? She thought about ringing Guy, but couldn't really see what purpose it would serve. It was unlikely he'd had time to see Chris Street yet. But then another wave of fear rolled over her. What if he had? What if Guy *had* already talked to the Streets and this was their nasty, sick response to the meeting?

Desperate for something else to occupy her mind, Iris grabbed the Elliot notes and continued typing up their details. When that was done she attacked the other letters William had left. As her fingers flew across the keyboard, she tried hard to keep the more worrying thoughts at bay. It was pointless to dwell on what she couldn't change. Until she heard from Guy Wilder, she wouldn't know for certain what the situation was.

Iris was still thinking about him, about their meeting the previous night, when the main door opened. She glanced up, expecting to see Toby or William, but her eyes made contact with someone else entirely. Her body froze as the terrifying figure of Danny Street sauntered towards her. Only her heart responded, its beat accelerating until she thought it would leap right out of her chest.

She was almost overcome with fright as he came up to the desk. His face was pale and covered in a thin film of sweat. A tiny glob of spittle nestled in the corner of his mouth. There was something about the way he moved, the way he looked at her – his gaze slightly out of focus – that told her he was high as a kite.

'Hey, sweetie,' he drawled. 'How's it going?' Although his voice was soft, it was filled with menace.

Iris was suddenly sure that *he* was the one who had made the calls. Abruptly, the adrenalin kicked in and she jumped to her feet. 'W-what do you want?' she stammered, almost knocking over the chair as she stood up and backed away from him.

'On your own, are you?'

Iris shook her head. Not for the first time, she inwardly cursed her father for what he'd done, for the legacy he'd left. How was she supposed to deal with the fallout, with this vicious thug who only wanted revenge? 'No,' she eventually managed to splutter, 'Mr . . . Mr Grand's in the office.'

Danny Street grinned. He continued to stare at her while he took a pack of cigarettes from his pocket, pulled one out and lit it. Squinting through the smoke, he said, 'Oh, I don't think so. Didn't he leave a while ago?'

Another wave of panic swept over her. So he'd been watching, waiting for an opportunity to catch her on her own.

'What's the matter, babe?' he said. 'You don't look too pleased to see me.'

There wasn't much she could say to that so she didn't bother trying. She could tell he was getting off on it all, enjoying the intimidation. And with him being over six foot, and bulky with it, there was plenty to be afraid of. Reversing a few steps closer to the wall, all she was thinking now was *God, I should have gone home. I should have gone home.*

'You could at least try and look pleased to see me. Ain't it your job to make people feel welcome?'

Glancing around the room, Iris was horribly aware of how alone she was, how vulnerable. There was nowhere to run, no one to help her. She could try to make a dash for the basement, but he was faster than her, faster and stronger. There was no chance she would get there before him. 'What do you want?' she said again.

'What do you think I want?'

He moved around the desk. He took a step closer to her. And then another. He was almost breathing into her face when William suddenly walked in. Iris cried out in relief. 'Please,' she begged, 'get him away from me.'

William, looking startled, glanced from one to the other. 'What's going on?'

Danny Street turned and shrugged his shoulders. 'No idea, mate.'

'He's lying,' she said.

William gestured towards the door. 'Perhaps it would be better if you left.'

'A pleasure,' Danny replied. He flicked his cigarette, depositing an offensive pile of ash on the carpet. 'But a word to the wise, mate: you should teach your staff some fuckin' manners. A bit of respect ain't too much to ask.'

William responded with a thin smile. 'Perhaps that works both ways, Mr Street.'

Danny paused. As if mentally processing the content of the answer, and trying to decide how insulting it was, a frown appeared on his forehead. After a moment, as if the effort of thinking was too much, he simply shrugged again. 'Yeah, right.' He took a moment to glare at William and then walked out, slamming the door behind him.

Once he was gone, Iris slumped down into the chair. 'Thank you,' she said.

William came over and stood beside her. 'Are you okay?'

She nodded. 'I am now. Thanks for that.'

'You want to tell me what just happened there?'

Iris wished she could, but that was hardly possible without relating the whole sordid story of the events of nineteen years ago. 'He was just . . . just being weird. I think he's on something. He . . .' She swallowed hard, trying to regain her calm. 'I don't know. Maybe I overreacted.'

'I doubt it,' William said. 'Danny Street's a piece of work. He's trouble, pure and simple. You shouldn't have had to deal with him on your own.' He laid a hand lightly on her shoulder. 'I can assure you it won't happen again. I won't have my staff threatened by the likes of that man.'

Iris, although she appreciated the sentiment, was immediately worried about what he was planning to do next. 'What do you mean?'

'I'm going to call the police,' William said. He reached for the phone. 'Perhaps they can keep him under control.'

'No!' Iris objected, quickly putting her hand over the receiver. 'There's no need for that.' Chris Street was hardly likely to be

217

amenable to Guy's attempts to smooth things over if he thought she'd been grassing up his brother. 'I mean, do you really think that's such a good idea? He was out of order, but he didn't actually *do* anything. Why waste your time? Not to mention the time of the police.' She looked at him pleadingly. 'To be honest, I'd rather we just forgot about it.'

William hesitated. 'Are you sure?'

'Yes, I'm sure.'

'I hate to see him getting away with it. It isn't right.' He gave an exasperated sigh. 'I don't suppose you have any idea where Toby is?'

'He had to go out. Some kind of emergency, I think.'

'Yes, I bet it was. Look, are you all right? You're white as a sheet. Can I get you anything? A cup of tea? A brandy?'

'Brandy?' she repeated, surprised by the suggestion.

'We usually keep a bottle in. Funerals aren't the easiest things to arrange and people can get upset. You never know when someone's going to need it.'

Like when Danny Street started shouting the odds, she thought. She smiled up at William. It was a somewhat faltering smile. His kindness towards her, his clear concern for her welfare, made her want to cry. 'Thanks, but if you want your letters typed with any degree of accuracy, I'd better keep off the hard stuff.'

'You don't have to stay. You've had a shock. I'll understand if you'd prefer to go home. Take the rest of the day off if you like. I can call you a taxi. You'll be there in five minutes.'

Iris was tempted by the offer – instead of going home, she could go round and see Guy – but decided against it. She couldn't go running to him every five minutes; he might get the impression that she was one of those hysterical females who fell to pieces at the first sign of trouble. Not that she didn't have good reason to be afraid. There was no doubt in her mind that

Danny Street would have gone further if William hadn't come back. But if she wasn't going to see Guy, what was she going to do? Faced with the prospect of spending the rest of the day alone in the flat, she decided to stay put. 'No, really, I'm fine. I'd rather just get on with things.'

'If that's what you want,' he said. He gave her shoulder one last pat before retreating to his office. At the door, he stopped and turned around. 'Let me know if you change your mind.'

Chapter Thirty-one

At lunchtime, Iris went to the kitchen. She toyed with the ham sandwich she'd thrown together that morning, but couldn't bring herself to eat it. The cold knot in her stomach kept on tightening.

All this because of some terrible mistake her father had made all those years ago. But it was more than a mistake, she thought. A boy had died. And if Liam had been *her* brother . . . well, maybe she wouldn't rest either until some kind of justice was seen to be done. Her father may not have pulled the trigger, but he had still been there. And being there was clearly enough for the Streets.

Iris took her mobile out of her bag and laid it on the table. At the very least she should call Guy, keep him in the loop. If he was seeing Chris Street today, he needed to know what had happened. Tentatively, she turned the phone on, instinctively flinching in case it suddenly started ringing again. But the only sound was the double beep of a text message.

Iris pressed the buttons and found a short note from Vita: *Hope all OK. R sent red roses to the office! V x*

She frowned at the words, recalling her earlier misgivings. Roses didn't come cheap. Had Rick used the money he'd got from . . . but she immediately stamped on the thought. No, she had to stop this. There were a hundred-and-one ways he could have got hold of that cash. And would Michael really have told him about her father's presence at a murder? Surely some family secrets stayed firmly locked in the closet. They had certainly been hidden from her for long enough.

She put her head in her hands and sighed. Vita, of course, knew all about her father, but she couldn't have been the one to have passed the information on. Iris had only told her the details last night – a good seven hours or so *after* Duggie had taken the wallet.

Raising her face, Iris decided that the only way forward was to do something positive. She'd go mad if she kept on chasing shadows. Accordingly, she took a deep breath, scrolled through the menu on her phone and called Guy Wilder. She swallowed her disappointment as she heard it switch instantly to voicemail. Then she hesitated. Should she leave a message? She decided not. The bar was open at lunchtime and he was probably busy. She'd try again later.

There were still fifty minutes left of her break. She twisted the phone between her fingers. What next? She tried Michael's number, but that was turned off too. This time she did leave a message. Trying to sound as cheery as possible, she said: 'Hi Michael, it's only me. Call me back, let me know how you are.' She had no intention of telling him about Danny Street's visit – he was so hot-headed he'd probably go off at the deep end again – but she did need to talk to him. She had to find out exactly *who* he'd told about her father.

Having drawn a blank on her first two calls, Iris was convinced that her third would have the same result. Still, she may as well give it a go. After pressing 1 on her keypad, she heard

Luke's phone start to ring. It seemed strange to think of it ringing all those miles away. She wasn't really expecting him to answer and when he did was entirely unprepared.

'Hi, babe! Great to hear from you. How are you?'

Iris could tell from his voice that he wasn't entirely sober. 'Oh, yes, hi. I'm okay. I'm fine, thanks. How's it going?'

'Pretty good,' he said. 'In fact, *very* good.'

She could hear the chink of glasses, of chatter and music in the background. 'That's great. You've clinched some profitable deals then?'

'On the brink,' he said. 'Here's hoping. And hey, I'm sorry I haven't called. I was going to catch up with you tonight. It's all been a bit manic here. You know what it's like.'

Iris *did* know what it was like. That was the trouble. She'd made a few business trips of her own in the past, spending half of them in various bars and restaurants. She remembered the easy atmosphere, the generous flow of wine and conversation. She remembered the men who had smiled and flattered and chatted her up. There had been plenty of opportunities if she'd wanted to take them. Of course, back then, she hadn't wanted to – Luke was the only man she'd been interested in – but she knew how much temptation there was when you were far away from home.

'Are you still there?' he said, hearing the silence.

'Yes,' she said breezily. 'So it's all going well?'

'Brilliant.'

He sounded happy, upbeat, like the Luke she'd fallen in love with five years ago. There hadn't been much sign of him over the last six months. She felt a tiny tug inside. His improved mood was probably down to the booze, to the heady excitement of deals being made, but maybe some of it – she couldn't pretend otherwise – was because he was away from her. Hearing his name being called, followed by a soft peal of laughter, her heart turned over. 'Who's that?'

'It's only Jasmine,' he said. 'Sorry, I've got to go. We're about to head in to lunch.'

Iris remembered the girl at the Christmas party, the girl she thought had been called Jade.

'Jasmine?' she repeated.

But if he'd heard the question mark, he didn't respond to it. 'Look, I'll give you a ring later, okay? I've got to go. You take care.'

'You too.'

'Bye then.'

'Take care,' Iris repeated softly as she put the phone back down on the table. He had no idea how much those words meant to her at the moment.

Chapter Thirty-two

Alice pulled up the hood on her red anorak as she scurried along the street. The snow was coming down in great swirling drifts, flying into her eyes and obscuring her vision. Not that she needed to see to find her way. She had made this journey so many times she could have done it blindfold. As she clutched her mother's dry cleaning to her chest – it was enclosed in a thin plastic cover that might not be entirely waterproof – she felt her throat making tiny gulping motions. She was trying hard not to cry.

Alice was almost overwhelmed by guilt. It was not an unfamiliar emotion – Janet Avery had made sure of that – but on this occasion it was more tangible than usual, the result of a *real* event. She had let herself down but, even worse, she'd betrayed a colleague too. Alice bit down on her lip. She had been halfway up the steps when she'd heard the voices coming from reception, and had instantly stopped dead. Consumed by fear, she had left Iris to face the wrath of Danny Street alone.

She hunched her shoulders, scowling at her own cowardice. All she could claim in her defence was that she might have made things worse if she'd joined the fray. But she knew it was a feeble excuse. What she'd been really afraid of was that he might turn on her, that in his drug-induced state he might let something slip about what had taken place in the basement. She shuddered at the thought. But still her conscience continued to nag. How could she have been so weak, so pathetic? If she had any backbone at all, she would have pushed through that door and stood beside Iris. She would have to try to find a way to make it up to her.

Alice's feet, following the well-travelled route, took a left and then a right. She had tried to call Toby but he hadn't picked up. She had left a breathless, warning message about the visit. Oh God, what would she do if Danny Street caught up with him and . . . Quickly, she shook her head, too afraid to finish the thought.

A few minutes later she arrived at Valentine Court. Why anyone had chosen to call a retirement complex by such a name was beyond her. The bland redbrick construction was four storeys high and overlooked a supermarket car park at the back. The only vaguely romantic thing about it was the layer of snow beginning to cover the scrubby patch of lawn.

Most of the apartments were occupied by women. She had only occasionally seen a man around. A few of these widows and 'spinsters' (as her mother insisted on calling any female who had not been fortunate enough to marry) appeared to spend a disproportionate amount of time staring aimlessly out of the window. In fact, there were several noses pressed to the glass at this very moment. Alice was aware of being watched, of being scrutinised. It made her even more self-conscious than usual.

Hurrying towards the glass doors, she jabbed in the security code. As Alice stepped into the entrance hall, she wrinkled her nose; a series of smells – none of them pleasant – assailed her nostrils. There was the slight odour of damp, of old cooking, and both of these were overlain by the cheap scent of an overly flowery air freshener. She walked across the lino floor and summoned the lift. While she waited, she glanced down at the large wooden table. There was a heap of leaflets sitting on it advertising Saga holidays, classes in yoga and Spanish, cheap meals at local restaurants, pizza takeaways, forthcoming theatre productions and private health insurance. There were even a few Tobias Grand & Sons flyers.

As she rode up to the top floor, Alice found herself pondering on the fate of those faces at the windows. They reminded her of prisoners trapped in their cells. The thought that this might one day be her own destiny filled her with horror.

Her mother was not one of the lonely watchers. Even as Alice knocked on the door she could hear a babble of voices coming from within. Her heart sank. The cronies, a vicious trio of witches, were regular visitors; their primary interest in life was the spreading of rumour and gossip, and this they did with alarming enthusiasm.

Janet Avery opened the door with a scornful expression. 'Oh, it's you,' she remarked, as if her daughter's visit was not only unexpected, but unwelcome too.

Alice held out the dry cleaning. 'You asked me to pick this up.'

Mrs Avery made no attempt to take it from her. Instead, she turned her back and walked off into the living room.

Alice had no choice but to follow. Gathered on the sofa were three women in their late sixties. Alice privately referred to them as The Coven. She wouldn't have been surprised to see them dressed in black and dancing round a cauldron.

'Hello,' Mrs Boyd said. 'You're looking different, Alice. Have you had your hair done? I think you've lost a bit of weight, haven't you?'

Alice forced a smile. Mrs Boyd was a thin, sharp-faced

woman who only ever threw out empty compliments. Before Alice had a chance to reply her mother jumped in.

'She's got herself a new young man, but she's being very secretive about him.'

'Oh,' Mrs Wilkinson said.

'Indeed!' Mrs Boyd said.

Alice knew that the term 'young man' was not meant literally, but still she felt a flutter of apprehension. Was it possible that her mother had found out about Toby? No, she couldn't have. They'd been too careful. 'I haven't,' she insisted quickly. 'There's nothing to tell.'

'Well, you've never shown much interest in your appearance before.'

Alice glared at her mother.

Sensing a spot of daughter-baiting, the other women sat forward, their beady eyes eagerly darting between the two protagonists.

But Alice was determined not to rise to it. After placing the dry cleaning over the back of a chair, she looked at her watch. 'I can't stay. I have to get back to work.'

'You've embarrassed the poor girl,' Mrs Boyd said slyly.

Alice knew that people only said such things when they wanted to embarrass you even more. 'Of course not.' But the words sounded curt and defensive. She swallowed hard, wishing she was somewhere else. Why couldn't she think of some witty retort?

'I've already told her,' Janet Avery said, 'if it's that Gerald Grand she's seeing, she wants to stay well away. There's no good ever comes from playing around with married men.'

'Gerald Grand?' Mrs Boyd repeated, almost licking her lips.

Oh Christ, Alice thought. By this time tomorrow it would be all over Kellston. She was mortified. 'I am *not* seeing Gerald Grand,' she almost shouted. 'I wouldn't. For heaven's sake, he's old enough to be my father! We just . . . we just work together, nothing else. I am not the slightest bit interested in him.'

There was a brief pregnant silence.

Alice immediately regretted having spoken. What was that saying about protesting too much? Now they were all going to think that she *was* seeing him. She could feel her face burning up and knew, without consulting the mirror, that her cheeks were two bright red tomatoes. She glared again at her mother. How could she do this to her? How could she be so despicable?

Mrs Tippett, who until now had been quiet, decided to chip in. 'Of course not, love. As if we'd believe anything like that.'

Mrs Boyd sniggered.

Alice shoved her hands down deep into her pockets, clenching them into two tight fists. She wasn't going to be the butt of their jokes forever. They'd treat her differently when they found out who she was *really* seeing. Abruptly, she came to a decision. There was a way out of all this and she was going to take it. The thought of their surprise, especially of her mother's, gave her a nice warm feeling inside. In a month or two, when things were sorted out, she could be engaged to Toby Grand – and then no one would be smirking.

Alice smiled down at the floor. She would do whatever Toby wanted in order to save him . . . and to save herself too.

Chapter Thirty-three

It was the second time in the space of a few days that Iris had found herself in William's car. The silver Volvo was warm inside and smelled of new leather. When he'd offered her a lift home at five o'clock, she hadn't thought twice. It was doubtful that Danny Street was still hanging around, but it wasn't a chance she wanted to take.

As they made their way slowly down the High Street – the traffic was jammed up as usual – Iris glanced at William. 'Thanks for this. I didn't fancy walking home in the snow.' She knew that wasn't why he'd offered. He was trying to make amends for what had happened that morning. Or perhaps he was just worried that she might decide to quit.

'It's no trouble. I always come this way.'

Iris gazed out through the windscreen. The wipers made a soft swishing sound as they travelled back and forth. The motion, along with the warmth of the car, made her feel almost sleepy. She yawned as a red light brought them to a halt.

'So how are you finding it, working at Tobias Grand & Sons?' William frowned at his own question and then gave a short laugh. 'Sorry, after what . . . This probably isn't the best time to ask, is it?'

Iris smiled. 'That's okay. It's not as though the likes of Danny Street walk through the door every day. And actually, on the whole, I rather enjoy the job.' She paused. 'Well, most of it. Some things are still a little unsettling.'

'Yes,' he agreed. 'It's not to everyone's taste.'

'But you don't mind? I suppose you've had more time to get used it.'

'Only a couple of years.'

Iris looked at him, surprised. 'But I thought—'

'That I've always worked there?' He shook his head. 'No, I couldn't stand the place when I was a kid; it gave me the creeps. Didn't care for it much when I grew up either. In all honesty, I couldn't wait to get away. Fortunately, Gerald was more than happy to carry on the family tradition.' As the lights turned to green, he edged the car forward. 'I was a broker in the City for twenty years. Perhaps I got out at the right time. Everyone hates brokers and bankers these days, don't they? All flash cars, too much cash and no morals. Public enemy number one.'

'I didn't realise,' she said.

'You thought I'd spent my whole life arranging funerals.'

Iris nodded. 'More or less.' She was curious as to what had brought him back. 'So why the change of career?'

He hesitated for a second, pretending to concentrate on his driving. She heard him draw a breath. 'Bad divorce,' he said.

'Oh, I'm sorry.'

William shrugged. 'It happens. And what do they say – any port in a storm? I wasn't . . . well, I wasn't dealing too well with things and Gerald suggested I came back here for a while. That was two years ago and I'm still trying to figure out what to do next.'

Iris gave a sigh. She understood how he felt. Perhaps Tobias Grand & Sons was a sanctuary for all the wounded souls of Kellston. Alice Avery never struck her as being overjoyed with the cards life had dealt her either.

William gave her a sideways glance. 'I suppose you'll be moving on before too long.'

'Are you trying to get rid of me?'

'No, of course not! I'd be . . . *we'd* be glad if you stayed. You wouldn't believe some of the temps we had in after Maggie went on leave. A nightmare. But I just presumed you'd be looking for something more challenging. You used to work in advertising, didn't you?'

'For my sins.'

'You don't want to get back into it?'

Iris shook her head. 'I'm not sure what I want, but I know it isn't that.' She remembered the conversation she'd had with Luke a week ago. He'd be none too pleased if she took the post at Tobias Grand & Sons on a more permanent basis. But so what? The decision had to be hers, not his.

'Well, you're welcome to stay for as long as you like. I don't know if you've heard, but Maggie isn't coming back.'

'Yes, Toby mentioned something.'

'So the job's yours if you want it.'

She grinned at him. 'Despite my rubbish typing?'

William laughed. 'I've seen worse.' He took a left into Silverstone Rd and pulled up outside the apartments. 'Have a think about it. Let me know.'

'I will.' Iris undid her seatbelt and got out of the car. She leaned down and said, 'Thanks again for the lift.'

'I'll see you tomorrow.'

It was only as he was driving off that Iris wondered whether she should have asked him in. Her social skills had gone to pot over the past six months. Still, he probably had plans for the evening. She, on the other hand, had a long empty night stretching ahead.

After checking her card through the security gates, Iris crossed the forecourt, punched in the code on the door and headed up the polished wooden steps. There was a lift but she rarely used it. It seemed too lazy when she was only going to the third floor. Really she ought to consider going to the gym again; she'd got out of condition recently. Trouble was she hated all that public exercising, all those sweaty bodies gathered together. Perhaps she'd invest in an exercise bike instead.

Iris reached the landing and pushed through the heavy fire doors. She walked along the corridor and stopped outside the flat. As she got out her key, she heard a slight scuffling sound coming from behind the door of the flat opposite. There would have been nothing unusual about it if it wasn't for the fact that the place was empty; it had been on the market for months and the 'For Sale' sign was still in the window. As Iris turned her head, her eyes focused on the tiny spyhole and the hairs on the back of her neck stood on end. She was being watched. She was sure of it.

For a second she stood absolutely still, rooted to the spot. She felt like a rabbit caught in the glare of oncoming headlamps. Something was wrong, very wrong. She could feel it in her bones, in every quivering nerve end. Danny Street flashed into her mind and she had a vision of his dark accusing eyes as he'd approached her desk this morning. And then suddenly her fight or flight instinct kicked in. Her body made a decision. There wasn't time to think. There wasn't time to hang around. She had to get the hell out!

Iris turned and ran back along the corridor. As she hurtled down the stairs she heard the ominous click as the fire doors closed again and then the sound of footsteps following close behind. They were heavy steps, a man's steps. She had a head start, but how long before he caught up with her? Her clammy palm grabbed the rail as she swung around the corners. She could stop at any floor, start screaming, start banging on doors – but what if no one was in? No, it was better to play safe, to keep on running, to keep on heading for the exit.

Her breath was coming in short, fast bursts as she got to the entrance hall, sped across it and flung open the doors. A blast of cold snowy air swept into her lungs. She raced across the court-yard, sprinting for the main gate. Her fingers fumbled with the lock. 'Come on!' she spluttered. Her hands slid along the icy metal. She shook the huge wrought-iron gates and glanced over her shoulder. He couldn't be far behind. 'Shit!' She tried the lock again and this time, thankfully, it gave way.

As she slammed the gate behind her, she looked back and saw the main door to the apartments open. A tall figure stepped out. Although there were lights in the courtyard, she couldn't see him clearly. He was hidden by the shadows of the porch. Danny Street? Or maybe the bruiser who'd accosted her in Columbia Market? She wasn't going to hang around to find out.

Taking to her heels again, she dashed up Silverstone Rd. Her lungs were pumping air, her heart thumping in her chest. At any moment she expected to hear footsteps behind and to feel the strong grip of fingers on her arms. As she hit the High Street, she looked around wildly. What next? She'd had a faint hope that she might see William's silver Volvo snarled up in the traffic, but he was well gone. However, there were lots of other people around. Should she tell someone there was a man fol-lowing her, ask for their help? But that would mean stopping and she might not have time to explain before he caught up with her. Seeing an empty black cab idling by the lights on the corner, she ran over and leapt into the back.

'Where to, love?'

She hadn't thought that far. Michael's flat? But he'd probably be in the pub. And Vita would still be at work. There was only one other person she could think of. 'Wilder's,' she said quickly. 'The wine bar. Do you know it?'

The cabbie, a thickset silver-haired man in his fifties, turned his head and pulled a face. 'That's only down the road,' he said, as if the fare was hardly worth his while.

Iris glared at him. Of all the times to come across some bloody awkward bastard. 'I know that, but I'm in a hurry. *Please*. As fast as you can.' Then, worried that he might refuse to take her, she said one of those things that she'd only ever heard before in movies. 'I'll make it worth your while.'

He thought about it for a second, gave a shrug, reset the meter and drove off.

Iris stared out of the back window. Was the man still chasing her? She couldn't see him, but the pavements were crowded with workers streaming off the trains. Fearfully, she scanned their faces, but didn't see anyone she recognised. She didn't see anyone who looked like a vicious thug either.

The cab took a left, escaping the High Street traffic, and twisted round the back streets. Iris still couldn't relax. What if her pursuer had a car? What if he was close behind? Scrabbling in her bag, she pulled out her phone and tried to call Guy. It went to voicemail again. *Damn*. She hoped that meant he was busy working and not that he'd gone out.

The driver pulled up outside the bar in less than two minutes. Iris shoved a ten-pound note into his hand. 'Here,' she said. And a second later she was out of the cab and running for the door.

'Hey, love,' he yelled out of the window, 'what about your change?'

'Keep it!' she shouted back.

As Iris rushed inside, she prayed that Guy would be there. But as she gazed around, there was no sign of him. It was still early and only one of the tables was occupied. The couple raised their heads to stare as she stumbled past. Catching sight of her reflection in the mirror behind the bar, Iris could see why. She looked like something the cat had dragged in: her eyes were too wide and bright, her cheeks flushed, and her hair was all over the place. But there was no time to worry about that now.

A slim, dark-haired girl was standing behind the counter, cleaning glasses.

'Is Guy here?' Iris said. Her voice was strained and croaky.

The girl looked her up and down. She shook her head. 'He's not working tonight.'

Iris felt her chest tighten. 'Do you know where he is? It's important, really important. I have to talk to him.'

'Sorry,' she said. 'I've no idea. Have you tried his phone?'

'Yes, he's not answering.'

The girl gave a shrug. From the bored and somewhat con-temptuous expression on her face, Iris got the impression that she was used to deflecting enquiries from desperate females. Perhaps Iris was only one in a long line of women who had come here searching for her boss. She was starting to despair when a door at the back of the bar marked 'Staff only' opened and Noah walked through it. He stopped and frowned, looking about as pleased to see her as on the last occasion they'd met.

But Iris didn't care. She hurried forward, grabbing hold of his arm. 'Thank God,' she said. 'I need to see Guy.'

Noah shook his head. 'He's not working tonight.'

'I know that,' she said, the frustration making her voice rise an octave or two. 'But is he here? Is he upstairs?' She could feel the panic gathering inside her again. 'Where is he? I have to see him.' She was aware of sounding like some mad stalking female, but couldn't stop herself. '*Please*, I have to see him.'

He stood back, abruptly shaking off her hand. 'It's his night off. I don't know where he is.'

'Oh, Jesus,' Iris said. She slumped down on a nearby chair. What now? She felt like bursting into tears.

Noah paused for a moment, gave a sigh and then sat down on the chair opposite to hers.

'It's Iris, isn't it?'

'Iris O'Donnell.'

'Yeah,' he said. 'I remember.'

She heard the distinct lack of enthusiasm in his voice. Not that she needed to hear it – she had seen it in his eyes the moment he'd caught sight of her. In a last ditch attempt to win him over, she leaned across the table. 'Look, I wouldn't ask if this wasn't urgent. I know you're only doing what you think is best but . . . Something's happened tonight, something bad. I really need to talk to Guy.'

Noah hesitated. He sighed again, running his hand over the top of his short wiry hair. His eyes gazed briefly back at her before skimming over the empty tables around them.

Should she say anything else? Iris decided not. He would make up his mind in his own time. As she waited, she looked over her shoulder, terrified that Danny Street might be about to walk in. He was the kind of man who wouldn't care about witnesses. He would do whatever he wanted, when he wanted. She anxiously turned to look at Noah again.

Perhaps as much through the desire to get rid of her than anything more sympathetic – distraught females were none too good for business – he finally relented. 'Okay. Wait here a minute. I can't promise anything but . . .'

'Thank you,' Iris said. 'Thank you so much.'

Noah stood up, walked over to the bar and murmured something to the dark-haired girl. She laughed, glanced at Iris and then pushed the phone towards him. He picked it up, jabbed at a button and spoke briefly into the receiver. Moments later he was back.

'This way,' he said with an abrupt wave of his hand.

Iris followed him through the door at the back of the bar. To her right was a short corridor leading to the kitchen. She could hear the clatter of plates and the sound of a radio playing. To the left was another door. Noah pushed it open and gestured towards the flight of stairs.

'Go on up,' he said. 'He's waiting for you.'

Iris gazed at the stairway, relief washing over her body. 'Thank you so much,' she said again. But as she turned her head, she realised she was talking to herself. Noah had already walked away.

Chapter Thirty-four

Iris was almost at the top of the stairs when the door to the flat opened and Guy Wilder appeared. She had almost, if not quite, forgotten how striking he was. She took a quick breath as he gazed down at her. He was smartly dressed in a dark grey suit, a white shirt and pale blue tie. Clearly, he wasn't intending to spend his night off in front of the TV.

'Hey,' he said, 'this is a nice surprise. How are you?'

She had one of those slightly hysterical thoughts about how crazy it was to be appreciating his looks at a time like this, but she was too stressed to ascertain how genuine he was being in his greeting. Turning up unannounced was hardly good manners. Not that manners came that high on the agenda when you had a psychotic gangster on your tail. 'I'm fine, I'm . . . er . . .' Although she'd embarked on the polite response, Iris couldn't maintain it. Her voice cracked and she shook her head. She could feel the tears welling up in her eyes and quickly raised a hand to cover her face. The day's events were starting to catch up with her.

Gently taking hold of her elbow, Guy led her into the flat. 'It's okay. Come on. Come inside.'

She was only vaguely aware of her surroundings as she dropped down on to a soft leather couch. Moments later she had a large glass of brandy in her hand.

'Just sip it slowly,' he said. 'Don't try to talk.'

Iris did as she was told. She could feel her throat gulping as she swallowed the drink. She had to keep herself together, maintain some level of control. If she started crying now, she might never stop.

Guy sat down beside her. After a few minutes, he said very softly, 'You want to tell me what's happened?'

Iris sniffled, reaching into her bag for a tissue. She turned her face away from him and blew her nose. Swallowing hard, she tried to get her thoughts in order. But all that came out was: 'He was there, I know he was. I heard him. I *felt* him.'

'Who was there?' he said.

'Danny Street,' she whimpered.

'What?'

Iris couldn't meet his eyes. Instead she studied the room over the rim of her glass. Her hands were shaking. The place was bigger than she'd expected, the living room stretching almost the entire length of the bar beneath. The walls were a bright crisp white and there were two large windows overlooking the High Street. The long green curtains hadn't been drawn and she could see the snow falling.

'*Where* was he?' Guy asked.

She continued to look around. The living room was smart but simple, a typically male kind of space. No fuss, no clutter. A large plasma TV had been attached to the wall above the fireplace. On the adjacent wall to the right were a couple of black and white prints, one of them a panoramic view of London, the other of a river that was probably the Seine. She'd never been to Paris, but the view was faintly familiar. 'I'm sorry. I shouldn't have turned up out of the blue like this. I tried to call you but—'

239

'Iris,' he said, taking her hand. 'It doesn't matter about that. You can talk to me. Just take a deep breath and start from the beginning.'

And so, at last, she did.

Guy scowled as she described the anonymous phone calls and Danny Street's visit to Tobias Grand & Sons that morning. 'If William hadn't come back . . . God, anything could have happened.' She had another sip of brandy. 'And then tonight, when I got home, I heard a noise coming from the empty flat opposite. I just had a feeling.' Iris screwed up her eyes. 'Do you know what I mean? It was weird. I could sense that someone was watching me.'

'Christ,' he said, squeezing her fingers.

'So I made a run for it. I could hear him following and . . . and I just . . . I just kept on going. I didn't look back. I managed to get out, to get to the High Street. I found a cab and—'

'And here you are.'

'I'm sorry,' she said. 'I couldn't think of where else to go.'

'Don't apologise. You did the right thing. I told you I wanted to help and I meant it.'

Iris remembered the look in Danny Street's eyes as he'd advanced towards her that morning. She shuddered. 'Well, maybe you can't. Maybe no one can.'

Guy frowned at her. 'So you're going to give up?'

Iris shook her head. She stared down at the carpet. 'I don't know. I can't think straight. All I *do* know is that I can't deal with this stuff any more.'

There was a short silence and then he said, 'So you're just going to let them walk all over you?'

Startled, she looked up. 'What?'

'I never took you for a coward.'

Iris shook her hand free and leapt to her feet. Her blood was boiling. After everything she'd been through, how could he be so callous, so crass? 'You're not the one being terrorised by some bloody psycho gangster. You think I like it? What the hell am I supposed to do?'

Guy sat back and smiled. 'Good,' he said. 'That's more like the *real* Iris O'Donnell, the one with guts, the one who doesn't allow herself to be pushed around. I was starting to wonder where she'd disappeared to.'

Iris glared at him for a second before her mouth slipped into a faltering smile. In her anger, she had temporarily lost her fear and that, she realised, was exactly what he'd intended. She folded her arms across her chest. 'Is that what you call shock tactics, Mr Wilder?'

Guy grinned. 'Tough love,' he said. 'I'm still working on my technique. You think it needs a little fine tuning?'

'More than a little.' She suspected he hadn't meant anything by the words 'tough love' – it was just a common phrase that was bandied around these days – but still felt a frisson of pleasure at his use of it.

'At least you haven't slapped me.'

'Not yet,' she said.

He laughed and patted the sofa. 'Now that I know you're not going to weep all over my soft furnishings, why don't you sit down again and we can start planning what to do next.'

Iris heaved out a breath that was half mock annoyance and half pure relief. She sat down and picked up her glass. 'This doesn't mean that I've forgiven you.'

Guy leaned back, clasped his hands behind his head and gazed briefly up at the ceiling. 'Well, the good news, if I can describe it as that, is that I haven't met up with Chris Street yet so at least we know this isn't a response to that. I'm supposed to be seeing him tomorrow morning.'

'But that's great,' Iris said. 'I'll come with you, explain to him face to face that I don't know where my father is. I can make him believe it. I'm sure I can.'

'And if Danny's there?'

Iris hesitated. Danny Street scared her to death, but this time she wouldn't be alone. 'I can deal with it.'

Guy shook his head. 'No, it's better if I go alone. They're not likely to give much ground if there's a female in the room.' He grinned at her again. 'It's that macho thing, hun. We men just can't help ourselves.'

Iris, although tempted, wasn't going to argue the point. 'So what's the bad news?'

He raised his brows.

'Isn't that how it works?' she said. 'You tell me the good news first and then spoil it all by telling me the bad.'

'Ah, well I think you already know about that. The Streets suspect you're in touch with your dad. And the Streets want to find out where he is. And the Streets are probably going to keep on pushing until . . . Can you see where I'm going with this?'

'Just about,' she sighed. 'What I don't understand is why they should even think that I've been in contact with him. I've been back for a year. It doesn't make any sense. I don't get why all this happening now.'

'Perhaps they've only just sussed out that you're here. Or perhaps someone's tipped them the nod that you know more than you're letting on.'

Iris thought of Rick again, of Rick and his unexplained wad of cash. All those unwanted suspicions crept back into her head. 'It's possible. But if it was true, I mean about knowing where my dad was, why would I be so stupid as to come back to Kellston? I could have met up with him anywhere.'

Guy shrugged. 'Well, we're not dealing with the sharpest knives in the drawer. Or maybe they figure that you came back here to search for him and have had a bit more luck than they ever did. Does it really matter? What we need to think about is what we do next.'

But it mattered to Iris. She had to know if someone had deliberately landed her in it. And there weren't too many suspects to choose from. Michael she could dismiss straight away – he was her uncle and she trusted him implicitly. He might have been a little economical with the truth in the past, but he'd never do anything to hurt her. Luke, of course, wasn't even in the reckoning. And then there was Vita. But Iris trusted her too. And that, apart from Rick, was about the sum total of her close contacts in Kellston.

Suddenly her mobile began to ring. Iris jumped and delved into her bag. Flipping the phone open, she checked out the caller. It was Luke. She stared down at the small blue screen. Should she answer it? No, she couldn't. Talk about bad timing. Quickly, she turned it off.

'You didn't have to do that,' Guy said. 'I can make myself scarce if you need some privacy.'

'No, no, it's nothing important.' She threw the phone back in her bag.

'To be honest, I'm not holding out that much hope for tomorrow,' Guy said. He saw her face fall and added, 'I'll do my best to persuade them to leave you alone – I think I can manage that – but whatever I say isn't going to stop them from trying to hunt down your dad. If he is out there somewhere, then we need to find him before they do.'

Iris nodded. 'It's all so mad. I want him to be alive. Jesus, I want that so much. I want him to make contact with me, but at the same time, if he does, then . . .'

'Yeah, I know. I understand. You're scared that if he does get in touch, he's only going to put himself in danger. But maybe we should have more faith in him. If he's managed to evade the Streets for this long, he's either very smart or very lucky.'

243

'Let's hope its smart,' Iris said. 'Luck has a habit of running out.'

Guy got to his feet. 'Are you hungry? I bet you haven't eaten all day. How about I rustle something up? What do you fancy?'

Iris looked at him. She looked at his smart grey suit. 'You don't need to do that. I don't want to spoil your evening.' She glanced at her watch. It was getting on for six and Vita would probably be home by now. She could give her a ring and ask if she could stay there for a night or two. There was no way she was going back to the flat until she was sure that it was safe. 'I don't want to hold you up. You're going out, aren't you?'

'Nothing urgent,' he said. 'It'll keep. As it happens, I'm starving and I don't like eating on my own. I also make it a rule never to plot on an empty stomach. So do you think you could manage to force something down? I make a mean carbonara even if I say so myself.'

Surprisingly, Iris found that she was quite hungry. Breakfast had only been a piece of toast and lunch, after Danny Street's unexpected appearance, had pretty well passed her by. 'Okay, if you're sure,' she said. 'Thanks. That would be nice.'

'Good,' he said. 'I'll get things started while you finish your drink.'

He went over to the CD player, pressed a button and the fluid notes of a jazz trumpet floated out across the room. She watched as he went through to the kitchen. She saw him take off his jacket and tie, put them over the back of a chair, and then remove his phone from the jacket pocket. He was about to make his excuses to whoever he had let down tonight. She thought of the call Luke had made a short while ago. Perhaps it was time to make her excuses too.

Chapter Thirty-five

Iris pressed the number for Luke and listened as the phone rang the other end. She felt calm enough to talk to him now. But the phone rang and rang and eventually went to voicemail. She didn't bother leaving a message. Instead, she switched the mobile off and dropped it back into her bag. Then she stood up and walked over to the window. The High Street was still busy and while she finished her brandy she automatically scanned the area, searching for would-be assailants hiding in the shadows or lurking in shop doorways. There was no one acting oddly. After a while, when she was sure that Guy had finished his call, she went through to the kitchen. 'Can I help?'

He was in the process of pouring some pasta into a pan. 'Sure. There's wine in the fridge. You can open a bottle and then you can sit down and keep me company.'

The kitchen was a decent size and was painted white. There was a poppy-coloured refrigerator in the corner, a set of expensive-looking pans hanging from the wall, and a pale wood table with four chairs. A couple of glasses were already sitting on the table along with a corkscrew.

'Or would you prefer red?' He gestured towards a wine rack in the corner.

'No, white's fine with me.' She opened the fridge and found a row of four bottles. 'Which one should I open?'

'Ah,' he said, glancing over. 'We'll start on the left, shall we, and work our way through.'

Iris stared at him.

Guy grinned back. 'Only kidding. There's no need to look so worried. I'm not planning on plying you with booze and then taking advantage.'

'I wouldn't mind,' Iris said. Then suddenly realising how that must have sounded, her cheeks flushed pink. She quickly added, 'I meant about having a few drinks, not—'

'I know what you meant,' he said, laughing. 'Just relax, will you?'

'Sorry. I still feel bad about ruining your evening.'

'Hardly that,' he said. 'In fact, you've probably done me a favour.'

She took the bottle across to the table. 'How do you work that one out?'

Guy carefully stirred the sauce. When he didn't reply, Iris began to feel awkward again. 'Sorry,' she said, sensing that she may have hit a raw nerve. 'It's none of my business.'

'No,' he said, 'I was only . . .' He looked up and shrugged. 'Well, some things just aren't meant to be, are they? And no matter how much you talk, how much you discuss it, that isn't going to change.'

Iris presumed he was talking about a relationship. What she had no way of knowing was whether the problem lay with him or the girl. Had tonight been earmarked for one of those make or break conversations? And was he the one who wanted out or was she? Iris thought of herself and Luke; they weren't exactly on the road to paradise either. 'Sorry,' she said again.

'Stop apologising. You've nothing to feel sorry for.'

Iris opened the bottle and poured out the Sauvignon blanc. 'Here,' she said, placing a glass beside him on the counter. 'Where do you keep the cutlery? I'll set the table while you're doing that.'

'Thanks,' he said. 'I can see you've been well raised.'

His comment reminded her that she hadn't called her mother yet. It was a call she'd been putting off. Iris still wanted to know, after all these years, why her mum had got in touch with Michael again – the only communication she usually had with him was the annual Christmas card – but was almost too afraid to ask. So many secrets from the past were coming to light and she was starting to worry about what might spring out next.

She watched as Guy moved around the kitchen. He was surprisingly graceful for a tall man. Through the fine cotton of his shirt, she could see the contours of the muscles at the top of his arms. She wondered who he'd been referring to earlier: a long-term girlfriend or someone more recent? Was he the type who played around? None of her business, she thought, although that didn't stop her from being curious.

A few minutes later the food was laid out. As well as the plates of carbonara, there was a fresh salad, a bowl of plump black olives and some garlic bread.

'It looks lovely,' she said, taking the chair opposite to his. 'Smells great too.'

'Thanks. I try to make an effort not to poison my guests.' He picked up his glass, leaned forward and chinked it against hers. 'No guarantees, mind.'

'I'll take my chances,' she said.

Guy forked a mouthful of pasta into his mouth, chewed and swallowed. 'Look, I'm sorry about earlier. I didn't mean to be cruel. I know you must be completely stressed out with everything that's been happening.'

Iris smiled. 'I thought apologising was off the agenda.'

'Off *your* agenda. I never said anything about mine.' He took a sip of wine. 'But seriously,' he continued, 'you have to think very hard about what to do next. There's still time to go to the cops.'

'No,' Iris said firmly. 'I don't want the police involved. What could they do anyway – give me a twenty-four hour guard? The Streets aren't going to admit to making threats so I'd just be back to square one, but with the added problem of them knowing that I've grassed them up.'

'You could have a point.'

'And the police would want to know *why* they've been threatening me and that would mean telling them about my dad.' Iris heaved out a sigh. 'I can't do that. It's bad enough that the Streets are trying to hunt him down. If he has the police on his back as well . . .'

'I just have to be sure,' Guy said, 'that you really understand what you're doing.'

Iris felt a shudder run through her. 'By which you mean it could get nasty. Or *nastier.*'

'Yeah. I'm not going to lie to you. Are you sure you're prepared for that?'

She tore off a piece of bread while she thought about it. 'What choice do I have?'

'There's always a choice,' he said. 'I can see why you don't want to go to the cops, but there's always the other option: you can pack your bags and get the hell out of Kellston.'

'Go on the run, you mean?'

Guy laughed. 'Well, I wouldn't put it quite as dramatically as that. I don't think the Streets would spend too much time looking for you. At the moment, you're just a means to an end. They've got no idea how much you know so they're putting on the pressure. Sometimes if you do a bit of stirring, things start to happen. People react: they talk to other people. Before you know it, all kind of shit starts to rise to the surface.'

'So they're using me to try and flush him out.'

'I'm only guessing,' Guy said. 'But if I was a dad and I knew my daughter was being threatened, I might be tempted to take risks I wouldn't normally take. I might also get a little careless.'

'What I don't get is how he'd even be aware of what's been happening.'

Guy gave a light shrug of his shoulders. 'Maybe he's closer than you think.'

The idea of that made Iris feel a little strange. 'Then why hasn't he been in touch? I've been back in Kellston for a year. He's had plenty of time.' Then she had another thought. 'You don't suppose—' But as she stared at Guy, she abruptly stopped, unwilling to bring up the subject of his mother's death.

'What is it?'

Iris hesitated.

'Go on,' he said. 'Please. We're supposed to be sharing ideas, aren't we? Trying to decide what to do next? We can't do that if you're not going to be open with me.'

He was right, of course. And now wasn't the time for undue sensitivity. 'I was just wondering if . . . Well, do you think all this sudden interest in my dad could have something to do with what happened to your mother? Michael said that she protected him from Terry, and now that she's . . .'

Guy put his head on one side and smiled. 'Been murdered?' he said. 'You are allowed to say the words. I'm not going to curl up on the floor and cry like a baby. We weren't close. You already know that.'

For all his apparent indifference, Iris still caught a defensive edge to his voice. She found the relationship he'd had with his mum difficult to fathom. It was hard to comprehend, even if the motives were as altruistic as Michael had suggested, why

Lizzie had given up her son for a villain like Terry Street. 'All I was thinking was . . . well, maybe her protection extended to me too. Which meant that for as long as she was alive, Terry wouldn't touch me, but as soon as . . .' She put down her fork and frowned. 'It would be a reason for my dad to come back, wouldn't it? If he'd heard about her death? He'd know I wasn't safe any more.'

'It's possible,' Guy agreed.

'But then why aren't they putting the pressure on Michael too? He's had a run-in with Danny Street, but he picked that fight himself. He went looking for Danny, not the other way round.'

Guy gave another of his shrugs. 'I suppose you're an easier target. Michael's a grown man and, from what I remember, a pretty tough one too. He can take care of himself. You, on the other hand, are—'

'A weak and helpless female?'

Guy smiled and shook his head. 'I doubt if anyone's ever described you as that. What I was going to say was that you're his *daughter*. He's naturally going to feel more protective of you. And that, I'm sure, is what the Streets are counting on. The more they put the screws on, the more likely your father is to try to protect you.'

'Do you really think he's out there somewhere?'

'Why not?' Guy said. 'He can't be dead or the Streets wouldn't be reacting the way they are. They're not the type to waste their time on idle gossip. Whatever they've heard, whatever they know, it must be enough to convince them that he's still around.'

'So why hasn't he been in touch? If he's that concerned about what might happen to me . . .'

'Because then you really would have something to hide. This way you don't have to lie about it. Perhaps he feels the less you know, the better.'

250

Iris finished her wine. She picked up the bottle and refilled both their glasses. The alcohol was starting to take effect and she was glad of it. She took a large gulp of the Sauvignon blanc. Would her fear levels drop in direct proportion to the amount of wine she drank? She decided that it was an experiment worth pursuing. 'I already know more than I want to.'

Guy gave her a rueful smile. 'Yeah, you have got kind of stuck in the middle of it all. You can't beat relations for landing you in the shit. Perhaps you should talk to that uncle of yours again. He may know more than he's saying.'

Iris had been planning on doing that anyway. 'It's the next thing on my list.' Then she went on to tell him about Rick Howard and the money he'd recently acquired. 'I don't want to jump to any conclusions, but it's a bit of a coincidence, isn't it?'

'Maybe that's all it is,' Guy replied. 'This girl, Vita, is she a good friend of yours?'

'The best. She's really helped me over the past six months. Ever since . . .' Iris paused, not wanting to mention the child she had lost. It wasn't that she was trying to hide anything from him, but talking about the miscarriage always made her emotional. Already that old dull ache had crawled back into her belly. 'She's been good to me.'

Guy, although he must have caught the hesitation, was sensitive enough to not pursue the cause of it. Instead he said, 'Well, maybe you should be careful about what you say to her. You start throwing accusations around about her husband and she may not stay a friend for long.'

Iris nodded. It was sound advice. If she had been left alone during the last year due to Lizzie Street's intervention, then Rick was hardly in the frame for informing the Streets that she was back in Kellston. 'Yes, you're right. And he could have got the money from anywhere. Maybe I'm just being paranoid.'

'Hard not to be with all this going on.'

As Iris finished the last of her pasta, she put down her fork and sighed. 'Thanks, that was lovely. And you weren't exaggerating: you *do* make an excellent carbonara.'

'There's no need to sound so surprised.'

'Well, some men tend to overegg their talents.'

Guy lifted his brows and his blue eyes widened. 'Heaven forbid.'

Iris grinned back at him. But then she thought of Luke. She felt a slight pang of guilt even though she wasn't doing anything wrong. People flirted all the time; it didn't mean anything more than what it was. Except in this case it wasn't strictly true. She *was* attracted to Guy Wilder. She'd felt drawn to him ever since the first day they'd met at Tobias Grand & Sons. Quickly, she got up to clear the plates, but Guy waved her back down. 'There's no rush,' he said. 'Sit and finish your drink.'

'You have to let me do the washing-up. It's the least I can do after you've taken all this trouble to feed me.'

'Later,' he insisted. 'You can help me with the arduous task of stacking the dishwasher. But first I need to tell you something.'

Iris could tell from his tone that what he had to say was important. Slowly she sank back into her seat. 'Why do I get the feeling that I'm not going to like this?'

'Maybe you won't,' he said, 'but before you make the final decision on what to do next, there's another fact that you have to consider. Terry Street's coming out of jail soon. I'm not quite sure when, but it's likely to be before Christmas. That's when the trouble could really start. I should be able to persuade Chris to lay off, but I can't predict what Terry's going to do.'

Iris felt her stomach shift. She reached for her glass again and took a few quick sips of wine before answering. 'You think he's going to come after me?'

Guy waited a moment before answering. 'I think you should seriously consider the possibility.'

Chapter Thirty-six

Iris sat on the leather sofa with her feet curled tidily under her. To say that she'd dismissed the threat of Terry Street would be an overstatement, but she had resolved to stay in Kellston. Running away wasn't a solution to her problems. And with Guy on her side, she felt capable of dealing with anything.

It was several hours since dinner and she couldn't recall the last time she'd talked so much. She had told him things about her life that she hadn't even discussed with Luke or Vita. Lifting her glass, she peered over the rim. 'How on earth do you do that?' she said, smiling. 'How do you get people to tell you all their darkest secrets?'

He grinned back at her. 'Ah, now that could be my incredible empathy with the female sex or . . .' He glanced towards the empty bottle on the coffee table. 'It might just be down to the amount of wine we've drunk.'

'I suspect that's a tactful way of saying I've been boring you to death.'

'You haven't been the slightest bit boring.'

Iris hoped that was true. She liked Guy Wilder and didn't

want to be remembered as his most tedious dinner guest ever. 'Well, I'm going to shut up now. I've been droning on about myself all night. Let's talk about you. How did you come to own the bar for starters?'

But instead of answering her directly, Guy looked at his watch. 'It's a long story,' he said, 'and it's getting late. Perhaps we should save that for another night.'

Iris could take a hint when she heard it. Appalled by the thought that she'd outstayed her welcome, she jumped to her feet. 'Oh, I'm sorry. I didn't realise the time. I should get going.'

'Hey, where's the fire?' he said.

But Iris was already struggling into her coat. Best to make her escape whilst she still had *some* dignity remaining. Anyway, if she didn't call Vita soon she might not have a bed for the night. There was no way she was returning to Silverstone Heights; the very idea made the hairs on the back of her neck stand on end.

'I wasn't suggesting you left,' he said. 'In fact, the very opposite. You're more than welcome to stay here.'

'Stay here?' she repeated, staring at him.

'You've got that look on your face again,' he said. 'Don't worry. I may have been lying about not plying you with booze, but the other part was true. I'm not going to try and take advantage. You can have my room and I'll sleep on the sofa.'

'I couldn't do that.' In case he thought she was turning down the offer – and that wasn't her intention, she felt safe here, safe and secure – Iris quickly added, 'I mean, you've already done enough for me. I can't kick you out of your own bed as well. I can take the sofa. I'll be fine.'

Guy shook his head. 'I think after what you've been through today you need a good night's sleep in a comfortable bed. Come on. Please stay. No strings attached, I promise. Then tomorrow morning, I'll come with you to the flat. You can pick up clean clothes and I can make sure there are no unsavoury characters hanging around.'

'Are you sure?' Iris said.

'You want to argue some more?'

Iris smiled. 'No, I'm prepared to give in gracefully. And thanks, I really appreciate it.'

'No problem.' He stood up and stretched his arms. 'Look, I need to go and check that everything's okay in the bar. I won't be long.'

As he headed downstairs, Iris took off her coat, picked up her bag and went over to the window. Guy had pulled the curtains across and she shifted one corner aside. It was quiet now outside with only the occasional person passing by. She took her phone from her bag and turned it on. There was a series of beeps. She frowned as she saw the message saying she had three missed calls. They were all from Luke and the last one was only ten minutes ago.

As she went to ring him back she paused, wondering what to say. If he'd called her mobile, he'd probably called the flat as well and would know she wasn't there. Was it safe to tell him she was at Vita's? Perhaps he'd tried there too. For a second she leaned her forehead against the coolness of glass. Her life was too full of secrets and lies. But now, when she was less than sober – and planning on staying the night in another man's flat – was probably not the moment to start trying to change things.

Luke's phone rang over six times before he eventually picked up. 'Oh, it's you,' he said, the irritation clear in his voice. '*At last*. Where are you? Where have you been? I've been trying to get you all night.'

Iris winced and stared out of the window. 'Sorry about that. I had my phone turned off.' The lie that followed slipped instantly out of her mouth. 'I've been for a drink with Alice.'

'Alice?' he said.

255

'Yes, you know Alice. She works at Tobias Grand & Sons.' Luke didn't actually know her at all – he'd barely been near the place since she'd started work there three months ago – but she had mentioned the name occasionally. She felt bad about lying to him, but couldn't see what else to do. The truth was too complicated and, on the surface, a little too compromising.

'Oh, right,' he said.

Then, before he could pursue the dubious matter of her whereabouts, she quickly said: 'So how are you? How's it going? Have you got those contracts signed yet?'

There was a brief silence.

Perhaps the connection had been cut. Iris pressed the phone closer to her ear. 'Luke? Are you still there?'

'Yeah,' he said. 'Hold on a sec.'

Iris could hear murmurings in the background – a woman's voice was saying something, something she couldn't quite make out.

Then Luke came back on the line and began to speak again. 'I just wanted to . . . I think we need to . . . erm . . . talk.'

'Talk?' Iris repeated blankly.

'For God's sake,' the female voice said clearly. 'There's no need to drag it out. Just tell her.'

Iris felt a jolt in her stomach. *Just tell her.* It didn't take a genius to figure what was coming next. The jolt was followed by a slow sinking sensation. 'Luke?'

'I was thinking it might be . . . might be better,' he said, 'if we took a break for a while. I'm sorry, but you know how it's been, babe. I mean . . . well, you know . . . we've not exactly . . .'

His excuses petered out into the ether. Iris could hear his embarrassment, or was it shame? Even though it was not completely unexpected, she still felt shocked. 'You're with someone else,' she murmured.

Luke didn't deny it, although she was sure that he would have tried if the fragrant Jasmine hadn't been standing at his shoulder. 'That's not why,' he blustered, attempting to justify himself. 'Even if I hadn't . . . I mean, it's not been working, has it? You know it hasn't. We've . . . er . . . grown apart. We both want different things.'

And Iris knew exactly what *he* wanted – a young, ambitious, fun-loving blonde with sexy curves and no emotional hang-ups. No complications. She scowled at her own stupidity. She should have taken more notice of that savvy woman at the party, the one who had warned her about the dangers of all the scheming bitches who worked at Rufus Rigby. Not to mention the fact that she'd failed to follow her own instincts. Hadn't she had her suspicions? Yes, but she'd pushed them aside, too distracted by what had been happening recently.

Luke cleared his throat. 'Iris? Are you all right?'

She didn't reply immediately. What he was saying about the state of their relationship might not be so far off the truth, but she wasn't going to give him the satisfaction of admitting it or of letting him off the hook so easily. This was five years of her life he was dismissing with a single cowardly phone call. He deserved to feel guilty for not having the guts to tell her face to face. 'How long?' she said coldly.

'What?'

'How long has it been going on for? I deserve to know that at least, don't I?'

He hesitated. 'Not long.'

Which probably meant months, Iris decided. So why the hell had he kicked up such a fuss about her going to the Christmas party? It had been a last chance gasp perhaps at *trying* to make things work. Or maybe she was being too generous. More likely it had been an opportunity to compare them both side-by-side and decide which one he really wanted. Her stomach gave another heave.

'Iris?' he said.

Iris turned off the phone and threw it on the chair. For the moment she had nothing left to say to him. For a while she stood motionless by the window. She felt angry. She felt sad and empty. What she didn't feel, however, was devastated. In fact, somewhere in the back of her mind there might even be a tiny glimmer of relief. She sighed as her mind skipped over the past twenty-four hours. There should be a law, she thought, as to how many shitty things could happen to a person in a day.

It was another fifteen minutes before Guy came back. By then she had helped herself to a brandy and was curled up in the corner of a sofa with her hands around the glass. He saw the expression on her face and frowned.

'What's up?'

'You don't want to know.'

He sat down beside her. 'I don't want to know or you don't want to tell me?'

'Both,' she said. 'Neither.' She shook her head. 'God, I've no idea.'

'Sounds confusing.'

She turned to look at him. His head was tilted to one side and his piercing blue eyes gazed steadily back into hers. Iris took a breath. 'Seems like I've just been dumped. Five years and all I get is a lousy phone call.' She laughed bitterly. 'In fact I didn't even get that. *I* called him.'

'Are you upset because he's dumped you or because he was graceless enough to do it over the phone?'

Iris shrugged. She opened her mouth but no words came out. It was perhaps a combination of all the day's events that finally brought the tears to her eyes.

'Hey.' Guy put his arms around her and pulled her close. 'If it's any consolation, I think the man's a fool.'

Iris leaned in against him. It felt like the most natural thing in the world. She could smell the light citrus scent of his after-shave. 'She's a blonde,' she snivelled into his shoulder.

'I've found, on the whole, that blondes are overrated.'

'You're just saying that.'

'Hand on heart,' he said.

She could sense his smile even though she couldn't see it. 'And now you're laughing at me.'

'Just trying to cheer you up. I have a sneaking suspicion that, given time, you may get over him.'

Iris lifted the glass and took a large gulp of brandy. What she needed most after Luke's unceremonious abandonment was to feel desired, to feel desirable. She snuggled closer to Guy. Here, in his arms, she was protected from all the people who wanted to hurt her. It was a good feeling. And then, almost instantly, another thought flashed through her head: one small upward movement of her face and her lips could be touching his . . .

Chapter Thirty-seven

It was almost one o'clock in the morning. Alice Avery had been asleep for over an hour when a sound pierced her troubled dreams, dragging her back to consciousness. She woke with a start, unable to grasp what was happening. Bewildered, she stared into the darkness until her brain eventually registered the ringing of the phone.

She leapt from the bed and ran barefoot into the living room. Calls at this time of day usually meant bad news. Could it be something to do with her mother? With a shaking hand she snatched up the receiver.

'Yes?'

'It's me.'

'Toby?' She thought it was him, but his voice sounded odd, kind of hoarse and distant. When he didn't answer she said his name again. 'Toby? Is that you?'

This time she heard him take a deep breath. Then a groan travelled down the line. 'I'm in trouble, babe,' he said. 'You've got to help me.'

Alice's heart began to thrash. She gripped the phone tighter to her ear. 'Oh my God, what's happened? Where are you?'

But it was only the latter question he answered. 'Shoreditch,' he mumbled. 'Shoreditch High Street. You have to come and pick me up.' He stopped and she heard a heaving noise. A few seconds passed. Then he said, 'Please babe, can you do that? Can you do that for me?'

'Whereabouts?' she said urgently.

There was another pause as if he was looking around. 'I'm . . . I'm not far from Belles. The nightclub. Do you know it? Near Bishopsgate.' He didn't wait for her to reply. 'There's a bus stop about fifty yards away. I'll be waiting there. You'll come, won't you, Alice? Promise me you'll come.'

She had never heard him sound so desperate. 'Of course I will. You stay there. I won't be long.' Before she could say anything else he'd hung up. 'Toby?' But the line was already dead. She thought about calling him back, but that would only waste more time.

Rushing back into the bedroom Alice flung off her pyjamas. She opened a drawer, took out some underwear and put it on. Then she quickly pulled on a pair of jeans and a jumper, and pushed her feet into the first pair of shoes she could find. In the hall she paused only to put on her coat and snatch up her keys.

It was cold outside, the snow still coming down. She shivered as she dashed along the slippery drive. The blue Nissan Micra was parked outside the gate, the same place it had been for the last two weeks. She rarely used the car unless it was to take her mother to the doctor or run her round to one of her friends. It was only a short bus ride into the centre of Kellston and from there Alice could easily walk to Tobias Grand & Sons. This saved her the cost of the petrol and the bother of trying to find somewhere to park.

But as she climbed into the Nissan, Alice acknowledged that these were only excuses. In truth, she was just not confident enough. It had taken her four attempts to pass her test and since that achievement over two years ago, she had clocked up fewer than five hundred miles. Heavy traffic made her nervous, as did the bully-boy tactics of the more aggressive London drivers.

She put the keys in the ignition, started the engine and hesitated. Driving during the day was bad enough, but driving at night and in this weather . . . Alice took a deep breath. Now wasn't the time to be getting the jitters. Toby was in need of help and she couldn't let him down. She could do this. She *would* do this.

After checking her mirror, she carefully pulled away from the kerb. She peered between the wipers as they swished back and forth. Her hands firmly gripped the wheel; they were placed precisely at ten to two as her instructor had drummed into her. She had not spent enough time in the car to develop bad habits.

The streets were quiet and within five minutes she had reached Bethnal Green Road. By now Alice had two conflicting emotions circling in her head: a chronic fear that Toby might be badly hurt, and a guilty tingling pleasure that she was the one he had turned to in his hour of need. That meant something, didn't it? He trusted her, relied on her. Her heart swelled at the very thought of it. It didn't even cross her mind that he might have tried to call others first.

The journey was not as bad as she'd anticipated. There was still some traffic but nothing too daunting; the lateness of the hour and the snow combined to give her a fairly clear run. For this she was grateful. She had no idea where Belles was, but would not give up until she found it . . . and found Toby.

She took a left on to Shoreditch High Street. As Alice passed through the junction with Commercial Street and Great Eastern Street, she noticed a couple of prostitutes standing on the corner. Whores, her mother would have called them. Despite the freezing temperatures they were dressed in skimpy tops, mini-skirts and short leather jackets. One of the girls was black, the other white. She wondered what kind of desperation had driven them out on a night like this – but already knew the answer. Their next fix wasn't going to pay for itself. Alice frowned as she drove, recalling some of the girls she'd worked on in the past. She remembered their skinny frames, the entry marks of the needle in their arms, legs and groins, but their faces were lost to her. After a while, they had all merged together into one sad bundle of misery.

Alice pushed the thought away. It was too terrible to dwell on. She slowed, glancing to the left and right. A nightclub should be easy enough to spot and once she'd found that, it shouldn't be too hard to locate Toby. She passed a building covered in scaffolding and then a long row of shops. Some of the properties were boarded up and covered in graffiti. It was not the kind of area to be roaming around on your own, she thought. She was glad of the protection of the car.

It was another minute before she came across the red neon sign. Outside the club, on the pavement, a couple of oversized bouncers were arguing with a guy. It wasn't Toby though. This man was taller and his hair was dark. She kept on driving, keeping her eyes peeled for a bus stop. The first one she passed had no one standing by it. Fifty yards away, wasn't that what he'd said? She was getting increasingly anxious. What if he wasn't there? What if he'd started walking and collapsed and . . .

But before her imagination could run riot, she spotted the bus shelter. It was on the other side of the street and she gave only one fast glance in her mirror before veering across and pulling up sharply beside it. The outside panels were covered in snow and she couldn't see if anyone was inside. Leaving the engine running, she jumped out of the car and called his name. There was no response.

But there was someone there.

For a second she paused, not sure if it was him or not. There was a man certainly, sitting hunched over with his head almost touching his thighs, but was it Toby? The light wasn't good and his face was obscured. She didn't recognise the clothes. This guy looked filthy, like a tramp. His hair was matted and he stank of alcohol.

'Toby?' she said again, this time more softly.

The man looked up and she gave a gasp. His face was battered and bruised and covered in blood. She instinctively took a step back. And then he smiled. It wasn't much of a smile, but it was enough. She would have known it anywhere. Alice rushed forward and went down on her knees. 'Oh God,' she said. 'What happened, love? Who did this to you?'

'You came,' he murmured.

'Of course I did.' As she took his swollen face in her hands, he flinched. She stared at him. He'd been so badly beaten that one of his eyes was closed. The other was only partly open. She made a fast survey of his injuries. His breathing was regular at least. There was no obvious damage to his skull, but concussion – or something worse – was still a possibility. From the way he was holding his chest, there could be broken ribs too. She had to get him seen to as quickly as she could. She took out her phone and began to punch in the number.

'What are you doing?' Toby said.

Alice stood up. 'Calling an ambulance.'

'No way,' he insisted, abruptly reaching out and snatching the phone from her. The physical effort made him groan. 'You can't. I'm not going to hospital.'

'What are you talking about? You need help.'

He shook his head. 'There'll be questions, babe. They'll want to know who . . .' He gave another low groan. 'Please,' he begged, gazing up at her. 'I just want to lie down, get warm. Can't we go back to your place?'

She hesitated. 'It's not a good idea.'

'You were a nurse, weren't you?'

'Yes, but—'

'So you can take care of me.' He passed the phone back to her. 'Please, Alice.'

She had to make a decision and quickly. If they stayed there arguing, Toby was as likely to die of hypothermia as anything else. 'All right then,' she said, deciding to take the chance. She prayed that there wasn't any internal damage. Still, if he showed signs of deterioration on the journey she could always take him straight to A&E.

Toby moaned as she carefully hauled him to his feet. With her arm around him, they half walked, half staggered to the car. She bundled him into the passenger seat and tried to pull the seatbelt across. 'Don't,' he said. 'It hurts too much.'

She didn't press the matter. Speed was of the essence now. She had to get him home as fast as she could. Running round the bonnet of the Nissan, she jumped into the driver's seat, slammed the door shut and set off for home.

Alice's attention was split between the road and Toby. She continually glanced at him, making sure that he was still conscious. A few minutes passed before she spoke again.

'It was him, wasn't it?'

Toby didn't reply. He gave a half-shrug, flinching as his shoulders lifted.

'Danny Street!' she spat out. 'It was that bastard, wasn't it? Didn't you get my call? I told you he was looking for you. I told you to be careful. What happened? Did he bring you here, force you to come with him? Christ, why didn't anyone help?' She knew she was asking too many questions, the words slipping hurriedly from her lips as each thought entered her mind.

Toby leaned his head against the back of the seat. 'He didn't take me anywhere. I went to the club to see him.'

Her eyes widened. 'You did what?'

'You can't hide from the likes of Danny Street.' He gave a soft laugh. 'Well, not forever. He was going to catch up with me eventually and the longer he had to wait, the angrier he was going to get. I figured it was better to face the music than spend the next few weeks hiding from him. I thought I could talk him round, buy myself some extra time.'

It was a tactic that quite patently hadn't worked. Alice felt hot tears prick her eyes. 'This is all my fault,' she murmured. There had been a chance for him to escape from Danny Street's sadistic clutches and she'd thrown the opportunity away. What price her conscience now? If only she'd done as he'd asked, if only she hadn't had those qualms about the cold, dead body of Catherine Macdonald . . .

Toby reached across and placed his hand on her arm. 'Don't,' he said. 'It wasn't your fault, babe. None of this is down to you.'

In the harshness of the bathroom light, Alice could clearly see all his injuries. There were dark purple bruises on his ribs and stomach. There were marks on his neck, the kind of marks that came from a hand being brutally placed around his throat. He was sitting in the bath and she was kneeling beside it, bathing him as gently as a mother would a child. She cleaned his face – his nose at least wasn't broken – and washed the blood from his hair. It was a sin, she thought, for anyone to intentionally inflict damage on so perfect a body. By nature she was usually a passive person, but she suddenly understood the vengeful anger that could rise up from the very depths of the soul. Had Danny Street walked through the door at that moment, she would have torn his eyes from their sockets.

'That thug should be locked up,' she said.

'I owe him money, babe.'

'That's no excuse.'

Toby gave a sigh. 'If he lets me get away with it, he's going to look like a pushover. He can't afford for that to happen. It's all to do with respect.'

Alice snorted. 'Respect. He doesn't know the meaning of the word. And you've done . . . well, other things for him.' She couldn't quite bring herself to say it out loud. 'Doesn't that count for anything?'

'Sure,' he said. 'It counts for half the debt, but only half – and the interest on the rest is growing by the day. Do you have any idea what their interest rates are like? Before long, I'll be back to square one.' He pulled up his knees and wrapped his arms around them. 'Shit, babe, I don't know what to do. He's crazy. He's off his head. He's going to kill me next time.'

'He won't,' Alice insisted. 'We'll find a way to sort this out. We'll give him what he wants. As soon as someone suitable turns up, we can—'

'But that could take weeks,' he wailed. 'Even months. He isn't going to wait. He's not what you'd call the patient type.' Toby let go of his knees and stared despairingly down at his bruises. 'And this was just a warning.'

'So we give him a down payment. I've got some savings. It's not much, only a few thousand, but it should be enough to keep him quiet for a while.'

He gazed at her, his blue eyes full of amazement. 'You'd really do that for me?' Then he quickly shook his head. 'No, I couldn't. It wouldn't be fair. God knows when I could pay you back.'

'You don't have to worry about that.' She'd been saving for a deposit on a flat, but what was the point of owning your own home when you had no one to share it with? Love, surely, was more important than cash. 'I want to do it. I won't take no for an answer.'

'You're incredible,' he said, grabbing hold of her hand and kissing it. 'Jesus, what would I do without you?'

Alice buried her face in the top of his head. His hair smelled of lemon shampoo. She could have stayed there forever, happy to know that she'd pleased him so much.

'But what about Grimm Senior?' he said, slowly pulling away. 'My dad will do his bloody nut when he sees the state of me.'

'You'd better keep out of his way for a while.'

'How am I going to do that? I live in the same house.'

Alice thought about it. 'Call him in the morning, say you've caught his flu and you're staying with a friend. He can hardly complain about you taking time off work when he's still at home himself.'

'You don't mind if I stay here?'

Alice felt a thrill at the thought of it. She couldn't have minded anything less. Leaning back, she picked up a towel. As she helped him from the bath, a smile played around her lips; she couldn't remember ever having been so happy. For once in her life she was needed. It was a feeling she'd never experienced before.

Chapter Thirty-eight

It was dark in the room but Iris knew it was morning. The first thing she was blearily aware of was the sound of running water, the second – and this jolted her fully awake – was that she was lying in someone else's bed. Suddenly, like a trailer for a movie, a sequence of images flashed through her mind: climbing the stairs to Guy Wilder's apartment, eating pasta in the kitchen, drinking wine in the spacious living room, hurling her phone on to the chair after talking to Luke, and then . . .

She could remember the need she'd felt for Guy, her desire to be comforted. With a groan, she scrabbled for the lamp on the bedside table. It took her a few seconds to find the switch and when the light came on she screwed up her eyes. They felt scratched and sore as if a sheet of sandpaper had been pulled across them. Turning her face, she squinted at the pillow beside her. There was no indentation, no sign that anyone had slept there. Then, through the hammering in her head – she had drunk way too much last night – her memory gradually cleared.

Nothing had happened.

She lay back with a sigh of relief. Sleeping with a man you

barely knew under the influence of alcohol didn't do much for a girl's self-respect. It didn't do much for her dignity either. And that dignity, after Luke's casual dumping of her, was already at an all-time low. She rolled the word around on her tongue. *Dumped.* She'd never had a boyfriend leave her before. She had always been the one to do the finishing. A guilty feeling crept across her conscience. Had she ever been as cruel as Luke? Well, perhaps occasionally, but then again there was a difference between a three-month fling and a five-year live-in relationship. The latter, surely, deserved a touch more respect than a long-distance phone call.

Her thoughts returned to the previous night. *Nothing had happened.* Except, she realised, that wasn't entirely true. As her memory wound remorselessly back through the details, Iris relived the moment when Guy had put his arms around her. She remembered the warmth she had felt, along with the glorious feeling of safety. But then there was that other moment, that vital moment when she had lifted her head and . . . Her heart sank like a stone. Oh God! With terrible clarity, she recalled how she'd made a clumsy pass at him.

Horrified, she stared up at the ceiling. Stupid, stupid, stupid! She shrank down beneath the duvet. What had she been thinking? The sound of running water stopped abruptly. There was a couple of minutes silence and then she heard Guy's footsteps. She ought to get up too, although she wasn't sure how she could face him.

What was the time? Dragging out her arm, she peered down at her wrist. It took a while for her eyes to focus, but when they did she leapt straight out of bed. She dashed out of the door, along the corridor to the living room and into the kitchen.

'It's half past eight,' she said. 'Why didn't you wake me?'

Guy was standing by the fridge with a carton of eggs in his

hand. 'And good morning to you too. I thought you could do with a lie-in.'

'I'm going to be late for work.'

'Give them a call,' he said.

'And tell them what?'

Guy put down the eggs and placed his hands on his hips. 'Women's troubles, flu, sore throat, toothache, emergency appointment.' He grinned. 'Cat ate the alarm clock. I've heard them all.'

'And did you believe any of them?'

'No,' he said, 'but that doesn't matter. It's the getting in touch that counts, letting them know that you're not coming in.'

'I have to go in,' she said. William had been good to her and with Gerald still off sick she didn't want to leave him in the lurch. There was only a faint chance that Toby might bother to turn up – he was hardly renowned for his reliability.

'Okay, so ring and tell them you'll be a couple of hours late. They can manage for that long, can't they? You can take a shower, have some breakfast and then we'll go over to the flat. I'll run you to work afterwards.'

Iris suddenly became aware of her state of dress, or more to the point the lack of it. She was standing in the doorway wearing only the white Nike T-shirt that he had given her to sleep in last night. That, however, was the least of her worries. She raised a hand to her mouth. She could hardly bear to ask the question, but it had to be done. 'Just how much of a fool did I make of myself last night?'

Guy grinned again. 'I was about to ask the very same thing. It all got a bit hazy after the third bottle. I can't recall a thing after twelve o'clock. Did I do anything I shouldn't?'

Iris suspected he was being more tactful than truthful. Whereas she'd been knocking them back like there was no tomorrow, he'd shown decidedly more restraint. And he certainly didn't appear to be suffering from a hangover. In fact he looked as fresh as a man who'd gone to bed early with a good book and a cup of cocoa.

'You grab that shower,' he said. 'Breakfast in ten minutes. And don't tell me you're not hungry. If you don't eat, you'll feel lousy for the rest of day.'

Iris knew she was going to feel lousy anyway, with or without the hammering in her head, but she nodded obediently and retreated to the bathroom. After a quick shower, she towelled herself dry and brushed her teeth. She wondered what to do with the toothbrush. Guy had given it to her last night, brand new and still in its wrapper. Was he the kind of man who always had a spare just in case someone stayed over? And if that was the case, how many did he get through in a month? Iris sighed. His sex life, whether promiscuous or otherwise, was nothing to do with her.

She left the toothbrush on the side of the sink and stared into the mirror. Her face fell. Yes, she really did look as bad as she felt. There were dark circles under her eyes and her skin had a greyish tinge. She made a mental note to *never* drink alcohol again. From now on she was a mineral water girl. At least she would be after she'd poured three cups of black coffee down her throat. She was going to need a lift to get her brain back in gear.

Iris rummaged though her bag but found only a few top-up cosmetics. With a stick of concealer, she did what she could to make herself look human, but knew she was fighting a losing battle. It would take twelve hours' peaceful sleep to even begin to repair the damage. And then there was her hair. She frowned. Without the benefit of straighteners, it was going to revert to its naturally tangled wavy mess.

As she was about to go, Iris glanced towards the cabinet on the wall. You could tell a lot about a man from the contents of his bathroom cabinet. Like whether there was sometimes a female in residence. She reached out a hand, but then withdrew it. No, it wasn't right to go snooping, not after all his kindness and support. But her attack of conscience didn't last. After all, it couldn't do any harm to sneak a quick peek. Before she could talk herself out of it, she whipped open the door and gazed inside. There was, she was pleased to see, no feminine items at all. There were only a comb, a razor, a can of shaving foam, a spare tube of toothpaste, dental floss and aftershave. She softly closed the door again and left the bathroom with a smile on her face.

In the bedroom, she took off the towel, folded it neatly over the back of a chair, and picked up her pants. She had washed them out the night before and left them to dry on the radiator. Now that was the true meaning of multitasking, she thought. It was amazing how practical she could be even when she was three sheets to the wind.

After getting dressed, Iris tidied the bed. She plumped up the pillows and straightened out the dark red duvet. Then she began to look around. The room was as masculine as the contents of the bathroom cabinet – and as sparse. Like the living room, it was painted a pure crisp white. There were a couple of pictures on the walls, Mediterranean scenes in shades of red and gold, but no photographs of family or friends. He was clearly a man who liked to keep things simple. A reaction to the dreadful mess of his childhood, perhaps. That was something she could relate to.

Iris checked her watch. It was ten to nine. William would probably be in work by now. She got out her mobile and scrolled through the menu. What was she going to say? She didn't want to tell an outright lie, but she could hardly tell the truth either. Sleeping in after a night of binge drinking was hardly acceptable behaviour for someone hoping to make their temporary post more permanent. And she needed that job now. With Luke gone, she'd be paying all the bills on her own.

The phone was answered after a couple of rings. 'Tobias Grand & Sons.'

'William?' she said. 'Hi, it's Iris. I'm really sorry, but I'm going to be a bit late.'

She must have sounded flustered because he said, 'Are you all right?'

'Yeah, yeah I'm fine. Something's just . . . er . . . something's . . .' She racked her brain, but it was still too sodden to come up with anything remotely plausible. 'Look, I'll explain later. I'm sorry to mess you about like this, but I'll be in about ten-thirty.'

'Are you sure—'

'I'll see you then,' Iris smartly interrupted, and hung up before he could ask any more awkward questions. She put the phone down with a small sigh of relief. He had seemed more concerned than annoyed. If it had been Gerald on the other end of the line, she would have got the third degree. Still, after what had happened with Danny Street yesterday, William was probably grateful that she was coming in at all.

As Iris headed for the door, she paused to study her reflection in the full-length mirror. There was no visible improvement: her face still had the pallor of cold porridge and her eyes were struggling to stay open. She blinked hard, wishing she had some drops to put in them. The creases in her clothes didn't do much for her appearance either. Still, she couldn't hide away forever. She took a deep breath, picked up her bag and went through to the kitchen.

'Scrambled eggs with smoked salmon,' Guy said, turning to smile at her. 'Toast and freshly ground coffee. Sit yourself down. I'll have it ready in a minute.' He picked up a bottle of aspirin from the counter and rattled it. 'You want some of these?'

Iris pulled out a chair and nodded.

'How many? One or two?'

'About fifty,' she said. 'And please don't shake that bottle so loudly. My head is in danger of exploding.'

He laughed and poured a glass of water. 'Here,' he said, placing a couple of tablets in the palm of her hand.

'Thanks.'

'Help yourself to coffee.'

Iris did. She poured herself a large mug and gulped down three fast mouthfuls, almost scalding her mouth in the process. Then she popped in the aspirin and washed them down with the water.

Guy brought over the plates and set one down in front of her. 'Eat!' he demanded.

Iris, although she knew she should, wasn't sure if she could. A faint wave of nausea was rising from her stomach. She stared down at her plate. It was the kind of breakfast that under different circumstances she would have viewed as rather special. It wasn't very often that scrambled egg with smoked salmon came her way. Even the toast, sitting in a rack, had been neatly cut into quarters and there were various pots of jam and marmalade on the table. All it needed was a bottle of champagne and . . . She quickly brushed aside the thought. For one, the very thought of alcohol made her feel ill, and for two it was perfectly possible that Guy Wilder always ate like this. She shouldn't go reading anything into it.

'This is very kind of you,' she said.

Guy raised his brows.

She saw the gesture and frowned. 'What?'

'Nothing,' he said, smiling. 'It just sounded very polite, as if we hardly know each other. And I suppose we don't, not really, but . . .'

Iris blanched as she thought about what had happened last

night. 'Well, I'm a polite kind of person.' Having made the claim, she then felt obliged to pick up her fork and at least try some of the food he had made. She put a small amount of egg in her mouth. She waited for a second but her stomach, thankfully, seemed to accept it.

'You don't have to eat it all. I won't be offended.'

Iris took another bite. 'No, it's good,' she said. And it *was* good. She only hoped that she could keep it down. What remained of her dignity would hardly be enhanced by a hasty dash to the bathroom.

'So how are you feeling? I mean, apart from the hangover.'

'If you're asking if I've changed my mind then no, I haven't. I'm going to stay. If my dad is out there somewhere, I have to find him.'

'I understand that,' he said. 'You should talk to Michael, see if he's got any ideas about where he could be staying: old haunts, friends, that type of thing. I know it's been going on twenty years, but people tend to return to places that are familiar. If we get some leads we can start asking around.'

'To be honest, I'm not sure he'd tell me even if he *could* think of anything. I don't mean that in a bad way, just that he wants to protect me.'

Guy leaned forward and refilled her mug with coffee. 'Winding up Danny Street probably isn't the smartest way to do that.'

'Yes, well, Michael doesn't always think before he acts. He has a kind heart, though. He's doesn't want me chasing after rainbows. He's convinced himself that Dad must be dead – even if Terry didn't catch up with him – and I doubt if anything I say or do will make him change his mind.'

'And what about Luke?'

Iris shrugged. 'What about him? It's finished. I'll get over it. There's nothing more to say.' That wasn't strictly true, but what she did have to say was for Luke's ears alone. 'What time are you seeing Chris Street?'

'Eleven-thirty.'

'Will you call me afterwards, let me know how it goes?'

'Of course,' he said. 'And try not to worry too much. I'm sure I can buy us a few weeks' grace.'

Iris noticed the 'us' and smiled. It felt good to have him on her side. 'Thank you.'

Chapter Thirty-nine

By ten o'clock Guy was pulling up outside Silverstone Heights. He parked the white Mercedes convertible a few spaces away from Luke's BMW. Iris turned and glanced wistfully out of the window; now that she and Luke had split, she would no longer have a car to borrow when she wanted to nip round to Vita's of an evening. The moment the thought entered her head, she pulled a face. It was hardly the kind of regret that should be uppermost in her mind after the break-up of a five-year relationship.

They went into the empty foyer and Iris pressed the button for the lift. 'I won't be long. I just need to get changed and grab a few things.' She had made up her mind to take refuge at Vita's for a while. Even though Guy seemed confident about persuading the Street brothers to leave her in peace, she still didn't fancy the prospect of being alone in the flat. Best, she decided, to give the dust time to settle.

'It's okay. There's no hurry.' He glanced around at the tiled terracotta floor, the spotless walls and the array of potted palms. 'I've never been in here before. Very plush. I'm impressed.'

Iris, who had never felt entirely comfortable in the complex, gave a light shrug of her shoulders. She wasn't sure how serious he was being. 'Well, there are plenty for sale if you fancy a change.'

'I don't imagine your neighbours would be too happy with one of the local plebs moving in. I might be accused of lowering the tone.'

'You could be right,' she agreed, 'especially with that old scrapheap of a car of yours.'

He grinned. 'I hope you're not suggesting that I'm some kind of flash bastard.'

'God forbid!'

The lift arrived and they got in. Guy leaned against the side and crossed his arms. As they ascended smoothly, he tilted his head to one side and stared at her. 'I've been trying to work out what's different about you this morning.'

'Different?' she said. 'What do you mean?'

'I've just figured it out. It's your hair.'

Iris self-consciously lifted a hand, fruitlessly trying to smooth her damp rampant waves. 'Thanks for reminding me.'

The lift drew to a halt, gave a delicate ping and opened its doors. They took a left into the corridor.

'I like it.' he said. 'It suits you. You look like one of those pale and mysterious pre-Raphaelite girls, like you've just stepped out of a Rossetti painting.'

She stared at him, faintly surprised that he had even heard of Dante Gabriel Rossetti. And then gave herself a mental kick for allowing such shallow presumptions to even enter her head. Why shouldn't Guy Wilder know about art? He might be an East End boy, born and bred, but was probably better educated than she was. 'So do you reckon they all had hangovers too?'

He laughed, gazing back at her. 'Maybe. It could account for those pensive expressions.'

Iris broke eye contact, glanced down at the floor and then up

279

again towards the flat. It was only at that moment she noticed. Stopping dead in her tracks, she reached out and gripped Guy's arm. 'The door,' she hissed softly.

It was open, only by an inch or two, but definitely open.

He shook off her hand. 'Stay here,' he said.

But Iris didn't. She followed him inside, aware as she entered the hallway of the small but distinctive sounds of someone moving around. A wave of fear rolled over her. Oh God, whoever had broken in was still here! Danny Street? The bruiser who had accosted her at Columbia Road? Or maybe just some drugged-up chancer who'd discovered that no one was in. Guy walked quietly into the living room. It was empty. He turned and came back into the hall. Iris pointed towards the bedroom.

'In there,' she mouthed silently.

There was a series of louder rattling sounds now, as if the intruder was rifling through her wardrobe. Iris reached for the phone in her bag. It would have been smarter, she realised, to have retreated, to have called the cops from outside the flat – outside the building even. She had heard about people confronting burglars and coming off the worse for it. Getting injured, even getting killed. And whoever was here could be far more brutal than a common thief. What if he was armed? What if he hurt Guy? She wanted to cry out, to tell him to come back, but it was already too late.

As he burst through the door she heard a startled yelp. It was followed by a thump, a dull heavy sound, and then a slight wheezing like a beach ball deflating. Iris dropped the phone back into her bag, picked up a large black umbrella from the stand in the hall, and hurried into the bedroom.

Relief was the first thing she felt. Guy was okay. More than okay. A man was lying face down on the carpet and Guy was straddling him, forcing the intruder's arm up behind his back. There was no doubt about who had won this particular battle.

A low futile grunting was the only noise emanating from the body on the floor. It was a few seconds before her gaze focused properly on the back of the head and the familiar brown silky hair. Instantly, she drew in a breath. 'Luke! What the hell are *you* doing here?'

Guy looked over his shoulder at her and then back down at the man he was restraining. Despite now knowing who he was, he didn't immediately release him. 'So I take it he isn't here to steal all your worldly possessions?'

'No,' she said, slowly lowering the umbrella. As she placed it on the bed, she thought how useless it would have been as a weapon. She noticed a suitcase already half filled lying on top of the duvet. So Luke had decided to sneak in and pack up all his stuff while he thought she'd be at work.

Luke squirmed and turned his head. His face was red and sweaty. 'For fuck's sake, Iris,' he croaked, 'tell this bloody goon to get off me.'

Iris didn't. In fact she'd have been more than happy for Guy to twist that arm even further up his back. She wasn't usually vindictive, but a little discomfort was the least he deserved after the way he'd treated her. 'What are you doing here?' she said again. 'You're supposed to be in Brussels.' But even as she spoke she was beginning to comprehend the truth. He hadn't gone away at all – well, not abroad at least. The whole business trip had been a lie from start to finish, just an excuse to spend some time with that bitch Jasmine.

'It's my bloody flat, isn't it,' Luke spluttered weakly. 'Why shouldn't I be here?'

Guy looked up at her. 'You want me to let him go?'

Iris paused for a second, but then reluctantly nodded. She watched as Guy released him and stood back. Luke stumbled to his feet, rubbing resentfully at his arm. He scowled at Guy, but only briefly. Guy was taller than him, broader and stronger. If

Luke had been expecting an apology for being manhandled in his own home, it wasn't forthcoming. Guy stared impassively at him for a few seconds and then turned and said to Iris, 'If you're okay, I'll wait in the car.'

'I'll be fine,' she said. 'Thanks.'

Luke waited until the front door had shut, until he was sure they were alone, before he spoke again. His voice had a bitter, nasty edge to it. 'And just who the hell was that?'

'A friend.'

He curled his lip. 'Well, it didn't take you long.'

Iris knew what he was implying. She was about to deny it, but then changed her mind. She didn't have to answer to him any more. And a part of her was glad that he *did* think that. It was a salve, albeit a small one, to her wounded pride. Guy Wilder was a very good-looking man and she wasn't comfortable with the role of the betrayed girlfriend.

'So I take it you're moving in with the lovely Jasmine,' she said.

Luke didn't answer directly. 'I'll just get my things and go.'

'Why didn't you tell me?' she said. 'I mean before. I presume this isn't love at first sight. You must have been seeing her for a while. When did it start? A month ago, three, six? How long has it been going on for?'

Luke shook his head. Unwilling to meet her eyes, he quickly looked away. 'Let's not do this now.'

'Why not? Will there be a better time?' She was aware that there was something almost masochistic about her desire to know the details. It could only bring her pain. But perhaps she needed that pain, needed the brutal clarity of the truth in order to draw a line under the whole relationship. Or perhaps that wasn't the reason at all. Maybe she just hated feeling like a fool for not having realised what had been going on.

'What does it matter?' Luke said.

Iris frowned. It did matter. If he told her when it had started she could look back, try to recall the signals, the clues that must have been there. That way she wouldn't make the same mistake twice. She'd had some suspicions last week, some nagging doubts, but had chosen to ignore them. She had put her head firmly in the sand and carried on regardless. 'I have the right to know, don't I?'

Luke shifted uncomfortably from one foot to another. 'A few weeks,' he said. 'A month.'

She knew he was lying. She could see it in his eyes, in the shifty way he glanced across the room. More like two months, she guessed – or even longer. Perhaps he had taken up with Jasmine soon after she'd lost the baby. That thought made her feel slightly sick.

'Right,' she said.

'I'll just finish packing,' he said.

Iris wrapped her arms around her chest, watching as he opened the drawers and threw T-shirts and underwear into his case. 'So what now?'

He spoke without looking at her. 'I'll pay the rent up to the end of January. That should give you enough time to find some-where else. Unless you want to stay here. If you want to keep on the lease, I'm sure—'

'No,' she said. 'I'll be moving out too.' She couldn't stay even if she'd wanted to; the rent here was way beyond her resources. And anyway she didn't like the place that much.

'Okay,' he said.

Iris wondered how it had come to this. Suddenly they were like strangers. Reaching into the wardrobe, she took out an overnight bag and quickly packed enough clothes to last for the next few days. She had wanted to get changed, but decided to do it when she got to work instead. The sooner she got out of here, the better.

'Well,' she said when she had gathered everything she needed.

Luke put his hands in his pockets and shuffled uneasily from one foot to another. 'Well,' he echoed awkwardly. 'Take care of yourself.'

Had Iris been in a more forgiving mood, she might have said 'You too', but she wasn't prepared to make it that easy for him. He deserved to feel guilt, to feel shame over the shabby way he'd treated her. People fell in and out of love, that was just a fact of life, but a bit of honesty wasn't too much to ask. Why couldn't he have sat her down and talked to her face-to-face? She found herself hoping that the delightful Jasmine would make his life hell.

'Bye then,' she said briskly. Despite her contempt, there was still a lump in her throat as she headed for the door.

Chapter Forty

There had been no conversation in the car as they made the short trip along the High Street from Silverstone Heights to Tobias Grand & Sons. The only sounds had come from the traffic outside and the occasional snuffle as Iris struggled to keep her emotions in check. She and Luke had been drifting apart for months, but there had been something special between them once. It was the end of a chapter and she couldn't help but feel regret.

As Guy pulled the Mercedes into the space usually reserved for the hearse, he said, 'Are you sure you want to do this? You could take the rest of the day off. I'm sure they'll understand. You're welcome to come back to the flat. You won't be disturbed, I promise. After I've been to see Chris Street, I'll be working in the bar. You can have some time to yourself.'

Iris shook her head. At the moment she didn't want to be alone. 'No, I'd rather get on with things, keep busy. You'll give me a call later, yeah? When you've talked to him.'

'Sure,' he said.

'Well, thanks for all your help.' Her voice had a slight waver to it. She wanted to say more, to explain how much she appreciated his support, but couldn't quite find the right words. Instead she undid her seatbelt and opened the door. As she went to leave, Guy laid a hand gently on her arm. 'It'll be okay,' he said.

She wasn't sure if he was referring to her problems with the Streets or her life in general so she simply nodded. After closing the door behind her, she gave a small wave and walked away.

Inside Tobias Grand & Sons, William was standing by her desk with the phone to his ear. He looked pale and harried, like a man on the edge. 'Mr Hills,' he was saying, 'as I've already explained, this really isn't—'. But the caller wasn't allowing him to finish. As he moved the phone away, Iris could hear an angry retort floating tinnily out of the receiver. William gave her a strained smile and raised his eyes to the ceiling.

'Two minutes,' she mouthed, before hurrying towards the staff area. She walked through the kitchen, flipping on the kettle as she passed, and went along the short corridor to the toilets. Here she quickly got changed into clean clothes: a pair of beige trousers and a cream cashmere jumper. She didn't normally wear cashmere to work, but she had grabbed the first things that had come to hand. In a few days, when she was feeling stronger, she would go back to the flat and retrieve the rest of her belongings.

Looking in the mirror, she wondered if she had made a mistake in turning down Guy's offer. She could have crashed on the sofa and got a few more hours of sleep. Despite eating breakfast, the inside of her head still felt squashed and pulpy. At least the banging had stopped. She pulled back her hair and secured it with a slide at the nape of her neck. Then she slapped on foundation, a lick of mascara and some lipstick. The improvement to her face was minimal, but it would have to do; no one expected glamour in a funeral parlour.

In the kitchen, Iris made two coffees but when she returned to reception, William had disappeared and Alice had taken his place. She was standing by the desk, rifling through a heap of papers.

'Morning,' Iris said.

Alice gave a startled jump. 'Oh, it's you,' she said. A few sheets fluttered to the floor and she hurriedly bent down to pick them up. 'I was just looking to see if anyone else might be coming in. Have you had any calls?'

Iris gave a shudder. What she meant was more *bodies*. And those cold corpses were the last thing she wanted to think about this morning. 'You'll have to ask William. I've only just got here.'

Alice didn't enquire as to why she was so late. Instead she said, 'It doesn't really matter. I was only . . . er . . . getting organised, you know, trying to sort out the day.'

Had she been less hung over, Iris might have been curious as to why Alice seemed even more jumpy than usual. As it was, she had other things on her mind. 'No sign of Toby, I suppose?'

'He's not in. He's got the flu.'

'That's original.'

'He really has,' Alice insisted. As if Iris were accusing her of something – of being overly gullible perhaps – her cheeks flushed a deep shade of pink. 'He rang earlier. William was busy so I took the call. He sounded terrible. I think he must have caught the bug off Gerald.' She placed the papers back on the desk. 'I don't think he'll be in for the rest of the week.'

Or next week either, Iris suspected. He'd skive off for as long as he could. Not that it made much difference. He never did any work when he was here. 'Okay,' she said, smiling. 'I believe you.'

Alice dipped her head in a small uncertain nod. This was followed by a few awkward seconds when Iris had the feeling she wanted to say more, but couldn't quite bring herself to do it. She waited, but Alice wasn't forthcoming.

'Well, I'm sure we'll manage.'

Alice gave her an uneasy smile. 'Yes. Yes, of course we will. I'd better get on.'

Iris watched as she scurried towards the stairs to the basement. One day she'd have to take that woman out for a drink and get her to loosen up a bit. As soon as the thought entered her head, she was reminded of the delicate state of her guts. Just the very thought of alcohol was enough to set her stomach churning.

Iris put one mug of coffee down and carried the other over to William's office. She knocked lightly on the door.

'Come in.'

William sat back with a sigh as she entered the room. Iris noticed the state of his desk – even more chaotic than her own – and felt a spasm of guilt. In Gerald's absence he had been burdened with far more work than he could manage and her going AWOL this morning could only have added to the pressure. Carefully avoiding the papers, she placed the mug in front of him. 'A peace offering,' she said. 'I'm really sorry about being late.'

'That's all right. After what happened yesterday, I'm surprised you're here at all.'

'It wasn't anything to do with that. More of a domestic really.' Then, having said that much, she decided she may as well finish the story. The truth spilled out before she could think too much about it. 'Actually, we've split up. Me and Luke, I mean. I had some . . . well, I just had some stuff to sort out.'

'I'm sorry,' he said, his grey eyes full of sympathy. 'Are you all right?' Then he shook his head. 'I don't know why I even asked you that. Look, there's nothing urgent to deal with. Why don't you go home, take some time out.'

Iris looked at the mess on his desk and smiled. It occurred to her that William Grand was too kind for his own good. This was the second time in two days that he'd urged her to go home. 'There's a limit, you know, as to how considerate any man should be. Are you telling me there's nothing important that needs attention here?'

'Nothing that can't wait.'

She knew he was lying, albeit in the nicest possible way. 'To be honest, I'd rather keep busy.'

William paused before giving her an understanding nod. 'If it's any consolation,' he said, 'it does get better. At the time it feels like—'

'It doesn't,' she quickly interrupted. Iris appreciated his concern, but didn't want his pity. Every girl had her pride and she wasn't prepared to tell him she'd been dumped. 'It's not like that. We've been having problems for ages. It was a mutual decision.' Before he could pursue the matter further, she smartly changed the subject. 'And if that offer's still open – the job, I mean – then I'd like to apply for it.'

'Good,' William said. 'Consider yourself hired.'

'You don't want to talk to Gerald first?'

'I'm sure he'll be as pleased as I am.'

Iris wasn't so certain. Ever since that trouble over Lizzie Street, she'd had the feeling she wasn't in Grimm Senior's best books. Still, as he wasn't around to argue, she may as well seize the opportunity while she could. Having just returned to singledom – and with a new home to find *and* fund – she needed every penny she could lay her hands on. 'Thank you. I appreciate it.'

It was after twelve before Guy Wilder called. Iris had been watching her mobile for the past twenty minutes. As soon as the phone started to ring, she snatched it up. 'Hi.'

289

'It's me,' he said. 'You don't have to worry. It's sorted.'

Iris, unaware that she'd been holding her breath, released it in a long sigh of relief. 'Are you sure?'

'Absolutely.'

'Oh, thank God for that.' She closed her eyes for a moment. 'So they believed you? They understand that I don't know where he is?'

'I wouldn't go as far as to say that, this is the Streets we're talking about, but they don't need me stirring up trouble for them. I'll spare you the details, but my mother was hardly discreet when she'd had a drink or two. She told me things they'd rather the law didn't get to hear about. One anonymous call and . . . well, I'm sure you get my drift. So they're prepared to lay off for a while although I wouldn't put it past them to try and keep tabs on you. They're convinced your father's out there somewhere and you're the person he's most likely to contact.'

'You think they'll have me followed?'

'It's possible,' he said, 'but if we get any promising leads I'm sure we'll find a way to shake them off.'

'I'm going to have a chat with Michael this evening, see if I can get the numbers and addresses of any of the people Dad used to hang about with.'

'Would you like me to pick you up after work?'

Iris thought about it. 'Thanks, but I'm better off talking to him on my own. I also have to explain about me and Luke splitting up.'

'Were they close?'

She gave a light laugh. 'Let's put it this way: I don't imagine he'll be crying into his beer. He thought Luke was an idiot – although he never admitted it – and Luke thought he was a useless drunk.'

'No love lost then.' Guy paused before he added, 'But look,

290

you will be careful, won't you? I know the Streets have promised to back off, but they're not exactly men of their word. So try not to go places on your own and give me a call if you ever get worried. I'm sure it'll be okay, but there's no point in taking unnecessary risks.'

'I won't,' she said. 'And I'll be staying at Vita's for a few days so I won't be alone.'

'That's good. And maybe you should contact the agents of that flat opposite and tell them you've heard noises. The last thing they'll want is squatters so I'm sure they'll check it out. They'll probably change the locks too.'

Iris hadn't thought of that. 'Good idea. I will.' She had no desire to go back to Silverstone Heights, but unless she found a new flat quickly she could well be forced to. Vita, she knew, would welcome her with open arms, but the little terraced house she occupied was barely big enough for her and Rick. With a third person in residence, they'd soon be falling over each other.

'I'll give you a ring tomorrow.'

'Hold on,' she said. 'Before you go, did they . . . did the Streets give you any idea of why they believe my dad's come back?'

'No. No details at least. But I got the distinct impression that he has been seen. Maybe it was Jenks who tipped them off. He never forgot a face; even after nineteen years he'd still have remembered him. Probably got a few quid from the brothers for the info and then decided to take another bite of the cherry by approaching you.'

'But if Jenks told them where he was, why haven't they found him?'

'Maybe the old Weasel was smart enough to keep something in reserve. He could have claimed that he'd seen him, but for one reason or another, hadn't been able to keep on his tail. That way, if he *had* followed him, he could play you off against each other – whoever offered him the most got to find out where your father was. That could be why Chris got so jumpy when he saw Jenks approach you at the Hope.'

Iris gave an inner groan. With Jenks now dead, she had lost her best lead to where her dad might be hiding. It was a horrible, selfish thing to be thinking, but she couldn't help herself. 'I'm so damn stupid. If only I'd gone after him.'

'Don't beat yourself up about it. He was a complete stranger, and a dubious one at that. He took you by surprise. In your shoes, I'd have probably done the same.'

Iris, although she doubted it was true, appreciated the sentiment. 'Thanks for everything. You've been a star. God knows how I'd have coped if you hadn't—'

'Hey,' he said. 'That's what friends are for. Don't go all slushy on me, girl. You take care, right, and we'll catch up soon.'

Iris said goodbye and put down the phone. She was grateful for all he'd done, but worried about it too. The Streets wouldn't have liked giving in to Guy's demands. In fact they'd have been downright furious. How long before they took the opportunity to get their own back on him? And it would all be her fault. She had drawn him into this mess and now he was in as much trouble as she was.

For a while she sat staring blindly in front of her. She didn't see the faded paper, the row of framed certificates or the old East End prints that lined the walls – her head was too full of other pictures. How easy it must be, if you were so inclined, to kill another person. You didn't even need to touch them. One tiny squeeze on the trigger of a gun and . . . A shiver ran through her. What was she getting into? There was still time to leave, to get the hell of here. If her father wanted to reach her, he could do it through Michael.

But then she felt ashamed of her cowardice. Guy had put

himself on the line for her. The least she could do was to show some bloody backbone! It was time to stop being so feeble. There and then she made a decision: whatever the cost, she was going to continue in her search. If her father was out there somewhere, she was going to find him. And a couple of gangsters, no matter how psychotic, were not going to stand in her way.

Chapter Forty-one

He breathes in the cold evening air as he tramps along the street. It gets to his chest, hurts his lungs, but he pushes the pain aside. He's waited too long for this return and the goddamn British weather isn't going to spoil it for him. Pushing his hands deep into his pockets, he carries on regardless. No one knows he is back. Well, not for certain. There may be rumours, but the East End is always full of those.

He stops, ostensibly to look in a shop window, but really just to catch his breath. Kellston has changed since he was last here, but only on the surface. It might look respectable, but underneath it still writhes with a sickness that can never be cured. There's been too much history, too much neglect, for the place ever to recover. History has left its mark. It's left its scars on him too.

He smiles as he sees the trays of jewellery: gold chains, diamond earrings, rubies and emeralds. Perhaps he should get something for Iris. What would she like? He feels a rush of shame at not knowing. He searches out the more subtle pieces, his gaze alighting on a sapphire bracelet. She always used to like the colour blue. Later, he swears, he will come back and buy her something beautiful.

294

As his eyes shift focus, he sees himself reflected in the glass of the shop window. The image startles him. An old grey man with lines on his face. Where have all the years gone? He aches for everything he's lost. He's like a ghost now, a man come back from the grave.

Moving slowly on, he meanders past the busy café. There's a sign outside advertising fancy coffees and freshly made sandwiches. Connolly's had been a greasy spoon in his day, all bacon and eggs and hot strong tea, with a pall of fag smoke hanging over the tables. He'd like to go inside, to sit down for a while, but it's too risky. Anyone could recognise him and this wasn't the time to be taking those kinds of chances.

A bitter wind sweeps along the High Street, making him grit his teeth. He moves on again, crosses the intersection with Station Road and keeps going south. He's almost there now. The next road is Beeston and the one after that is Silverstone. He takes a left when he arrives at Silverstone Road and quickens his pace. The building looms suddenly out of the darkness, a high-walled fortress illuminated by spotlights. He stops in surprise. He hasn't expected anything quite so dramatic.

He walks up to the entrance and stares through the tall wrought-iron gates at all the rows of windows. So this is where his daughter lives. This is Silverstone Heights. It had been an asylum once, he recalls, and some of the original structure is still there, a small squat block to the right and the ornate redbrick arch over the front door. But most of it is new. Scanning the third-floor windows with their neat little balconies, he wonders which ones belong to her flat. There's no way of knowing.

Still, he's glad she's so well protected. It will help him sleep more peacefully tonight. He's tempted to shake the gates, make sure that they're as secure as they look, but can see the CCTV cameras poised on the pillars either side of the gates. He shouldn't hang around. Best to take off before some jumpy security guard picks up the phone and calls the filth.

Chapter Forty-two

A freezing wind was whipping through the dark streets of Kellston. Iris shivered, her hands raw with cold, as she stopped to cross another number off the list. She was getting used to the odd looks she received as she enquired at each house or flat for a man called Fin. This wasn't the kind of area that welcomed casual callers or too much curiosity about the people who lived there. She'd already had a few doors slammed in her face.

It was three days now since she'd talked to her uncle and the third time she had come out to roam the district with Guy. Michael hadn't been too keen on sharing what he knew and it had cost her four pints of Old Peculiar and a spot of gentle blackmail to finally squeeze the information out of him. Didn't he owe her something for all the secrets he'd kept, all the lies she'd been fed?

Out of the short list he'd provided of her father's closest pals, they'd been able to eliminate three of them immediately: Jimmy Neal had been killed in a car crash, Bob Layton had emigrated and Paddy Morris was currently residing at Her Majesty's Pleasure. Only one had remained as a likely prospect. Finlay –

more commonly known as Fin – had been her dad's best mate since school. What Michael wasn't so sure about, however, was whether Finlay had been his Christian or surname. And he couldn't (or so he claimed) recall exactly where he'd lived.

'Somewhere off the High Street,' he'd said unhelpfully. 'I dunno, love. I went there once but it was years ago.'

Iris had got out her pocket A-Z, found the right page and reeled off a dozen street names, but no joy. If anywhere had rung a bell with him, he hadn't been prepared to say. She knew what Michael thought – that she was wasting her time – but she refused to be deterred. Following up any lead was better than doing nothing. It might be a shot in the dark, but it was still worth a go.

Of course, she had done the logical thing first and rung round all the Finlays she could find listed in the phone book. It had been a futile exercise, yielding no results. So many people were ex-directory these days or only using mobiles. And then, apart from the fact that Finlay might not have been his surname, there was also the distinct possibility that he could have moved away. She had tried the electoral register too, noting down the addresses of any local Finlays. They had managed to talk to some of these, but still no fifty-year-old Fin had come to light.

Iris looked up at Guy and pulled a face. 'I'm starting to get that needle in a haystack feeling.'

'Ah,' he said. 'The technical name for that, hun, is coffee deprivation. Come on, let's find somewhere to rest out feet and review our options.'

Iris wasn't going to argue. They'd spent three hours on Thursday evening and another three on Friday slogging round these streets and knocking on doors. All to no avail. Today was Saturday, getting on for five o'clock, and her spirits were beginning to sink. They had been on the go since twelve.

As they tramped along the snowy pavements, Iris was careful

to watch her footing. Only a few days ago a twenty-year-old girl had slipped on the ice and banged her head against the kerb. It had been a freak accident and a fatal one. One moment Jenni Brookner had been happily looking forward to the festive season, the next she'd been whisked off in an ambulance. Now she was down in the basement of Tobias Grand & Sons awaiting Alice's attention.

They stopped outside Connolly's and peered in through the window. The café was busy, packed with Christmas shoppers, but they could see one empty table. They went inside and Guy took off his thick dark overcoat, carefully hanging it over the back of his chair. Underneath he was wearing black jeans and a pale blue sweater. Iris gazed at him. The sweater complemented the intense blueness of his eyes and she wondered if that was why he'd chosen it. And why not? She wasn't without vanity herself. He caught her looking and grinned. Iris quickly sat down, picked up the menu and pretended to examine it.

'Are you hungry?' he said.

Iris shook her head. 'Not really.' Disappointment had blunted her appetite. She thought of all the blank stares she'd experienced over the past few hours, all the undisguised suspicion and downright hostility. Not that she was surprised by any of it. Had some stranger turned up on her own doorstep asking questions, she would have been less than welcoming too.

'Don't let it get you down,' he said. 'For all we know, we might have already hit the jackpot.'

She frowned. 'What do you mean?'

'If your father is hiding out in one of the houses we've been to, he's hardly likely to show himself, is he?' Guy put his elbows on the table, steepled his fingers and lowered his chin on to their tips. 'And this man Fin isn't going to come clean about his identity either, at least not if he's been asked to keep shtum.'

Iris thought back to all the places they had visited, trying to remember if anyone had given even the tiniest indication that they knew what she was talking about. No one came to mind. What would she have done if her dad *had* suddenly appeared? The idea simultaneously alarmed and excited her.

'The point is,' Guy continued, 'that we just don't know. People in the East End are used to keeping quiet, to being less than trusting of strangers. There's a chance we've already stumbled on the right address but just don't realise it. If we have – and if your father *is* there – then by now he's going to know that you're searching for him.'

Iris gave a sigh. 'I'm not even sure I'm doing the right thing, I mean trying to flush him out like this. What if we lead the Streets straight to him?'

'We haven't been followed, I'm pretty certain of that. And what other choice is there? If we wait until Terry gets out of the nick, it's going to be too late. This way we force your father's hand. He's going to be worried about exactly the same thing – that the Streets *are* watching – and if he wants to keep his hiding place secret, he's going to have to find some way of contacting you, of warning you to stay away.'

Iris nodded. She and Guy had done a lot of talking over the past few days. It seemed more than likely that her dad had come back in response to Lizzie's death. 'So you really think he's planning on confronting Terry?'

'Perhaps he feels it's the only way of keeping you safe. Terry's an old-fashioned kind of villain, an-eye-for-an-eye and all that. He's dealt with Tyler, but there were two men at his house the night that Liam was killed. He isn't ever going to let that go. And if he can't find your father, then . . .'

Iris understood without him spelling it out. Terry had lost a son, and she was Sean O'Donnell's daughter. There was more than one way of getting revenge. She shuddered at the thought of it.

'Hey,' Guy said, seeing her expression. 'I don't think you're in any real danger. And especially not at the moment. But the threat of it, of what Terry *might* do when he gets out, could well be enough to push your dad into showing himself. That's probably why Terry's had the boys hassling you, threatening you just enough to prove they mean business.'

Iris dropped her face into her hands. 'Jesus,' she said, 'I should never have come back. If I wasn't here then Terry couldn't—'

'None of this is your fault, Iris. Don't start thinking that way. We need to concentrate, stay focused. We have to try and find your dad before he does something stupid.'

Iris couldn't help speculating on what that something stupid was likely to be. 'But he must know that Terry's going to kill him if he ever shows his face. So what *can* he do?' She already suspected what the answer was likely to be. Her breath caught in her throat as she said, 'You reckon he's going to try and kill Terry, don't you?'

'Do you think your father's capable of that?'

'I don't know,' she replied. 'If you'd asked me two weeks ago I'd have said no, but now I'm not so sure. I don't have a clue as to who he actually is any more.'

'Well, he must have some finer feelings or he wouldn't have bothered coming back. It's you he's trying to protect. '

'Or he just feels guilty,' she said sceptically. 'Does that count as a finer feeling?'

'Maybe you shouldn't be so hard on him. Whatever he did, he lost his family through it. That's a big price for any man to pay.'

Iris knew he was right. It was unfair to pass judgement on someone she hadn't even seen for nineteen years. She was grateful to Guy for defending him, an action she didn't seem capable of at the moment. Maybe she was just too scared to admit to herself how much she wanted to see her father – and how afraid she was of losing him again.

The waitress arrived at their table with her notepad. She was a skinny middle-aged woman with the weary, fretful appearance of someone who'd been on their feet since the crack of dawn.

'Yeah?' she said. 'What's it to be?'

'A latte,' Guy said. 'And a couple of toasted sandwiches. Cheese is fine.' He looked over at Iris. 'You can manage a sandwich, can't you?'

Iris glanced at her watch. It would be another few hours before she got anything substantial to eat, so she nodded. Then, as the waitress hovered impatiently, she tried to decide what to drink. She considered a hot chocolate, but decided she was more in need of energy than comfort. 'And a large cappuccino, thanks.'

Iris waited until the woman had left and then turned her face back towards Guy. 'I wish I knew how your mother had managed to persuade Terry to leave us alone all those years ago. Did she ever say anything to you?'

Guy shook his head. 'You'll have to talk to Michael about that.'

'Believe me, I've tried. He isn't shifting from his original story. He just keeps on insisting that because he was at the Hope that night, Lizzie was able to provide him with an alibi. But that doesn't explain why Terry didn't have a go at Mum – or me, come to that. I doubt if Terry Street's got too many scruples about terrifying children.'

Guy, unable to refute the suggestion, gave a light shrug of his shoulders. 'So what does your mother say?'

'I haven't asked her.'

He looked surprised. 'Why ever not?'

'Don't get me wrong, she's great, she really is, but this would only freak her out. It took me over an hour to persuade her that I wasn't going to fall apart after splitting up with Luke. If I told

301

her what I was doing now, she'd be on the next train down. She's convinced that Dad's dead, has been for years, and thinks I should accept it too. She doesn't even know that Michael's told me about what he did that night.'

'Isn't he going to tell her?'

'Are you kidding?' she said. Her mouth broke into a grin. 'No sane man would willingly bring down the wrath of Kathleen O'Donnell on his head.'

'Is she that scary?'

Iris gave a soft laugh. 'Not unless she's roused, but this would certainly rouse her. She'll be mad as hell if she thinks he's been giving away the family secrets. Anyway, I've made a deal with Michael – I'll keep quiet about it if he does. She's not likely to ring him again in a hurry; she only called him last week because she got worried about all the questions I was asking. At that point he hadn't told me anything so he didn't need to lie about it.'

'But at some point you're going to have to—'

'I'll cross that bridge when I come to it,' Iris said quickly. She couldn't afford to have her mother on her back right now. And she couldn't face that difficult conversation they would need to have either – about why she'd been lied to, about why she'd never been told the full story of her father's disappearance. She knew what her mother would claim – that it had been done to protect her – but the whole deceit still rankled. Iris had grown up wondering if it was her fault that he'd left. If only she'd been told just a little of the truth . . .

She was about to try to explain this to Guy when the waitress came back with their order. The woman plonked the tray gracelessly in the middle of the table, dumped the bill in a saucer and left without a word.

Guy grinned. 'Well, you can't fault the quality of the service.'

Iris picked up her cappuccino, took a sip and smiled. 'They're renowned for it. You could learn a lot about customer service from the staff in here.'

'I'll bear it in mind.'

Iris, after the interruption, decided it was time to stop talking about herself. It was all she ever seemed to do these days. Despite all the hours they'd spent together, she still knew very little about Guy Wilder; he was extremely good at deflecting questions about his own life and feelings.

'So what about *your* dad?' she said. 'Do you ever see him?'

Guy bit into his toasted sandwich, chewed it for a while and swallowed. 'No,' he said shortly.

Iris tore off a corner of her own sandwich and waited.

Guy let out a sigh. 'You want the truth?' he said. He paused for a second. 'I don't know who he is and I don't give a damn. His name's not even on my birth certificate. From what I can gather, I'm the result of a five-minute fumble in the backseat of a car. She was only a kid. What kind of a man sleeps with a fourteen-year-old?'

Iris lifted the piece of sandwich to her mouth, and then abruptly put it back down on to her plate again. She had just had an uncomfortable thought. 'What if it wasn't a man?' she said. She remembered the way Michael had talked about Lizzie, his obvious affection for her. Perhaps this connection she felt to Guy had its roots in something closer to home. 'I mean, what if it was a boy, someone the same age as herself?'

Guy looked at her for a moment before he started to laugh. 'No way,' he said. 'Don't even go there. Your uncle isn't my father, I can assure you of that.'

'But how can you be sure? They were friends, they used to hang out together.'

'Mates, yeah,' he said, 'but nothing more. For one, Michael was too young to drive and for two, my mother – even at that tender age – wouldn't have dreamed of sleeping with someone

303

who wasn't useful to her.' He picked up his coffee and gazed at her over the rim of the mug. 'We're not cousins, Iris. The man who fathered me was just some lowlife who flashed a few quid, had his wicked way and buggered off.'

Iris felt a wave of relief wash over her. Had there been a blood tie, it would have changed the way she felt about him. Although even if they were cousins it wouldn't have been illegal for them to . . . She stopped the thought in its tracks, feeling her cheeks begin to burn. What was she doing? It was only days since she had split up from Luke and with everything else that was going on, now was hardly the time to be considering another relationship.

'Let's just concentrate on finding *your* father,' Guy said.

'And when we do?' She paused. 'Well, *if* we do.'

'Then we can all work together to try and sort this out.'

Iris suddenly became aware of a quartet of pretty girls, young women really – they must have been in their early twenties – sitting nearby. Their eyes were all fixed on Guy and he was clearly the topic of their conversation. A ripple of giggles emanated from the table.

'I think you have a fan club,' she said.

Guy glanced sideways and then back at Iris. 'What makes you so sure it's me they're interested in? Perhaps they're in the Sappho club. They could be admiring your stunning red hair.'

Iris smiled. 'Oh, spare me the false modesty.'

He grinned back, leaned forward and took her hand. 'Then perhaps you should pretend to be my girlfriend in case they try to rob me of my innocence.'

'Well, should that unfortunate situation arise, I'm sure you'll find a way to cope,' she said, although she didn't immediately move her hand away.

Chapter Forty-three

Alice Avery had a smile on her face as she walked along the supermarket aisle. Pausing by the men's toiletries, she scrutinised the vast display of shampoo, shaving foam and razors. She picked up jars and bottles and put them down again. It pleased her to be choosing things for Toby, to be making the kind of purchases that other women took for granted.

Alice had never lived with a man before. Not that they were, strictly speaking, living together, but Toby had been in her flat for the last three days and was likely to be staying for most of the following week. His bruises were starting to fade but were still too obvious for him to return to the family home and the scrutiny of Gerald Grand. Secretly, she hoped that he would never go back, and to this end – having heard that the way to a man's heart is through his stomach – she was feeding him three large meals a day.

Unsure of what he used in the bathroom, Alice went for the more expensive products rather than the supermarket own-brands. She had a moment's hesitation. Perhaps, after lending Toby all her savings, she should be taking more care over how much she was spending. But she quickly pushed the thought aside. She was working, wasn't she? She could afford a few luxuries. As Alice dropped the items into the trolley, she felt a thrill sweep through her body. How odd, she thought, that something as mundane as shopping could make her heart beat so fast.

At the chill section, Alice studied what was on offer, her eyes sweeping over the meat, fish and poultry. She was a good cook, had even gone on a few courses in the past, but the opportunities to show off her expertise had all but disappeared in recent years. Her mother didn't care for what she referred to as 'that fancy stuff' and making complicated meals for one never seemed worth the effort. Still, perhaps she shouldn't be too experimental. Toby's tastes seemed to run more towards burgers and Chinese takeaways than anything more exotic. Eventually, she plumped for two large steaks and a corn-fed chicken. She would grill the steaks tonight and make a roast dinner tomorrow.

At the thought of what would happen tomorrow, her stomach began to churn. But there was no going back now. She had told Toby, and Toby had called Danny Street so she had no choice but to go through with it. And perhaps it was meant to be, for why else would God have delivered poor Jenni Brookner so fortuitously? The moment this profane thought entered her head, her eyes automatically rose towards the heavens and her fingers gripped the trolley. But there was no clap of thunder, no divine retribution, and gradually she relaxed again.

Alice made her way to the shelves of alcohol and picked out three bottles of wine, a bottle of vodka and twelve cans of lager. She wasn't sure when she'd get the chance to shop again and Toby was always in a better mood after a few drinks. Not that she blamed him for getting tetchy. While she was out at work, he was trapped in the flat all day with nothing but the TV for company. Still, he'd been decidedly more upbeat since she'd got home last night and told him about Jenni Brookner. Well, at least he had been after that one small altercation.

'Is she a looker?' he'd asked.

The question had made her squirm. 'A what?'

'You know,' he said. 'Not a dog or anything?'

'What's the matter with you?' Alice had snapped back. She had found his question both insensitive and crude. Or maybe she was just old-fashioned when it came to that kind of talk.

'I was only asking,' he'd said. 'There's no need to have a fit about it.'

'I'm not having a fit. I just don't think we should be . . . well, discussing her like this.'

And then, of course, Toby had gone into a sulk, the corners of his mouth turning down in that all too familiar style. 'You mean *I* shouldn't.' He'd glared at her for a second. 'I'm not asking for my own benefit. I'm not some kind of perv. Only if Danny Street gets there on Sunday and finds that we've provided some old crone—'

'He won't,' Alice had insisted. 'For heaven's sake, she's only twenty.'

Toby had shrugged, turned away and given her the silent treatment. And of course she had backed down. She couldn't bear it when he was cross with her. And she dreaded him leaving. What would she do if he walked out? Therefore, in order to placate him, to please him, she'd spent the next ten minutes describing the tragic Jenni Brookner in intimate detail. He'd been happy after that, and when he was happy he was affectionate.

Alice headed for the checkout, smiling again. Had that been their first major row? All serious couples had rows; it was normal, natural. And it was almost worth the pain for the making up that came after. She blushed a little at the memory.

With Toby she did things she had never even imagined before. But it was all right, wasn't it, because he loved her and she loved him. It was just the two of them now against the world.

As Alice waited in the queue, her thoughts inevitably returned to Sunday night. She was supposed to do the embalming on Monday, but William would be none the wiser. Toby had keys and they would use the rear door. No one would see the lights unless they came round the back. Her only concern – well, not perhaps her only one, but the only one she could face at the moment – was that Gerald Grand, if he'd recovered from his flu, might come in early on Monday morning and start poking around. William, like Iris, rarely came down to the basement, but Gerald liked to keep an eye on things. He was always looking over her shoulder, always checking up on her. How would she explain that a job booked in for nine o'clock had already been completed? They would need a cover story just in case.

The awfulness of what they were doing descended on her again, the horror swooping down like a devilish crow pecking at her conscience. She closed her eyes briefly and took a deep breath. She had sworn she would never do it again, but what choice did she have? She had to remind herself that no one was getting hurt. Yes, it was dubious, certainly immoral, but it wasn't strictly illegal. And it had to be endured if Toby was to be saved. He had made a mistake, that was all, a stupid mistake. Villains like the Streets knew how to exploit people, how to take advantage. None of this was really Toby's fault. All he had done was to play a few games of cards – a game that was probably fixed – and now that blood-sucking leech Danny had latched on to him and wouldn't let go.

The thought of seeing Danny Street again filled her with dread. She still felt guilty over leaving Iris to deal with him on her own. She remembered standing on the stairs at Tobias

Grand & Sons and listening to him rant. He was vile, wrong in the head. She had seen what he'd done to Toby and it made her sick with fear.

The queue shifted forward and Alice found herself next in line. Forcing her worries from her mind, she started to empty the trolley. She wondered if the middle-aged woman behind her carrying a basket containing a few microwave meals for one, a pint of milk and three small tins of cat food, was examining what she'd bought. Alice often stared at the shopping of the person in front, gauging from their purchases whether they were single or attached, always envying those who were buying for two. And now, incredibly, she was one of those people. She was part of a couple. She had Toby, beautiful Toby, and for all her fears she wouldn't change that for anything.

Chapter Forty-four

Despite the apparently casual nature of the gathering, Iris had the feeling she was about to go on trial. It was eight o'clock on Saturday night and she'd returned to the little terraced house in Lemon Road to find Vita, Rick and Michael installed in the kitchen. The sudden silence as she entered the room was enough to inform her that she'd been the subject of their conversation.

'Don't stop on my account,' Iris said.

'We were just . . .' Vita began. She paused and chewed on her lip for a moment. 'Well, we're worried about you. All this stuff about your dad.'

'Stuff?' Iris repeated abruptly.

'You know, knocking on doors and everything. Are you sure it's safe? There are some odd people living round here. And you look exhausted. You've been out for the past couple of nights and most of today. You'll drop if you don't start taking care of yourself.'

Iris sighed. She really didn't need this. Her feet were aching and she was desperate for a long, hot soak in the bath. 'I'm fine.'

'You're not fine. Grab a chair and sit down.'

Iris, too tired to argue, did as she was told. Whatever they had to say, she would be forced to listen to at some time or another. Better to get it over and done with. She glanced at Michael. He shifted in his seat and looked uncomfortable. 'So?' she said. 'I take it you're not here to offer your support and ask me how it's going.'

Michael frowned. He made a shrugging gesture, lifting and dropping his heavy shoulders. 'It's like Vita said. We're just worried about you, love. You're going to make yourself ill if you carry on like this.'

'So why don't you do something useful instead of criticising? You could come out and help us look. You're the only one who might actually recognise this Fin guy if we come across him.'

'No one's criticising you,' Vita said. 'But don't you think that if your dad wanted to be found he'd get in touch? All he has to do is pick up the phone.'

'It's not that simple, is it? You all know what he did, and that Terry Street isn't going to forgive him for it. He has to be careful. If he contacts me and the Streets find out about it then—'

'But you've got no proof that he *is* back,' Michael interrupted. 'Where's the proof, love? There's not one bit of evidence to suggest he's come within shouting distance of Kellston in the last nineteen years.'

'I've been threatened,' Iris said, 'and more than once. What does that tell you?' She looked around at their faces and her heart sank. 'Or do you think that I've been making all that up, that I'm going quietly crazy? Is that what's going on here?'

'No,' Vita said quickly. 'Of course not.'

But Iris could imagine what they'd been discussing before she came back: her loss of the baby, depression, problems with

311

Luke . . . She shook her head and stared at Michael. 'You had a fight with Danny Street over this.'

'Not because I thought Sean was back. I've never thought that. It was only because of what that kid from Tobias Grand & Sons told me.' The kid, Iris realised, being Toby. 'He said Danny had a go at you the day before the funeral. I wasn't having that. And I was upset over what'd happened to Lizzie. It was stupid. I wasn't thinking straight.'

Vita, who was sitting next to her, gently touched Iris on the wrist. 'No one's saying that the threats weren't real. But maybe they just stemmed from idle rumours. Maybe someone, someone like that old guy Jenks, thought he saw your dad – or maybe he made the whole thing up to try and squeeze some money out of the Streets, and out of you. I mean, that would explain why they've been bothering you, wouldn't it? With Jenks dead, the Streets have no way of knowing whether what he'd told them was true or not.'

'Is that what you think?' Iris said, turning to Michael. 'Do you really believe they'd be hassling me this much, wasting so much time on me, because of a few idle rumours?'

Michael didn't answer directly. He folded his arms across his chest and deliberately avoided her gaze. 'Your dad's got no reason to come back.'

Me! Iris wanted to shout at him. *Aren't I reason enough?* Instead she took a deep breath and counted to ten. Getting mad wasn't going to help; in fact it would only add credence to what they already suspected – that she was in the midst of some kind of nervous breakdown, even suffering from delusions about the extent of the danger she was actually in. She had thought they were on her side, but that was clearly not the case. But she mustn't lose her cool. She had to try and stay calm, to answer all their objections quietly and rationally. 'Because of Lizzie,' she explained softly. 'Now she's dead, there's nothing to stop Terry

Street from doing whatever he wants. Guy thinks he wants revenge and that the way to get it is through me. And it makes sense. You have to see that.'

'But you have no actual *evidence*,' Vita said, echoing Michael's use of the word.

Iris looked at her despairingly. 'What kind of evidence do you want? For Dad to walk in through the door? For me to be found murdered in some dark alley?'

It had been a stupid thing to say. She heard the gasp that came from Vita's throat. 'If you're that worried, Iris, you need to go to the police.'

'I've told you why I can't do that. And Guy thinks that if we can find Dad, find him before he tries to get to Terry Street, then we can stop him from doing anything stupid.'

'Guy thinks, Guy thinks,' Michael repeated roughly. He took a swig from the can of beer that was in front of him and replaced it with a bang on the table. 'I don't get what any of this has to do with him.'

Iris moved her hand out of sight, laying it on her thigh as her fingers clenched into a fist of frustration. 'He's Lizzie's son, isn't he? He knows things. Like the fact that she made sure Terry never came after you after Liam was killed.'

'He didn't come after me because I had nothing to do with it.'

'And since when did that ever stop a thug like Terry Street? You helped Dad get away, didn't you? You gave him money and clothes. He might even have told you where he was planning on going.'

'He didn't.'

'Yes, but Terry wouldn't have known that, would he? You're Dad's brother, the first person he'd turn to when he was in trouble. Well, apart from Mum, but that option wasn't open to him after what he'd done.'

313

There was a short silence. Iris looked around again, hoping to find a person who might actually support her. Rick was the only one who hadn't spoken. When she'd talked to Michael on Wednesday night, he'd told her that, until recently, Rick hadn't known anything about the past, but she wasn't so sure. Once Michael had had a few drinks his tongue tended to run away with him. He could have told Rick the whole story, every gory detail, and not recalled a thing about it the following morning.

'So what do you think?'

Rick hesitated, glancing at his wife as if he wasn't sure of what to say. 'Er . . . well, I think Vita's got a point. Whether your dad's back or not, you should tell the cops if you think you need protecting.'

'But I can't do that, can I? Why isn't anyone listening to me? If he gets arrested by the police then—'

'Oh, for fuck's sake, Iris!' Michael's voice was filled with exasperation. 'This has to stop. Your dad was a selfish bastard. He ran away because he was too scared to take responsibility for what he'd done. He abandoned you and your mother and didn't give a toss about the consequences. He's never coming back, not in a million years, and it's time that you accepted that.'

Iris stared at him, feeling the blood drain from her face. She couldn't believe what she was hearing. A lump rose to her throat and she tried to swallow it down. 'You're wrong,' she eventually managed to mumble through her tears. 'You're all wrong.' Then she pushed back the chair, dashed out of the kitchen and ran quickly up the short staircase. As she reached the top she heard Vita say reprovingly, 'Jesus, Michael, there was no need for that.'

Iris went into her bedroom and shut the door. She slumped down on the single bed, leaned forward and put her head in her hands. She and Michael had never argued before, had never even exchanged a cross word. Her whole body was trembling.

Michael didn't know what he was talking about. Her dad *was* out there somewhere. She was as sure of it as she was her own name. She was his little girl, wasn't she? He wouldn't let her down. And he wouldn't let Terry Street hurt her.

After a while she heard the front door slam. Wiping the tears from her face, she stood up and went over to the window. Michael and Rick were striding down the road, probably heading for The Dog. That was Michael's solution to everything, she thought bitterly. Just put your head in the sand, have another drink and pretend that nothing's happened.

'Iris?' Vita called up the stairs. 'Are you okay?'

Iris shouted through the closed door, 'I'll be down in a minute.' She wanted some time alone to gather her thoughts. She couldn't stay here, she decided, not with everyone against her. Even Vita didn't believe that her father was in Kellston. Not that she'd said it in so many words, but it didn't take much to read between the lines.

Iris took off her boots and socks and flexed her aching feet. She gazed around the room that had been decorated according to Candice's taste: everything in shades of pink, the paintwork and the curtains, the built-in cupboards. There were posters of boy bands pinned above the bed along with some photographs. A couple of Barbies, dolls Candice had probably grown out of, lay discarded on the dresser. Iris sighed and turned again to the window. It was time for her to move on and at the moment there was only one place she could go – back to Silverstone Heights. The thought filled her with dread, but what was the alternative?

Lemon Road was bathed in a thin orangey light from the streetlamps. The remains of the last snowfall still lay on the ground, a stripe of crisp white ice by the front garden walls, a grey dirty slush on the rest of the pavement and in the gutters. She watched as Michael and Rick turned the corner and disappeared. Were they talking about her, she wondered, discussing her state of mind, her terrible *obsessions*? She felt a spurt of frustration. But this was swiftly followed by a wave of sadness and regret. She didn't want to fall out with her uncle. The past, which he must have tried so hard to leave behind, was coming back to haunt him too. Perhaps she shouldn't judge him too harshly.

She was about to go downstairs when her eyes alighted on a man walking slowly along the road. He was on the other side, coming from the opposite direction to the one that Michael and Rick had taken, and was stopping occasionally to peer through the gloom at the houses. Checking the numbers, she thought. He was tall and broad-shouldered, wearing a dark overcoat and a hat that was pulled down low on his forehead. When he was about twenty yards away, he paused again to light a cigarette. She saw the match blaze briefly before he extinguished it with a flick of his wrist and dropped it on the ground. There was something about that gesture that set off a spark in her memory. Then he looked up and stared directly at her window. She only caught a fleeting glimpse of his face, but it was enough to send her pulse racing: a face of middle age, with a strong chin, heavy brows and a full mouth. He was the right height too and the right build. It was him! Oh Jesus Christ, it was him!

Iris dashed down the stairs, flung open the front door and ran outside.

'What is it?' she heard Vita call out. 'What's going on?'

The slush was icy beneath her bare feet, but Iris hardly noticed. She sprinted along the short path, out of the gate and into the street. Her breath was coming in short, excited bursts and she could feel her heart pumping. 'Dad!' she yelled.

The man had already passed the house. At the sound of her voice he stopped and looked over his shoulder.

Iris dodged between the parked cars and ran across the road, not even thinking about traffic. She was only feet from him now and in seconds she would be able to touch him, to throw herself into his arms. He'd come back! Her daddy had come back for her!

But then she saw him clearly for the first time. He was about the right age, but his features were completely wrong. The eyes were small and brown, the nose too flat and wide. Even his mouth, which at a distance had seemed so familiar, was quite different to her father's. She stopped dead in her tracks, anguish sweeping through her.

'I . . . I'm sorry,' she stuttered. 'I thought . . .'

The man looked confused and then embarrassed. His gaze quickly swept over her, taking in her dishevelled state, her wide eyes and naked feet. *A loony*, she could almost hear him thinking. *A mad woman. One of those Care in the Community cases.*

'I thought . . .' she began again, but her mouth was too dry to continue.

Suddenly Vita was beside her, gently taking her arm. 'Sorry,' she said briskly to the man. 'We thought you were someone else.'

Iris felt absurdly grateful for the 'We', as if its utterance somehow proved that she was not insane, not the only one to have mistaken his identity. She felt the tears gathering under her lashes and tried to blink them away.

The man stared at them both for a moment, gave an uneasy nod and continued on his way.

'Come on,' Vita said softly, 'let's get inside before we both freeze to death.'

'I was sure it was him,' Iris managed to murmur.

'I know. It's dark. It was an easy mistake to make.'

Iris nodded. Her disappointment was almost too much to bear. She felt like a kid at Christmas, a kid who'd been given the present she'd always wanted and then had it cruelly snatched away.

They crossed the road and went back into the house. Vita shut the door. 'Look, why don't you run yourself a bath and relax for half an hour. I'll order a takeaway. It'll be here by the time you come down.'

'Thanks,' Iris said. She was aware now of the coldness of her feet, of the ice between her toes. She wrapped her arms around her, starting to shiver despite the warmth of the hall.

'And then we can have a chat,' Vita said. She patted Iris on the arm.

There was something overly solicitous in the gesture, something that set alarm bells off in Iris's head. 'A chat?'

'Just the two of us.'

Iris frowned at her, the truth gradually dawning. 'Christ, you think I'm losing the plot, don't you?'

'No,' Vita said. 'Don't be daft. I don't think that at all. But you've got to admit that you've been through a tough time recently. These things can get to you. They all add up, one stress piling on another, and before you know it—'

'So did you ever find out where Rick really got that money from?' Iris snapped back defensively.

Vita looked puzzled. 'What's that got to do with anything?'

The words sprang out of her mouth before Iris had time to consider them properly. 'You don't think it's odd, that thief nicking his wallet from outside a club owned by the Streets?'

'For God's sake, Iris, what are you suggesting?'

This would have been the time for Iris to apologise, to claim she was upset and didn't know what she was saying, but a streak of stubbornness prevented her from going there. She was sick of being judged, of being on the receiving end of other people's pity. *Poor old Iris who lost her baby and her boyfriend and now imagines that her father's coming home to rescue her.* Turning away, she started walking up the stairs. 'I'm just saying that it's odd, a bit too much of a coincidence.'

Vita followed her up and into the bedroom. 'You can't say something like that and then just walk away. What's going on in that head of yours? What exactly are you accusing Rick of?'

Iris pulled on her boots and began to gather her belongings. She had to get out of here before she really did go mad. She glanced at Vita, saw the mixture of anger and bewilderment in her friend's dark eyes, and hesitated. But she was too wound up, too despairing to stop now. 'You do the maths. The Streets have been threatening me. Rick's been getting cash from the Streets. I tell you things, you probably pass them on to Rick. People like the Streets tend to pay for their information.'

'You're crazy,' Vita retorted. And then, realising what she'd said, her long slender hand rose quickly to her mouth.

Iris forced out a laugh. 'Well then, it's probably better if I go and be crazy somewhere else.'

'But you can't actually believe . . . God, we're your friends, Iris. Rick would never do something like that.'

Iris could cope with the anger, but the pain on Vita's face cut her to the quick. What had she done? It had been stupid, hurtful. But there was no way to salvage the situation. The words had been uttered and couldn't be taken back. 'I'm sorry,' she said stiffly. 'I really am, but the truth is I don't know what to believe any more. That's why it's better if I leave.'

'And go where?'

'Back to the Heights. Luke's paid the rent to the end of January. The place is sitting there empty so I may as well use it.'

Vita didn't argue. 'If that's how you feel.' She stood watching silently as Iris stuffed her clothes and make-up into a bag. When the packing was done, she said, 'Let me call you a cab at least. I can't give you a lift. I had a few drinks earlier on.'

Iris shook her head. 'Thanks, but I'd rather walk. I need some air.'

They went downstairs together and stood for a few awkward seconds in the hall before Iris opened the door and stepped outside. She looked back at Vita, but couldn't think of anything to say. There wasn't anything *to* say. She had crossed a line. She had broken the bond between them and shattered their friendship into a thousand tiny pieces.

Chapter Forty-five

Iris shifted the bag on to her shoulder and began to walk. By the time she got to the High Street she was filled with remorse. She wanted to turn around, to run back to Vita's and tell her she was sorry. But she couldn't. Until she found her father there was no going back. It was only then, when the truth was out, that bridges might eventually start to be rebuilt. But would Vita ever forgive her for what she'd said? Iris screwed up her face. Whether her suspicions about Rick Howard were right or wrong, she should never have voiced them.

A few snowflakes had begun to fall. They gathered on her hair and the shoulders of her coat. She wiped her eyes and marched steadily on. It was still early, not yet nine o'clock, and there were plenty of people around. Most of them were girls dressed in their Saturday night attire: short skirts, high heels and slogan-carrying skimpy tops. Apparently immune to the cold, they were standing at the bus stops, laughing and joking, waiting to be transported to the glories of the West End. Some of them were drinking, their hands clasped around bottles of cheap cider and cans of Special Brew. It was too expensive to drink much in the clubs, more economical to get smashed before they got there.

Iris let out a sigh, trying to remember the last time *she'd* been so carefree. The wild days of her youth felt like a million years ago. How had everything become so complicated, so serious? She yearned for the superficial pleasures of the past. Since returning to Kellston, every part of her life had started to unravel. And yet she couldn't be entirely sorry about coming back, not if it meant that she would, eventually, be reunited with her father.

Five minutes later, as she was approaching the corner of Silverstone Road, a dark blue car slowed and drew up beside her. Iris glanced at it nervously. The windows were tinted and she couldn't see the driver. She walked a little faster, moving in towards the shelter of the shops, but the car continued to cruise along beside her. It was a fancy low-slung motor, the kind of car that Chris or Danny Street might drive. Her whole body tensed with a shudder of fright. She was about to make a run for it when she heard the faint whir of a descending window. A voice called out, 'Iris!'

Iris recognised the voice. She stopped abruptly, looked over her shoulder and saw Guy Wilder leaning over the passenger seat. Trying to appear casual, as if she hadn't been about to attempt a one-hundred-metre sprint, she strolled over to the car and leaned down. 'What are you doing here?'

'Your friend – Vita is it? – rang me at the bar. She's worried about you.'

'Oh.' Iris wasn't sure whether to be annoyed or pleased. On the one hand it was galling that Vita felt her incapable of coping, but on the other it was reassuring that she had taken the trouble to call. Surely that meant she still cared? Or at the very least, cared enough not to want her to be on her own.

'Well, don't just stand there,' he said.

'Where are we going?'

'My place,' he said. 'Unless you've had enough of me for today. I thought you might be in need of some company.'

Iris hesitated. She *did* want to be with him, but not through some misguided sense of responsibility. She'd had her fill of other people's concern for one night. 'I'm all right, you know. You don't have to do this.'

'I'm not doing it because I have to.' He grinned and pushed open the door. 'Can you stop being so damn proud for just a minute and get in the goddamn car? I'm getting snow on the upholstery.'

She smiled, climbed in and pulled her seatbelt across. 'So why are you driving this? What happened to your car?'

'My keys were upstairs so I borrowed Noah's.'

Which meant he must have rushed straight out to find her after Vita's call. She sank back into the seat, trying not to look too pleased about this snippet of information. As he pulled away from the kerb she said, 'Did Vita tell you what happened?'

'Only the edited version. Something about a row with your uncle?'

Iris nodded. 'That's how it started. They were all waiting for me when I got back tonight, Vita, Rick and Michael, gathered round the table like the three wise men.' She gave a short mirthless laugh. 'Well, two men and a woman. They've got it into their heads that all this "stuff" about my dad is garbage, that he hasn't come back, isn't ever likely to, and that I shouldn't be searching for him. We had what might be called a frank exchange of views. It all got a bit out of hand.'

'Jesus,' he said. 'Poor you.'

'And then . . .' She paused, unsure about telling him the rest of the story. But now wasn't the time to be holding back - she either trusted him or she didn't. 'Well, I was upstairs, looking out of the window, and I thought I saw him. Dad, I mean.'

323

Guy turned his head sharply. 'What?'

'Except it wasn't him,' Iris quickly admitted. 'I went rushing out into the street like a madwoman, no shoes or anything, ran up to this total stranger and made a complete and utter ass of myself.'

'And now Vita thinks that you're losing your marbles.'

'Pretty much.' She waited a moment and then asked in a small voice, 'Do you?'

'No,' he said, touching her lightly on the shoulder. 'God, of course not! Don't ever think that. You've been knocking on doors, searching for him all day. Then you have a row about him. I get it. I really do. He was bound to be on your mind.'

'Thanks,' she said, relieved. Somehow the fact that one person believed in her sanity was enough.

'And that's when you decided to leave?'

Iris pulled a face. 'Not exactly. Vita got all . . . well, anxious about it. Not that I blame her, it must have seemed pretty nuts my rushing out into the street like that. But by then I'd had enough. I knew I was on the brink of another of *those* conversations and I just couldn't face it and . . .'

He waited for her to go on. When she didn't he said, 'And?'

She took a deep breath. 'And I then made it ten times worse by accusing Rick of collaborating with the Streets.'

'Ouch,' Guy said. 'You don't do things by halves, do you?'

Iris groaned. 'I wish I'd kept my big mouth shut. I don't think she'll ever forgive me.'

'Give it time,' he said softly. 'Once the dust has had time to settle . . .'

'You think?'

'She called me, didn't she? She can't hate you that much.'

Iris hoped it was true. She was quiet as Guy took a left, swung into the small car park belonging to Wilder's and pulled up. He switched off the ignition and the lights but didn't make

324

any attempt to get out. The snow was falling faster now, obscuring their view out of the windscreen. He seemed lost in thought and it was a while before he turned to look at her again. 'Is this all my fault?'

'What do you mean?' Iris said.

'If you'd never met me, if we'd never talked, then . . .'

'Then what?' she said, suddenly worried that he was regretting ever having come to find her. 'I'd still be in the same place, still looking for my father whether I'd met you or not.'

'Would you?'

Iris thought back to that moment in the Hope & Anchor, to those few fateful seconds when Albert Jenks had leaned down and said those words: *Don't you want to know where your daddy is?* 'Yes,' she said firmly.

Guy leaned over the wheel and his face twisted. 'But you don't know what Terry Street's really like.'

'I've got a pretty good idea. If his sons are anything to go by . . .'

'Except he's smarter than his sons.'

'He can't be that smart,' she said, with more courage than she felt. 'Bearing in mind where he is.'

'Clever enough to get away with the murder of my mother.'

Iris remembered the lean grey-haired man with the cold eyes and the scars on his throat. She shivered, wrapping her arms around her chest.

'You're not on your own,' Guy said. 'Don't ever think that.'

Their eyes met and some kind of understanding passed between them. He smiled. 'So, ready to face the world?'

'As I'll ever be.'

They got out of the car and walked across the snowy forecourt. When they were almost at the door, Guy reached out and slipped his hand into hers.

Chapter Forty-six

By ten o'clock the bar had filled up and there was barely space to move. Iris was sitting at a table near the back, picking distractedly at a plate of tapas whilst turning over the events of the day. Every now and again she delved into her bag, took out her phone and checked to see whether there were any messages. But no one, it appeared, had anything more to say to her.

Guy was making one of his regular circuits of the room, meeting and greeting the customers, making everyone feel welcome. She raised her eyes to follow his progress. It was easy to see why the place was so popular: the bar was friendly, laid-back, but it also had a buzz to it. It was Guy, she thought, who created the atmosphere, his presence like a fizzing current of electricity.

Iris sipped carefully on a glass of wine – after her recent indulgences she was taking it easy – and forced herself to look away. She didn't want him to catch her staring. On a screen on the far wall, a clip of an old black and white movie was playing. She concentrated on this for a while, peering through the crowd, before turning her attention to the counter. Noah was perched on a high-backed chrome stool with a slender, very beautiful black girl sitting beside him. The one who'd been giving him grief perhaps? Iris could see how she might be high maintenance.

Noah, if not exactly effusive, had been a little friendlier on her arrival than on previous occasions. He'd even managed a smile so she supposed that was progress. She wondered how much he knew about the situation. Had he been told the truth about Guy's recent absences, about their daily slog around the streets of Kellston, or did he just think she was the latest in what was possibly a long line of conquests? She wasn't sure why it mattered, but it did. She wanted him to like her, to accept her.

It was another ten minutes before Guy came back and slid into the seat across the table. 'Are you sure you're okay down here?'

'More than okay.' She could have gone to the flat upstairs, but preferred, for the moment, to be in the company of others. Solitude would only give her time to dwell on what had happened. Not that she could chase it from her mind even if she wanted to, but at least there were distractions in the bar. 'You've got a job to do. Don't worry about me.'

'Well, I'm on a break now so you have my undivided attention.'

Iris was pleased to have him to herself, even if was only for half an hour. 'So tell me about Noah. You never said how the two of you met.'

Guy glanced over at his friend, looked back at Iris and grinned. 'It was at that fancy school of ours. We were the two misfits, the ones who were always in trouble. He was the only black kid in the year and I was the only pleb. Those things still mattered back then.' He raised his eyes to the ceiling. 'God, what am I talking about? I'm sure they still do. Neither of us belonged so we were natural allies.'

'Is that his girlfriend?' Iris said.

'Ah, the lovely Serena. She's a model in case you hadn't guessed.'

'She's very beautiful.'

'On the outside,' he said.

Iris heard the note of hostility in his voice. 'You don't like her.'

Guy gave a shrug, that familiar closed look coming over his face. Iris was curious now about Serena: was his dislike of her down to the simple fact she was always messing Noah around or was it rooted in a more personal experience? She would have liked to find out, but sensing the bad blood between them quickly changed the subject. 'So, back to this fancy school of yours - did you actually manage to survive without getting expelled?'

'Yeah,' he said, 'despite my finest efforts. I can only presume that they needed the fees.' He leaned forward, put his elbows on the table and gave her one of his wry smiles. 'Or maybe the headmaster was too terrified of my mother to even think about going there.'

Iris lifted her brows. From what she'd heard about Lizzie Street, that might not be too far off the truth. 'So when did you get this place?' She knew she was asking a lot of questions, but this was the first time since they'd met that Guy actually seemed prepared to talk about himself. She wasn't going to waste the opportunity.

'It came on the market about three years ago. To be honest it was a bit of a dump, but we could see it had potential. Noah's the one with the nous – he's got a business degree – and he reckoned we could make it work, but we didn't have enough cash so . . .'

'So?' Iris urged.

'I knew someone who had.' He bowed his head for a second

as if the memory pained him. 'I went cap in hand to my mother and begged for a loan. It wasn't my proudest moment, but there was no bank in the world that was going to touch me.'

Iris, knowing how he felt about Lizzie, could imagine how much that had cost him. 'But you made a success of it,' she said. 'It doesn't matter where the money came from. Look at this place, it's heaving.'

Guy frowned as if all the success in the world couldn't make up for the way it had been bankrolled. 'You wouldn't say that if you truly understood the nature of Terry's business. We're talking prostitution, extortion, drugs – and that's just for starters. Would you really want all that on your conscience?'

'But you didn't get the cash from Terry,' she said. Even as she spoke she knew how disingenuous the argument was. 'Well, even if it did have dodgy origins, you created something good out of it. You can't hate yourself for doing that.'

Guy shook his head. 'You have no idea how vile that man is.'

Iris, aware that she was probably near the top of Terry Street's list of 'Things to Do' when he got out of jail, suppressed a shudder. 'I'm hardly his number one fan myself.'

'You don't know the half of it. Even when I was a kid . . .' He stopped suddenly, as if he'd said too much. Picking up the bottle of wine, he added a splash to her almost full glass and poured himself a large one. He sighed. 'Sorry. You don't want to hear all this. You've been through enough already.'

'No,' she said, 'Don't stop. I want to know about him.' Even as she said it, she wondered if it was true. Was it better to know what he was capable of or not? Sometimes ignorance *was* bliss.

Guy hesitated. He lifted the glass to his mouth and as if he needed some Dutch courage, drained half the wine in a single gulp. 'What can I say? After my mother hitched up with Terry I went to live with them for a while. It only lasted for about six months. He couldn't stand the sight of me and never bothered to pretend otherwise. I was the cuckoo in the nest, the little prissy blond in his tribe of dark-haired boys.' He took another drink, laughed softly and said, 'Oh Christ, this is old history. Let's talk about something else.'

But Iris wanted to hear. And it wasn't just Terry she was interested in. If she was ever to understand Guy Wilder she needed to know about his past. 'No, go on. *Please.*'

'Well, you've got some idea of what he's like. You can probably guess the rest.'

'I don't want to guess.'

Guy's mouth twisted at the corners and Iris almost regretted her persistence. Perhaps it was just too painful for him to talk about. But after a few seconds he took a quick breath and continued. 'Terry never had much patience. It started with an angry word here or there, but then he started talking with his fists. Everything I did was wrong – the way I ate, the way I ran, even the bloody way I breathed. By the time he'd broken my arm, even my mother had to face the fact that it wasn't really working out.'

Iris gasped in outrage, a wave of disgust rolling over her. That anyone could deliberately hurt a child was beyond her. Instinctively, she reached out and wrapped her hands around his. 'Why the hell did she stay with him? Why didn't she protect you?'

He shrugged. 'I guess her maternal instincts came a poor second to a lifestyle she'd always dreamed about. If it ever came into her head to leave, it would have been a thought so fleeting that it barely registered.'

Iris stared at him, saddened and amazed. Recalling what he'd told her that first time they'd met at Tobias Grand & Sons, she said, 'And so she farmed you out to live with your grandmother.'

'There are worse fates,' he said with artificial brightness.

'Gran was a feisty old dear, I'll give her that. No one ever got the better of her. We didn't make a bad team, the two of us. It wasn't perfect, but hey, what is? We rubbed along okay.' He focused on the wall behind her before slowly lowering his eyes to look at her again. He tried a smile that didn't quite come off. 'She died when I was twelve and that's when I was shipped off to school. I was a boarder for the next four years, left when I was sixteen, got a job and . . .' He lifted his shoulders again. 'And there you have it. The life and times of the infamous Guy Wilder.'

Iris was about to pursue the missing years – he was in his early thirties now – when Noah appeared by their table. 'Sorry to interrupt,' he said, leaning down to address Guy, 'but Tommy Holland's just arrived.'

Guy looked at Iris and gave a groan. 'Sorry. So much for being off duty. Do you mind? He's a local businessman who brings a lot of clients here. I'd better go over and say hello.' He gently withdrew his hands from her grasp. 'I'll be as quick as I can.'

'You go,' she said, waving him away. 'Take as long as you like. I'll be fine.'

Guy stood up and within a few seconds the two of them had been swallowed up by the crowd. Iris sipped on her wine and did some people-watching. Eventually her gaze slid back to the bar where Noah's girlfriend was also sitting on her own. Serena was one of the most striking women she had ever seen: her dark hair, cropped close to her skull, accentuated her razor-sharp cheekbones and wide almond eyes. She had a long graceful neck, the type that was usually described as swan-like, and her lips were full and sensuous. Iris wondered what it was like to be so perfectly formed, to have one of those faces that could never be forgotten.

Their eyes met and Serena smiled. Iris, embarrassed at having

331

been caught out staring (although she was probably used to it), returned the smile and then glanced down briefly at the table. When she looked up again, Serena was already heading towards her. She was wearing a short red dress that clung to every slender curve of her body. She was a lot taller than Iris had realised, over six foot, although a few inches of that was down to her high heels. Her walk was the model's walk, a fluid swaying motion that drew attention to her impossibly long legs. As she made her way across the room, the crowd – as if instinctively obeying some fundamental if unspoken law – moved apart to let her through. No pushing or squeezing past for her. No bruised toes or elbows in her ribs. Her beauty gave her rights that were not bestowed on lesser mortals.

When she reached the table she held out a hand. 'Hi, I'm Serena,' she said. Her voice was low, slightly husky. 'Seeing as we've both been so rudely abandoned, I thought we could keep each other company.'

Iris took the hand and lightly shook it. The fingers were dry and cool.

'So you're the mysterious Iris,' Serena said. She didn't wait for an invitation, but sat down in the seat recently vacated by Guy. She took a sip of the drink she had carried over, something transparent with ice and a slice in a long glass. It might have been water. Perhaps she never drank anything but water – it would account for that smooth, unblemished skin. Models probably couldn't afford the luxury of hangovers.

'Mysterious?' Iris said.

'Well, you have been seeing Guy, haven't you?' She didn't wait for a reply. 'And as he hasn't bothered to introduce us, I'm presuming you're more than just a passing fancy. He tends to become rather secretive when he's getting involved.'

Iris stared steadily back at her, unsure as to how to respond. Yes, she felt a tiny thrill at that word 'involved' – it was true that

332

she and Guy had grown closer, there was no denying it – but she was also alert to the slight edge in the other woman's voice. There was something almost proprietorial about it. Or was her imagination running riot again? The evening had been an emotional one, and her judgement, as Vita could easily testify, had flown out of the window hours ago.

'You're not his usual type,' Serena said, looking her up and down.

Iris bristled. 'Really.'

'Sorry,' Serena said. 'I didn't mean that to come out sounding like it did. You're just . . .' She stopped and smiled again. 'Am I being disgustingly nosy? Only Noah never asks Guy anything. It's that weird male thing. I don't think they have a curious bone in their bodies.'

Iris relaxed a little. Serena was Noah's girlfriend and was probably, in her own individual way, just trying to be friendly. She would have liked to have asked what Guy's type usually was, but didn't want to seem too concerned. Instead she gave a small casual shrug of her shoulders. 'Well, it's early days . . .'

'So how did you two meet?'

'Through work,' Iris said. She paused, thinking back to that fateful afternoon at Tobias Grand & Sons. Lizzie Street, through her death, had been the catalyst for almost everything that had happened since. If it hadn't been for her, she and Guy would never have met. It was a disconcerting thought. She could see that Serena was waiting for her to go on and wondered how much more to tell her. She didn't want to seem evasive, but wasn't prepared to be too forthcoming either. Guy might not appreciate her revelations. 'It was just one of those chance encounters.'

'So what do you think of him?'

'What do you mean?' Iris said, although she knew exactly what she meant. She was starting to feel uncomfortable again.

Serena and subtlety were clearly strangers to each other. And she sensed something sharp and brittle underpinning her questions, something more than mere curiosity.

'He's complicated, isn't he? You never know what's going on in that head of his. Is it serious between the two of you?'

'Maybe you should ask him that,' Iris retorted, wanting to put an end to what was beginning to feel like her second interrogation of the night. She glanced around but couldn't see him. 'I don't think he'll be too long.'

Serena parted her lips and expelled a noise that was partway between a sigh and a snort. 'I wouldn't count on it. The number of times I've heard that *I'll only be five minutes* line. Once Tommy Holland digs in his claws, it's damn near impossible to get away. He likes to click his fingers and have everyone come running.' She smiled. 'Although personally I don't jump through hoops for any man.'

Iris could well believe it. When you looked like she did, hoop-jumping would never be one of life's requirements. 'I guess its part of the job. If you run a place like this, you have to cater for all the egos, inflated or otherwise, that come walking through the door.'

Serena's smile wavered. Perhaps she was trying to decide if Iris was having a dig. She lifted her glass again and stared at Iris over its rim, one of those close assessing looks that females tend to practise when they're weighing up the opposition. Except they weren't in competition, were they? Iris was with Guy, and Serena was with Noah.

'So what about you?' Iris said, deciding to remind her of this fact. 'How long have you and Noah been an item?'

Serena threw back her head and burst out laughing. 'What?' She had tiny diamonds in her ears and they sparkled as they caught the light. 'Whatever made you think that? God, no. He's not my other half – he's my brother!'

334

'Oh,' Iris said, feeling like an idiot. She frowned, thinking back to her earlier conversation with Guy. It was true, come to think of it, that he hadn't actually said that Serena was Noah's girlfriend. *She* was the one who had made the presumption. But he hadn't put her right either. 'Sorry, I just saw you together and . . .'

Iris was saved from any further explanations by Guy's timely reappearance. Despite Serena's pessimistic prediction, he'd only been gone for ten minutes. His blue eyes narrowed on seeing who she was sitting with.

'Serena,' he said, giving her a small nod.

'Guy,' she replied with the same level of coolness. 'I thought I'd keep your poor friend company while you were sucking up to Tommy Holland.'

'How very . . . *considerate* of you. Still, don't let us keep you. I believe Noah's back at the bar now.'

But Serena made no attempt to move. Indeed, she even settled back a little in the seat. The message was clear: she would leave if and when she wanted to.

Iris looked from one to the other. She was trying to work out if their animosity was down to genuine dislike or if they shared one of those odd, sparky attractions that was only ever expressed through a constant pretence of mutual loathing. The former she hoped, not relishing the thought of having Serena as a rival.

'Come on,' Guy said, holding out a hand to Iris. 'I've had enough of this place for one night. Let's go upstairs.'

Iris didn't need to be asked twice. Taking his hand, she got up and stood beside him. Aware of his closeness, she felt a sudden quickening of her heart. 'Bye then,' she said to Serena, not wanting to appear too hostile. She had enough enemies already without adding to the list.

'Bye, hun,' Serena said, arching her perfectly plucked brows. 'Have a nice evening and . . . good luck.'

Iris was still thinking about that 'good luck' as they climbed the stairs. They were almost at the top when Guy asked, 'So what did the delightful Serena have to say for herself?'

Iris could hear the barely disguised irritation in his voice. 'Nothing much. You know, just small talk.' Was he worried that Serena might have been badmouthing him? Or warning her off? 'Why didn't you tell me she was Noah's sister?'

'Does it matter?'

Iris, walking in front, looked over her shoulder. 'Just curious,' she said, trying to sound as if she didn't really care.

Suddenly his mouth broke into a grin. 'Hey, it's not what you think. We had a brief fling, but that was years ago. That's not what this is about.'

Iris was a step above him, which put them almost at the same height. Gazing straight into his eyes, she said, 'You don't need to explain.' She wanted him to tell her, but at the same time she didn't want to come across as one of those needy, jealous women who demanded to know every detail. She had a horror, especially after being dumped by Luke, of coming across as in any way desperate.

'I want to,' he said. 'You've got a right.' Wrapping his arms around her waist, he turned her around and pulled her closer. 'Truth is, she's not too pleased about the company I've been keeping recently.'

'Ah,' Iris murmured. 'I presume that means me . . . or am I being oversensitive?'

'She thinks you're going to get me into trouble.'

'So she knows about my dad?'

Guy shook his head. 'Not the details. Only that you're searching for him, and that I'm helping you. Oh, and that Terry Street's quite keen to have a word with him too.' He pulled a face. 'She's not too keen on the Terry Street angle. Everyone knows him round here, and what he's capable of.'

'I suppose she's just looking out for you and Noah.'

'Serena never looks out for anyone other than herself. She lent her big brother some cash so he could buy a share of the business. Now she's worried that we'll have the Streets on our backs. She's just stressing about her investment.'

Iris opened her mouth to ask another question, but Guy quickly put a finger to her lips. 'Enough,' he said, smiling. 'Let's not waste our time talking about things we can't change. Serena isn't important. It's just you and me now.' He swept back a strand of her hair, coiled it between his fingertips and gazed solemnly into her face. 'You know how I feel about you, Iris O'Donnell.'

Iris held her breath. 'Do I?' Had she said the words aloud? She wasn't sure. There was a tiny fluttering at the base of her throat.

'Yes,' he whispered.

As he bent to kiss her, Iris closed her eyes.

Chapter Forty-seven

There was a cold, hard stone in the pit of Alice Avery's stomach. She had spent over forty-eight hours dreading this moment and now it had finally arrived. As she walked behind Toby, stumbling occasionally, her heart was thumping in her chest. Beyond the reach of the streetlamps, the alley that ran along the back of Tobias Grand & Sons and its neighbours was pitch-black. She looked up. Even the night sky was starless. The only light came from the thin, wavering beam of Toby's torch.

A skinny cat leapt out of the darkness and hurtled past them. Alice stifled a cry and her hand sprung out to touch the back of Toby's jacket.

He gave a soft laugh as if her fear amused him. 'Almost there,' he whispered.

They could have gone in through the front door – who was likely to see them at this time of night? – but he'd insisted on this half-blind journey through the alley. She suspected that he liked the subterfuge, the idea of prowling around like a burglar. It was an unwelcome reminder of just how young he was.

Toby stopped suddenly and she almost crashed into him.

338

She heard the jangle of his keys as he took them from his pocket. Then the beam of the torch sought out the lock. Seconds later they were inside and Alice breathed out a sigh of relief. The first part was over. Now they only had to descend to the basement, start the preparations and wait for Danny Street to arrive . . .

Twenty minutes later, everything was ready. Jenni Brookner had been removed from the refrigeration unit and was laid out on the table, her nakedness covered by a crisp white sheet. Alice had put on her scrubs and latex gloves. She was checking and rechecking her tools, trying to keep busy, to keep her mind off what was coming next – but her eyes kept straying towards the table. She shivered. Guilt, as bitter as bile, was eating away at her.

Alice embarked on yet another unwelcome battle with her conscience. There was still time to say no, wasn't there? She didn't have to go through with it. They could find another way of repaying the debt. But she knew it wasn't just about the cash: Danny Street wouldn't release his hold on them until he'd got exactly what he wanted.

Toby paced the floor, glancing impatiently at his watch. 'Where is he? Where is he, for fuck's sake?'

Alice thought about the first time they'd done this. How had she ever let Toby talk her into it? But looking at him, at his lean supple frame and shock of fair hair, she knew exactly why. Love made people do the most outrageous of things. Even ugly things. 'He only wants to watch,' he'd said to her. 'You wouldn't mind, would you? Only he's fascinated by it, by the process, you know, of . . . er . . . embalming.' And yes, Danny Street had been fascinated all right, but not in any way that could be described as healthy. She remembered his cruel dark eyes following her every movement, the lick of sweat on his forehead, the quickening of his breath as he watched her make the incisions. It was the thrill, the excitement he'd so clearly felt, that had filled her with horror. He hadn't even touched the body, but that didn't make a difference. It was what had been in his mind that revolted her.

No, she should never have agreed to do it again. But then she thought about the consequences of backing out. She recalled driving to Shoreditch and finding Toby battered and bruised; he still bore the scars from that beating. Sometimes, when she touched him, he flinched and pulled away. The idea of his being hurt again was just too much too take. Instantly, she made her decision. Removing the sheet from Jenni Brookner's corpse, she gently began to massage the limbs. The sooner she got started, the sooner she could be finished. But she was still holding on to a glimmer of hope. Street was already late. Perhaps he wouldn't turn up at all. Perhaps, God willing, something terrible had happened to him.

Toby swore again and continued to pace.

The minutes slowly passed.

The knock when it came sounded unnaturally loud. It seemed to reverberate, sending off a series of shocks that the whole neighbourhood must hear. Alice almost jumped out of her skin. Her heart began to thump and a trembling started in her knees. She wanted to run away, but even if her legs could have carried her there was nowhere to go.

Toby headed for the steps but then stopped, turned around and laid a hand on her arm. As if he guessed that her resolve might be faltering, his blue eyes gazed pleadingly into hers. 'You won't let me down, will you?'

She shook her head.

'You swear?'

'I swear,' she croaked.

He bent and kissed her softly on the lips. 'I love you.'

Alice watched him disappear up the steps. Her heart was still missing beats, but it wasn't just from fear. It was worth doing almost anything to hear those three precious words. She thought of her mother and her cronies gathered in the flat at Valentine Court. It wouldn't be long now before she could wipe those mocking smiles off their faces.

She heard Toby open and close the back door. This was followed by a murmuring of voices. She waited, but still they didn't come down to the basement. What were they doing?

She shifted restively from one foot to another. Now the time had come, she wanted to get it over and done with.

It felt like forever before she finally heard their descending footsteps, although in reality it was probably no more than three or four minutes. Danny Street came first. He strutted in wearing a white jacket and tie, his attire more suited to a cocktail party than the cool, sterile basement of Tobias Grand & Sons. His eyes alighted on her briefly. He gave a slight nod, enough to acknowledge her presence without taking the trouble to open his mouth. She could have taken offence – no one liked being greeted with indifference – but Alice had more pressing worries. She didn't give a damn whether he was polite to her or not. In fact, she was glad that they didn't have to talk – he had nothing to say that she wanted to hear.

As Toby followed behind, he shot her a reassuring smile. She smiled tentatively back before returning her attention to Danny Street, watching closely as his gaze gradually focused on the pale naked body of Jenni Brookner. She found herself holding her breath, suddenly afraid that he would find something to complain about. What if Jenni's figure was all wrong, her hair the wrong colour? The moment these thoughts entered her head, she felt disgusted by them. She shouldn't be entertaining such ideas - they were evil, sick.

But Danny Street appeared more than happy with what he was seeing. A glimmer of a smile snaked on to his lips. 'Well, we'll get started then, shall we,' he said. He didn't address her directly, didn't even glance in her direction, but simply uttered the words into the space that lay between them.

Alice looked over at Toby, but he had his eyes firmly fixed on the floor. He'd moved away from the table and was standing by the sink. His face was drawn, his arms wrapped around his chest and his hands clenched under his armpits. He looked like a scared little boy and her heart went out to him. If she bottled it now, there was no saying what Danny Street might do. Well, she wasn't going to let him be hurt again. They were in this together. She gulped down her panic and stepped forward.

Alice could see only one way to get through this and that was to get it over and done with as quickly as possible. If she put her mind to it, she could complete the job in less than an hour. Yes, that's how she had to think about it – just another job, nothing else. She had to hold her nerve. Last time she had told Danny Street exactly what she was doing, taking him through the process step by step, almost treating him like a student, but on this occasion she sensed it was smarter to stay silent. Unless he asked her something, she would keep her mouth firmly shut.

As Alice went to shoot the formaldehyde into Jenni Brookner's carotid artery, she realised her hand was shaking. She had to lower the needle and take a few seconds to calm herself. It didn't help that Danny Street was standing so close, almost breathing down her neck. She could smell his sweat and the stale lingering stench of cigarettes. She glanced at him, noting the sheen on his upper lip. *Concentrate,* she told herself. For Toby's sake, she had to stay calm. Once this was over, they'd be free of the creep forever.

The next forty-five minutes were possibly the longest of Alice's life. She was trying to work as efficiently as she could, but her fingers, usually so nimble, had become thick and clumsy. All the procedures that had once been second nature, now felt so complicated she was barely able to perform them. She stumbled over the simplest of manoeuvres, dropping hooks, spilling chemicals. With every action she performed, something seemed to go wrong.

She tried to ignore Danny Street, to pretend he wasn't there, but his presence was too solid, too overwhelming for this to be possible. He was like a long, vile shadow attached to her shoulder. Every tiny movement he made, every clearing of his throat, induced a desire in her to scream. She could feel the hairs standing up on the back of her neck.

Alice paused for a moment. She looked down at Jenni Brookner, at her pale flawless skin and long fair hair. This was a young woman whose life had been cruelly snatched away before she'd even reached her twenty-first birthday. Usually Alice would have pondered on what that life had been like, searched for clues on the body, but she had no time for idle ruminations tonight. She knew what she should be feeling – pity and compassion – but there was no space left in her heart. Fear had consumed her, pushing all other emotions aside. She closed her eyes for a second. If only this was a bad dream, a nightmare she could eventually wake up from.

Danny Street shifted impatiently behind her, his black shiny shoes making a tiny scuffing sound against the lino.

Alice blinked open her eyes again. *Concentrate.* She had to wipe her mind clean of everything, everyone. It was the only way she was going to get through this. She straightened her shoulders and breathed in deeply. Then in one quick easy motion she leaned down, picked up the trocar and pierced the girl's abdomen just above the navel . . .

Somehow, she got through it – and in record time too. By one o'clock Alice had completed the emptying, the washing, the replacing, even the sewing-up of all the loose ends. She stood back and gave a sigh of relief. It was over. Jenni Brookner was perfectly embalmed. Now all that was left was for her to apply a little make-up . . . and for Danny Street to walk away and leave them in peace.

But as Alice reached for her bag of cosmetics, Toby moved forward and took her hand. 'Let's go upstairs,' he said. 'Take a break.'

She glared at him. A break was the last thing she needed. All she wanted was to get out of here and as soon as possible. 'What?'

'A drink,' Toby said.

Oh, great! As if she hadn't had enough to endure of the crazy Danny Street already. Now she was expected to sit across a table from the lunatic and act as if nothing out of the ordinary had happened. She frowned at Toby, not able to say what she was thinking out loud. Then when this had no effect, she peered deliberately at her watch. 'It's getting late. Don't you think . . .?'

Toby didn't take the hint. Instead he propelled her firmly up the stairs. 'Just one drink,' he said. 'That's not going to make much difference, is it?'

When they reached the kitchen, Toby switched on the over-head light. As always the neon tube flickered and hummed before coming on properly. She presumed it was safe to have the light on – the kitchen was at the back of the building – but as she sat down she still looked warily towards the two frosted windows.

Toby took a half bottle of vodka from his pocket, unscrewed the cap and slopped a generous measure into a couple of mugs. 'Here,' he said, placing one in front of her. He bent and kissed her neck. 'You deserve this. You were brilliant.'

But Alice didn't want congratulations. There was nothing praiseworthy about sneaking around in the middle of the night, pandering to the dubious interests of a local thug. What she had done was wrong and there was no getting over it. She glanced anxiously towards the door and then back at Toby. 'Where is he? What's he doing?'

Toby shrugged and looked away.

Alice frowned. There was something furtive about him, about the way he wouldn't meet her eyes that set alarm bells ringing in her head. Suddenly she had one of those revelatory moments. It was like a bright, vivid light illuminating the impossible. Her body went hot and cold and her mouth fell open. Goosebumps gathered on her arms. 'Oh my God,' she murmured. Why hadn't it occurred to her? Why hadn't she realised that this time watching might not be enough for a monster like Danny Street? That's how it worked, wasn't it? First there was the interest in corpses, then there was the obsession, and then . . . She shot up out of her chair and headed towards the door.

Toby grabbed hold of her arm, forcibly restraining her. 'What are you doing?'

'What do you think? We have to stop him. We can't . . .' She couldn't bring herself to finish the sentence. 'We *can't*.'

'We have to.'

'D-don't you care?' she stammered out.

Toby gave a low frustrated growl. 'Of course I care, but what do you want me to do? Go down there and tell him he's a fucking freak? We just sit here and wait. This is our one and only chance to get clear of him forever.'

'But—'

'But nothing,' he said fiercely. Two bright red spots had appeared on his cheeks. 'Do you want him to kill me? To kill *you*?'

Alice had begun to shake again. This was worse than the trembling that had overtaken her in the basement, a hundred thousand times worse. It racked her body and made her teeth chatter. She felt the nausea rise up from her stomach. Shaking herself free of Toby's grasp, she rushed across the room and threw up in the sink.

345

Chapter Forty-eight

Iris couldn't remember the last time she'd felt so happy. Bearing in mind the ominously dark cloud that still hung over her, this was probably tempting fate, but she didn't care. Love and optimism went hand in hand, and with Guy beside her she could get through anything. It was as though she'd turned a corner and from this point on life could only get better. Was it possible to fall in love overnight? She smiled to herself. Except, of course, it hadn't just happened overnight; there had been a spark there, a chemistry, from the very first moment they'd met.

She looked around reception, aware that if it hadn't been for this job she might never have set eyes on him. God bless Tobias Grand & Sons! It was Monday morning, nine-thirty, and even Gerald Grand's reappearance – and his insistence on reviewing every bit of paperwork for the past week – couldn't blunt her good mood. All she had to do now was to start building some bridges with Vita . . . She wasn't too worried about Michael, *that* spat would blow over, but her friend was a different matter altogether. She suspected it would take more than a heartfelt apology to heal the rift.

Iris wondered if she should have called her yesterday. Giving the dust time to settle was all very well, but the longer she let things drift, the worse they might become. Would Vita have told Rick what she'd said? Of course she would. It was too serious, too inflammatory to ignore. Iris felt a flush invade her cheeks. How would she ever look him in the face again? It seemed doubtful that the truth about where he'd got the money from would ever come out – but her hasty accusation would never be forgotten. Still, she had to at least try and make amends. She would ring tonight; Guy would be working and, if Vita was willing, they could have a long talk.

The main door opened and Toby Grand bounced in. He shook the snow from his leather jacket and came over to perch on the corner of her desk. 'How's it going, babe? Have you missed me?'

Iris stared up at him. 'God, what happened to your face?'

His fingers rose to flutter over the fading bruises. 'Oh, this?' he said. 'Nothing. I just slipped on the ice. I was a bit bladdered to be honest. So there's no need for any sympathy; I didn't feel a thing.'

Iris wondered if Toby lied about *everything*. It was a habit, perhaps, and one he found impossible to break. There was no way he could have got those bruises from a fall. It was a natural instinct, even when you were drunk, to put out your hands if you were hurtling towards the ground. Anyway, it wasn't that long since she'd tended to Michael's cuts and bruises; these, she thought, looked pretty similar. 'I heard you had the flu.'

He grinned. 'What's the rule that says you can't be sick *and* have a few bevies?'

'No rule. Only most people refrain from fighting when they're up to ears in Lemsips and tissues.'

Toby grinned. 'Well, I'll try to remember that in future.'

'Something to do with your new best friend, was it?' Iris

asked, trying to sound casual. With all the trouble going on at the moment any dirt she could get on Danny Street might be useful.

'And who would that be?'

'The charming Mr Street,' she said. 'Or, how was it you referred to him on the day of his stepmother's funeral? Deadhead?'

'Oh, him.' He gave a light unconvincing laugh. 'What makes you think I've seen him again?'

'You seemed pretty close that evening at the Hope & Anchor.'

'Part of the job description, hunnybun,' he said. 'Schmoozing the clients, keeping them happy. The Brothers Grimm don't appreciate the amount of effort I put into this business. There's a lot more to the funeral trade than preserving bodies and choosing coffins. You need to keep people happy if they're going to pay their bills on time. You need to offer them that little extra bit of service.'

'And has he?' Iris said.

'What?'

'Paid his bill.'

Toby gave an indifferent shrug of his shoulders. 'Not my department, love. You'd have to ask Grimm Junior about that.'

But William, even if she'd wanted to ask, had been closeted in his office all morning. Now that Gerald was back, he'd retreated into the place he felt most comfortable: safely in the background. 'Right,' she said. 'So this . . .' She gestured towards his face. 'This has got nothing to do with Danny Street?'

'As if! I hardly know the guy. I told you - I slipped. It was an accident.'

Iris, realising that he wasn't going to change his story, gave up and returned her attention to the papers on her desk. She shuffled them into the proper order for typing. Then, for the second time in half an hour, she checked the diary. With Gerald on the rampage, and her full-time position only recently confirmed, she couldn't afford to make any mistakes.

'Anything I should know about?' Toby said.

'Three appointments this morning – I presume your dad's going to deal with those – and a viewing for this afternoon. Jenni Brookner's parents are coming in at four. Do you know about her?'

'Is she the girl who fell on the ice, the one who cracked open her skull?'

'That's her. She was only twenty. Sad, isn't it? Do you think I should chase Alice up, make sure that everything's on schedule?'

Toby shook his head. 'I wouldn't bother. She'd probably take it as an insult. Since when was Alice ever *not* on schedule?'

'True enough,' Iris said. 'God, I can't imagine what that girl's parents are going through. It must be terrible to lose your daughter like that.'

'She was a bit of a looker too,' Toby remarked, with his familiar sensitivity. 'A blonde, yeah? I saw her picture in the paper.' He left a short pause and then added, 'Apparently, if a beautiful or famous woman died in ancient Egypt, they'd keep her away from the embalmers for a few days – you know, leave her out in the heat to rot for a while.'

Iris frowned at him. 'What?'

Toby laughed, his blue eyes dancing. 'Just in case those horny guys got any unsuitable ideas.'

'Ugh,' Iris said. 'Delightful!'

'Isn't it?'

There was a sudden sharp intake of breath and they both turned their heads. Unheard by either of them, Alice Avery had come up from the basement and was standing close behind. Her face was deathly pale, her eyes wide open as if she'd seen a ghost. She was staring hard at Toby. For a few seconds she stood there, the only movement in her body a visible heaving of her chest. Then a stifled sound, something halfway between a cry and a sob, escaped from her lips, and she turned and ran back towards the stairs.

Iris, unsure of what had happened, jumped up from her chair. 'What the . . .?' Bewildered, she gazed after the departing figure and then turned to look accusingly at Toby. 'What the hell have you done now?'

Toby raised his hands defensively. 'Hey, this is nothing to do with me. I only just got here, remember. Didn't you see me walk in through that door five minutes ago?'

Iris couldn't deny it. And he hadn't been in the office for most of last week either. But Alice had definitely been staring straight at him. 'Maybe it was what you said, that weird stuff about the Egyptians.'

'Why should that bother her?' He gave a snort. 'Bearing in mind what she does for a living, she can hardly be the squeamish sort.'

But something had clearly upset Alice. 'Should I go after her, try to find out what's up?'

'I wouldn't. She'll calm down soon enough; this isn't the first time she's thrown a wobbly.' He glanced towards the stairs as if to make sure she wasn't still in earshot. Then he lowered his voice. 'She's probably at that time of life, you know, the *change* or whatever it is you women go through.'

Iris glared at him. 'For Christ's sake Toby, she's not that old.'

He shrugged. 'Well, go after her if you like, but she won't thank you for it. In fact, you could make things worse.'

Iris wondered if he had a point. Alice was hardly forthcoming at the best of times and this obviously wasn't one of them. Would she really welcome someone fussing round? Maybe, for once, Toby was right. It might be better to leave the poor woman alone.

'Oh well, things to do,' Toby said cheerily. He dumped his empty cup in her bin and sauntered off towards the kitchen. 'Catch you later, babe.'

Slowly, Iris sat back down. She shuffled the papers on her desk and attempted to concentrate, but try as she might, she couldn't get the incident out of her head. What was it that had upset Alice so much? There had been shock on her face, fear and disappointment. Iris sighed. Her earlier good mood had evaporated. As if everything had been spoilt, she had an odd, sour feeling in her guts.

Chapter Forty-nine

Toby muttered under his breath as he trudged reluctantly down to the basement. What the hell was wrong with the woman? Well, he knew what was wrong – she'd overheard what he'd said to Iris – but that was no reason to get hysterical, to draw attention to herself in such a very public way. And okay, so maybe she hadn't realised *exactly* what Danny Street was planning last night, but at some level, some subconscious level at least, she must have guessed what his ultimate intentions were.

As he reached the bottom of the steps, Toby stopped and took a moment to run his fingers through his hair. Irritation tightened the corners of his mouth. After rearranging his expression into one of absolute sincerity, he pushed open the door and strode inside.

Alice was leaning against the sink with her arms folded across her chest. As he approached, she kept her eyes fixed firmly on the floor. She was wearing a black skirt that was too short for her. He noticed the heaviness in her thighs, the overly pale and slightly flabby flesh on her upper arms. Sleeping with her had amused him at first – it was true what they said about a certain type of older woman being both enthusiastic and grateful – but now she only filled him with disgust.

'Alice, love,' he said. 'Are you all right?'

He went to put his hands around her waist, but she pushed him away. Her tearstained face was red and splotchy. 'How could you joke about a thing like that? How could you?'

'I'm sorry. I was only messing about, trying to deal with it in my own stupid way. I didn't mean anything. You think I'm not as upset as you are? I am. I truly am. I had no idea that he . . .' Toby tried to look as shocked as possible. 'Jesus, I still can't believe it.'

Alice didn't say anything. She gave a series of sniffles and glared down at the lino.

'I should have stopped him. I know that now.' Toby bowed his head. 'Do you have any idea how ashamed I am? It was cowardly of me. I should have had the courage to stand up and be counted – no matter what he did to me.'

Her eyes slowly flickered up to meet his. He could sense a slight thawing in her attitude. The vulnerable little-boy-lost act usually did the trick.

'I wouldn't have wanted you to get hurt,' Alice said more softly. 'That's not what—'

'No, I've behaved like a bloody idiot. And what you heard me say upstairs . . . that was terrible, dreadful. I don't know what I was thinking. I'd understand if you didn't want anything more to do with me.'

But Alice wasn't going to let him off the hook that easily. 'You're not the only one to blame. I didn't try to stop him either. It's something we're both going to have to live with.' A weary sigh slipped from her lips. 'So long as we have each other, we can get through this.'

'Of course.'

'You do still love me, don't you?'

Staring down into her desperate eyes, Toby felt a shudder of revulsion. If he could have dumped her then and there he would, but what if she went squealing to his father or, even worse, to the cops? Not that she'd come out of it smelling of roses – she was as guilty as he was – but he suddenly knew that wouldn't stop her. In her present emotional state, she was more than capable of landing them both in the shit. 'You know I do.'

'And we'll always be together?'

'Always,' he repeated through gritted teeth. 'So are we . . .' he'd been about to say 'friends again', but it didn't sound quite right. 'Am I forgiven?'

Alice gave a tiny nod. 'Let's never mention it again. It'll be our secret.' And then an odd look crept over her face. It was part beseeching, part cunning. 'All married couples have secrets, don't they?'

Toby's jaw dropped. Married? What was she talking about? Christ, the woman was mad. It occurred to him, rather late in the day he had to admit, that he hadn't really thought the relationship through. He'd somehow imagined he would disentangle himself from this liaison as effortlessly as he had all the others, but now he saw that it wasn't going to be that easy.

'I'm so happy,' she said. 'Just wait until I tell my mother . . .'

As Alice leaned in heavily against him, Toby felt more than the bulk of her body. He suddenly realised what it meant to have a millstone round your neck. How would he ever get free of her? He could feel himself drowning, being sucked into the depths of a cold, greedy sea of despair. As he stared miserably down at the top of her head, an idea suddenly popped into his own. He shoved it quickly away – it was unthinkable – but it bounced straight back. This time he gave it a little more consideration. Perhaps the only way to draw a line under this whole unfortunate episode was to get rid of Alice Avery forever . . .

Chapter Fifty

It was shortly after ten o'clock when the main door opened and two uniformed police officers, a middle-aged man and a much younger woman, stepped into the warmth of Tobias Grand & Sons. Iris raised her head and smiled as they approached her desk. The man was fairly bland-looking, his features not of the type she'd ever recognise again, but the woman was more memorable. She had a thin, angular face with a halo of blonde frizzy hair.

'I'm PC Grove, this is PC Matlock,' the woman said, briefly flashing her card and badge. 'We're looking for an Iris O'Donnell.'

'That's me,' Iris said, her smile gradually fading as she became aware of the seriousness of their expressions. She felt a flutter of panic. Oh no, had something happened to her mum? Or was this connected to her father? Had they heard he was back, discovered what he'd done all those years ago?

'And you live at Silverstone Heights?' PC Grove said.

Iris nodded. 'That's right. What's this about?' At the mention of the Heights, her fears veered off in another direction. Maybe

355

the flat had been broken into. Maybe the thug who'd been waiting for her had come back for another go. So many anxious
thoughts were running through her head, she didn't know
which one to concentrate on.

'And are you related to Michael O'Donnell?'

'Yes, he's my uncle.'

PC Grove bit down on her lower lip. She had small, wary
brown eyes and they darted sideways towards her companion.
He gave an almost imperceptible nod. 'Er . . .' she began, and
then stopped and swallowed hard. 'We're really sorry to inform
you that there was . . . there was an incident in the early hours
of this morning. Mr O'Donnell was hit by a car and—'

'Is he hurt? Is he in hospital?' Iris said, shooting up out of her
chair. 'Oh God, is he . . .?' She instinctively knew the answer to
this last question, but couldn't bear to acknowledge it. Sweat
prickled on her forehead and her hands began to shake. If she
could just delay the moment of truth, even for a few seconds,
maybe she could make this whole nightmare go away. Gazing at
the woman, she silently pleaded with her to tell her anything
but the cold, brutal facts.

The young PC gazed sadly back at her. 'I'm really sorry, but
I'm afraid he died at the scene.'

'No,' Iris murmured. 'He can't be. He can't.' Her legs gave
way and she slumped back into her chair. She covered her face
with her hands and let out a mighty groan. She felt like she was
falling, hurtling down into a dark, deep pit of despair. And she
knew, like in one of those peculiar dreams she sometimes had,
that she was going to hit the ground at any second, and that
when she did, the pain would be unendurable.

'I'm sorry,' PC Grove said, moving around the desk and placing a hand lightly on her shoulder. 'Is there someone we can
call, someone you'd like to be with you?'

Iris thought the man said something too, but she couldn't be sure. She could barely hear their voices any more. All she was thinking was *No, no, no.* The word revolved in her head, a spinning mantra blocking out everything else. This wasn't right. It wasn't possible. Michael couldn't be dead. The last year streamed through her head like a jumbled reel of film, a series of disconnected scenes from the very first day she'd met him again, through all the times they'd spent together since.

It was only the appearance of Gerald Grand that jolted Iris back to the present. 'Officers,' he said, striding brusquely out of his office. 'Is there something I can help you with?'

Iris ignored him. She stared up at the woman PC. Suddenly she had to know the details. 'Where did it happen? When?'

It was at this point that PC Matlock took over. Sensing perhaps that his younger partner was struggling, he said to her, 'Why don't you explain everything to Mr Grand.' Then he turned back to Iris. 'It was in Mansfield Road, near the estate. He was found this morning, about six, but we think the accident happened much earlier – probably around eleven, twelve o'clock. Unfortunately, he was hit by a vehicle that didn't stop.'

Michael would have been on his way back from the pub, Iris thought. Drunk after drowning his sorrows. And why did he have sorrows to drown? Because of all the grief *she'd* been causing him. Her hands clenched into two tight fists, her fingernails digging into the skin of her palms. 'So he could have been lying there for hours.'

'No,' Matlock said. 'He didn't suffer. The medical examiner believes he died instantly.'

Iris tried to conjure up that moment, that fateful second when life ceased to be. How could there be no suffering involved in that? She felt a tightening in her throat as she struggled to take it in. One minute he'd been there and the next . . .

'We found a card in his wallet,' Matlock continued. 'It had your name and address on it and a couple of numbers. One of them was for Silverstone Heights – we tried there first – the other was for here.' He left a short pause during which she was vaguely aware of Gerald hovering in the background, of a thin muttering of other voices.

'Are you his closest relative? Only I'm afraid we'll need someone to identify the body.'

'I think that can wait, can't it?'

Until she heard him, Iris hadn't even realised that William was there. She looked over in surprise. Toby was standing beside him. 'No,' she said. 'It's all right. Someone has to do it. I want to do it.' And she did. She felt a desperate yearning to see Michael again, to touch him, to let him know that he hadn't been abandoned. The thought of him lying alone in the morgue was almost too much too bear.

'Then I'll take you in my car,' William said, 'and I can drop you home after.' He paused. 'That's if you want me to.'

'Thank you,' Iris murmured gratefully.

Gerald opened his mouth as if about to object to this careless abandonment of the business, but then thought better of it. He glanced at William and gave a thin smile. 'Very well.'

It was only as she was rising to her feet that Iris was struck by a thought so obvious she couldn't believe it had only just entered her head. 'Are you sure this was an accident? You said the driver didn't stop, right?'

PC Matlock raised his brows. 'Do you have any reason to think it might not have been?'

'Yes,' Iris said, the accusation tumbling from her lips before she had time to think twice about it. 'You want to talk to that nutter Danny Street, find out where he was at midnight last night. You know who he is, don't you?'

'We're aware of the Street family,' Matlock said. 'Was your uncle involved with them in some way?'

'Not like you're thinking,' Iris snapped. She knew what he

was hinting at, knew that they'd probably checked him out on the computer already. 'Michael hasn't been in trouble for years. He had a fight with Danny Street about a week ago. It was in the Hope & Anchor. My uncle took a beating. You don't need to take my word for it; there were plenty of witnesses.' Her throat felt tight and strained. She stopped for a second and gulped in a lungful of air. 'And then last Tuesday, Danny Street came here and started threatening me. William knows. He saw him.'

This was clearly news to Gerald. His face took on a pinkish tinge and he stared at his brother. The two PCs looked at William too. 'Is this true, sir?'

'Well, yes, Danny Street was here. I didn't actually hear what he said, but Iris was upset, very upset. I could see that he'd frightened her. I asked him to leave and he did.'

It was then that Toby piped up, 'I know he's a bit on the crazy side, but perhaps we shouldn't jump to any hasty conclusions.'

Iris's mouth fell open. Hadn't she just explained about the fight, the threats? What was wrong with him? She couldn't understand why he was trying to protect that nasty, vicious creep. 'And what would you know about it?'

Toby pushed his hands in his pockets and gave a light shrug. As if it was only *her* interests he had at heart, he smiled at her sympathetically. 'I'm sorry Iris, but you've had a shock. I just think you should be careful about making any wild accusations. I mean, where's the actual evidence?'

'When you say threatening you?' Matlock asked.

The two questions came at her virtually simultaneously. Iris realised that she couldn't give a convincing answer to either of them without explaining about her father. Was now the time to come clean about everything? But if her dad was out there, and if Danny Street had murdered Michael, then he was in more danger than ever. A warning voice whispered in her ear: *Think about it. Don't make any reckless decisions. What you say now can never be taken back.*

Shunning Toby – she had no idea what he was playing at – Iris addressed her response purely to Matlock. 'He was just being intimidating, throwing his weight around. It wasn't anything specific.' She knew how thin it sounded, how pathetic, like a grieving relative desperately grasping at straws. 'All I'm saying is that you should talk to Danny Street, check out where he was last night.'

Toby gave a small heartfelt shake of his head as though in her present state she couldn't, and shouldn't, be taken too seriously.

'I'll get your coat,' William said.

The morgue, on the east side of Kellston, was only a ten-minute drive away. For the duration of the journey, Iris sat very still and stared blankly through the windscreen. She was faintly aware of the traffic, of the bright glare of the snow in the gutters, but most of her senses seemed to have shut down. Cocooned in a web of disbelief, she was having trouble even breathing. William had the sensitivity to keep quiet, to give her the time she needed to prepare, but when they arrived she still felt a jolt of surprise. It was as if only seconds had passed since they'd left Tobias Grand & Sons.

The morgue was an anonymous grey brick and steel construction that she had passed a hundred times without ever taking in what it was. Iris released her seatbelt but made no further attempt to move. Her eyes raked the car park. She saw the two PCs get out of their blue Peugeot, glance over their shoulders and head into the building. Now, suddenly, it all began to rush in on her again. Michael was in there. Michael had been hit by a car that hadn't stopped. Michael was dead.

Iris wrapped her arms tightly around her chest. She felt a pain deep inside, like a knife slowly twisting. All she could think about were the harsh words that had been exchanged between them. How could she go inside that place? She looked across at William. Her voice, when it finally fought its way out, was barely more than a whisper. 'We had a row on Saturday night. I said things I shouldn't. That was the last time I saw him. I should have called. I should have. I should have made it up with him.'

William didn't ask what the argument was about. Instead, he said, 'People often have rows, especially when they care about each other. It doesn't mean anything.'

'I didn't even get to say sorry.'

'I know,' he said gently. 'But you have the chance to do that now.'

Iris could feel the tears stinging under her lids and tried to blink them away. She stared at the glass doors of the morgue, trying to gather the strength to move. The minutes ticked by. Then realising that she couldn't put it off any longer, she roughly wiped her eyes, and nodded. 'Okay. I'm ready.'

Inside, the building smelled like a hospital. It didn't feel like one though. There was none of the hustle and bustle, no doctors and nurses going about their business, no solemn visitors steadfastly clutching flowers and grapes. In fact, not that many people at all. The two PCs were patiently waiting and they all traipsed silently down a corridor until they reached the room where Michael was lying. It was explained to her that there was a viewing window she could look through, that she didn't need to go in, but that was too impersonal for Iris. She quickly shook her head. This wasn't something to be done from a distance.

Iris looked up at William. 'Will you come in with me?'

'Of course I will.'

There was a moment, as the man pulled down the sheet, when she prayed that a dreadful mistake had been made. It was possible, wasn't it? These things happened. Maybe Michael had been mugged, had his wallet stolen as he lurched drunkenly back from the pub. Maybe this man was just someone who bore an uncanny resemblance to him. But she knew it wasn't true even before his face was revealed.

Iris gazed down at the man she had grown to love so much over the past twelve months. Apart from the fading cuts and bruises from his run-in with Danny Street, there was no other damage to his face. With her eyes she traced the heavy brows, the strong chin, the wide O'Donnell mouth and thick, dark curly hair. Did he look peaceful? Not really. But then peacefulness and Michael had never been bedfellows. He'd always been the type of man who'd roared through life rather than meekly accepting it.

She looked up at PC Grove, her lips dry and trembling. 'Yes, it's Michael.'

William moved closer as if to offer some comfort, but then, uncertain perhaps as to how such support might be received, stopped short of doing anything more.

Iris continued to stare down at Michael.

Eventually she reached out to touch his hand. Her fingertips rested on the cold, lifeless flesh. A memory of him sitting in the Hope & Anchor leapt into her head. She remembered his laugh, the way he'd swept away her worries over cancelling his birthday meal. She remembered the way he'd smiled when he'd talked about Lizzie Street. And then – and she could barely stand to think of it – there was that last terrible time they'd talked in Vita's kitchen. Oh Christ, why had she said those things? How had it come to this? It was all wrong, impossible.

Leaning down, Iris kissed him softly on the forehead. 'I'm sorry,' she murmured. 'I'm so sorry.' Squeezing shut her eyes, she felt a splintering inside her, a gradual splitting open as though every part of her was being slowly torn apart. *Please God*, she prayed. *Don't let this be happening.*

Chapter Fifty-one

Iris stood in the bedroom at Silverstone Heights, gazing into the mirror. The face that stared back at her was so pale as to be almost ghostly. She wondered how she'd got through the past ten days. Some parts were a blur, others so distinct that she flinched even to think of them. If it hadn't been for Guy, she would have fallen apart; he had helped her survive the empty mornings, the bitter afternoons, and the sleepless haunted nights.

The police had been in touch with the results of the autopsy. No big surprises there: Michael had died as the result of severe internal injuries. There had been little progress to date on finding the car involved, thought to be a stolen black Vauxhall caught on CCTV speeding down the High Street. The cameras on Mansfield Road had been vandalised yet again, so there was no coverage of the actual 'incident'.

PC Matlock had informed her that Danny Street had provided an alibi, swearing he'd been working at Belles from eight o'clock on the Saturday night until after two the following morning. His brother and other members of staff had backed up the claim – no big surprises there either. Personally, Iris didn't see that as much of an alibi, but hadn't voiced her dissent. She had come to the conclusion, and Guy had agreed, that it might be better not to pursue it right now in case some curious copper started digging out old files and trying to work out just *why* the Streets might want to threaten her. If they went back far enough they might spot the connection between Liam Street's killing and the disappearance of Sean O'Donnell. For the time being she had to do whatever she could to protect her father; he didn't need the law getting interested in him too. So, if the cops wanted to believe that the cause of Michael's death was an accidental hit-and-run, she wasn't going to dispute it. This deception made her feel guilty as if she was turning her back on justice for him. But it was only temporary, she kept on reminding herself. Once she was sure her dad was out of danger, she wouldn't rest until Michael's killer had been exposed and brought to justice.

Iris smoothed down her long red hair. Now there was the funeral to endure and after that the drinks at the Dog. The day stretched in front of her, interminable hours of talking, of listening, of forcing her mouth into thank-you-for-coming smiles. She understood the significance of the rituals, but recoiled at the thought of them. What she really wanted to do was to crawl back into bed and pull the duvet over her head.

'Iris? Are you ready?'

She sighed and turned away from the mirror. Her mother had come down on the train and was now waiting in the living room. Despite Iris's resolve to never argue again with someone she loved, they'd almost had a falling out last week.

'The crematorium?' Kathleen had repeated tightly over the phone. 'What's wrong with St Anne's? It's still there, isn't it?'

'When was the last time Michael ever set foot in a church?'

'But there has to be a funeral mass.'

Iris was well aware that Michael hadn't cared much for religion. He may have been raised as a Catholic, but had long ago lost whatever faith he had. She'd been forced to listen to his drunken, although always amusing, ramblings on priests and rites and sin on more than one occasion. 'I don't think it's what he would have wanted.'

'But it's important, Iris.'

'It would just be hypocritical.'

Her mother's sharp intake of breath had been clearly audible. 'Well, I think you're wrong. And I don't think it's up to you to make such a serious decision. Unless Michael left specific instructions, put something in writing . . .'

But of course, not having the foresight to know he was about to get run over, Michael hadn't. He hadn't even left a will. And Iris couldn't put her hand on her heart and claim that he'd actually come right out and said what he did or didn't want done in the event of going to meet his maker. It was more a matter of what had been patently obvious. She'd been about to point out that, as his next-of-kin, it *was* actually up to her to make the final decision, but had had the sense to bite down on her tongue at the very last second. She had spoken in haste before and lived to regret it. 'Okay, okay, I'll think it over.'

Iris had discussed it with William – Tobias Grand & Sons were organising the funeral – and a compromise had been suggested: there could be a mass, but with the service taking place in the crematorium. 'Do you think that would offend him?' William had asked. It was the first time since Michael's death that Iris could remember smiling. It was partly because William has referred to him in the present rather than the past tense, but mainly because she suddenly realised that Michael wouldn't give a damn as to how he was buried so long as everyone had the decency to raise a pint of Guinness to him later.

In the living room her mother was sitting bolt upright on the sofa, her shoulders back and her hands placed demurely in her lap. Even when no one else was around, Kathleen O'Donnell wouldn't slouch. As Iris gazed at her, she was aware of how physically similar they were: the same height and body shape, the same greeny-grey eyes, even the same colour hair. It was as if she had got all her genes from the maternal side and none from the paternal. Maybe what she had inherited from him wasn't visible to the naked eye; it was on the inside rather than the out.

Iris glanced down at her watch. There were ten minutes to go, but she had a sudden desperate need to get out of the flat. She felt stifled by its walls, by its memories. The bare Christmas tree, still leaning pathetically to one side, had begun to shed its needles on the carpet. She felt her heart sink as she stared at it; it was hard to believe Christmas was only a week away. 'We may as well wait by the gate. Guy should be here soon.'

Kathleen's nose wrinkled at the mention of his name. 'I still don't understand why he's coming. It's not as though he knew Michael particularly well; you said yourself he hadn't seen him since he was a child.'

'You know perfectly well why he's coming. We're together and I want him to be there with me. *He* wants to be there for me.'

'But Lizzie Street's son,' Kathleen said, her tone flagrantly disapproving. 'Of all the men you could have chosen . . .'

Iris felt her hackles rise. Her mother hadn't met him yet, but had already formed a negative opinion. 'He's nothing like her. I've already explained that to you. He didn't even live with her while he was growing up. He's his own man, a decent man, and he runs a perfectly legitimate business. He's not an offshoot of some criminal dynasty.' She wanted to go on, to sing his praises, to say how amazing he'd been – especially in the hunt for her father – but couldn't do that without opening a can of worms.

Of course she would have to have *that* tricky conversation eventually, to reveal that she was aware of the robbery, of what her dad had done, but not today. It wasn't the right time, although the Lord alone knew when it would be right.

Kathleen pursed her lips. 'Have you even spoken to Luke about Michael?'

Iris walked through to the hall, opened the door and went out into the corridor. 'Why should he care? It's nothing to do with him any more. We've split up, Mum, and we're not getting back together. It's over.'

'But all couples have their differences. A relationship needs to be worked at. You can't give up at the first hint of trouble.'

Iris snorted as she turned to lock the door behind them. 'Hint? I'd call it more than that. He was the one who left me, remember. Dumped me for a champagne blonde with an overflowing bank account and a taste for other women's men.' She actually had no idea of the state of Jasmine's finances, but it made her feel better to cast some additional doubt on Luke's motives for leaving. Anyway, the girl looked the type to have a wealthy papa lurking somewhere in the background, a rich city slicker perhaps who wouldn't think twice about bankrolling his little angel's lifestyle. Not that Iris really cared. Not any more. She'd been hurt not so much by what Luke had done, but by his way of doing it.

Kathleen gave a weary sigh. 'All I'm saying is—'

'Yes, I know exactly what you're saying.'

They were silent as they descended in the lift. Iris looked at the floor and then glanced sideways at her mother, regretting the sharpness of the exchange. This wasn't a day for recriminations or bad feeling. Kathleen had liked Luke, had grown accustomed to him, and it was understandable that she wasn't comfortable with this sudden change in her daughter's situation.

Iris found herself wondering how her mother had managed

after Sean's abrupt departure. She'd been forced to make a new life for herself, to start over in an unknown city with a small child and no friends or family for support. It couldn't have been easy. That she'd survived was a testimony to her strength of character. She had worked hard to provide a decent home, to always put food on the table, to make Iris's childhood as happy as possible. And it had been happy, at least as happy as it could be with a father-sized space slap bang in the middle of it. Iris felt a stab of guilt. Perhaps it was time to stop blaming her for the things she hadn't done – like telling the truth about the past – and to start appreciating the things she had.

The lift came to a halt and they stepped into the coolness of the foyer.

'Let's not fall out,' Iris said, linking her arm through her mother's. 'I'm really glad you came. It means a lot to me.' Her mother might have let her down in some ways, but in others she was always there for her. Iris briefly leaned her head against her shoulder. It was at times like these you really needed your family.

Chapter Fifty-two

Iris sat in the front pew at the crematorium with her mother to her left and Guy to her right. They hadn't talked much in the car. When Guy had shaken hands with Kathleen and said that he was pleased to meet her, she had been polite but distant. Iris hoped he hadn't been offended. Perhaps he would presume that her mind, understandably, was somewhat preoccupied.

The chapel was filled with flowers and Iris breathed in the heady scent of lilies. She looked over her shoulder as the seats gradually filled. It was gratifying that there was such a good turnout. Michael, with his good sense of humour and generous ways, had been popular not just with his peers, but with many other members of the community too. He might occasionally have strayed on to the wrong side of the law, but his heart had always been a kind one. Iris held in a groan as that familiar ache rolled through her body. It was still impossible to accept that she would never see him again.

Vita had chosen to sit a few rows back. Rick wasn't with her – he was one of the pall bearers – and Iris tried to catch her eye, but she was staring determinedly down at the Order of Service sheet. Michael's death, coming so soon after the row, had meant that any serious attempts at reconciliation were on hold. They'd talked briefly on the phone and exchanged an awkward hug when they'd met at the entrance, but things were still strained between them. How to put it right? Iris didn't know. She wasn't even sure if she had the energy to try.

Turning back to face the front, she glanced at her mother. 'I never realised Michael knew so many people.'

Kathleen gave a shrug of her shoulders. Her voice was hard, almost cynical. 'All his drinking buddies, no doubt. He spent more time in the pub than anywhere else.'

Iris felt a spurt of annoyance. She wondered why her mother had even bothered to come if she had nothing better to say about him; it wasn't as if she'd had any time for Michael while he was alive. But then, like before, she felt ashamed of judging her too harshly. Everyone dealt with loss in their own way. For all the water that had passed under the bridge, some of it turbulent, he had still been her brother-in-law. She supposed they must have been close once.

Guy reached out and took her hand as the coffin was carried in. She grasped his fingers tightly, barely able to contain her emotions. As they laid the coffin on the plinth, she blinked back the tears. Rick turned around and walked back past without looking in her direction; keeping his gaze focused straight ahead.

As the mass began, Iris stared over at the stained-glass windows. The sun had come out and it was slanting through the glass, making multi-coloured rainbows at her feet. She found herself thinking of all the trials she'd put Michael through, all the secrets she'd forced him to reveal. What if the Streets hadn't been responsible for his death? Maybe she was just trying to shift the blame on to someone else. What if he'd got blind drunk and staggered out into the road because of everything

370

she'd said and done? Her obsession with finding her father had clearly driven him to distraction. Iris bowed her head, suddenly overwhelmed with memories of that last argument at Vita's.

As the service continued, Iris automatically went through the responses, slipping in the Hail Marys where she was supposed to. She was only half listening. Her mind was distracted. Another thought had popped into her head and she kept turning and glancing quickly over her shoulder to scour the faces of the assembled mourners. Surely her father wouldn't miss his own brother's funeral? But at the same time she knew it would be madness for him to come here. If the Streets were still searching – and why shouldn't they be? – this would be the obvious place to look. But still, she couldn't help wondering, hoping, that he might be close, at the same time willing him to stay away, to keep safe.

She caught sight of William Grand standing at the back. He gave her a tiny nod, his eyes full of concern. Over the last ten days, she had relied on him almost as much as she'd relied on Guy. He had taken her through the funeral arrangements, endlessly kind and sympathetic. He'd helped her choose the coffin, the hymns and readings, never losing patience as she hesitated, dithered and frequently changed her mind. Each decision had felt so momentous she could hardly bear to take it.

Guy leaned in a little closer and she felt the warmth and comfort of his body. As she looked at him, he mouthed, 'Are you okay?' She tried to smile but didn't quite succeed. Her lips felt dry, almost frozen.

The priest was talking about Michael. Iris tried to concentrate, to listen to what he was saying, but her thoughts kept floating away. How had this happened? Why? But she knew why – the past had finally caught up with them all. Michael had paid the price for all her father's terrible mistakes.

As the final prayers were said, Iris bent her face and gazed at the polished wooden floor. So this was it. She glanced sideways at the coffin with its raised crucifix. She thought of Michael lying motionless inside, dressed in his crisp white shirt and dark grey suit. She wanted to believe in God and heaven, but wasn't sure if she could. What if this was it? What if there was nothing else?

Outside, the sunlight was glinting on the snow. The sudden brightness made Iris screw up her eyes. Guy put his arm around her and kissed the top of her head. 'It's over now,' he said. She nodded, even though nothing much did feel over. The funeral, yes, that had been survived, but it had done little to assuage her grief. The pain rolled over her again in waves so strong that she thought she might drown.

'It will get easier,' Guy said. 'I promise you.'

But Iris wasn't in a place where she could imagine such a thing. She gulped down a sob and brushed the tears away with the back of her hand. 'Will it?'

'What I mean,' he continued softly, 'is that there'll come a point when you can look back on the happy times and not the sad ones. You'll be able to remember the Michael you loved and not just the agony of losing him.'

She buried her face for a moment in his shoulder. Was he speaking from personal experience? It wasn't that long since he'd lost his mother. They may have lived separate lives, but she knew that he missed her. 'Do you . . . do you wish that you'd gone to your mum's funeral?'

Guy shook his head. 'She made a new family for herself. I wasn't part of that. I wouldn't have been welcome.'

She raised her face, frowning as she looked into his eyes. 'But you had every right to be there.'

'Yes,' he agreed, 'but it wouldn't have made me feel better about anything. The only kind of closure I'd have been looking

372

for would have involved my fists and Terry Street's hypocritical jaw. And I've always thought there's something rather undignified about scrapping in church.'

Iris smiled despite herself. 'But not in funeral parlours?'

'Ah, but I didn't start that.'

As Iris looked back towards the door of the chapel, she saw her mother talking to the priest. She would be doing the decent thing, expressing her thanks, saying how nice the service had been. Iris felt a rush of both gratitude and guilt. Enclosed in her bubble of grief, clinging on to Guy, she had forgotten all about the common courtesies. She should be putting on a brave face, talking to people. She should be looking for William and thanking him for everything he'd done. She should be searching out Vita and trying to build some bridges.

But Iris couldn't see either of them in the crowd that was gathering outside the chapel. Already some of the mourners were starting to drift away, to get into their cars, heading for the Dog & Duck. She looked towards the road, wondering if the Streets were watching. She thought again about her father and her eyes quickly raked the memorial gardens in case he might be viewing the proceedings from a safe distance. But there was no one there.

'He won't come here,' Guy said. 'Not today.'

She looked up at him, startled by how easily he had read her mind. 'I just thought—'

'I know,' he said.

Iris didn't get the chance to say anything else. Her mother had left the priest and was walking towards them. As she came closer, Guy slipped his arm from her waist. 'I'll be in the car,' he said.

'You don't have to go.'

He bent and kissed her again, this time on the lips. 'I'll be waiting. Take your time. Take as much time as you need.'

373

As he left he smiled at Kathleen, but she didn't smile back. Iris watched as her mother's eyes narrowed into two thin slits.

'What's the matter?' Iris said.

Kathleen pursed her lips, watching as Guy walked towards the car park. 'How much do you really know about that man?'

'Enough,' Iris said sharply.

The exchange was interrupted by the ringing of her mother's phone. 'Heavens,' Kathleen said, 'I thought I'd turned that off.' She took it from her bag and checked the screen. 'It's work. I'd better take it.'

'Don't they realise you're at a funeral?'

But she'd already turned, moved a few steps away and was speaking softly to the caller. Iris didn't get a chance to hear what she was saying. A couple of Michael's friends came over to shake her hand and express their condolences. Iris went through the motions, saying, yes, it had been a lovely service; yes, there had been a good turnout; yes, she would see them shortly in the Dog & Duck. All the time she was watching her mother: Kathleen had her head bent to the phone, a small smile playing around her lips. If that was work, Iris thought, she was the Queen of Siberia. There was more than business being discussed in that conversation. Still, why shouldn't she have someone special in her life? She was only in her late forties and still a very attractive woman.

'Something important?' Iris asked as her mother hung up and put the phone in her pocket.

'Oh, just some papers that had gone astray.'

Kathleen worked as a PA for one of the senior partners in a large legal firm in Manchester. Iris could still remember her learning to type, her fingers tap-tapping away on the keyboard of a second-hand computer. That memory sparked off others too: a tiny kitchen with a damp patch on the ceiling, the roar of traffic from a main road, the strange sights and smells of an unfamiliar city. Which city had it been? They had lived in so many, especially in those early years. There had never been boyfriends, at least none that she knew of. Her mother must have been lonely with only a young child for company.

'That's all?' Iris said. 'Just some papers?'

'It's a busy office. Things go missing.'

'Well, I suppose it goes to show how indispensable you are. Was that your boss?'

But Kathleen wouldn't be drawn. She looked down at her watch. 'We'd better go. We don't want to be late.'

Iris didn't see how they could be late – it wasn't as if the guest of honour was even going to be there – but she didn't say anything. If her mother didn't want to talk about her mystery caller, then so be it. Everyone was entitled to a private life. Not that she was giving up on finding out. Maybe later, after a few drinks, she might be more forthcoming. As they walked towards the car, Iris took her hand and gave it a squeeze.

Chapter Fifty-three

Vita and Rick had organised the post-funeral gathering, for which Iris was grateful. It had been one less thing to worry about. The Dog & Duck was packed and they had to squeeze through the crowd to get to the bar. Their progress was slow; every few feet or so they were stopped by somebody wanting to shake their hands, to express their sympathy, to talk about Michael. Eventually, Guy had taken their drink orders and proceeded on his own.

By the time he got back, Iris had become separated from her mother. It seemed that Kathleen had not been forgotten despite her long absence from Kellston. Old friends and neighbours had hugged and kissed her and whisked her away for a catch-up. Iris took the glass of wine from Guy and knocked half of it back in one.

'Hey,' he said, 'take it easy. You carry on like that and you'll be legless before you know it.'

'My homage to Michael,' she said. 'I think he'd approve.'

'In that case I'll get a bottle next time.'

'Now that sounds like the best idea I've heard all day.' She suddenly wanted to be drunk, very drunk, to be removed from everything that was going on around her. The gathering served to remind her of that evening, not so long ago, when she had met Michael in the Hope for Lizzie's wake. Had Lizzie been the love of his life? Was that why he'd never married? No, she thought, with a little shake of her head, she was just romanticising. She wasn't sure if she really believed in soulmates, in there being just one other person in the world who you were meant to be with . . . and yet when she looked at Guy she felt a quickening of her pulse, a stirring in her heart that she'd never experienced before.

'Do you believe in . . .' She had been about to say fate, but stopped and bit down on her tongue. In the circumstances, there was something decidedly tasteless about the question, and anyway it was way too early to be thinking of her and Guy as a long-term prospect.

'Believe in?'

'Oh, nothing,' she said. 'It doesn't matter.' She glanced around the pub and spotted Rick in the adjoining room. He had taken off his black jacket and was playing pool in a half-hearted sort of fashion. She should have a chat with him. But not right now. She wasn't ready yet. Half a glass of wine wasn't nearly enough to banish her embarrassment over what she'd accused him of. Shifting her gaze, she saw William Grand in conversation with a couple of tearful middle-aged blondes. Michael had been popular with the ladies and this pair, she suspected, were just two of his many conquests. How he had always managed to disentangle himself without causing any lasting bad feeling was beyond her. As she was looking, William raised his gaze and gave her a rueful smile. He had the forlorn expression of a man in need of rescuing.

Iris turned to Guy. 'I'd better go and thank William for everything he's done.'

377

He nodded. 'Sure. I'll wait for you here. In fact, no, I'll head back to the bar and get us that bottle I was talking about.'

'You're an angel. I won't be long.'

William nodded at the two women, excusing himself as Iris approached. 'How's it going?' he said to her.

Iris pulled a face. 'Not too bad. I just don't know what to say to people.' She frowned. 'Well, I do know, but it all seems so trite, so glib. I feel like I'm just going through the motions. And that doesn't seem right. It's like I'm being fake, just pretending but . . .' She paused, surprised by this sudden articulation of thoughts she hadn't even realised were in her head.

William placed his hand lightly on her arm. 'You're doing fine. None of this is easy. No one expects you to be the perfect hostess. It's not a party,' he said.

She kept her voice low. 'But I thought these things were supposed to help, to provide some kind of *closure*.'

'Not closure,' William said. 'It isn't about that. It's about . . . I don't know . . . celebrating the man he was, appreciating the memories he's left you with.'

Iris drained her glass and put it down on a table. 'Except all I can think about is that we argued on the night he died. He got mad at me and . . . I should have made things right. I shouldn't have just left it.' She could feel the tears pricking her eyes and swiftly wiped them away.

'And do you think that's how he'd like you to remember him – that one single moment above all others?'

She sighed. 'No, I guess not.'

'I take it this was his favourite pub?'

'You could say that.' She looked around at the shabby wallpaper, at the peeling paint around the windows. She glanced towards the other room where Rick was still playing pool. 'Come to think of it, I'm surprised they didn't charge him rent.'

William smiled. 'So you do have some good memories.'

'Of course I do, but . . . but it doesn't make anything right, does it? I mean how it ended. I never got the chance to tell him how much I cared, how much I loved him.' Iris picked up her glass, found that it was empty and put it down again.

'Here,' William said, passing her his own glass. 'Have this. I shouldn't be drinking – I've got to get back soon.'

Iris peered into the glass. It looked like whisky. She lowered her nose and took a sniff. Yes, it was definitely whisky. Mixing her drinks probably wasn't such a great idea, but she took a sip nonetheless. 'I wanted to say thanks for everything you've done. You know, for today and all the arrangements and coming to the mortuary with me.'

'There's no need.'

'All in a day's work?'

'No, I didn't mean that.' He turned his face away. Just before he did, she saw something flash into his eyes.

'William?'

After a second, he turned back to her, his features perfectly composed. 'I want you to know that I'm here if you need me. I don't just mean as an employer, although that too, but as a friend.'

'Thank you,' she said. 'I appreciate it.'

'I didn't realise that you knew Guy Wilder.'

There was something slightly strained about his tone. 'Yes,' Iris said. 'We're . . . we've known each other for a while.'

'I see.'

Iris was about to ask exactly what *I see* meant when Toby suddenly descended on them. And he was clearly well ahead on the drinks front. From the way he was talking, he'd probably shifted a few lines of coke too. 'Shit,' he said, wrapping an arm around her shoulder. 'I know you must be mad at me. I can't blame you for that. But the only reason I said that stuff about Danny was because I was worried about you getting involved

379

with the cops and all. I mean, you weren't thinking straight. And you don't want to get mixed up with the Streets. They're crazy, babe. And God, you don't mind me being here, do you? I didn't know Michael that well, but he was a great guy.'

'It's fine,' she said, pushing him gently away. 'Or at least it would be if you could give me a tiny bit of space.'

'I should be going,' William said. 'Take care of yourself, okay?'

'I will. And thanks again.'

Toby watched him leave with a big grin on his face. 'Grimm Junior trying to lure you back into work, is he? I tell you, that place has been falling apart without you.'

'I doubt that very much,' Iris said, sipping on the whisky. She felt the warmth as it slid down her throat. Having skipped breakfast, she could feel the effects of it too. Already a slight haziness was starting to invade her thoughts. She liked the feeling, the way it took the edge off the pain.

'We've got a temp in of course, but she hardly brightens up the place. She's as bloody old as the hills. I don't think telephones were even invented when she was born.' He picked up a sandwich from a plate on the table, bit into it and chewed. 'So are you coming back soon?'

'After the weekend,' Iris said. 'Can you survive until then?'

'It's not me I'm worried about. I spend as little time in that damn place as I possibly can. I think Grimm Junior might be pining though. He walks around all day looking like a sick puppy dog.'

'Don't be ridiculous,' Iris said.

Toby laughed. 'The trouble with some women is that they can't see what's right in front of their noses.'

'And the trouble with some men is that they don't understand the meaning of friendship.'

'Have it your way,' he said, stuffing the rest of the sandwich into his mouth. 'But don't say I didn't warn you.'

Despite her dismissive tone, a part of Iris couldn't help considering if he was right. Hadn't William been rather attentive over the past few weeks? And what was that he'd said only a few minutes ago – *I'm here if you need me?* She frowned, thinking how difficult this might make things at work. But no, Toby was probably just trying to wind her up. He wouldn't let anything as inconvenient as a funeral get in the way of his entertainment. And it wasn't five minutes since he'd been convinced that something was going on between Alice Avery and William. 'Well, it's been lovely to have a chat, but I'd better start circulating. Duties to perform and all.'

'Sure. Catch you later, hun.'

'If you can still stand up,' Iris said. Although she was one to talk. She had every intention of getting blind drunk herself. By now she'd finished the last few drops of whisky and was in desperate need of a refill.

Toby sloped off, nudging his way through the crowd, and Iris looked around for Guy, but couldn't see him. He must have got caught up in the queue at the bar. She was about to head that way herself when Vita appeared by her side.

'Hey, how are you bearing up?'

'It still feels unreal,' Iris said. 'Thanks for doing all this.' She gave a wave of her hand, taking in their surroundings. 'It was really good of you.'

'That's okay.'

'How's Rick?'

'Oh, you know,' Vita said. 'He's taking it pretty hard. Michael's been his best mate for years. The two of them were virtually inseparable. He hardly knows what to do with himself.'

Iris wondered if Vita was making some kind of point – that Rick had known Michael for much longer than she had and was perhaps more family to him than she, his niece, had ever been. Or maybe she was being too thin-skinned, imagining slights where none were intended. Either way, she had to admit that twelve months was hardly long enough to form the kind of bonds that came from years of friendship. 'I'm so sorry about what I said, about Rick and the money. I suppose you told him?'

Vita stared down at her shoes. There was a small awkward silence. 'I had to,' she said. 'You do understand that, don't you?'

'Of course I do, but . . . but I was wrong. I was way off the mark. He'd never do anything like that. I was just upset, confused. Everything's been such a mess and now . . .' Iris shrugged. 'I can't figure out how to put things right. Do you think I should talk to him?'

'Some time,' Vita said, 'but not today, not when emotions are running so high. Maybe later, in a week or two, when things have calmed down a bit.'

Iris nodded. 'But you'll tell him, won't you? You'll let him know I'm sorry?'

'Sure.'

'I don't want there to be all this bad feeling between us. It's entirely my fault, I know it is, and I'll do anything to put it right.'

'Try not to worry. I'm sure we'll sort it out.' But there was something in her eyes that told Iris it might not be that easy. A bond of trust had been broken and it would take more than a few apologies to weld it back together again.

'Thanks.'

Vita changed the subject. 'So I see you've brought the beautiful Daniel Craig with you. How's that going?'

Once upon a time, and it wasn't that long ago, Iris would have opened up and told her everything – about how she felt, about how this might finally be the real thing – but at the moment there were too many barriers between them. Now wasn't the time to be sharing confidences. 'It's early days,' she said, 'but I like him. He's good to me.'

'So long as he makes you happy.'

'Try telling that to my mother.'

'She's probably worried. I mean, you and Luke have only just split up. She's bound to be concerned.'

'We didn't split up. He dumped me.'

Vita swept back her long dark hair. 'All the more reason to be cautious about getting involved with someone else so quickly.'

'You don't like him,' Iris said defensively.

'I don't know him,' Vita said, 'and neither do you, not really. How long has it been – a few weeks? All I'm saying is that maybe you shouldn't rely on him too much.'

Iris, sensing that they could be on the verge of another row, had to fight the urge to snap back a retort. Why couldn't the people she was close to actually be happy for her? Through all the recent bad times – and had there ever been worse ones? – Guy had been the one person who'd continued to believe in her. Still, she couldn't expect Vita or her mother to understand. Guy was a stranger to them and maybe, if she was in their shoes, looking in from the outside, she might be tempted to give the same kind of advice.

'He's a good man,' Iris said calmly. 'There are lots of blokes who'd have run a mile at the prospect of dealing with the kind of things I've been through recently.'

'Talk of the devil,' Vita said.

Iris glanced over her shoulder. Guy was approaching with a bottle of wine in one hand and two clean glasses in the other.

Vita leaned forward and patted her on the arm. 'You take care, okay?'

'There's no need to rush off.'

'No, I'd best get back to Rick. I'll see you later.'

Guy watched her as she left and then put the bottle down on the table. 'Another one of my fans?'

'What?'

'Your friend saw me coming and couldn't get away fast enough.'

'It's not like that,' Iris said quickly. She didn't want him to feel disliked or rejected. 'It's me she's upset with, not you. She had to get back to Rick; Michael's death has hit him pretty hard.'

'I'm only kidding. Although a less secure man could start to develop a complex. Your mother didn't seem that overjoyed at meeting me either.'

'She'll like you,' Iris said, 'once she gets to know you. She's not that keen on change and with everything that's happened . . .'

Guy passed her a glass of wine. 'It's okay. I understand.'

Iris stood on her toes and peered around, searching for her mum. Perhaps now would be a good time for her and Guy to get acquainted. With so many people squashed into the pub, it took a while to locate her. She was standing across the other side of the room, near the door, with the phone glued to her ear again. Iris saw her mouth the words '*Hold on a minute*' into the silver mobile before she pulled open the door and went outside.

Ten minutes later she still hadn't come back. Iris waited impatiently, shifting from foot to foot. Just how many papers went missing in that office? Or was this a different caller? She sipped some more wine. A few people approached, expressed their sympathy, and wandered off again.

Iris put her glass down on the table. 'I'm going to see where my mother's got to.'

Outside, the cold air hit her like a slap. The sun had gone in and the sky had turned an ominous shade of grey. Iris shivered, her arms hugging her chest, as she looked to the left and the right. There was no sign of her. The Dog & Duck was on a corner so she hurried around the side and gazed down the street. Yes, there she was, standing near the bank, deep in conversation with some bloke. He was one of the mourners perhaps, who had caught her on his way in or out of the pub.

Despite the cold, Iris hung back, not wanting to interrupt. There was something intense about the exchange, something almost intimate. They were standing very close together, their bodies almost touching. A few minutes passed and still the two of them were talking. She couldn't see the man's face, only the back of his silver-haired head. Should she leave them to it or wait? She kept hoping that her mother might look up and notice her, but she was clearly too preoccupied.

Iris was about to return to the pub when Guy appeared. He was carrying her coat and he placed it carefully around her shoulders. His voice, although light-hearted on the surface, had undertones of worry. 'Ah, here you are. I was beginning to think you'd done a runner.'

'Sorry,' she said.

It was Guy's arrival that must have alerted her mother. She suddenly glanced to one side and spotted her daughter. Iris saw panic enter her eyes and didn't understand. Why would she . . .? But then the man turned his head and Iris saw him clearly for the first time. The shock was so great that for a second she could neither think nor move. Horror immobilised her body. And then a howl, a sound that was almost primitive, rose up from the depths of her soul and echoed around the street.

Chapter Fifty-four

As the adrenalin kicked in, Iris launched herself forward. It was the scars she had noticed first, those fierce white lines rising up from the collar of his shirt. *Terry Street!* She couldn't believe it. Terry bloody Street out of jail and standing chatting to her mother as if it was the most natural thing in the world. She had never fully understood that phrase *seeing red* before, but now she did. If she'd had a knife to hand she'd have picked it up and plunged it through his heart. A crimson fury was burning in her brain.

'You bastard!' she screamed, grabbing hold of the lapels of his overcoat. 'You fucking bastard!' Almost immediately she let go and began to hammer on his chest with her fists. 'Come here to make sure he's dead, have you? Come to gloat?'

Either surprised by the ferocity of the attack, or unwilling to use undue force against a woman in public, Terry did little to defend himself. His face looked white, almost as shocked as hers. His mouth opened, but no words came out.

'I hate you!' Iris screamed.

It was Kathleen who grasped her arms and tried to pull her off. 'What are you doing? Stop it! Leave him alone!'

Iris was breathing heavily, her lungs pumping out only rage and bitterness. She continued to beat at him. 'Yes, he's dead! He's dead! Are you satisfied now? Are you happy? You couldn't kill my father so you killed Michael instead!' She pummelled his chest, her fists beating against the thick cloth of his overcoat. 'You bastard!'

'Stop it!' her mother insisted again. This time she managed to drag Iris off. 'What are you doing?'

Iris struggled, desperately trying to get free. 'What are *you* doing? Let go of me!' But Kathleen held on tight. Iris turned, wide-eyed, to her mother. 'He murdered Michael, for fuck's sake!'

'Of course he didn't. Michael was killed in a hit-and-run.'

Iris stared at her, tears running down at her cheeks. Why was she defending him? It didn't make any sense. It didn't make any sense that she'd been talking to him in the first place. 'So what's he doing here?'

Kathleen hesitated, the colour rising in her cheeks. 'We had things to discuss.'

'What things? What bloody things?' Iris was aware of a twisting in her stomach, like a burning rope coiling through her guts. It made her almost double up. 'We haven't got anything to say to him – other than we hope he rots in hell.' She finally wrenched her arms free. Her eyes were blazing. She would have gone for Terry again if Guy hadn't stepped in and gently restrained her.

Bending close to her ear, he whispered, 'Don't give him the satisfaction, babe.'

By now a small crowd had gathered, fascinated by the spectacle. It wasn't every day you got a free show like this and they were making the most of it. Guy turned to them, his voice full of contempt. 'Fuck off!' he said. 'There's nothing more to see here.'

A few of them drifted away, but most of them ignored him.

Iris glared at Terry Street. 'You're sick,' she said. 'You're mad. You're a fucking psycho.'

He straightened out his collar and stared straight back at her. His cold grey eyes gave nothing away.

'Leave it,' her mother said to her. 'You don't know what you're talking about.'

Iris felt her heart thrashing against her ribs. Confusion battled with the pain and the anger. 'Is he threatening you? Is that was this is all about?'

Kathleen shook her head. 'He didn't kill Michael.'

Iris didn't like the way her mother was still defending Terry; she couldn't understand it. Suddenly she wanted some distance from them both. Holding on to Guy's arm, she took a few steps back. 'What's going on here?'

'Nothing,' Kathleen said. 'I already told you. We just needed to talk.'

'To talk?' Iris hissed. She spat out the words contemptuously. 'What the hell is there to talk about? You know what he is, what he's done. How can you even bear to look at him?'

Kathleen covered her face with her hands. 'Stop it,' she pleaded, 'please stop it.'

'Is there somewhere we can go?' Terry said. 'Somewhere we can talk in private.'

It was the first time since Lizzie's funeral that Iris had heard that rasping voice. It sent a chill down her spine. 'Don't you get it? No one has anything to say to you. *No one.* Leave us alone. We don't want you here.'

Guy moved forward slightly, his lips set in a snarl. 'You heard what the lady said.'

Terry gave a snort. 'And what the fuck's it got to do with you?'

Iris felt the muscles in Guy's arm flex as his right hand clenched into a fist. She could feel the hostility oozing from him, his hatred almost as great as her own. 'Don't,' she said warningly. 'He isn't worth it.' Her own attack had been instinctive, unpremeditated. Terry Street hadn't seen it coming. But with Guy he'd be ready, and who knew what he was carrying – a knife, a gun? And although her head told her that Terry wouldn't be so stupid as to kill him with so many witnesses present, her heart wasn't willing to take the risk.

Terry Street looked at Guy for a few seconds, gave a shrug and then returned his attention to Iris. 'Don't you want to know about your father?'

Iris drew in her breath. 'What?'

At the same time as she spoke, her mother gasped, 'No!'

'She's got a right, hasn't she?' Terry said.

Kathleen was shaking her head. 'For God's sake, we've just buried Michael. You can't do this. You *can't*.'

'I'm sorry, but it's not your decision.' He turned his cold gaze back on to Iris. 'Yes or no?'

Iris hesitated. What was she supposed to do? A part of her wanted to scream at him to go, to leave them all in peace, but another part – the greater part – was desperate to hear what he might have to say. It could be something she already knew, like the fact that her father had been present when Liam had been shot. But what if it was something else? What if the Streets had found out where he was hiding? What if they'd already killed him? But no, Terry Street wouldn't be standing here now if that was the case.

Kathleen rushed over and grabbed Iris by her free arm. 'Come on. We're leaving.'

But Iris didn't budge. Clinging tighter to Guy, she said to Terry, 'Is this about what happened to your son? Because if it is, then I know, okay? Michael told me all about it.'

This revelation shocked her mother into releasing her grasp. 'He told you?'

'Not willingly,' Iris said, 'I had to force it out of him. And I understand why you kept it a secret but . . . but I think I had the right to know.' Just like she had the right to know whatever else Terry Street might be thinking of telling her.

'There's more,' Terry said. 'A lot more. You want to hear it or not? Say no and I won't bother you again. But there're no second chances – it's now or never.'

Kathleen stared at him. 'Don't do this,' she said pleadingly. 'You promised. You said—'

But Terry wouldn't even meet her gaze. He kept his eyes firmly fixed on Iris. 'If the truth means anything to you . . .'

'He doesn't know what the truth means,' Kathleen said urgently. 'Don't listen to him, love. Don't listen to a word he says.'

Which made Iris all the more determined to go ahead. She was sick of all the secrets and lies. She hated Terry Street, but was no longer prepared to live out her life in ignorance. However hard it was, she had to hear him out. 'We can go to the flat. We can talk in private there.'

Terry nodded. 'Just the three of us: you, me and your mother. That's the deal. Take it or leave it.'

'You're not in any position to make deals,' Guy said.

'I'll let your new girlfriend be the judge of that.'

'I want Guy there,' Iris said. 'There's nothing you can say to me that I wouldn't want him to hear.'

Terry Street lifted his chin and Iris became aware of those brutal scars again. 'No,' he said. 'If you want to tell him later, then fine, that's up to you. But you can spare me twenty minutes first.'

Iris became overly aware of all the people gathered round, of everything they'd already seen and heard. She was reluctant to back down, but could see that Terry Street was adamant. She glanced at her mother, but her face was impossible to read. Oh, she could see the worry, the anxiety, but she wasn't entirely sure what underpinned it. All that was clear was that there was something she didn't want her to know. 'Okay,' Iris said. 'It's a deal.'

'No,' her mother said. 'Iris, *please.*'

'I'll see you at the flat.' Having the feeling that if they travelled together she might try to talk her out of it, Iris added, 'I'll meet you there. Guy can drop me off.' She rummaged through her bag and took out Luke's set of keys and his security card for the gate. 'Here,' she said, pushing them into her mother's hand. Then, without meeting her eyes again, she turned on her heel and walked away.

Kathleen called out, 'Iris?' but she didn't turn around. She didn't look back.

As they got into the car, Guy gave a sigh. 'You don't have to do this.'

'I do.'

'You can't trust him.'

Iris pulled her seatbelt across. Her hands were trembling, her whole body still reeling from the shock of what had happened. 'I don't like it any more than you do, but what options do I have? Spending the rest of my life looking over my shoulder? Always wondering what he knows and I don't? I can't live like that. I just can't.'

Guy thought about it for a moment, and then he nodded. 'You're right. You deserve to know the truth.' He started the engine and they pulled away from the kerb.

Chapter Fifty-five

Iris paced the flat, roaming from room to room, returning always to the kitchen where she could gaze down on the parking bays. She had a sudden desire for a cigarette, although she'd given up smoking when she'd found out she was pregnant. There was a bottle of wine in the fridge; she opened it and poured herself a glass. Raising it to her lips, she hesitated. Wouldn't it be better to keep a clear head? Yes, she decided, but took a gulp anyway. The fear of what was coming next was almost too much to endure.

A dark red sports car, low and sleek, rolled into the courtyard and Iris watched as Terry Street and her mother got out. She quickly drank some more wine. They didn't immediately make their way towards the entrance, but stood for a while and talked. Well, her mother talked. Terry didn't seem to be saying much at all. Iris could see her mouth moving, could see the pleading in her eyes, but he just shook his head.

After a while they stopped talking, moved towards the flats and disappeared from view.

A few minutes later there was a knock on the door. Iris

jumped even though she'd been expecting it. As Kathleen came inside, she wore a defeated expression. Iris felt a pang of remorse that she'd forced her into this situation. She was clearly upset, but had acquired an air of resignation too. It was as if she'd given up, as if all the fight had gone out of her.

'I'm sorry,' Iris said.

Her mother gave her a wavering smile. 'It's not too late. You can still—'

'I can't. I'm sorry, but I can't.' Iris wanted to say more, to try to explain, but Terry Street was right behind. She didn't speak to him. Instead, she simply waved him towards the kitchen. Had she still thought of this as her home, she'd never have invited him here but she'd long since ceased to feel much attachment to Silverstone Heights.

Iris didn't offer him a drink – this was hardly a social occasion – but she gestured towards the table and chairs. It was Kathleen who went to the cupboard and took out the bottle of brandy. She must have seen it when Iris was making coffee that morning. Kathleen found two glasses and poured a large shot into each of them. She glanced over at Iris. Iris shook her head; she still had the wine and she'd mixed enough drinks for the day. The brandy reminded her of Michael, of the drink he'd had here after being beaten up by Danny Street. And then she thought about the gathering at the Dog that would still be going on. This wasn't the way she should be celebrating Michael's life. Wasn't she meeting with the man who had probably murdered him?

There was an uncomfortable silence where no one knew where to start. Iris was aware of the aura Terry Street gave off, that air of power and control. He wasn't a young man but he wasn't spent either. There was still strength in his body, a sturdy determination to get what he wanted.

393

'So?' Iris said. They had both taken a seat, but she remained standing, leaning against the sink.

'Why don't you sit down?' her mother said.

But Iris couldn't. There was something fundamentally wrong about the three of them sitting around the table. She wanted to make it clear that although she may have invited Terry here, it didn't mean that he was welcome. The sooner he spat out what he had to say, the better.

'So what do you know?' he said.

Iris took a deep breath. She didn't look at her mother as she spoke – she might lose her nerve if she did – but kept her eyes focused on Terry Street. 'I know that my father broke into your house nineteen years ago. I know that your son was killed.' She paused for a second. 'And I'm sorry about what happened to him, I truly am, but my dad had no idea that Tyler was carrying a gun.' She could have added that she was sorry about what had happened to Terry too – those scars on his throat bore witness to how he'd also been a victim – but somehow couldn't bring herself to articulate the words. There was a part of her, a part she wasn't proud of, that wished Davey Tyler had been a better shot.

'Right,' Terry said. He glanced at Kathleen but she kept her eyes lowered, staring down at the table. 'And Michael told you this?'

'Yes,' Iris said. 'But my dad's not a bad man. You do understand that, don't you? He was there, he agreed to do something stupid, but he didn't know Davey Tyler was armed.'

'It was your father who had the gun,' Terry said bluntly.

Iris stared at him, her jaw falling open. She shook her head. 'No, no, you've got it all wrong. He was there but—'

'Ask your mother,' Terry said.

As Iris quickly turned to look at her, to recruit her in some defence against this vile accusation – it wasn't true, it couldn't be – she felt a sinking in her heart. She waited, but no rebuttals came, no expressions of outrage. Kathleen now had her face firmly buried in her hands.

'*He* had the gun?' Iris repeated faintly.

'He wanted to kill me,' Terry said, 'but his hand was shaking so much he killed my son instead.'

'No,' Iris remonstrated, still trying to cling on to hope. 'You're lying! I don't believe it. He'd never do anything like that.'

Kathleen raised her head. 'He was upset,' she murmured.

'Upset?' Iris repeated, her voice filling with anger and bewilderment. 'People get drunk when they're upset, they shout or cry or throw things around the room – they don't take a bloody gun and shoot someone!'

'I'm so sorry, love,' she said.

And at that moment, at that terrible moment, Iris knew Terry Street was telling the truth.

Kathleen drank some of the brandy and clattered the glass back down on the table. 'Your father didn't mean to do it. I swear. He'd never have . . . Yes, he went there to rob the place, I'm not denying that, but he didn't know that Terry and Liam were going to come back in the middle of it. They were supposed to be out for the evening. Sean panicked. The gun went off and—'

'No,' Iris interrupted. A sharp pain was spreading across her temples, like a knife being stabbed into her forehead. 'That doesn't make any sense. Why would he take a gun with him if he didn't expect to use it?'

'Because he wanted to kill me,' Terry said again. He stopped, as if trying to get his thoughts together. 'I'm not saying he *intended* to kill me, only that he wanted to. Having the gun made him feel like that was possible. It gave him power, even if it was only imaginary power.'

'He was angry,' her mother added. 'He was hurt.'

'Why?' Iris said. Even as the question slipped from her lips, she knew she would regret asking it.

Terry was the one to answer. 'Because he'd found out something.'

'Found out what?'

Terry glanced at Kathleen. She shook her head. 'No,' she whispered. 'Please don't.'

'She has a right to know,' Terry said.

'Tell me!' Iris demanded.

Terry hesitated, but then took a breath and said: 'Because he found out we were having an affair.'

In the silence that followed, Iris barked out a laugh. It was a nervous reaction. What had he just claimed? It was too mad, too ridiculous. Her mother, her nice respectable mother, and this murderous thug? Why would she do anything like that? It was vile. It was disgusting. But again her mother wasn't protesting and gradually the truth began to sink in. She felt a groan rise up from the pit of her stomach. No wonder her father had felt so betrayed.

'How . . . how could you?' Iris spluttered.

It wasn't her mother who answered but Terry. 'That's why he came to my house. That's why he wanted to rob me. It was payback time.'

Iris stared at the two people in front of her. Her mother suddenly felt like a stranger. She wanted to ask how she could have done it, how she could have willingly slept with this cold reptilian man. The very thought of it sent a shudder through her. And there were so many other questions, but they were all tumbling into her head in a crazy jumble, one crashing on top of another until she could barely think straight. 'So what's happened to my dad? What's *really* happened to him?'

Terry Street gave a brief dismissive shrug. 'I've no idea.'

'Don't lie to me,' Iris hissed. 'He killed your son. He shot you in the throat. You're not the type of man to let that go.'

'I promised your mother. I gave my word, swore I wouldn't go after him. She thought it was all her fault. She blamed herself for everything.'

And with due cause, Iris thought bitterly. If it hadn't been for her sordid little affair . . . 'So what's changed?'

'What do you mean?'

'You said you swore to leave him alone, but you're not doing that, are you? He's come back to Kellston and you can't wait to find out where he is.' Iris gave a snort. 'Perhaps you've found him already. So much for promises.'

Terry frowned. 'Why the hell would he come back? There's nothing here for him.'

'There's me!' Iris yelped, barely able to believe her ears. What was the matter with the bastard? Surely, if nothing else, he should be able to understand the urge of a parent to try to protect their child.

Terry opened his mouth to speak, but Kathleen jumped to her feet. There were tears running down her face. 'Stop it! That's enough!'

'No,' Terry said, his features finally taking on some animation. A light blazed into his eyes. 'It's *not* enough. I've done everything you've asked of me. I've stayed away. I've kept my silence all these years. Well, not any more. I've had enough of all the fucking lies, all the secrets. It ends here. It has to.' His high, sharp cheekbones were stained with red. 'If you don't tell her, Kathleen, I will.'

Iris looked quickly from one to the other. Her heart had started to thump. She raised her left hand to her mouth and bit down on her thumb. She could feel the four walls starting to close in on her. Oh God, what was coming next?

Kathleen stood very still. For a moment it seemed as if she'd turned to stone. Then, with her legs no longer able to support her, she slumped back into the chair. Like a trapped animal her gaze darted around the room as if there might still be some means of escape. Her lips opened but no sound came out.

Iris couldn't bear the silence. 'What are you trying to tell me?'

'What happened between us all those years ago,' Kathleen eventually said, glancing at Terry. 'It wasn't . . . wasn't just a fling.' Her voice was very low, barely audible. She swallowed hard, struggling to get the words out. 'It was more than that. Terry and me, we were . . . we were together for ten years.'

'Ten years?' Iris repeated dully. She couldn't take it in. Shock battled with confusion. 'But that's not possible. How could it be? We moved away, hundreds of miles away.'

'I don't mean then,' Kathleen said.

It took a few seconds for what it did mean to register in Iris's brain. When it did she gave a start. Her mother was referring to the time *before* they'd moved away. And that meant the relationship had been going on before Iris was even born. And then suddenly the full horror of what she was being told kicked in. Her eyes widened with fear and disgust. 'No,' she said hurriedly. 'It's not true. Tell me it's not true.'

Kathleen bowed her head. 'I'm so sorry.'

'You can't be sure,' Iris said. Her frantic gaze shifted to Terry. 'You can't be.'

'We had a blood test done,' he said. 'There isn't any doubt.'

Iris was still holding the wine glass. As her grip tightened, the glass suddenly shattered in her hand. She stared down at the cut on her palm, at the blood seeping between her fingers. She could feel the bottom slowly falling out of her world. Panic was gathering inside her. She couldn't breathe properly. Sweat was starting to run down her back. 'No,' she muttered, 'no, no, no.' If she repeated it often enough, it might eventually be true.

Kathleen stood up again, made as if to move towards her, but Iris shook her head. 'Stay away! Don't come near me.'

'Please,' her mother begged. 'You have to—'

'No, I don't want to hear it.' Iris turned and ran from the flat, slamming the door behind her. She stumbled along the corridor. As she half ran, half fell down the stairs, she felt a scream rising up inside her. It was too much to bear. She wanted to be sick. She was Terry Street's child, his flesh and blood. *She was a murderer's daughter!*

Chapter Fifty-six

It was over four hours now since Iris had learnt the terrible truth. She played with the bandage that Guy had wrapped around her hand, picking at the corners. She felt lost, disconnected, as if all her foundations had been wrenched up by the roots. Her mother had tried to call but Iris had turned off the phone. She couldn't talk to her, not yet. She was too upset, too enraged by what she'd done. There were so many things she wanted to ask but . . .

Unable to stay still, she jumped up from the sofa and went over to the window. It was dark outside and the street was jammed with rush-hour traffic. She saw a group of people cross the road and walk into the bar downstairs. She stared down at the long line of cars, wishing she had nothing more to worry about than when the lights would turn to green.

'You must hate me,' Iris said, glancing over her shoulder. 'How can you even bear to be near me?'

Guy stood up and came to stand behind her. 'What are you talking about?' He wrapped his arms around her waist. 'You're still the same person, Iris.'

400

'But I'm not,' she said bitterly. 'You know I'm not. I'm the daughter of the man you hate, of the man *I* hate. It's sick. It's disgusting.' She shuddered as she spoke the words out loud. If she could have reached into her body and ripped out every vile strand of Terry Street's DNA, she would.

'No,' Guy said tenderly, pulling her closer. 'You're Iris O'Donnell. You're *you*. You're not defined by who your parents are. I'm the son of Lizzie Street and God knows what piece of shit. Does that make me a blood-sucking leech? Does it make me a drug dealer, a pimp, a heartless bastard?'

'Of course not,' she said quickly.

'So?'

She shook her head. 'It's not the same.'

'Of course it's the same.' He turned her around. 'Look at me.' When she wouldn't, he gently lifted up her chin. 'You're young, intelligent, beautiful. What the fuck has any of that to do with Terry Street? Don't let him do this to you. You've got your own identity. If you let him get under your skin like this, he'll destroy you.'

Iris wanted to believe what he was saying, but shock had blunted her ability to reason in any logical fashion. Coherent thought, at least for the moment, was completely beyond her. Too many questions were whirling around in her head. 'I just . . . I can't get anything straight. Nothing makes any sense. He's not out there, is he? My dad.' She squeezed shut her eyes and opened them again. 'The man I *thought* was my dad. He hasn't come back. Why would he? He knew I wasn't his. He's never coming back. All that knocking on doors, all that searching – it's been a waste of time.'

Guy leaned down and kissed her forehead. 'It looks that way. I'm sorry.'

'But if he hasn't come back, why was I being threatened?'

'Maybe someone started a rumour. Maybe it was the Weasel

who set the ball rolling. He needed a few quid, knew Terry was coming out of jail soon, and decided to stir up a hornet's nest. If he claimed he'd seen Sean—'

'So Jenks must have known that my dad . . .' She paused, the word sounding suddenly weird on her lips. 'He must have known that he'd been involved in Liam's murder.'

'Well, he worked for Terry for long enough. I doubt if there was much he didn't know . . . except for who your real father was, of course. That was one little secret that Terry managed to keep well hidden.'

Iris frowned. 'But that still doesn't explain why the Streets were threatening me. Why did Danny come to Tobias Grand & Sons? Why did they hire some thug to follow me around? Why would Terry let them do that? Why would he allow them to scare me half to death?'

Guy gave a sigh, his lips briefly touching her forehead again. 'If I'm giving him the benefit of the doubt, I guess it's just about possible that he wasn't aware of what was going on. He was still inside when all this started, wasn't he? The last time he saw the boys, before being released, was probably at my mother's funeral. Jenks turning up with some news about their brother's killer isn't the type of thing they'd have wanted to discuss over the phone so maybe Chris and Danny went ahead on their own. Terry might have only found out about it when he got home.'

'And if you're not giving him the benefit of the doubt?'

Guy gave a light shrug. 'He gets his scumbag sons to do his dirty work, to put the fear of God in you, and then he tells them to back off. The great long lost father comes riding to the rescue. It would be one way to get you on side, wouldn't it?'

'Jesus,' Iris said, a hand rising to her mouth. She felt the revulsion rise in her again. How could she be that man's child? 'I don't even understand why he *wants* me to know I'm his daughter. What's the point after all these years? Why couldn't he just leave me alone?'

'Because you're his, Iris. You're a piece of property, a possession, something that *belongs* to him. It's nothing to do with love. That man wouldn't recognise love if it kicked him in the balls. I guess while my mother was alive, he didn't have much choice in the matter, but now . . .'

'Do you think she knew about the affair, about me?'

Guy gave another shrug. 'There wasn't much she didn't know when it came to that bastard.'

'So why did she stay with him?'

His voice, when he answered, was filled with bitterness. 'Why do you think? Christ, she was willing to give up her own son if it meant she could live in comfort for the rest of her life. You think she'd have left him, sacrificed her entire future, just because Terry couldn't keep it in his pants?' He stopped and mumbled 'Sorry' into the crown of her head. 'I shouldn't be talking like this. I just wish I'd known, that she'd told me, and I could have saved you all this grief.'

Iris lifted her face to look at him. Her mouth was trembling. 'Nothing could have made this any easier. No matter how I heard it, or who I heard it from.'

'No,' he said. 'I guess not. But at least you could have been prepared.'

Another thought rose quickly to the surface. 'God, they don't know who I am, do they? Chris and Danny, I mean. They don't know I'm their half-sister.' They would be as happy, she was sure, to hear the news as she had been.

'If they don't, they soon will. It's not as though he can keep it from them now.'

Iris groaned into his shoulder. If only she could make it all go away. 'How could she?' Iris whispered. 'She's my mother and I thought I knew her but . . . God, ten years of skulking around behind my dad's back.' And Sean O'Donnell *had* been her father in every real sense. He'd been the one to read her bedtime stories, to hold her hand as they crossed the road, to comfort her when she fell over. She thought of how he must have felt when he'd found out. No wonder he'd gone out and bought himself a gun. She could sympathise with the desire to shoot Terry Street straight through the bloody heart. 'He should have taken me with him when he left. I wish he had.'

'I'm glad he didn't,' Guy said. He lifted her face again and his eyes sought out hers. 'We can get through this. I promise.'

Iris began to cry, great heaving sobs as if all her emotions had suddenly been unleashed. She gripped the back of his shirt with her hands. 'I'm scared,' she wailed through her tears. 'I don't know who I am any more. I don't know what Terry wants. I don't know—'

Guy wrapped her tightly in his arms. 'I won't let him anywhere near you. I promise. I'll take care of you, Iris. I swear I'll never let anything bad happen to you ever again.'

Chapter Fifty-seven

It took Vita a while to find her husband. Rick was slumped in a corner of the Dog & Duck, looking somewhat the worse for wear. She sat down beside him and he immediately started to talk about Michael. His eyes were tired and bloodshot, his face slightly sweaty, and there was a damp stain on the front of his white shirt where someone had spilt half a glass of red wine as they pushed past. He'd been drinking heavily all afternoon and had now fallen into that rather rambling state of mind where one road led on to another but no destination ever seemed to be reached.

'I don't suppose you've seen Iris?' Vita said, interrupting his monologue.

'Iris?' he repeated. For a second he appeared confused as if the name didn't mean anything to him, but then sighed into his pint and said, 'She thinks Michael was murdered, doesn't she?'

'Don't worry, she's not pinning it on you. Not yet at least.'

'She thinks the Streets did it.'

Vita stared at him. 'Who told you that?'

His heavy shoulders lifted in a shrug. 'Bound to, isn't she.' He lifted the glass to his mouth, took a drink and placed it back on the table. 'Perhaps she's right. I wouldn't put anything past Danny Street. That bastard would have done it with a smile on his face.'

'Oh, come on,' Vita said. 'I thought you didn't believe in all that stuff about her dad coming back. Michael certainly didn't.' She paused. 'Unless he told you something he didn't tell me.'

'It might not have been to do with that.'

'What are you talking about?'

Rick seemed about to tell her, but then clearly changed his mind. 'Nothing,' he murmured. 'It doesn't matter.'

'It obviously does matter or you wouldn't have mentioned it.'

He peered at the wall for a few seconds, at a spot just above her head and then slowly lowered his gaze. Suddenly, his whole body stiffened and his eyes widened in alarm. 'Shit, Vita. What if I'm next? What if Danny Street's coming for me too?'

Thinking all this was down to some drunken leap of the imagination, she started to laugh. 'Don't be crazy. Why on earth would he—'

'Michael just wanted a bit of cash,' Rick said quickly. He leaned forward, the words tumbling out of him. 'An emergency fund. You know, in case he had to scarper. With Terry coming out of jail and . . . he couldn't be sure, you see . . . it was different when Lizzie was alive, but when she was killed, it changed everything. All deals were off. You know what I mean?'

Now Vita was starting to get worried. Her stomach twisted a little.

'Michael said he'd give me half if I helped him. I needed the cash. With Candice wanting this ski trip, with all the bills and everything . . . well, it's not right that you have to pay out all the time.'

'Helped you with what? Jesus, what are you saying?'

Rick looked quickly around, checking that no one was within earshot. 'It's to do with Toby Grand,' he said. 'Gerald Grand's son.'

'What about him?' Vita had never been introduced but knew him by sight. In fact, she was sure he'd been here earlier. He was a young blond guy who Iris had occasionally talked about – a guy, if she remembered rightly, who had a pretty high opinion of himself.

Rick took a deep breath. Then he took another drink. 'Shit,' he said again.

'Tell me. Tell me what's going on.'

He stared at her for a while, his fear of Danny Street clearly vying with the consequences of confession. 'It was at Lizzie's do,' he finally said, 'at the Hope & Anchor. Toby was high as a kite, completely off his head. He got talking to Michael after Iris had left, started dropping hints about Danny Street and his *unusual* interests.'

Vita frowned. 'What kind of interests?'

'You don't want to know.'

Vita was starting to lose patience. 'For God's sake, just spit it out. I'm a lawyer for Christ's sake. You think I haven't heard it all before?'

'Okay, okay. He had a fascination with bodies, women's bodies, and I don't mean the living breathing kind.'

Despite her earlier protestations, Vita started. She jumped back in surprise. She hadn't been expecting anything quite as gross as that. 'What?'

'Yeah,' Rick said. 'He's a fucking nutter.' He stopped briefly, ran his tongue across his lips and then continued. 'Anyway, Michael kept on at him – at Toby I mean – trying to wheedle out whatever information he could. He said he didn't believe him, that he was making it all up. Which, of course, made Toby even the more determined to prove it. He ended up by telling

407

Michael that Danny Street had offered him five grand if he'd let him . . .'

Vita shook her head. She felt sick inside. 'You're kidding?'

Rick dropped his head into his hands. 'I wish I was.' He grabbed for his glass again and sank most of what remained of the pint. 'Michael decided it might be worth following Toby around, just to see if he might actually . . . and found out rather more than he expected. That he was seeing that woman for example – you know, the one who does all the embalming.'

Vita's head was starting to spin. 'Alice Avery?' she said.

'Yeah. Not Toby's type at all. And then Michael saw the three of them coming out of Tobias Grand & Sons late at night. And I mean late. After midnight. There was no good reason for them to be there. He put two and two together and figured that Toby might just have made all Danny Street's dreams come true.'

'No,' Vita said. Her chest felt tight. 'He couldn't have. He *wouldn't*.'

Rick, as if unwilling to meet her eyes, glanced up at that spot on the wall again. 'Michael figured we could use it, you know, to put a bit of pressure on.'

As the penny gradually dropped, Vita stared at him, aghast. 'You were blackmailing Danny Street?'

'No,' he hissed, 'of course not. And keep your voice down.' He looked around again. 'It was Toby we went for. You think I'm bloody stupid?'

'You want an honest answer to that?' Vita wasn't just feeling scared now, she was feeling angry too. And something else was welling up inside her: a deep and ugly disappointment. Five minutes ago she'd had a husband who . . . well, she couldn't have said that she trusted him absolutely, but she wouldn't have believed him capable of anything as morally corrupt as blackmail.

408

'Okay, so it wasn't the smartest move in the world,' Rick said bitterly. 'And I know it was wrong. But that kid gets paid for doing fuck all. He struts around like he owns the place – which he will one day, without ever having lifted a finger. And I get paid a pittance for whatever scraps of work they decide to throw my way.'

'And that's a good enough reason to blackmail him?'

Rick pulled a face. 'It wasn't as if he was going to miss a couple of grand. We didn't really have anything on him, except for his rather dodgy relationship with Alice. And we figured that had to be connected to this business with Danny Street. I mean, why else would he be screwing her?'

'Perhaps he likes older women.'

'Yeah, right. She's hardly Joan Collins, is she?'

'No,' Vita said, 'she's about twenty years younger. And perhaps she has other qualities like honesty and kindness.' Vita couldn't keep the contempt from her voice. 'So you asked him for money in exchange for keeping your mouth shut.'

Rick was either too drunk or too self-absorbed to realise how disgusted she was. 'It had to be me who approached him. Michael didn't want Toby to know he was involved. He was worried about Iris, about the kid making things difficult for her at work.'

Very considerate, Vita thought to herself.

'I told Toby I knew what he'd been doing, that I'd seen the two of them coming out of Tobias Grand & Sons in the early hours. I said I'd tell his old man everything unless he paid up. He laughed it off at first, said I was talking crap until I mentioned about how I'd seen Alice Avery too – and how they seemed to have got pretty cosy recently – and that perhaps, if pushed, she might be more forthcoming than he was. He started to panic then, said it wasn't what I thought, that they'd actually been buying some coke off Danny. However, as he

409

didn't want his father to know about it, he was willing to pay just this once.'

Vita put her head in her hands. She thought about how she'd defended him against Iris's accusations. When she glanced up again, she wasn't sure who she was looking at. Where had her husband gone? Where was the funny, charming man she'd been sharing her life with for the past four years?

'You knew what he'd been doing and yet you still . . .'

'I'm not proud of it, love,' Rick said. 'And as it happened, Toby didn't come up with the two grand anyway. I met him outside Belles. He only gave me twelve hundred, swore that was all he could lay his hands on. I gave half of it to Michael and the rest was . . . shit, you know what happened to the rest. It was lifted by some little toerag.'

Vita sighed as she remembered Duggie handing over Rick's wallet in her office. She'd had all sorts of ideas about where the cash might have come from, but never in her wildest dreams could she have imagined the truth. 'And you didn't think, not even for a minute, that Danny Street was going to get the hump over this?'

'No, he wasn't supposed to know about it. I told Toby that if he ever breathed a word, I'd expose him, tell everyone what he and Alice had allowed that pervert Street to do. I might get done for blackmail, but it was nothing compared to what they'd be facing.'

There were lots of things Vita could have said, none of them reassuring or in any way supportive. Rick didn't seem to comprehend that he was equally culpable. By taking Toby's money, by keeping silent, he'd allowed the whole vile business to continue. How could he? But that was something to be dealt with later. No matter how painful it was, she had to temporarily push it to the back of her mind. For the moment, she had to concentrate on getting the whole story out of him.

410

'So why did Michael go and pick a fight with Danny Street? That was hardly a smart thing to do in the circumstances.'

Rick shrugged again. 'It wasn't anything to do with this. He was still pissed off over what Toby had told him that night at the Hope, about how Danny had had a go at Iris when he went to view Lizzie Street's body. You know what Michael was like – act first and think later. I tried to talk him out of it, but he thought that Danny might be punishing her for what Sean had done. He was worried that it was personal, that Danny might not stop there, that he might go on and seriously hurt her.'

'And now you think what? That Danny Street found out about the blackmail and murdered Michael as a result of it?'

Rick's eyes got that scared expression in them again. 'I don't know. Maybe.'

'But I thought you said you were the one who approached Toby. How would he have found out that Michael was involved?'

'It wouldn't have been that hard to figure out. I mean, we were friends, weren't we? The little shit might have guessed I wasn't working alone. He might have remembered what he'd told Michael that night at the Hope.' Rick started gnawing on his knuckles. 'What am I going to do, Vita?'

'We're going home,' she said, standing up. 'We're getting out of here right now.' She walked around the table, grabbed his arm and hauled him to his feet. 'First you're going to sober up, and then we're going to talk to Toby Grand. We'll find out what's going on. I'll shake the bloody truth out of him if I have to.' Vita gazed angrily up at her husband. 'And we're going to pay that money back, every last damn penny.'

Chapter Fifty-eight

It was past eight o'clock by the time Iris got out of bed later that evening. She pulled on the white towelling robe, wandered back into Guy's living room and went to stand by the window again. The traffic was lighter now, only a thin stream of cars passing by. It was snowing, great white flakes that fell against the glass, and she laid her fingertips against the pane willing the flakes to cling on, to grasp whatever was left of their slight ephemeral lives. She was feeling . . . What was she feeling exactly? Shame, guilt, confusion – and all of it intermingled with a strange exhilaration. She could still feel Guy's touch on her skin, could still smell the scent of his body. How could they have made love at a time like this?

And yet she knew why. It was to do with that primitive connection between sex and death. *La petite mort* – the small death – wasn't that how climax was referred to by the French? She had needed to get lost for a while, to lose touch with reality, to enter that place where nothing mattered but the touch of a hand, the sound of a voice, the slipping away from time and space.

She slowly ran her fingers down the glass.

Today, she had been overwhelmed by loss. Death had been all around her. She hadn't just had to acknowledge the loss of one person she'd loved but two. Michael was gone and so was her father. Terry Street had taken him away as surely as if he'd stabbed him through the heart.

She jumped as Guy's mobile started ringing.

'Can you grab that, babe?' he called out from the kitchen. 'I'll be through in a sec.'

Iris picked up the phone. 'Hello?'

'Your mother's here,' Noah said.

Iris could tell from his tone that he wasn't too happy. 'I don't want to see her. I can't. Just tell her to leave me alone.'

There was a short pause at the other end of the line. 'I don't think so,' Noah said sharply. 'If you want her to leave, you can tell her yourself.' And he slammed the phone down before she had the chance to say anything else.

Guy appeared at the door. 'Who was it?'

'Apparently my mother is downstairs.'

'Oh. You don't have to talk to her if you don't want to.'

'Try telling that to Noah.'

'Why? What did he say?'

Iris shook her head. She couldn't blame Noah for being peeved about it all. He was just trying to run his business, to keep things running smoothly. From the moment she'd arrived on the scene she'd brought nothing but trouble for Guy – and, by association, trouble for the bar too. Guy was spending way too much time on her problems and not nearly enough on the business. 'Nothing. It was just a bit of surprise, that's all. I didn't expect her to come here.'

'You don't have to talk to her,' Guy said again.

'No, I'd better go down.' She walked through to the bedroom, slipped off the white robe and started to get dressed. Guy followed her in. He stood watching while she pulled on her jeans and a T-shirt.

'Are you sure you want to do this?'

'No, but what choice do I have?' Iris looked in the mirror and ran her fingers through her hair. 'Unless you want her camped on the doorstep for the next twenty-four hours. I know what she's like. She's not going to leave until she's had her say.'

'You can bring her up here if you like. I'll make myself scarce.'

Iris shook her head again. This flat was the only place she felt safe and secure. She didn't want it associated with anyone but Guy. As she went to leave, he put his arms around her and kissed her softly on the lips.

'If you need me, just shout, okay?'

'I won't be long.'

Downstairs was busy and for the first time Iris noticed all the decorations. They'd probably been there when she'd come back earlier, but she'd been too distracted to take them in. The long strings of tiny lights glittered and blinked. She tried not to think about what kind of Christmas she'd be having this year.

Iris pushed through the crowd searching for her mother. She eventually found her at the very same table she had sat at with Guy the first time she'd come to Wilder's. Kathleen had a cup of coffee in front of her but she was stirring it rather than drinking it, her hand moving the spoon in a motion of which she seemed barely aware.

'I don't know what you're doing here,' Iris said. 'We've got nothing to say to each other. Or at least I've got nothing to say to you.'

Her mother looked up. Her face was pale, stricken. Iris could tell she'd been crying and had to fight the impulse to comfort her. Why the hell should she? This was the woman who'd lied to her for most of her life, who'd carried on a secret affair, who'd landed her with a murderous gangster for a father.

'I had to see you,' Kathleen said. 'I couldn't leave without . . . Please. Give me five minutes.'

'Five minutes? You think that's all it's going to take to sort this out?'

Kathleen put her hand over her mouth. She stared at Iris, the tears glistening in her eyes. 'I'm so sorry,' she mumbled.

Iris, despite her determination to stay strong, to be unforgiving, felt a weakening of her will. She couldn't bear to see her mother looking so distraught. Sliding into the seat opposite, she rummaged in her jeans pocket, pulled out a tissue and pushed it into her hand. 'Here,' she said brusquely. 'Your mascara's running.'

Kathleen smiled weakly and dabbed at her eyes with the tissue. 'I never meant to hurt you. That's why I didn't . . . *Should* I have told you? You loved Sean so much. I didn't want to take all that away from you.'

Iris put her elbows on the table and glared at her. 'Oh, for God's sake, Mum. You didn't do it for me. You did it to hide your dirty little secret, to cover up your own shame and guilt. If nothing else, you can be honest about that.'

'That's not true,' Kathleen said, her mouth twisting at the corners. 'You think I care about what people think?' She snuffled into the tissue. 'Well, I care about what *you* think, of course I do, but that's not the same thing.'

'But you must have realised that it was all going to come out one day. Secrets like these don't stay buried ever.'

'He swore he'd never tell. He promised me.'

Iris snorted. 'And you believed him?'

Kathleen stared down into her cooling cup of coffee. 'It's been over twenty-six years. Why should he break his silence now?'

415

'I don't know,' Iris said. 'Why don't you tell me? I should think it has something to do with his wife being conveniently murdered a short while ago.'

'He had nothing to do with that.' Kathleen suddenly leaned forward, grasping her daughter's wrist. Iris jerked it away.

As if she'd been stung, Kathleen quickly withdrew her own hand. 'He wasn't responsible for Lizzie's death,' she said firmly. 'How could he be? He was in jail when she was killed.'

Iris thought her mother at best naïve, at worst almost chronically deluded. Even now, after all this time, she didn't seem able to see Terry Street for what he really was. 'That wouldn't stop him. You think he couldn't organise a hit from a prison cell? He's got contacts, he's got money. He's even got two grown sons who are probably more than happy to carry out his dirty work for him.'

Kathleen picked up her coffee and sighed into the cup. 'Who's been putting all these ideas in your head? That son of hers – is that it? You really think you can trust anything that he tells you? He always hated Terry.'

'And with good reason,' Iris said.

'Well, you've only his word for that. There are two sides to every story. Guy was never exactly—'

'I'm not here to discuss Guy Wilder. If you came to say sorry, then fine, you've done it. Perhaps it would be best if you went back to Manchester now.'

Kathleen twisted the tissue between her fingers. 'I haven't come to make excuses, Iris. I only want to try to explain. What I did – what *we* did, me and Terry – it was unforgivable. We got married when we were young, your dad and me. Too young. We didn't really know each other, not properly. We should have waited, hung on a few years, but we thought we knew best.'

'And then you met the charming Terry Street.'

Kathleen winced at the sarcasm but nodded anyway. 'Sean used to go out with his mates on a Friday night and I'd see my girlfriends. Sometimes we'd go to one of Terry's clubs. He used to flirt with me, buy me drinks. I was flattered, but I didn't take it seriously. It was just a bit of fun, you know.'

'Until you decided to sleep with him.'

'That wasn't for ages,' Kathleen said. 'And it wasn't just sex. It was more than a casual fling. We knew we shouldn't be together, that it was wrong, but . . . we fell in love.'

Iris raised her eyes to the ceiling. 'Oh, spare me the violins! You were hardly Romeo and Juliet. You were both married to other people. He had a wife and three kids. Didn't you think about what it would mean, about how much damage you could cause?'

'You think I didn't feel guilty?' Kathleen said. 'Of course I did. I still do. If I could go back and change things I would. But it's too late for that now.'

Iris couldn't argue with that. 'So why not make a complete break? When you knew it was serious, why didn't you get a divorce? You were with Terry for ten years. *Ten years* of lying and cheating, of creeping around behind Dad's back.' Iris paused. 'Am I even allowed to call him that now? I don't know what to call him.'

'Sean *was* your dad,' Kathleen said. 'He adored you. He did everything he could for you. And he tried his best to make me happy too. It wasn't his fault that—'

'That you fell out of love with him? That you found someone more exciting?' Iris was reminded of Luke's betrayal and felt her stomach tighten. Poor Sean. Had he had his niggling suspicions too, vague shadowy notions that he constantly pushed to the back of his mind?

'If you want the truth,' Kathleen said. 'I was too scared to leave. I loved Terry, but I was never sure if I could trust him. I

417

knew what he was involved in . . . Well, not all the details, but enough to make me worried. I wanted him, but I didn't want that kind of life. And then when I found out I was pregnant, I had you to think about too.'

'So you thought you'd just lie to your gullible husband about the baby being his.'

'Sean was overjoyed when he heard the news. I didn't know then whether you were his or not.' Kathleen's cheeks burned red as she made the admission. She dropped her eyes and picked up the spoon again, stirring the coffee that she still hadn't begun to drink. 'It was Terry who arranged the blood test. You were a few weeks old at the time. I should have told Sean when I found out – Terry wanted me too, he wanted us to be together – but I couldn't do it. And the longer it went on, the more impossible it became. The years passed by. Sean loved you so much. You loved him. How could I destroy all that?'

Iris hissed through her teeth. 'You were the one who allowed it to happen in the first place.'

Kathleen gave a short abrupt nod of her head. 'You're right. But I tried to make it work with your dad. I swear I did. I stopped seeing Terry for a while, stayed away from him. I wanted us to be a family, a proper family.'

'You obviously didn't try hard enough.'

'No,' Kathleen said softly, dropping the spoon and lifting the ragged piece of tissue to her eyes again. 'I'm sorry.'

Noah walked by the table, stopped and looked at Kathleen. 'Is everything all right?' He glanced at Iris, his gaze dark and hostile. It was at that moment that she realised his animosity was personal. It was nothing to do with the business, with her connection to the Streets. He disliked her, pure and simple.

Iris stared at him. 'Everything's fine.'

'Mrs O'Donnell?' he said, as if Iris's word could not be trusted.

'Yes, yes,' Kathleen murmured. 'We're fine.'

'Let me get you a fresh coffee,' Noah said to her solicitously, as if she was the victim in all this, and Iris the feckless daughter causing her unnecessary grief. 'That one must be cold by now.' Before she could answer he waved at a waitress who brought a couple of fresh cups and a pot of coffee over to the table.

Iris wanted to scream at him to go away, to leave them alone. He didn't know anything about what was really going on. She felt confused by his attitude. What had she ever done to provoke such antagonism? It had been the same from the very beginning.

The waitress looked over at Iris, the pot poised in her hand. She shook her head. 'No thanks.'

'Thank you,' Kathleen said to Noah. 'That was very kind.'

He gave her a friendly smile before he withdrew. It wasn't a smile that he extended to Iris.

Iris watched as he walked away. She took a few seconds to ponder on the source of his contempt, but then wiped it from her mind. Turning her attention back to her mother, she took a quick breath. 'So how did my father . . . how did *Sean* . . . find out about the affair?'

'Does it matter?'

'Yes.'

Kathleen finally took a sip of coffee. 'Michael told him. He found out from Lizzie.'

'Michael?' Iris frowned. Somehow it wasn't the answer she'd been expecting.

'She told him how long it had been going on for. Apparently she'd known for years. If it hadn't been for that – and for the fact that she told him you were Terry's daughter – he might have come to me first, talked to me about it. He knew how much it was going to hurt Sean, but what could he do? He couldn't keep it from him. He was his brother.'

419

Iris had a flashback to sitting in Michael's kitchen, drinking the watered down whisky while he told her a story that was full of lies. 'That's how he knew Sean was never coming back.'

'Michael was only trying to protect you. He gave you a version that was credible. I suppose he hoped it would be enough to stop you digging any further.'

Iris tugged at a strand of hair, wrapping it around her fingers. No wonder her mother had made that call to Michael. She remembered seeing the number lying on the notepad by the phone. Kathleen must have been desperate to talk to him, to make sure the truth remained hidden.

They didn't need to go over what had happened next. Iris already knew about Sean's response to the revelations – the acquisition of a gun, the robbery, the terrible shooting of Liam Street. But there were still other questions that needed to be answered. She started with the most obvious one. 'When did Terry get out of jail?'

Kathleen gave a light shrug of her shoulders. 'I'm not sure.'

Iris didn't believe her. 'A week, two weeks? You must have some idea.'

'I know what you're thinking, but he didn't kill Michael. I've already told you. He wouldn't—'

'How can you be so sure? He had good reason to want him dead. And to want his wife dead too, come to that. If Sean hadn't found out about the affair, if Michael hadn't told him, then Liam would still be alive today.'

Kathleen leaned forward again, her eyes full of denial. 'No, you're wrong. He promised me. I went to see him in the hospital after . . . after . . .' A shaky hand rose up to cover her mouth. It was a few seconds before she removed it again. 'I told him it was over. And it wasn't Michael or Sean or Lizzie who were to blame. It was only us, the two of us, who were responsible. And me most of all. If it hadn't been for my cowardice, my mistakes,

420

that poor boy would still be alive. I should have finished the affair before you were born. It was wrong. It was always wrong. I should never have . . . Sean was devastated when he found out. He went out of his mind; he didn't know what he was doing.'

Iris could see the pain flowering on her mother's face. She suddenly understood the extent of her feelings of guilt. But that didn't mean she could forgive her. She was still angry over all the lies, all the deceit. Trying hard to cut herself off from any feelings of sympathy, she quickly said: 'And what about Lizzie? How did Terry persuade her to keep her mouth shut? Her stepson had just been killed. She knew who'd done it. Michael had told her, hadn't he? So why didn't she tell the police?'

Kathleen's expression instantly changed, her face taking on a harder look. 'I've no idea what Michael told you, but Lizzie wasn't what you'd call the sentimental sort. Or the motherly sort. She had her own agenda. She saw an opportunity and grasped it with both hands. If there was one thing she dreaded, it was Terry leaving her. She could put up with his infidelity, his lies, but not a divorce. She'd sacrificed too much to let him just walk away.'

'Yeah, well she had every reason to be resentful. You'd been sleeping with her husband for the past ten years.'

Kathleen blushed again. 'I'm not trying to excuse my own behaviour, but hers wasn't exactly praiseworthy either. She knew how it would look if it all came out – how his kids would react, how much they'd hate him. And she realised that she'd finally got the hold on him that she'd always wanted. She said she'd tell the boys that what he'd done – what *we'd* done – had been the cause of Liam's death. They'd never forgive him for it. She said she'd shout it from the rooftops unless he agreed to stay with her.'

'And so he dumped you,' Iris said.

Her mother shook her head. 'No, he was prepared to risk all that, to take the chance on his boys possibly hating him forever if we could still be together. But it was impossible, wasn't it? After what had happened, we could never go back there. It was too late.'

'And so you just took off, ran away.'

'There wasn't anything else I could do. He found us of course – eventually. But I wouldn't change my mind. I begged him to leave us alone, to let us get on with our lives. We'd caused too much damage. It was over between us.'

'Except you still had his daughter.'

'You might not believe this,' Kathleen said softly, 'but he *did* love you. He loved you enough to let you go.'

But Iris wasn't having any of this romantic claptrap. 'Well, at least it saved him the cost of maintenance.'

'You'll never know what it cost him,' Kathleen said sharply.

Iris stared at her mother across the table. 'God, you still love him, don't you?'

'No.'

But Iris had seen the way the two of them had been talking when she'd come out of the Dog that afternoon. She had seen the way they'd been standing too close to each other. It had all been in the body language. 'I don't believe you.'

'If you want to know if I still have feelings for him, then yes, of course I do. He's your biological father. If it hadn't been for him, you wouldn't even be here.'

There was a short silence.

Iris became aware of the bar again, of the people in it, of the music that was playing. All the other lives that were going on around her. A girl in a very short skirt slid by the table and went into the Ladies.

'Are you in love with Guy?' Kathleen asked.

Iris frowned. 'What's that got to do with anything?'

'Sometimes love makes us do stupid things, things we can spend the rest of our lives regretting.'

Iris had heard enough. She got to her feet and looked down on her mother. 'Actually, if you want to help there is something you can do.'

'Anything,' Kathleen said eagerly.

'Tell Terry Street to stay away from me. I don't want to see him. I don't want to talk to him.'

'But—'

'I mean it,' Iris said. 'He's nothing to me. I won't ever acknowledge him as my father.'

Chapter Fifty-nine

On Monday morning Iris was back at her desk at Tobias Grand & Sons. The shock of discovering who her real father was had still not worn off – she wasn't sure if it ever would – but she couldn't put her life on hold. The busier she kept, the less time she'd have to think about it. She was hoping her mother had made that phone call and that Terry Street was clear on where he stood: she had no intention of ever seeing him again. She might be his daughter, but there weren't going be any happy reunions. The knowledge that she was related to him still made her shudder. What would she have done if it hadn't been for Guy? Fallen apart, she thought. It was only his love and support that was keeping her going.

Gerald Grand walked past her and nodded. 'How are you today, Iris?'

'Bearing up,' she replied politely. She had to prove that she was capable of doing this job if she wanted to hold on to it. Gerald's sympathy for her recent loss wasn't likely to last very long.

'Yes,' he said, 'erm . . . good, very good.'

Iris returned to her work. Although she was trying to concentrate, her mind kept wandering. She returned over and over again to what Michael's motives had really been in telling Sean about the affair. Was it possible that they'd been less to do with brotherly love and more with self-interest? Michael had always had a strong attachment to Lizzie Street; by spilling the beans, he may simply have been hoping to split the two marriages up. If Terry left Lizzie for Kathleen, then Lizzie would be free to be with someone else. But then again, could she really believe that he'd be so selfish? And would Lizzie have been interested anyway? Iris didn't want to think badly of him, but when Michael had revealed the truth all those years ago he had set in motion a chain of terrible events, the repercussions of which were still being felt.

Iris gave herself a mental kick. No matter what Michael had done, no matter what his motives, there were only two people who were ultimately responsible for the mess that had ensued – her mother and Terry Street. It was *their* selfishness, and theirs alone, that had ruined the lives of so many other people.

At ten to eleven, William came out of his office and placed some papers on her desk. 'Good news,' he said. 'It appears that our longstanding resident Mr Hills is finally leaving us.'

Iris looked up at him, surprised. The last time she'd typed up any correspondence on the matter, mother and son had still been at loggerheads. 'How on earth did that come about?'

'I've no idea,' he said, 'although I did have a conversation with the son on Friday. It seems he's reconsidered and has now agreed to his mother's wishes that the body be returned to Ireland.'

Iris smiled. 'And that had nothing to do with your powers of persuasion?'

'I shouldn't think so,' he replied modestly. 'Actually, there's quite an interesting story behind it all.' William, clearly in no hurry to get back to work, leaned against the corner of the desk and folded his arms. 'It seems that Connor Hills was born in Kellston, lived here for the first thirty-odd years of his life, but then moved to Dublin. He set up an import and export business, got married, had a family and then twelve months ago came over on a visit with his wife to see their oldest son. The boy's at university in London. There was nothing unusual about the visit – they'd been here a few times before – but on this occasion Connor stayed on, claiming that he wanted to look up some old friends. There wasn't a problem at first but, as the weeks went by, the phone calls gradually became less frequent and then he just disappeared. The family alerted the police, but of course a man who chooses not to return to his home isn't exactly top priority.'

'And then?' Iris said, her curiosity roused.

'Well, eventually the son tracked him down, living rough near Kellston Station. That was about three months ago. And that's where it all gets even odder. He said his father was perfectly coherent, if not entirely clean, but that he made him promise not to tell his mother where he was. Connor swore he'd disappear forever if he broke his word or if anyone else came sniffing round.' William paused, reflecting perhaps on his own recent difficulties. 'Maybe it was some kind of breakdown.'

'And the son agreed to keep quiet?'

'Yes. The two of them were close and he made the decision, rightly or wrongly, to do as his father asked. He was hoping he could talk him round, persuade him to get some help if nothing else. He wanted to tell his mother, of course he did, but he knew she'd be on the next flight over. So instead he went to see him every day, took him food and blankets, and tried to find out what was going on. And then one morning he arrived and he wasn't there. He asked around and eventually discovered that his father had died the night before. Apparently it was a heart attack. There were no suspicious circumstances.'

Whilst William had been relating the story, Iris had started to experience one of those weird tingling sensations on the back of her neck. She knew it was ridiculous, but the story was beginning to echo parts of her own past. 'So why all the fuss about where he was going to be buried?'

William gave a sigh. 'It was something his father told him. During one of their conversations, Connor Hills had said that he wanted to die in Kellston, to be buried here. He was quite insistent.'

'Did he explain why?'

'Not exactly. He just said that this was where he belonged, that he should never have left.'

'How old is he? The son?'

'I'm not sure. About nineteen, I think.'

Iris frowned. 'So how can he afford a lawyer at that age? He must have been racking up the legal fees over the past few weeks. You said he was a student, didn't you?'

'Yes, but he doesn't seem to have any money worries. Mr Hills, it appears, left him well provided for.'

Iris thought about the cash Sean had taken from Terry Street's house. Michael had said it was only a few thousand, but had he been telling the truth? Maybe it had been a lot more than that. Enough perhaps for Sean to change his identity, set himself up in a nice little business in Ireland . . . and leave his kids a tidy inheritance.

'What does he look like?' Iris said. 'The father, I mean.'

William tilted his head to one side. 'Look like?'

Iris realised how odd the question must have sounded and quickly tried to come up with a rational explanation for it. 'It *is* an interesting story. I was just wondering if I'd ever seen him at Kellston Station.'

'Sorry, it was Gerald who made all the original arrangements.'

Iris nodded as if it didn't really matter. What were the odds of Connor Hills and Sean O'Donnell being one and the same? Pretty slight. And if Sean had come back, surely he would have got in touch with Michael. Although with Michael's track record on straight-talking, there was no saying that he hadn't. There was only one way of finding out for sure. She could go downstairs and ask Alice to show her the body. No sooner had the thought entered her head than Iris instantly dismissed it. She was only being fanciful. This was just another sad story in a city full of private sorrows.

'Are you all right?' William said.

Iris forced a smile. 'Yes, yes I'm okay. I was just thinking about all these lives that are going on around us, and how little we know about them all. So how did you manage to get the son to change his mind?'

'I'm not sure if it was down to me. I simply mentioned that whatever was driving his father was connected to the past – and that sometimes, if you can't let go, the past can destroy you. And the people around you too.'

That he was talking from personal experience, Iris had no doubt at all. She kept quiet while he continued.

'I asked him to think very hard about the consequences of what he was doing, about how it would affect his mother. I also asked him to consider the fact that his father was clearly unwell when he was talking about where he wanted to be buried. And that if he'd been in his normal state of mind, would Connor really have wanted to inflict that kind of pain on his wife? Wouldn't it mean that in some ways he was turning his back on the life they'd shared together?' He gave a shrug of his shoulders. 'I just asked the questions and left him to work out the answers.'

'And do you think he made the right decision?'

William didn't immediately answer. 'For her, yes. For himself? I don't know. I suspect he's always going to feel guilty about not carrying out his father's wishes.'

Iris thought of all the secrets and lies that had dominated her own life. Could she ever bring herself to forgive her mother? At the moment her feelings were still too raw, too painful, to even begin to make steps in that direction. 'I wonder what it was all about, what it was that drew him back to Kellston.'

'That's something we'll never know.'

'I'm glad it's sorted,' Iris said.

'So am I. It's for the best. Although I don't think Gerald's quite as convinced. I probably shouldn't be telling you this, but he wasn't exactly overjoyed at my intervention. For as long as the dispute continued, the bill for keeping the body here was steadily mounting. I've probably cost him a small fortune. Still, I understand how he feels; these are tricky times and everyone's feeling the pinch.'

'Maybe you're in the wrong job,' Iris said.

William shifted, glanced down at the floor and looked up at Iris again. 'Now you mention it, I've finally made a decision on that front. I've decided to join Mr Hills.'

'What?'

'Oh,' he laughed, 'not on the burial side of things. I'm not quite *that* depressed, but I've decided to leave Tobias Grand & Sons, to make a fresh start. He's being flown over to Ireland next week and when he goes – well, I've decided to go there too.'

'To Ireland?'

'What's wrong with Ireland?'

'Nothing,' Iris said. 'But there are countries where it doesn't rain quite so much. Spain, Portugal, Italy?' She was trying to keep her tone light, but her heart was sinking. This place wouldn't be the same without William. She'd grown used to having him around, to having someone to talk to. In fact she wasn't even sure if she'd want to stay in the job if he wasn't here. Gerald wasn't exactly her biggest fan and Toby only came in when he felt like it.

'I've got friends living there. I'm not saying I'll stay forever, but I think it's time to move on.'

'I see,' Iris said. If there was any way she could have made an escape from Kellston, she would have grasped it with both hands, but that was hardly possible – at least in the short term – with Guy's business being here. 'Well, good luck. I hope it all works out for you.'

William got up from the desk. 'Thank you. Anyway, I'd better get on.' He was halfway to his office when he glanced over his shoulder and said casually, 'So you and Guy Wilder. You're . . . ?'

'Yes, we're together.' She recalled Toby suggesting that William had feelings for her. She still wasn't sure if it was true or not.

William hesitated as if he might be about to say more, but didn't. He gave her an odd look, went back into his office and closed the door.

It was getting on for twelve when Iris's mobile started to judder across the desk. Gerald didn't like his staff taking private calls during work hours, so she usually kept the phone on silent. Glancing quickly back along the corridor – Gerald was in the middle of some funeral arrangements – she quickly snatched up the mobile and checked the caller. It was Vita. They hadn't talked since Michael's wake and Iris didn't know if she'd heard about the altercation with Terry Street.

'Hi,' Vita said.

'Hi, it's good to hear from you.'

But Vita didn't seem in the mood for niceties. 'Look, can we meet up? It's important. Can you get to Connolly's?'

'Of course. What's it about? Is it—'

'I'll be waiting for you,' Vita said abruptly and hung up.

Chapter Sixty

Fifteen minutes later, having arranged an early lunch break, Iris slid into the seat by the window. Vita Howard was hunched over the table, absent-mindedly stirring a small cup of espresso. Iris was reminded of her mother's distraction a few days earlier and felt her heart sink; whatever was coming next was serious and in her present frame of mind, she wasn't sure if she could cope with more bad news.

Vita looked up and gave a curt nod. Her normally open face was tight and there were worry lines on her forehead. 'Thanks for coming.'

'It sounded urgent.'

'It is.'

They were immediately interrupted by the waitress. Iris ordered a cappuccino and then turned back to Vita. A few seconds passed. Vita continued to fiddle with the spoon. Eventually she lifted the cup to her lips, but then abruptly put it down again.

'It's about Rick and that six hundred quid.'

Iris felt the colour rise in her cheeks. Why had she spoken so impulsively that night at Lemon Road? She would regret it for the rest of her life.

'You were wrong,' Vita said, 'about where he got it from.'

'I should never have said those things. I'm sorry. I should have—'

'But you weren't wrong about *him*.' Vita bit down on her lip and her face twisted. 'It seems I'm married to a man I don't even know.'

Iris stared at her, startled. 'What?'

'There I was defending him against all your wild accusations, believing that my husband had certain moral boundaries, had a few principles at least, when all the time . . .' She stopped and gave a soft, bitter laugh. 'You'd better prepare yourself for what I'm about to tell you next.'

Iris's first thought was that Rick had been cheating on her. It would account for the expression in her eyes, that mixture of disgust and betrayal. Iris recognised that look - she had seen it herself when she glanced in the mirror. Before Vita had a chance to continue, the waitress reappeared with the coffee.

'Thank you,' Iris said.

There was a moment of silence as the woman walked away. The lunchtime rush was only just beginning and the tables either side of them were still unoccupied. Vita cleared her throat. Despite their relative isolation, she kept her voice low as she began to recite the story that Rick had told her the day of Michael's wake. Usually so articulate, Vita stumbled over the words, stopping and starting, her lips clearly reluctant to relay the horror of what she had learnt.

When she got to the end, Iris vehemently shook her head. Her thoughts were reeling and her first response was denial. 'No, not Alice. That can't be true. No way! She wouldn't.'

'Yeah, well, I never thought Rick was a blackmailer.'

But Iris still had trouble in believing that Alice would have

432

colluded in such a monstrosity. Allowing Danny Street to . . . It was too vile, too revolting. No, it went beyond that: it was inhuman, the breaking of the final taboo. 'She isn't like that. And there's nothing going on between her and Toby.'

'Are you sure?'

'Yes, of course. She doesn't even like him. It's ridiculous!' But then Iris frowned as she remembered the remark Toby had made about the ancient Egyptian embalmers – and the way Alice had reacted to it. Gradually, a string of doubt began to coil around her trust in Alice Avery. She recalled those times when Alice had tried to talk to her. What was it she'd said? *Have you ever done something . . .* And then there was the new hairdo, the make-up, the diet, all the awkwardness around Toby that Iris had put down to embarrassment, to the fear of being teased. Even William had remarked on the oddness of her behaviour, but she had brushed his concerns aside.

'People do all kinds of crazy things for love,' Vita said.

'But not *that*. No decent person could ever allow that.' And yet Iris wasn't certain if she believed her own protestations. Danny Street was capable of anything, and there was a vulnerability about Alice, a kind of innocence that left her open to the exploitation of others - even her own mother ran rings around her. Maybe Toby had somehow managed to persuade her, or bully her, into going along with it all. With his idle lifestyle, his clubs and his girls, he was always desperate for cash. And he had the moral values of an alley cat. But that was still a long step away from taking money for . . . 'Look, perhaps Toby was telling the truth about buying the drugs. I've known him high as a kite on more than one occasion. He wouldn't have wanted Gerald to know about it.'

Vita gave a sigh. 'Twelve hundred quid to keep quiet about a few lines of coke? I don't think so. And why do the deal at

Tobias Grand & Sons? Why take that risk? You could do it on any street corner.'

Iris stared down into her coffee. Vita was right. And hadn't she seen Toby's green Toyota parked outside work that Sunday she'd gone round to see Michael? And hadn't Toby denied being anywhere near the building when she'd talked to him the next day? 'So what do we do?' she said. 'It's not as though we've got any actual proof.'

Vita hoisted her handbag on to the table, unzipped it and took out a yellow padded envelope. 'I want you to give this to Toby Grand.'

'What is it?'

'The twelve hundred quid that Rick and Michael took from him.'

'I can't just hand it over to him.'

'Of course you can. Tell him it was dropped off by a courier or . . . I don't know, some stranger who came through the door. It's not going to change what Rick did – nothing will ever do that – but at least it makes *me* feel less guilty. I've got no idea what happened to Michael's share, but I imagine most of it's sitting in the till at the Dog and Duck.'

Iris could understand her desire to return the cash. 'I'll give you Michael's half,' she said quickly. 'There's no reason why you should pay back all of it. But then what? I mean, this could still be going on. And even if it isn't, we have to do something about it.'

Vita glanced away, unable or perhaps unwilling to meet her eyes. 'I have done something. I've given back the money. If Toby Grand's got any sense, he'll realise he's in trouble. If the deal with Rick no longer stands, he's going to be worried. It should make him think twice about doing it again.'

Iris looked at her.

'I know what you're thinking,' Vita said, 'and I find all this as disgusting as you, but there's nothing I can do to change what's already happened. If we go to the cops, tell them what we *think* has gone on – and don't forget we haven't got any actual evidence – then what chance is there of actually getting a conviction? And if by some miracle we do, Rick might end up in jail again. And despite how I feel about him at the moment, I just can't go there. I can't be responsible for that.'

'But what about Danny Street,' Iris said. 'What about Toby? They can't be allowed to get away with it.'

'That's up to you.'

'Me?'

'I don't mean the cops,' Vita said, 'but you could talk to William Grand, have a quiet word. You get on with him, don't you? You could tell him what's been happening and try to put a stop to it.'

Iris couldn't even imagine how that conversation might go. 'I can't start accusing Toby of something like that with nothing to back it up. It's going to be his word against mine and who the hell is going to believe me? Toby's going to deny it. Alice is going to deny it. I'm going to end up sounding like some deranged fantasist.'

'I suppose,' Vita said. 'And that's the problem. There really isn't any proof.'

And suddenly Iris realised that doing nothing was exactly what Vita wanted. She might not like what Rick had got involved in, but she was prepared to brush it under the carpet if she had to. 'But we can't just let it go. It's too . . . it's too . . .'

'Gross?' Vita suggested.

Iris stared at her. 'Just because you're giving the money back, doesn't mean it's over. It doesn't mean it's going to stop either.'

'No,' Vita said.

'At Tobias Grand & Sons perhaps, but what if it carries on somewhere else?'

Vita ran her fingers through her hair. 'Do you think Danny

Street would ever let this get to a courtroom? If he even suspects we're on to him, our lives aren't going to be worth living. I don't want to let it go, but he's worse than mad, Iris. He's capable of anything.'

And suddenly Iris thought about who Danny Street really was. He was Terry's son. And that meant he was her half-brother. A wave of nausea rolled up from her stomach. That she was actually related to him made her lower her head in shame. Vita still didn't know the truth about who her father really was. Should she tell her? No, she couldn't. Not today, at least. There was too much else to deal with.

Vita briefly put her hand on Iris's arm. 'I'm sorry. I know this is the last thing you need at the moment.' She pushed the envelope across the table. 'So will you give it to him?'

Iris nodded.

As if she couldn't wait to get away, Vita jumped to her feet. 'Thanks. I'll give you a call, okay?'

Iris finished her cappuccino while she pondered on what to do next. Should she try and talk to Alice? But if she did, Alice might run straight to Toby – and who would he turn to? There was no saying how Danny Street might react if he discovered that his vile little secret was about to be exposed. Maybe she could talk to William, but once those wheels were set in motion, there was no going back. But doing nothing was intolerable too. What if it all became public? She imagined the scandal that would follow and the pain of the relatives. How many women had Danny Street . . . But she couldn't even bring herself to finish the thought.

Ten minutes later, Iris set off along the High Street. She could feel the weight of the money in her bag, a burden of guilt that seemed to grow heavier as she approached the funeral parlour. Her palms were clammy, her lips starting to dry. What was she going to do?

But when she got back to work the only person around was Gerald. Iris quickly removed the envelope from her bag and slipped it into the desk drawer. As he passed through reception, she opened the drawer and passed the package to him. 'This came for Toby earlier. Could you make sure he gets it?' She glanced at her watch. She still had half an hour left of her lunch break. 'I have to go out again. I'll be back by one.'

Iris had suddenly realised that she didn't need to deal with this alone. There *was* someone she could talk it over with before making any final decisions. If she grabbed a cab, she could be at Guy's in five minutes.

Chapter Sixty-one

Toby took the padded envelope and ripped it open. Seeing the cash, he quickly closed the flap before his father could see. 'When did this arrive?'

'Some time this morning.'

It hadn't been posted. There wasn't even an address on the outside. Just his name in bold black print. 'So someone delivered it by hand?'

Gerald frowned at him. 'I've no idea. You'll have to ask Iris. Why, what is it? Is there a problem?'

'No, not at all,' Toby said as casually as he could. He chucked the envelope down on the desk as if its contents were of no importance. 'It's just a few CDs. My mate was telling me about this new band he's promoting and . . . well, you wouldn't like them. They're not your cup of tea at all. He works near here so . . .' Toby shrugged. 'I thought I might be able to catch up with him, say thanks, if he'd only just dropped them off.'

'Or you could send him a text,' Gerald said dryly, 'and consider doing something truly revolutionary – like some work, for instance.'

As soon as his father had returned to his office, Toby picked up the envelope again. There was no note inside, nothing but the cash. He flipped through the notes, fifties and twenties, already guessing how much was going to be there. Twelve hundred quid. He could feel his heart beginning to race. This was trouble, serious trouble. If it meant what he thought it meant . . . God, what was he going to do? Should he warn Danny Street? No, not yet, not until he'd thought through all the implications. He mustn't do anything rash, anything stupid. He had to try and keep his cool. And before he made any decisions, he had to talk to Alice.

Toby hurtled down the steps to the basement as if the Devil himself was on his heels. Alice was writing up some notes, and she turned, startled, as he crashed into the embalming room.

'We're in the shit!' Toby said. 'We're in the fucking shit!'

Alice jumped to her feet, her mouth falling open.

Toby upended the envelope and let its contents spill out across the counter. 'It was left for me at reception.'

'I don't understand,' Alice said. Wide-eyed, she stared down at the notes. 'Where has it come from? *Who* has it come from?'

'That Howard bastard.'

'Howard?'

'Rick Howard,' Toby said impatiently. 'The big bastard, the one who works as a pall bearer. The one who does some driving.'

'I know who he is, but why's he giving you money?'

'He's not giving it to me, he's giving it back. He's changed his fucking mind, hasn't he?' Toby raked his fingers through his hair. He could feel the blood pounding in his temples. 'Christ, do you think he's going to the cops?'

At the mention of the police, Alice went pale. Her legs gave way and she slumped back on to the stool. 'What . . . what do you mean?'

'He found out, didn't he? Fuck knows how. Found out about Danny Street being here, about . . . Shit, I don't need to spell it out for you. He wanted two grand to keep his mouth shut.'

'And you paid him?'

'Of course I fucking paid him – well, I gave him twelve hundred. What else was I going to do? If I'd told Danny Street, he'd have thought one of us had been blabbing. I did it for you, Alice, to keep you safe, to stop that nutter coming after you.'

Alice continued to gaze at the money. 'Why didn't you say? Why didn't you tell me?'

'And what would you have done if I had? There wasn't any point in two of us being stressed out of our heads. I thought I'd got it sorted. I used some of the cash you lent me to pay him off.' Toby began pacing the room, up and down, up and down, his boots beating out a steady rhythm on the linoleum. There had to be a way out of this. There had to be. And then he suddenly stopped. 'Perhaps I've got it wrong. Perhaps the greedy bastard's only playing with us. He waits for a while, gives back the money, and then asks for the full amount – or more. He might just be making a point, trying to put the thumbscrews on. What do you think?'

Alice raised her pale face to look at him. 'I think it's time to put a stop to all this. I think we should go to the police.'

Toby stared at her, hardly believing what he was hearing. 'What?'

'If we get there first, tell *our* side of the story . . .'

'Our side?'

'Yes,' she said. 'Don't you see? We can explain about how you lost the money at a card game, how Danny Street threatened you, how he beat you up, how we were forced into doing what we did. There were mitigating circumstances, Toby.'

'Oh, and you think that'll make it all right?' Toby felt a shudder run through him. The woman was a fucking liability. He

440

might have guessed she'd cave in at the first sign of pressure. 'I don't think so, love. I don't know about you, but personally I don't fancy spending the next five years of my life banged up. And what about my father's business? You think anyone's going to commit their nearest and dearest into his tender loving care when they know what Danny Street's been up to?'

Alice got to her feet and grabbed hold of his arm. 'But if Rick Howard's going to tell, isn't it better that we get there first? It has to be. It's all going to come out, isn't it? There's nothing we can do to stop it.' Her voice was steadily rising in pitch, her grip tightening on his arm. 'Everyone's going to know what he did, what we allowed him to do. My mother's going to find out, and Gerald, and—'

Toby could hear the rising panic in her voice. Scared that she was about to scream, he freed himself from her grasp, took hold of her shoulders and shook them. 'For one, it wasn't a card game. It was drugs, okay? I owe Danny Street for drugs. I like to do a few lines of coke every now and again and the bill – well, it got a bit out of hand. And how do you think that's going to look to the cops? And for two, I've got no intention of being gangbanged by a pile of sex-starved six-foot bruisers. So if you've still got any ideas about going to the law you can think again. I won't let it happen. I won't. You understand?'

Alice stared at him. She glanced down, looking more puzzled than threatened, as if she hadn't quite grasped what was going on. 'Look, we have to deal with this together. When we're married—'

Toby's grip tightened around her shoulders, his fingers digging hard into her flesh. 'Oh, for fuck's sake, Alice! There is no *us*. There isn't going to be any bloody marriage. It was just a bit of fun, okay? And now it's over. And everything else is going to be over too, if you don't keep your big mouth shut.'

Alice shook her head. 'You don't mean that.'

'I've never been more bloody serious.'

'You don't,' she said again. Her brown eyes stared up at him, pleadingly. 'You can't.'

Toby looked into her face. He should have felt guilt or pity, but all he felt was desperation. If the bitch went to the police, his whole life would be ruined. 'Just keep your fucking mouth shut, right?'

Alice shook herself free and walked away. She went to stand by the sink, her shoulders hunched. Her voice when she spoke again was little more than a whisper. 'So you don't love me?'

Toby laughed. It was a question that seemed to him quite ridiculous. Had the woman no grasp on reality at all? She only had to look at him, to look at herself, to realise how deluded she was. 'I'm a young man,' he sneered. 'I've got my whole life ahead of me. Why the hell would I want to be with someone like you?'

It was only as she turned, as she began to slowly walk back towards him, that Toby recalled the idea he'd had the last time they'd spoken – that the only way to cover his back was to get rid of Alice Avery forever.

She was only inches away when she lifted her hand. It was only then he saw the knife, the flash of silver as it sliced through the air. Toby opened his mouth to protest, but already it was too late. His very last thought as the blade slid between his ribs was that he should have made that call. He really should have.

Chapter Sixty-two

Iris got out of the cab, paid the driver and went into the bar. There was no sign of Guy so she hurried through to the back and took the stairs two at a time. He would know what to do, wouldn't he? And even if he didn't, she needed someone to share the burden with. The decisions she had to make were too great to cope with on her own. As she unlocked the door to the flat she could hear music coming from the bedroom. Leonard Cohen's 'Dance me to the end of love,' was playing, and she smiled. It was one of her favourites. Guy must be getting changed before going down to work.

She was about to call out when she suddenly heard him laugh. The sound rose above the music and she quickly closed her mouth again. She listened, her head tilted to one side, wondering if she'd imagined it. And then it came again, this time followed by the murmur of voices. More than one voice. *More than one person in the bedroom.* It took a moment for this to sink in and when it did a cold wave of fear swept over her. Suddenly her legs felt leaden. Forcing herself to move, she took a step inside.

As Iris softly pushed open the door to the bedroom, her heart was pumping. *Please God,* she prayed silently, *let there be an innocent explanation for this.* But her prayer went unanswered. She froze as she saw the two of them lying naked on the bed. It was Guy she focused on first, his lean, taut body tangled in the sheets, his arms looking pale against the much darker skin of his partner. Iris couldn't see her face, but she guessed who it was. *Serena. That bitch Serena!* So much for Guy's promises to her, for all his protestations of love. Iris lifted a clenched hand to her mouth. Her head was filling with so many emotions she could barely acknowledge them: anger was quickly followed by hurt, by rejection, by despair . . .

She must have gasped because they both abruptly turned to look at her. And it was then that she was hit by a second thunderbolt. It wasn't Serena's cat-like eyes that were gazing back at her, but Noah's. The shock was like a physical pain, so sharp it took her breath away. It was as though her chest was caving in, squeezing the life from her heart, from her lungs. Turning, she dashed from the room and sprinted for the front door.

Guy shouted, 'Iris! Wait!' but she didn't stop. She stumbled down the flight of stairs, desperate to make her escape. Pushing aside anyone who got in her way, she fled through the bar. Outside, she ran straight into the street, indifferent to any thoughts of safety, and forced a black cab to stop only inches from her.

'What the . . . You trying to kill yerself, lady!'

'Tobias Grand,' she yelped, falling into the back.

Had her destination been anywhere else, the cabbie might have refused to take her or at the very least subjected her to a tirade on the dangers of blindly stepping out in front of a moving vehicle. As it was, Tobias Grand & Sons was associated with death, with funerals, and from the look on her face he must have surmised that she'd just received some pretty bad news. Accordingly, he held his tongue, contenting himself with a few exasperated mumbles as he drove along the High Street.

Iris sat back in the seat, her arms hugging her chest, her body shivering. It was all too much to take in. She felt sick, despairing, as if she'd entered a nightmare she couldn't wake up from. Now, finally, Noah's antagonism made sense to her. How long had it been going on for? How long had the two of them been together? And then she remembered that strange conversation with Serena, that final 'Good luck,' as Guy had led her upstairs.

The cab pulled up and Iris got out. She took her purse from her bag to pay the driver. 'Thank you.'

'You all right, love?'

Iris forced her lips into an unconvincing smile. The concern in his voice was almost too much to bear. 'Yes, yes. Thank you.' Before he could say anything else that might come close to kindness, anything that might cause her to burst into tears, she quickly pushed the note into his hand. 'Keep the change.'

She must have looked like a ghost as she walked in through the door to Tobias Grand & Sons. The initial shock had abated and now she felt like she was sleepwalking, as if everything was taking place in slow motion. Even her thoughts were starting to fragment, splitting off in a hundred different directions.

It was William who was standing in reception. He took one look at her and asked, 'What's happened?'

Chapter Sixty-three

Iris, with the help of a large glass of brandy, finally came to the end of her story. It had been a disjointed tale with frequent pauses and hesitations, interspersed with a series of perhaps unanswerable questions. Even while she'd been reciting the horrors, she'd still been trying to put all the pieces of the jigsaw together. There hadn't been any tears. She felt incapable of crying. It was as if she'd been wrung out and drained of all emotion.

William hadn't interrupted. He'd kept quiet while she told him everything about Sean, the robbery, her mother's affair, the fact that Terry Street was actually her father . . . and finally, the humiliating truth of what she'd just discovered about Guy. The lyrics of Leonard Cohen were still revolving in her head. *Dance me through the panic 'til I'm safely gathered in.* Taunting her, they refused to go away, adding to her agony. She leaned forward, burying her head in her hands. If anyone had been danced to the end of love, it was her.

Eventually, she looked up at William. 'Did you know? Did you know about Guy Wilder?'

He gave a small embarrassed shrug. 'I'd heard a few rumours but . . .'

Iris nodded. William wasn't the type to repeat gossip – and would she have believed him even if he had? 'I've been so blind, so bloody stupid!'

'No,' he said. 'You've been used.'

They were in the room at the back, the room where relatives were usually taken to discuss funeral arrangements. The walls were a pale wishy-washy green and the paintwork was chipped. Even the furniture was past its best; the arm of the chair Iris was sitting on was frayed and she picked distractedly at the threads. 'No wonder Noah couldn't bear the sight of me.' She barked out a short, slightly hysterical laugh. 'And there was me thinking it was Serena I had to worry about. Maybe she was trying to warn me that night at the bar. Guy certainly wasn't happy about her talking to me.'

'Or maybe it was her brother she was trying to protect.'

Iris thought about that for a second before she nodded. 'I never could figure out why Noah disliked me so much. I thought it was to do with Terry but—'

She was interrupted by the phone ringing in reception.

'Sorry,' William said. 'I'd better get that.'

Iris heard the murmur of his voice and then the sound of one of the office doors opening and closing.

A short while later he came back. 'I'm afraid I have to go out for a while. Will you be all right here or would you like me to give you a lift home?'

Iris couldn't think of anywhere she currently thought of as home. She shook her head. 'If it's okay, I'd rather stay here for a while.'

'Of course it is. I shouldn't be too long, an hour or so.'

'I'll be fine,' she said. 'Don't worry about me. I just need a little time to . . . you know, think things through.'

'I'll ask Gerald to keep an eye on reception.'

'Thank you.'

As soon as he'd gone, Iris got to her feet. She walked up and down the room for a few minutes trying to figure out what to do next. The paralysing shock she had felt on finding Guy with Noah was gradually being replaced by anger. It was clear to her now that she'd just been a pawn in a game he'd been playing, a game that had little to do with sexual conquests and everything to do with power and revenge. It was connected to the past, with old simmering resentments, with betrayals that could never be forgiven.

Iris knew she had a choice. She could wallow in self-pity, accept the role of victim for the rest of her life or she could try to take back some control. Grabbing her mobile from her bag, the first call she made was to Guy.

'Iris,' he said as he picked up. 'Christ, I've been trying to ring you. I'm so sorry. What you saw, it wasn't . . . Look, I've got to talk to you. I need to explain. It's not—'

Iris cut him short. 'I'm at work. Be here in fifteen minutes if you've got anything to say.' She hung up before he could make a response. Then she took a few deep breaths. Hearing his voice again had revived the pain and she squeezed her eyes shut, trying to blot out the image of him and Noah on the bed. Why was she so bloody gullible! Of all the men she could have fallen in love with . . .

The next call she made was to her mother. 'I need Terry's number.'

'Oh,' Kathleen said, sounding surprised. 'So you've decided to contact him again. I didn't think—'

'Will you give it me or not?' Iris said curtly. 'I can't hang about. I'm in a hurry.'

Kathleen sighed and gave her the number. Iris scribbled it down and said a quick goodbye. She stared at the digits for a while, wondering if she really had the courage to go through with this. But then, remembering that Guy was probably already on his way, she punched the number into her phone. It rang a couple of times before he answered.

'Terry Street.'

'It's Iris,' she said. 'I need to see you. Can you come to Tobias Grand & Sons?'

'Now?'

'No second chances,' she said, echoing his own words that last time they'd met. 'It's now or never.'

'I'll be there,' he said.

Iris's hand started to shake as she dialled the final number. She had another brief moment of doubt. But there was no going back now. The wheels had already been set in motion.

A young woman answered. 'Good afternoon. Belles. How can I help?'

'Put me through to Chris Street,' Iris said.

'Who's calling?'

'Just put me through,' Iris said insistently. 'Believe me, love, he'll want to talk to me. And he won't thank *you* for keeping me waiting.'

Perhaps there was something suitably threatening about her tone because after a short pause the girl did exactly as requested. There were a series of clicks at the other end of the line.

'Yeah? Chris Street.'

'It's Iris O'Donnell.'

'Who?'

Iris frowned. It wasn't quite the response she'd been expecting. Why was he pretending he didn't know who she was? Perhaps he was worried that the cops were listening in. 'Iris O'Donnell,' she repeated. In case she was right about the phone being tapped, and not wanting the cops to know any more than they should, she quickly added: 'We've met before, at Tobias Grand & Sons.'

449

Chris Street gave a hiss of frustration. 'Look, if it's about the bill for the funeral, I've already spoken to your boss. I'll have it with you by the end of the week.'

Iris raised her eyes to the ceiling. Was he being deliberately obtuse? 'It's not about the funeral.' She had to think of something that would get him here – and get him here in a hurry. 'It's to do with Liam. If you want to know the truth about how your brother died, then get yourself over to Tobias Grand.'

That got his attention. Instantly, his voice took on a harsher edge. 'What? What are you talking about?'

'You heard. And I wouldn't hang about. Your father's already on his way.' Iris cut the connection and turned off the phone. She walked through to reception, sat down behind the desk and waited for it all to begin.

Chapter Sixty-four

Guy was the first to arrive. As he came through the door, Iris was painfully aware of all the reasons she'd loved him. It wasn't just his good looks and charm – although any woman could be forgiven for falling for those – but the way he looked at her, *into* her, with those intense blue eyes. Even now, after knowing what he'd done, a tiny part of her still desired him.

'I'm so sorry, Iris,' he said. 'What happened with Noah today, it was a terrible mistake. No, a mistake doesn't even begin to describe it. We should never have . . .' He stepped forward, reaching out his hand, but Iris shrank away. She couldn't bear to be touched by him.

'Come through to the back,' she said coolly. 'We can't talk here.'

Guy didn't sit down and nor did she. They circled around each other for a few seconds and then met in the centre of the room. Guy was the first to speak again. 'I don't know where to begin. I know you can't ever forgive me, but it didn't mean anything.'

'Is that supposed to make me feel better? That you had some meaningless romp with your business partner?'

'What I'm trying to say is—'

'How long have the two of you been together?' She remembered the laughter she'd heard as she'd opened the door to the flat. They'd probably been laughing at her. 'Did it start in school? Have the two of you been together since then?'

'It's not like that. I swear to you. It was the first and only time. It's never happened before and it never will again. It was a moment of madness. I can't tell you how disgusted I feel, how ashamed.'

'Just how stupid do you think I am?' Iris shook her head. 'No, you'd better not answer that. It can't have been easy for him, watching while you . . . Or is he so besotted that he'll put up with anything?'

Guy gave a groan, pulling his hand down the length of his face. 'It was the first time,' he repeated. 'I'd had a few drinks – more than a few. I'm not trying to make excuses, but with everything that's been going on recently . . . We got talking about stuff, about my mother, about the past, about the way she died. It all got a bit emotional.'

Iris could hardly bear to listen to him. All she could keep thinking about was what she'd lost. But what she'd lost was something that she'd never really had. 'It was all to do with Terry Street, wasn't it? You knew I was his daughter. You always knew, right from the beginning. You had everything planned from the very first day you came here. God, I bet you even made sure that fight took place.'

'No!' He vehemently shook his head. 'That's not true.' He reached out and this time managed to take hold of her arms. His eyes were bright, almost tearful with pleading. 'You're the only woman, the only *person*, I've ever truly loved. Please don't throw it all away. Give me a second chance, Iris. I'm begging you. I need you. You're everything to me.'

For a second, Iris faltered. Every atom of her rational being was screaming out that he was lying. It was only her heart that refused to comply. What if he *was* telling the truth?

'Don't believe a word he says. The only person that bastard loves is himself.'

The rasping voice came from behind and Iris quickly turned. Terry Street was standing by the door. She wondered how long he'd been there, how much he'd heard.

'What are you doing here?' Guy said fiercely. 'You're not wanted. Get out and leave us alone!'

Terry gazed at him, a cold, thin smile on his lips. He glanced at Iris before looking back at him again. 'What's the matter, son? Trouble in paradise?'

'Get out!' Guy shouted. 'Get out or I'll fucking throw you out.'

'Come on then,' Terry taunted. 'I'm waiting.'

Guy's hands were still grasping Iris's arms and she felt his grip tighten. Just like that time outside the Dog, she could feel the rage running through him. 'You're nothing to her,' Guy said. 'Nothing! You're just a murderous shit who happens to have screwed her mother.'

'And what are you?' Terry retorted. 'Just a useless shit who wanted to screw his own mother.'

Guy released his hold on Iris, his eyes blazing with hate.

As the two men advanced towards each other, Gerald Grand appeared. His voice was sharp with irritation. 'What's going on here? What's . . .' And then, recognising Terry, he instinctively moved back. 'Oh, Mr Street. I didn't realise it was you.' As if he wasn't sure if Terry had been legally released from prison or had somehow managed an audacious escape, his face took on an anxious expression. His tone, however, became more benign. 'Er . . . is there something I can help you with?'

'Yes,' Terry said sharply. 'You can fuck off and let me talk to my daughter.'

453

Gerald's eyes grew large and round and his cheeks took on a purplish hue. His pronounced Adam's apple bounced up and down in his throat. He stared at Iris. She could see the shock on his face and knew exactly what he was thinking: it was no problem organising a funeral for the wife of a local gangster, but employing his offspring was a step too far. Finding out that she was related to a minor villain like Michael had been bad enough, but discovering she was the daughter of Terry Street . . .

Iris might have been amused if she hadn't had more pressing things on her mind. As it was, she didn't give a damn about what Gerald thought of her any more. No matter what happened next, she would never work for Tobias Grand & Sons again. Her life in Kellston was over. 'If you could just give us a few minutes?' she said. 'There won't be any trouble. I promise.'

Gerald, understandably, didn't look that convinced but was smart enough to withdraw from the scene. Everyone was silent until the door had closed on his office again.

Iris turned to the two men left in the room. She narrowed her eyes and glared at them. 'If you want to beat the shit out of each other you can do it somewhere else. You've both messed up my life in one way or another so the least you can do is give me some answers.'

'What do you want to know?' Terry said. Ignoring the 'No Smoking' sign on the wall, he took a pack of cigarettes from his pocket, tapped one out and lit it. He took a drag and blew the smoke through his nose in one long, thin stream. 'I presume you've already discovered that you're not his one true love, that the only reason he took up with you was to get at me? It was all about revenge. He knew that I wanted to make contact again: his drunken witch of a mother must have told him that. And he also knew that the one way he could get at me was to form a relationship with you.'

Iris knew that what he actually meant was to *sleep with her*, to use and abuse her in the way that would hurt Terry most. Her stomach made a heaving motion.

'You're perverted,' Guy said. 'A fucking liar! It's serious between me and Iris. I love her. I want to be with her. It's got nothing to do with her being your daughter.'

'Like hell it hasn't,' Terry said. 'You don't give a damn about her. You never did. All you ever wanted was to take her away from me.'

'As if she was ever with you. You think she wants a man like you for her father? You disgust her. You make her sick.'

'And how do you think you make her feel?'

'Stop it!' Iris snapped. She already knew that she'd been used and didn't need it rubbing in. She looked at Guy. 'You can stop pretending now. It's over.'

'You heard her,' Terry said. 'She doesn't want to listen to your lies.'

'Or yours,' Iris said. She stared at Terry's gaunt face, searching - as she had searched so many times before when she'd studied the photographs of Sean – for some signs of a family resemblance. But now, instead of wanting to find some features they might have in common, she wanted to find nothing. Terry's eyes were dark, his lips much thinner than hers, his cheeks sunken. Her gaze slid quickly down over the rest of his body. Although he wasn't as tall or broad as his two sons, he still gave the impression of a sinewy strength. As he lifted the cigarette to his mouth again, she noticed his misshapen knuckles, evidence no doubt of the amount of jaws he'd broken. 'Guy's not the only one who's deceived me.'

'That wasn't my fault. Ask your mother. I *wanted* to see you. She was the one who wouldn't allow it.'

'He's lying,' Guy said. 'He paid your mother to leave. He was desperate to keep his filthy little secret quiet. That's all you ever were to him – something dirty to be swept under the carpet, to be hidden away. If he could have drowned you at birth, he would. Even after he got his own son killed, he couldn't face up to what he'd done. He crawled back to Lizzie and got her to cover everything up. He made her lie to the cops about what really happened that night.'

It was at that moment, as she heard those dreadful words, that Iris realised just how bitter and twisted Guy Wilder really was. She'd heard a different story from her mother and it was a version, despite all the deceit that had gone before, that she was certain was true.

'He's the one who's lying,' Terry said. 'It wasn't like that.' There was an almost desperate edge to his tone as if he was genuinely distraught at the thought of her believing Guy's lies.

Iris nodded. She had no desire to take Terry's side, to take anyone's side, but she was determined to get to the truth. 'I know.'

Guy looked at her. 'So you're going to trust him over me? You're going to believe that vicious bastard?'

'Dad? What's going on?'

All three of them turned to see Terry's two sons standing in the doorway. It was Chris who had spoken. Iris took a breath. So now everyone was here. It was like one of those scenes in an old-fashioned drama, an Agatha Christie perhaps, where everything finally came to a head.

'Thanks for coming,' she said.

'What is this?' Guy said. 'What the hell are they doing here?'

Iris smiled at him. 'I thought it might be nice for us all to get together.'

Guy's face hardened. It suddenly became cold and calculating. 'You've set me up, you bitch!'

Iris didn't bother to reply. After what he'd done, she didn't feel the need to justify herself.

Chris Street stared at her. 'Are you the one who called me? You said it was about Liam.'

'Yeah, meet your sister,' Guy said. 'If you want to know why Liam died, the answer's standing right in front of you.'

'They know that already,' Iris said. 'Why do you think they hired their thugs to follow me around?'

But Chris Street just looked confused. 'What thugs? Sister? What the fuck are you talking about?'

'The boys don't know about Sean,' Terry said to her softly. 'Or about you. I haven't had the chance to talk to them yet.'

'Oh,' Guy said, 'that's classic! He hasn't even got the guts to tell his own kids about you. *That's* how much he cares about his beloved daughter.'

'They must know about him,' Iris said. 'Guy talked to them. I was threatened – at the flat, at Columbia Road market; they even had someone following me around. And *he* came here.' Iris nodded towards Danny. 'He came here and had a go at me.'

Terry, looking bemused, glared at his son. 'Danny?'

Danny Street was shifting from one foot to another, gazing around the room. He had a shifty nervous look in his eyes and Iris recalled what Vita had told her. If it was true about what he'd been up to in the basement, then perhaps he was only concerned that *his* gruesome secret might be about to be revealed.

'Danny?' Terry said again.

Danny slowly focused his attention back on his father. 'Shit, I don't know what's she's going on about. She's talkin' crap. I don't know nothin' about any Sean geezer. Yeah, I came here, but it wasn't to do with her. I was looking for that Toby Grand. The little ponce owes me money.'

Iris frowned, thinking back to that day. Was it possible that she'd made a mistake? He'd never actually mentioned Sean. Perhaps, already on edge, she'd jumped to an entirely wrong conclusion.

Terry took another deep drag on his cigarette. 'It wasn't my boys,' he said. He turned his stony gaze on Guy. 'There's only one person who'd have wanted to scare you like that, someone who wanted you to rely on him, to *need* him.'

Iris shook her head as she followed Terry's gaze. 'No, tell me that it wasn't you,' she whispered. 'Christ, it was, wasn't it?' She lifted her hands to momentarily cover her face. Suddenly it was all so utterly clear to her. '*You* hired those men to threaten me! *You* made me believe that my father was in Kellston, that he was in danger, that I needed you to help me find him.'

Guy gave a small dismissive shrug. 'It was all so easy, babe. You were so fucking desperate to believe that he was back.'

'You did what?' Terry growled.

Iris heard the anger in his voice. It was an echo of her own personal rage and frustration and just for a second, for an unexpected second, she felt grateful that he was standing up for her. No sooner had the thought entered her head than she pushed it abruptly away. He might be her biological father, but she refused to feel any kind of connection to him.

'You heard,' Guy said.

Realising that one or the other might be about to turn this into a more physical argument, Iris quickly stepped between the two of them again. The settling of their differences could wait until she'd got the answers she needed. 'But why? Why would you want to do that to me?'

'It was nothing personal,' Guy said. 'I like you, I really do.'

'It's just that he hates me more,' Terry said.

'And Jenks,' she murmured, still trying to come to terms with the depth of Guy's betrayal. 'What about him?'

Guy grinned. 'Ah, the Weasel would do anything for money. All I had to do was slip him a few bob and get him to approach you in the pub.'

'Like mother, like son,' Terry spat out contemptuously. 'I might have guessed.'

'Yeah,' Guy said, 'the Weasel came to see my mother a few

months back, told her that Terry here was paying him to sniff around some girl in Kellston. He didn't know who she was of course, but my mother did. Iris O'Donnell, her husband's bastard child.' He grinned at Terry. 'Is that why you killed her, because she wasn't going to put up with it? Did she threaten to tell your precious boys the truth?'

'She's our sister?' Chris Street suddenly said, as if the fact had only just sunk in. He looked Iris up and down as if she was something he'd scraped off the bottom of his shoe.

'Half-sister,' Iris corrected him. 'And I'm as overjoyed about it as you are.'

'It's complicated,' Terry said.

Guy sneered. 'Oh, it's not that complicated. Lizzie was drinking a lot, wasn't she? That loose mouth of hers could have got you in all sorts of trouble. I mean, shit, she was even talking to me, telling me all about your sordid little affair. She was going to blow the lid on what really happened with Liam, wasn't she?'

'I didn't kill her,' Terry said.

'No,' Guy said. 'You got someone else to do your dirty work for you. Not that I'm complaining – it's nothing more than the whore deserved and it saved me the trouble of doing it myself.'

'What's he saying?' Chris asked. 'What does he mean about Liam?'

Guy's grin grew even wider. 'He knows who murdered your brother. He's always known. And it wasn't Davey bloody Tyler. No, he was just the poor sod who your daddy took his frustration out on because he couldn't kill the real culprit.'

Terry threw his cigarette butt on to the carpet and ground it in with his heel. 'He's talking shite.'

'No, he isn't,' Iris said, determined to have the whole truth revealed. She glanced over at Chris. 'My father, the man I once *thought* was my father, was called Sean O'Donnell. He was a good man, a decent man, but he was destroyed when he found out Terry had been having a long-term affair with my mother, and that I was the product of that affair. Sean bought a gun – I don't think he meant to use it, but that's beside the point – and went with Tyler to your house. He only intended to rob it but . . .'

'Is this true?' Chris said, glaring at his father.

'What?' Danny said.

Terry ignored them both. As if his only desire was for Iris to hear his side of the story, he addressed himself purely to her. 'Did Guy tell you about how I broke his arm? Poor little boy, seven years old. I bet he laid that on thick, didn't he? Terry Street, the brutal kiddie-beater. What he probably forgot to mention was that I found him in the living room in the middle of the night with a can of petrol and a box of matches. If he had his way, we'd have all been ashes by the morning.'

Guy laughed. It was a nasty brutish sound that sent a chill though Iris. 'You deserved to burn in hell, the whole bloody lot of you!'

'Is it true?' Chris said again, advancing on his father. 'You let the bastard who murdered Liam get away with it?'

'Of course he did,' Guy said, trying to stir things up even more. 'What kind of justice is that for your brother? Iris's mother – she's called Kathleen by the way – made him promise not to tell the law, or go after her husband. And you know what else? Even after everything that had happened, that pathetic excuse for a man still wanted to be with her. He thought more of his slut of a mistress than he did of Liam.'

Chris stared into his father's face. Suddenly his hands whipped up from his sides and grabbed the lapels of his suit. His eyes flashed with rage. 'All this time,' he hissed, 'and you never said a word.'

Terry took hold of his wrists. 'For God's sake, you don't know the half of it.'

'He was your fuckin' son!'

Breaking free, Chris lashed out and caught him with two quick blows to the jaw. Terry staggered back against the cabinet. A tray containing cups and saucers clattered to the floor. Chris launched himself forward again, grabbed Terry and began to shake him. 'What about Liam? What about Liam?' Terry tried to fight him off and the two of them, caught in an unholy embrace, staggered around the room, crashing into furniture. A vase of flowers toppled over and smashed, spilling water and white chrysanthemums over the faded carpet.

Iris, unable to control the situation, stood well back. She could understand Chris's rage: she might have felt the same way if it was her brother who'd been killed and her father who had chosen not to tell the truth about it. Danny was usually the first to resort to violence, but this time he'd been caught unawares. Perhaps he was too out of his head, or too busy worrying about his own secrets, to really comprehend what was going on.

Guy, enjoying the conflict he'd caused, laughed again. Perhaps it was that derisive laugh that reminded Danny Street of what he should be doing. Turning suddenly, he delivered a low ferocious blow to his stomach. Guy doubled over, the breath flying out of him, but as Danny went in to finish the job he recovered enough to grab hold of his legs. There was a brief ungainly struggle before the two of them thudded to the ground.

Within seconds the room had dissolved into chaos. Grunting, spitting, cursing, the four angry men screamed abuse at each other. Fists started to fly haphazardly. It was hard to know exactly who was fighting who. Somehow they had all got entangled in a vicious knot of rage and bitterness.

Iris withdrew to the safety of the corridor. She saw Gerald poke his head out of the door, and then rapidly retreat again. He'd be straight on the phone to the cops, but by the time they got here it would all be over. As she looked back into the room,

Iris experienced one of those déjà vu sensations. There was something overly familiar about the scene. It was as if she'd come full circle from that first day, not so long ago, when Guy had come to view the body of his mother. As she witnessed the growing devastation, the smashed furniture, the crushed white petals of the flowers, she could see it all as a fitting metaphor for the wreckage of her own life.

Iris slowly shook her head. There was only one thing left to do. She went through to reception, picked up her coat and her bag, and without a backward glance walked away from it all.

Epilogue

It was a snowy Christmas Eve. As the plane rose up into the sky, Iris took a final look at the city of London. She didn't know when, if ever, she'd see the place again, and couldn't put a name to the emotion she was feeling as she gazed down on the myriad of lights beneath her. Exhilaration, relief, anxiety? She wasn't even sure why she was doing this – except that doing something, going somewhere, was better than doing nothing. William's offer had come out of the blue and she'd accepted it without a second thought.

He put down his newspaper. 'You will get through this.'

'Yes,' she said.

'You could try and say it like you meant it.'

Iris forced a smile. 'Am I doing the right thing?' She suddenly felt scared, disturbed by the notion that she was simply running away from it all. Wherever she went, the truth would always follow her.

'It's a bit late if you want to get off now.'

Aware of the other passengers sitting around them, Iris lowered her voice. 'I don't,' she said, 'but Terry Street's never going to pay for what he did, is he? There's no proof that he arranged to have Lizzie killed, or that he murdered Michael.' And there was nothing she could do to change the situation. She couldn't even pursue the accusations without dragging her mother's name through the mud, and she wasn't prepared to do that. 'He just gets away with it.'

'Does he?' William said. 'It depends on how you look at it.' He paused, his grey eyes becoming thoughtful. 'From what you've told me, his one desire was to be reunited with his daughter. He's spent the last nineteen years believing that would happen. You've deprived him of the only thing that he can't buy or steal.'

Iris still hadn't come to terms with who her father really was. She scowled as Terry's thin, gaunt face rose up into her mind. 'It's not enough.'

'What would be enough? Terry Street rotting in jail for the rest of his life? This might not be justice, but it's the closest you're going to get.'

Iris sat back in her seat and considered his reply. Perhaps he was right. After what Terry had said that final day at Tobias Grand & Sons, she had no doubt that his feelings for her were genuine. He *had* always hoped that there would be a happy ending. And perhaps there could have been if, long ago, different choices had been made.

'Did you call your mother before you left?'

Iris nodded. 'I told her I was going away for a few weeks. I didn't say where in case she took it into her head to get on the next plane out. Believe me, she's more than capable. I need a bit of space from her, time to think things through.' It hadn't been an easy conversation; there was still a gulf between them, an ocean of awkwardness. It was painful to look back over those years, to count the lies she'd been told, but at least it was all out in the open now.

'Tell me,' William said, 'would you have started the affair with Guy if you'd still been with Luke?'

She was surprised by the question. 'Of course not.'

'Truthfully?'

Iris hesitated. She understood what he was getting at. Sometimes, even when you knew what you were doing was wrong, you still went ahead and did it. There were people who got under your skin, who connected in a way that went beyond good sense or morality. Isn't that what had happened to her mother? And could she really put her hand on her heart and claim that she wouldn't have succumbed to Guy Wilder's charms even if she had still been attached? 'You think I'm being a hypocrite.'

'No,' he said, 'not a hypocrite. I didn't mean that. But we all make mistakes, and then occasionally make even worse ones trying to put them right. Your mother never intended to hurt you. What she did was wrong, but she's had to live with that for a very long time. I'm not saying it's going to be easy, but maybe one day you can begin to make your peace with her.'

They were silent for a few minutes. Iris gazed out of the window again. All this talk of mistakes, of the terrible things people did, had got her thinking about someone else. 'What will happen to Alice?'

'It's hard to say. Hopefully, she'll get the help she needs.' William frowned down at his paper. 'I know Toby was my nephew but . . . well, he wasn't the nicest person in the world. And I'm not saying he deserved that kind of end, but after what he did to her, what he put her through, I find it hard to look on him as a completely innocent victim.'

Despite the warmth of the plane, Iris shivered. 'But will she even be able to give evidence? I mean, will anyone trust her word after what she's done?'

It was Gerald Grand who had made the gruesome discovery.

After the police had arrested Guy and the Streets, he had gone down to the basement to make sure the rest of the building was clear. What he'd found there had been beyond his worst nightmare: Alice Avery standing calmly by the counter . . . and laid out on the table, the perfectly embalmed body of his son. 'Poor Gerald,' she said. 'God, it must have been horrific! I should have told you what Vita said – about Rick's blackmail, about Danny Street. I could have—'

'It wouldn't have made any difference. It was already too late. Toby was dead before you even got back from Guy's.'

'Why did she do it?' Iris murmured. But it was a purely rhetorical question. Others would claim it was down to hatred or revenge, to bitterness at being dumped, but the truth was much more disturbing. Alice, tragically, had done it for love.

'I doubt if Danny Street will ever go to trial,' William said. 'He's been questioned by the police, but he's denying everything. There's no physical evidence – the body of Jenni Brookner's already been cremated – so it's her word against his and with her current mental state . . .'

Iris, knowing he was right, gave a small groan of despair. Alice Avery had been driven to the edge, and then Toby Grand had pushed her over. She had given a statement to the police backing up Alice's story – but what she'd been able to tell them was only hearsay, a reiteration of what Vita had said to her. Before she'd left, she'd posted a cheque to Vita for six hundred pounds. It had been a final goodbye, a severing of all links between them. It was unlikely that any action would be taken against Rick Howard; although the money had been found on the floor of the embalming room, Vita was denying ever giving it to her to pass on to Toby, Toby was no longer around to confirm or deny its source and Alice was hardly a reliable witness.

And Guy – what would happen to him? Iris gritted her teeth.

Every time she thought of him, her body stiffened with revulsion. All those things he'd done, all the ways he'd used her, his callous and twisted manipulation. He wouldn't have to answer to anyone. He wouldn't even have to take responsibility for the damage caused to the room at Tobias Grand & Sons. Gerald had more important things on his mind than pressing charges against a load of scrapping thugs. The business had closed down and would never reopen. 'And Guy's another one who's just going to walk away from it all,' she said bitterly.

'Not exactly.'

'What's that supposed to mean?'

'Do you think he'll ever be happy?' William said.

Iris didn't need to think twice about it. Guy was empty inside, dead and empty. 'No.'

'Well then.'

Iris sighed. He had a point. Guy would spend the rest of his life battling with his demons. Nothing and no one could ever give him back what he really wanted: his mother's love had been lost long ago.

Alice Avery sat down in the chair, neatly crossed her legs and before opening the letter took a moment to survey the room. Other people might have considered it rather bare, spartan even, but she was pleased by its simplicity. It was small and neat and she didn't have to share it with anyone else. Here, away from all the trappings of modern life, she was finally able to relax.

Alice talked to the psychiatrist every day. These were meetings she looked forward to: no one had listened to her quite so intently before. For the first time in her life she felt able to speak openly. She liked to talk about Toby most of all, the things he'd said, the way he'd made her laugh, the time they'd spent together. When she was doing that she felt close to him again.

She was less happy to discuss Danny Street. Even now, as his name came into her head, she shuddered. She drew her knees up to her chin and wrapped her arms around them. It was Danny who'd made Toby say all those terrible things, who'd corrupted his mind with the coke and the crack and all the other vile substances he'd encouraged him to buy. The *real* Toby would never have abandoned her. It was the real Toby that she'd reconstructed on the embalming table. It had been her finest piece of work and she didn't regret it. He had never looked more beautiful.

Alice glanced down at the letter. Her mother's thin spidery handwriting crawled across the envelope. She didn't need to open it to know what was written inside: all the letters were the same, filled with anger, outrage and disgust. *That any daughter of mine could be so evil, could do something so perverse . . .* But none of it mattered any more. Alice smiled as she pushed the envelope aside. Her mother couldn't touch her now. Nobody could.

Terry Street gazed gloomily down into the glass of whisky. He didn't get much past breakfast these days before having a drink. In his head, he went over and over what had happened, always starting with the very first night he had seen Kathleen, always ending with the horrifying contempt in Iris's eyes when they'd met for the final time in that room at Tobias Grand & Sons.

He wasn't sorry that he'd killed Michael O'Donnell. How could he be? The bastard had deserved it. If he hadn't gone shooting his mouth off all those years ago everything would have been different – Liam would still be alive, Kathleen would still be at his side and he wouldn't have a daughter who despised him. He stared at the wall, reliving the almost climactic feeling he'd had as he'd put his foot down on the pedal, as he'd felt the acceleration of the car, the moment of impact, the dull, satisfying thump of hard metal against soft flesh . . .

And okay, so he'd broken his promise, but he'd made that promise at another time, in another life. Kathleen had no hold over him any more. She'd relinquished that loyalty from the moment she'd walked away. He should have taken his revenge years ago. If he could have run the bloody car over Sean O'Donnell, he would have; he owed her murdering, scumbag of a husband absolutely nothing.

Terry knocked back his drink, got up and poured another. He could hear someone moving around in the kitchen. Chris? Chris's wife? Not Danny. Danny had been avoiding him ever since that trouble at Tobias Grand & Sons. The rumours were still circulating . . . crazy rumours that he couldn't control. They were enough to send Terry demented. That mad Avery woman spilling all her bile and filth. He slammed his fist down on the table. That's what women were like. Full of lies! Full of shit! No son of his was capable of what that bitch was accusing him of.

Terry poured himself another whisky. Lizzie was probably enjoying this, laughing at him from her grave. The thought of it filled him with a rage he could barely control. And then he thought of Guy Wilder and how he'd violated his daughter. If it hadn't been for him filling her head with all those lies . . . This was all *his* fault! Terry got to his feet and hurled the glass against the wall, feeling a brief rush of satisfaction as it smashed into a thousand pieces. Well, he wasn't going to let him get away with it. He'd make him pay. He'd make him fuckin' pay!

There were only ten minutes left before they were due to touch down. Iris found herself thinking about Michael again. She missed him. She always would. He'd known all along that she wasn't really his niece, not by blood at least, and yet he'd never shown her anything but affection. And even though he'd lied, she felt his lies had been spoken more out of a desire to protect than anything more sinister. There had been kindness there, love and tenderness. He could have turned his back on her, but he hadn't. He'd made her feel like she belonged.

But now it was time to move on, to start again. She felt a brief rush of excitement, of anticipation, as the plane started its descent. Ireland – home of her ancestors. She'd never even been here before. By the time she was born, both sets of her grand-parents were dead. Iris, despite her more hopeful mood, made a resolution not to expect too much. She turned to William, trying to keep her voice light. 'If it's raining, I'm on the next flight out to Spain.'

'If it didn't rain so much, the grass wouldn't be so green.'

Iris pulled a face. 'Is that one of those fatuous clichés about how the good wouldn't be so good if it wasn't for the bad?'

'No,' he said smiling. 'It's a simple fact. Sometimes there aren't any lines to read between.'

Iris wrinkled her nose. She still wasn't sure what William expected of her. Was he after something more than friendship? He might possess a wealth of kindness and a certain quirky charm, but she had no intention of getting involved with any man, ever again. From now on she was resolutely single. The only person she was going to rely on was herself. If he imagined, even for a second, that she was going to . . . but as soon as the thought crossed her mind, she felt an echo of his smile creeping to her lips. Who exactly was she trying to convince? And there was nothing remotely predatory about William; whatever his feelings for her, he wouldn't act on them unless she gave him some encouragement. She had a long way to go before she could trust anyone again, but it might be a journey worth taking if a man as good and decent as William Grand was at the end of it.

In the meantime her life was a patchwork of lies she would need to unpick. She thought of Connor Hills, travelling with them in the hold. Had he found happiness in Ireland? Had he come to terms, discovered some peace, before his past – whatever it was – had come back to haunt him? She knew it was fanciful, but she couldn't help hoping that Connor Hills and Sean O'Donnell might be one and the same person. If that was the case, perhaps a part of Sean had never let go. Perhaps he had come back to find her. It was a romantic notion – even an implausible one – but it would be a fitting end if she was the one who was finally taking him home.